SHADOWS
of
PERL

J. Elle is the *New York Times*, and indie, bestselling and award-winning author of multiple books including *Against The Tide*, an original prequel tie-in to *The Little Mermaid* live-action film. Her debut duology, Wings of Ebony, dubbed "an incredible debut" by NPR and best fantasy book by POPSUGAR, was a 2022 NAACP Image Award Nominee for Outstanding Literary Work for Youth and Teens, an Amazon Editor's pick for Best Science Fiction and Fantasy, and a Barnes and Noble YA Book Club Pick. The former educator credits her nomadic lifestyle and humble inner-city beginnings as inspiration for her novels. When she's not writing, Elle can be found on the hunt for desserts without chocolate, drowning herself in regency romance reads and shows, and looking for any excuse to wear a tiara.

SHADOWS

of

PERL

HOUSE OF MARIONNE
BOOK TWO

J. ELLE

MICHAEL JOSEPH
PENGUIN
Est. 1935

PENGUIN MICHAEL JOSEPH

UK | USA | Canada | Ireland | Australia
India | New Zealand | South Africa

Penguin Michael Joseph is part of the Penguin Random House group of companies
whose addresses can be found at global.penguinrandomhouse.com

First published in the United States of America by Razorbill,
an imprint of Penguin Random House LLC 2024
First published in Great Britain by Penguin Michael Joseph 2024
001

Design by Alex Campbell
Text set in Adobe Garamond Pro
Printed and bound in Great Britain by Clays Ltd, Elcograf S.p.A.

The authorized representative in the EEA is Penguin Random House Ireland,
Morrison Chambers, 32 Nassau Street, Dublin D02 YH68

A CIP catalogue record for this book is available from the British Library

HARDBACK ISBN: 978–0–241–68153–4

TRADE PAPERBACK ISBN: 978–0–241–68154–1

www.greenpenguin.co.uk

For Naomi,
find your wings, unleash your power.

I

HOUSE OF PERL

SPECIALTIES OFFERED

ANATOMER

Transfigurer of anatomy

AUDIOR

Transfigurer of sound

SHIFTER

Transfigurer of matter

RETENTOR

Remover of magic

CULTIVATOR

Transferer of knowledge

DRAGUN

By invitation only

KNOWN SPECIALTIES

TRACER

MEMENTAUR

PERL DISTINCTIONS OF VIRTUE

DISCRETION

VALOR

HONOR

SACRIFICE

LOYALTY

DUTY

Labor operarii difficile est

THE UNMARKED GIRL

————— ✳ —————

The only thing colder than the crisp fall air thumped an easy cadence against the girl's ribs. She closed her eyes a moment before she strode across the snowy mountainside. A warm curl of memories tried to unfurl in her chest, but they froze against her cold, dead heart. Once, it had fluttered, raging with an appetite for things she had never thought possible for someone with her position and in her condition.

But the boy she'd loved was gone.

And whatever they'd had had faded like the names etched into the headstones littered around her. She had to forget him. Her fist tightened on the black rose bouquet as she ventured deeper into Ambrose territory. Where other Houses were like crown jewels on lush, manicured lawns, Dlaminaugh Estate was a fortress built into a steep mountainside and shrouded in acres upon acres of graveyards.

Something shifted. She stopped, bumps skittering up her arms. The fog around her moved like a flag billowing in the wind. She inhaled for a rancid scent, but the altitude robbed her of the confirmation she was after. They were here, too. She could feel their presence like needles on her skin. The dead of House Ambrose lingered on the estate grounds to protect it from intruders. And that evening they were rightly suspicious of her.

With her free hand, she slipped an ornate vial from her pocket and held it tight in her fist, urging herself to move, to keep her blood warm and her courage hot, but fear locked her knees. The old crone who sold her the vial said that Sun Dust in the eyes obscures the vision permanently. She seemed certain. She also seemed desperate for money.

The girl pushed forward with an urgent stride. Her hands were stiff and icy despite her gloves. She sighed. Perhaps she should have taken the horse the groundskeeper had offered her. But she wasn't going to sign in or do anything asinine like give him her name. Besides, she was there for only one reason—to force her mother to heal her affliction.

Her head swiveled, but there was no sign of the severe woman who'd birthed her, not just yet. Her thighs burned as she shoved one boot forward, then the next. The cold had seeped through her leather shoes hours ago. The climb was steep, and this late in the year it snowed at least once a week, so nothing had time to melt. The higher she climbed, the more violently her coattails flailed in the clutches of the wind. As if the Ambrose ancestors had every intention to pull her off that mountainside.

She cleared her throat and yelled at them, "Get back to the estate!" The hovering shadows didn't move. "I can see you." The ancestors tended to hide from human eyes.

But the pull at her clothes only grew more insistent. The girl kept going, remembering her mother's disdain. She had leverage now. Headmistress Isla Ambrose would do what *she* wanted for a change, or else. Shadows whipped around her as if they could hear the secret whispers of her heart. She leaned into the wind, grabbing at any strong roots she could find to pull herself along. When she reached a plateau, she surveyed the new stretch of graves. "Thirtieth row, second from right when facing west," she said to herself. The gravestones were so odd. The land was up and down, with stretches of flat areas dotted sporadically with cement plaques, like a puzzle someone started but never finished. Some plaques were stuck to the side of the hill like bricks hastily laid, scattered and crooked. One was completely upside down. She dusted away a chunk of snow.

WILMA ERO GHINSON

She wasn't even close. She tightened her woolen coat and kept going. When she finally rounded on the *W*s, her foot clipped the edge of a tombstone and her gaze snapped to its epitaph.

HERE LIES RED WILLOW

OF NO NAME, OF NO ONE'S BLOOD

SHE DIED FREE, SHE DIED LOVED

She set the black roses beside the tombstone and lingered. Her heart began to sink as she traced its carved letters, going back and forth over the same few. Depthless slivers of shade lingered between the branches of the trees—the ancestors, still watching her. But when the sound of hooves pounding earth broke through the forest, the dead vanished. She blew out a sharp breath and removed her hood, revealing her simple raised headband of brushed silver. She scanned for the ancestors once more before pressing the headband into her scalp until it hurt to ensure it didn't move; to make sure it looked like an actual diadem. To ensure *she* looked like a Marked person—someone born with magic.

In the distance she made out a white-socked shire with a gleaming black coat, not unlike Daring: her seventh birthday present, the one thing her mother ever did right. Her mother never ventured into the woods. She loathed graveyards, which was odd considering her obsessive fascination with the dead.

The girl's mouth bowed in anticipation as she squinted. She recognized her horse's leaning gait, his agile canter as he navigated the uneven ground with ease. Riding him here today was a bit desperate, but definitely clever. This was really happening. *Her mother was really here.* The girl's hand holding the vial trembled as she replayed her plan in her head.

Daring came to a stop with a huff, and she clenched her fists. Mother was fully hooded in House robes, but a tripointed sun threaded into her outer coat could still be seen from far away. One tip for each of the gods. They were the only House who knew Sola Sfenti was the Sovereign, but not the only deity. Their ancestors had worshiped the Sovereign, the Wielder, and the Sage for as long as her bloodline existed, before her House ever existed, in their darkest days. But she couldn't care less about any of the gods. What had they done for her?

Draped across Daring's back was another cloak, this one in royal blue.

The girl's lip twitched. Her mother swung around and hopped off, and the thud of her boots hitting the ground ricocheted like a bullet in the girl's chest. But something was all together odd. Her mother moved stiffly and was too tall . . .

Wait—

Her heart leapt as her brother's long brown hair spilled out of his hood across his shoulders. His amber robe shone like copper against the depthless forest as his brushed silver mask seeped back into his skin. Her fists tightened. Her shoulders tried to sink, but her brother's arms opened wide, and she was twelve again, hopping onto his back to be snuck out of their estate.

"Ellery!" She dashed to him and he caught her in a hug. It had been so many months since he'd helped her run away from Dlaminaugh to the farm he'd discreetly bought for her. She hadn't seen him since she narrowly escaped being killed by Draguns. Ellery squeezed her tight, and his warmth stilled her like an anchor.

"Little sister." He planted a kiss on her head. His strong Ambrose jaw; his turned-up nose, which they both had in common; and those deep-set, gentle eyes, a mirror to her own. His, blue. Hers, stormy gray—the same as all the women in her family. She ran her thumb across a jagged scar etched across his jaw just below his earlobe. Scars were the one thing even House of Ambrose Anatomers couldn't change. She studied his every feature. It was really him.

"It's me, in the flesh."

She held her brother tighter. If the boy she'd loved for the last several months had taught her anything, it was that family had less to do with blood and more to do with loyalty. Now that he was gone, Ell was the only family she had left. She felt tears well in her eyes but blinked them away and rotated the vial in her hand. "You're alone?"

"Not alone." He patted her horse on his thick neck. "He missed you."

She tickled Daring's velvety nose and he nuzzled her hand. "Where is Mother?"

The mirth drained from Ellery's expression like the horizon drinking in a sunset. He grabbed her wrist. "Open up."

She tugged away, but her brother's grip, though gentle, was firm. He was built like an Ambrose fellow, stocky with meaty arms and devilishly strong. He pulled at her fingers to pry her fist open, but she held tight. Until he wiggled a knuckle into her ribs. Her grip slacked and a begrudging laugh burst from her lips.

"Ellery! Give that back," she said, centering her faux diadem in her nest of auburn curls. He would not take her only weapon against their mother. He had to see reason.

He unscrewed the vial's top, and she couldn't miss the tally marks on the back of his hands. Her gaze lingered.

"A vial of Sun Dust? Could you be any more predictable? And what were you going to do with it? Force it down her throat?"

"Threaten to throw it in her eyes," she shoved out through gritted teeth. "Make her undo this poison she put in me." Now that she said the idea aloud, it sounded so dumb. Her cheeks flushed.

"You really don't know anything about magic, do you?" He threw an arm around her shoulders and mussed up her hair.

"I'm clever, I don't need magic." She searched for words to prove to him her plan was a good one. To make him help her or get out of the way. But she came up empty.

"You are clever. My favorite little sister."

"I'm your only sister."

He was the one grinning this time.

"Why are you here, Ellery? Out with it."

"To convince you to see clearly." He rolled the vial between his fingers. "Mother would have never fallen for this anyway."

She growled. "It's mine. Give it back."

"Technically it's property of House Ambrose." He showed her the sigil engraved on its sleek, polished side. "Three yew leaves, intertwined, one for each god." Then he tossed the vial in the air. She snatched at it, but he was quicker, opening his robes so it slid right into a hidden pocket.

She pulled at his arm in a last-ditch effort at getting it back, and his sleeve rose. Her jaw dropped at the endless rows of tally marks up and down his forearms. The last time she saw him, they'd only covered one arm. She pushed his sleeve higher: nearly every inch of skin up to his elbow was covered in marks. He tugged down on his collar, and more were all over his chest.

"I'm sure Mother's proud," she said, eyeing his marks—one for each new magical discovery. When she was little, when her hope had not yet been crushed, she'd dreamed to debut at Cotillion with a few dozen tally marks. That was an admirable number, most Ambrose débutants managed only a fraction of that. But not a single tally mark was ever etched into her skin.

She was Unmarked. Not magical. Powerless.

And now, thanks to their mother—poisoned.

She glared at Red's grave. "And destined to be alone," she muttered.

"I don't do any of this for her," he said. "You know that." Ellery re-adjusted his clothes, and she sighed. Her brother loved her, but he was just as stubborn as she was. He wasn't giving that vial back. He wasn't there to help her coerce Mother. Silence blew between them. She twisted her boot in the snow, eyeing the forgotten royal-blue robe draped across Daring. Ell wasn't just there to stop her. It was far worse: he wanted her to come home. A scream bounced around in her head. Heat built in her chest. Him here, refusing to help, wanting to take her back to that *place* . . . Just the thought was infuriating.

"You steal that vial of Dust before you left?" Ellery asked.

"That's none of your business." She'd have to find another way to threaten her mother. *And* keep her brother out of her way.

"Oh, so we keep secrets from each other now?"

She rolled her eyes. "Remember when Mother lost her transport compact."

Ell's brows bounced. "That was you!"

"It was set out to be refilled when the estate was being cleaned. But Mother was pulled away for an urgent matter. I took it and tucked it away for safekeeping."

Ellery's gaze fell to the headstone beside them, and his warmth returned with the comfort of a summer breeze. His blue eyes gleamed with apology. She shook her head. That was the thing she loved most about her brother: how they could communicate without a word. He knew her. He'd lived through what she'd lived through at Dlaminaugh. But he came out of it with high marks—the perfect, prodigious son. She was thankful she'd come out of it *alive*. Her breath came shorter; the urge to sob scraped against her ribs.

"It's not your fault," she said before he could get a word out.

His jaw clenched. "I'm your brother. I should have protected you from her."

"You did well with the plaque and wording and such. It all looks nice." It was his idea to put a burial plaque here for Red. She folded her arms.

"I thought you'd like that."

Pressure built in her chest. She wasn't sure how much longer she could stand there beside Red's headstone before the memories took over and broke her, before the happy life she'd buried beneath a mask rose to the surface and choked her. She turned away, and they walked through a clearing in the trees where a river rushed between two mountains. The sky's dull gray had lifted. Now a pale blue stretched over them and the sun winked from the clouds.

"She is going to fix this poison she put in me," she said, moved by the good omen.

"Don't count on that."

She balled her fists. "Then I will go to *Debs Daily* and out all this House's illicit secrets. The twisted things she allows in the name of discovery!"

Her brother squeezed her shoulders, towering over her in that way he did. She felt small and even more powerless. She clenched her fists tighter. He stroked her cheek. "You will not do anything that could get you killed."

She stormed off.

"I've been looking into some things. You *have* to come home. There's so much we need to talk about." The urgency in her brother's voice sent her heart thudding. Her ears perked, though she kept her back to him. "Mother never saw your letter. When I intercepted your note, I decided to come myself. And—" His voice cracked.

"You've come to convince me to return home, but you can save yourself the trouble," she said to his face.

"I am still looking into it, but I have come to believe there are"—he gazed around—"many reasons you need to be at Dlaminaugh."

She folded her arms. "And what are these reasons?"

"Not here."

"Ellery, don't try to stop me. *Help* me."

"Mother would never admit it, but I don't think she actually knows *how* to undo what she gave you."

"*Toushana.* Call it what it is."

He closed the distance between them. "Keep it down."

"I did not come all the way here to *keep it down.*" She held his tattooed arm to his face. "Somewhere in the centuries of our House's legacy and all their heralded discoveries, *someone* must know how to get this stuff out of me. I won't hear excuses. *Intellectus secat acutissimum.* Intellect cuts the sharpest. Our maezres always said there is no puzzle magic cannot solve. Is it true or not? Is Ambrose superior in intellect or are we not?"

Her brother held his chin in deep consternation.

"She was trying to anoint me with the Dust, Ell, hoping for the millionth time it would wake something in me. Me—her *Unmarked* daughter, the heir to her House, with *no* magic. But all her desperation did was poison me!"

Tears welled again in her eyes. She hated her mother for countless reasons. But the top of the list was infecting her with toushana. Before that, she'd just been the Unmarked daughter of a House Headmistress. But as the lies to cover her lack of performance grew stale, more became suspicious. A private tutor on the grounds, a private cottage. Eventually, people began to question why they hadn't seen the heir *do* magic. But instead of admitting that her daughter had none, Isla Ambrose listened to her old, dusty books.

"She can hate me forever for not being what she wanted, but she will *not* control my life." Her mind wandered to Yagrin: how she showed him her wildest, most ridiculous non-magical ambitions and he didn't mock a single one. How he reveled in the fact that she wasn't part of the Order—or so he thought. How he loved that most about her! How, with him, she was free and loved in that unbridled existence. How he never asked her to change a single thing, not her hair, not the way she dressed, not the things she thought were funny, or the weird way she ate her eggs—with ketchup and lettuce. How he loved every piece of the person she was on the inside. The person she'd dared show no one else. Her heart raged in her chest. She could still picture the way he looked at her—imperfect, Unmarked *her*—like she was the sun itself. She felt the tiny bump in her pocket where she kept a gift he gave her.

"I swear to the Wielder, the Sage, and Sola Sfenti himself, I *will* have a life, Ellery. A regular life away from Mother's ridiculous expectations."

"Is the"—he lowered his voice—"*toushana* causing problems?"

"No. It's such a small amount inside me. It's only flared up once or twice. But I've done my research; one day it will get worse."

"So we have time."

"It appears so." She folded her arms. "If she would have just left me alone, I was happy . . ."

"Your happiness is not Mother's concern. Your fitness to usher the House forward is."

"And you agree with that?"

"You *know* I don't agree with that," he chastised in a loud whisper. "But you are her firstborn daughter. The seat passes to you, whether you want it or not!" Fear flickered in her brother's eyes. "The Order is fracturing. Have you had your head so deep in those cornfields you haven't noticed? The Sphere has *cracked*." He pulled a copy of *Debs Daily* from his robes and tossed it at her. A sketch of the orb that encompassed the balance of all magic took up most of the front page. The headline took away her next breath.

THE FUTURE OF MAGIC UNCERTAIN

She swallowed. "It's bleeding out?"

"Not yet. But it's only a matter of time."

If the Sphere bled out, magic would be lost for half a century at least. It was written. *Could that be a good thing?* But what would that mean for her family? She wanted nothing to do with the Order or its problems. She just wanted toushana out of her so she could move on with her life as if the Order didn't exist.

"Members are angry," he went on. "And rumors are that House of Marionne is an entire disaster." He raked a hand through his hair, and they walked back to Daring in silence. He grabbed the brilliant blue robe and laid it carefully across his arm before kneeling at her feet.

"Please, come home."

For several moments she said nothing. "I do care about my life. That's why I want anything tying me to the Order *gone*."

"Off-Season balls have started."

"I don't care."

He stood, draping the House color worn exclusively by the heir across her back. "Not even a little? I have to attend and I'd much prefer to take you than one of the Hargrove daughters."

"Mother's *still* trying to force that family down your throat? I mean, they do have seven unmarried Marked daughters, can you really blame them for being desperate?"

He grimaced. "Come on. Name anyone in the entire House who can dance a waltz better than you."

She smirked.

"The annual Fall Harvest Gala is in a few weeks." Ellery's hand hovered before her face. She braced for the familiar feeling she knew was coming. He worked his Anatomer magic, and she felt nostalgic at the shift of her eyes widening, the prickle of her lashes lengthening. It always felt like a sneeze was scratching her nose when he changed her face. Only House of Ambrose had stretched the bounds of appearance-changing magic to be able to change *others'* appearances, not just oneself. Her House had stretched the bounds of most strands of magic. Her jaw softened as her lips filled to pout in the way Red's did. Her hair crawled down her back in darker red ringlets, shifting from her natural auburn to burgundy. She closed her eyes and inhaled, wishing this appearance could still be real. Wishing her Red persona didn't have to go away, too.

"You know we can't use her anymore," she said. It all went south after the Draguns followed her home from the Tidwell Ball, determined to make the boy she loved suffer. They intended to kill Red with the farm, but they never found her. She hid beneath the barn as they searched. When they set the whole place ablaze, she escaped through a tunnel beneath the house that led to her cornfields. She had the secret passage put in for that very reason. She was technically Unmarked: not born with magic. And an Unmarked cannot look on magic and live. In the field is where the other Headmistress found her several days later, persona wiped away, shaking with terror.

Darragh Marionne offered her a real way to disappear: by erasing her name from the Book of Names. She could have a life that didn't require a persona. "Nore Ambrose would be—on paper—dead," she promised. Nore shook on it immediately.

But she'd since botched their agreement.

She was trapped in the Order. Nore had duties and expectations. Nore had a horrid mother. Nore wasn't who she wanted to be anymore, but Red wasn't safe either. Draguns could still be hunting for Red. For Yagrin's safety, too, the persona Red was dead and it had to stay that way.

"I know, but I also know how much you loved being her," her brother said.

"And how Mother hated it." She'd hoped to taunt their mother today with Red's headstone. Reminding her that even though she didn't have magic, she would always outsmart her and find a way to live freely. But she'd have to wait a bit longer to satiate that desire.

She pulled away from her brother's magic and it dissolved. "No use dwelling on the impossible. That game is over," she said. "Red is dead." She shrugged off the Ambrose heir robes and tossed them at her brother before petting Daring once more. "I'll go to the Harvest Gala with you if you can ensure Mother will be there." She turned to walk away.

Ellery groaned.

"Those are my terms," she shouted over her shoulder.

"*Nore!*" he yelled at her back. "Threatening to hurt Mother won't work."

"Then it won't be a threat."

PART ONE

ONE

Quell

Every time I close my eyes, he is there.

I blink away the face of the boy I used to love and focus instead on the buzz of the streetlamps as they flicker off, one after another. The city lights always remind me of my mother, and the busy street fogs through my tears. We had nothing. We had no one. And somehow everything's changed and yet nothing has.

I hug around myself. When she and I first started running from the Order, before we could afford an apartment, before my mother could find a job, those first several weeks, we would sleep wherever we could: a random unlocked car, a boarded-up building, an alleyway. Each night she'd leave to find food or other things we might need. *It's easier to go unnoticed without a little one at my side,* she'd say. A lot of things would have been easier without me at her side. *But I'll be back before the streetlights are off, I promise.*

I wish she knew how strong I am now. How I can protect *her,* once I find her. Magic prickles the crown of my head, and on the back of my eyelids I can see my regal black diadem encrusted with bloody, dark-pink gems. I wish I could show it. I wish I could show everyone. But I hold the tightness at my center to keep my diadem hidden, a skill I saw Abby do the first day I met her, one I've finally mastered.

I settle deeper into the park bench and watch as strangers scamper across the street and enter the park on East Capitol. Car horns usher them hastily. I groan, checking my watch. *One last test.* The sky continues to brighten until all the streetlights I've stared at the last few hours, as far as I can see, are off.

Octos clears his throat next to me, his face hidden behind a giant newspaper. Its outer pages are from *The Washington Post*; its inner pages, *Debs Daily.* It's been a couple of months since I fled Chateau Soleil, where I shared my grandmother's tethering secret with Cotillion guests before plunging my dagger into my chest to bind with my toushana. And yet, the chaos that engulfed House of Marionne still haunts me. There's been no official word about any of it—my grandmother or her House.

"Anything yet?" I ask him. He leans over the paper, his blackened-bluish fingernails curled tightly over a magnifying glass held up to a few lines of text. Then he furiously jots down notes on a pad of paper.

"Almost," he says. Despite his attempt to blend in, his withered olive skin, tally marks beneath the rolled sleeves of his threadbare coat, and greasy straight hair crawling over his shoulders have won us a few quizzical glances. "How's Lincoln looking?"

"Still a few stragglers."

Octos has been training me while Abby looks for my mom. We've spent the recent weeks hunting for places I can push my toushana to its limits without hurting myself. Today's the final test. After that I'm going to meet Abby, and then we'll find my mom.

I flex my hands and pull on the hum of cold lurking in my bones. It shoves through me like a tide swallowing a shore, until iciness pools beneath every inch of my skin. I picture the release of my magic, and tiny plumes of smoke seep from my pores. I tighten at my center and draw in a deep breath. As my lungs fill with air, my shadows retreat back inside me. Sometimes I just call on my toushana to feel its nearness.

"Save your strength, you'll need it," Octos says. His tone is even. Always calm.

My training has gone well. But he insists we try my dark, destructive magic in various environments and under different amounts of stress.

Once he had me bring down an abandoned multistory building. Purple bruises covered my arms from using the toushana for too long, and it was several days before I could even get out of bed without blinding pain.

"And those are only the bruises you can *see*," he'd said.

My control over my dark magic, balancing the oscillating cycle of release-release-rest, has grown over the past several weeks. I still have splinters from the walls I collapsed to trap a robber in a basement. But he was apprehended and I left there without a single bruise. I thought Octos's and my time together would be over then. But today he insisted on one last big test to push my toushana harder than I ever have. The only place in this city with enough tree cover to do magic is Lincoln Park, which was closed to the public for construction last night.

"And you're sure about this place?" I ask, wary of being in a big city. It was his idea to get far away from Louisiana, or any place my grand-mother could stumble upon us. Crossing into new territory was safer, and everything on the East Coast north of the James River is House of Perl country. We settled at a safe house in a rural town several hours from Washington, DC, in the middle of nowhere, but you can't use magic in or close to a safe house, so DC it is.

"As sure as I can be."

I leave Octos to his newspaper decoding. Cars whoosh by and I peer at the drivers, foolishly searching for a face that looks like my mom's. She'd take me to time the streetlamps early in the morning and at night so that I'd know she was paying close attention. Then she'd return me to wherever we were staying and tuck me in. I would rarely sleep. Instead I would stare at the glow the lights cast on the walls outside, imagining it was the light in a hallway outside my room, in a real home somewhere. A reminder that my mother was never far, always just a few steps away. The hum of the lamps was her voice, I told myself. Any moment, she'd come back and we'd be together again.

What will she think of what I've done? Binding to toushana. Leaving House of Marionne in complete chaos.

"Did you hear me?" Octos folds his paper into a tidy rectangle. The fedora on his head shades his dark hair and sloped cheeks. But I can still make out the circles around his eyes. The way he fidgets.

"No mistakes today," he repeats.

"Right." I am not Octos's hostage, but sometimes it feels that way. *I* want to know how to use this magic coursing through my veins more than anyone. *Without* harming myself or people I love, but he seems to forget that.

I thought Octos might be bound to toushana, like me. Though I've never seen him use dark magic, his instruction is always intimately detailed. But no, he told me he just dabbled in it and studied it for a long time at House of Ambrose. That earned him a slew of tally marks *and* expulsion. Only Draguns are permitted to use toushana. Anyone else is executed.

So maybe it's jealousy. Sometimes there's a shadow to his encouragement. A fatigue to his smile. An odd gleam in his eye. I'm not sure why, but at times it just feels like he's holding on to me, too tightly. I survey my hands and arms, which, thanks to his help, have only ghosts of healed bruises. He transfigured my black diadem at Chateau Soleil. Even if he is jealous, Octos was the only person willing to show me how to use toushana.

"Thank you for helping me."

He meets my eyes. And for several moments says nothing.

"Of course."

"Three minutes," I tell him.

He slides me a fold of the paper and taps a tiny byline.

I don't recognize the name, but I skim the article; it's a blur of meaning. Some Houses are restructuring their leadership, lengthening term limits for Headmistresses, refreshing their security protocols.

"This means nothing to me."

"This article is written by Amelia Brendalin. She usually covers entertainment and gossip. But she's written the top story this week." Octos flips to the obituaries and points to some guy. "Frank was young and healthy, the hotshot headliner at the *Daily*, but now he's—"

"Dead."

He nods and it sends a shiver down my spine.

He shows me his notepad, where he has written in block letters the message he decoded from the paper.

HEKNEWTOOMUCH

"The dead guy knew too much about what?"

"Your guess is as good as mine."

Worry carves Octos's face. I try to find some concern for this reporter I've never met, for this Order that has never accepted me. But the only thoughts that come to mind are how my mother and I were forced to live our entire lives on the run because of my toushana, and how my grandmother—Headmistress of House of Marionne—was binding débutants to her House in servitude. How the boy who I let see pieces of me that I'd never shared with anyone found out my dark secret and betrayed me to my witch of a grandmother.

"I don't care, Octos. About any of it. We finish my training. Then I find my mom." If Abby doesn't find her first.

His mouth parts, but he closes it when we see the street empty. I stand, buttoning my coat.

"The park is clear. Let's get this over with."

Lincoln Park is an oasis of trees and a natural clearing in the otherwise concrete desert of Washington, DC. The rustle of leaves accompanies our footsteps as Octos and I slip through the barricade. There are no buildings or residences inside the park's gates. Only tiny outhouse structures, monuments, and objects that I could disintegrate in a blink.

I think about the last note I got from Abby weeks ago. I've read it a hundred times. *Nothing to report. I'll tell you the minute I get eyes on her so that you can come meet us.* I honestly thought Mom would be easier to find. That she would be waiting nearby, waiting for the streetlights to turn off. A lump rises in my throat and I can't force it back down. I pick up my pace, hustling through the park. To prepare for this moment, Octos would not let me use my magic for days.

"What's the test?"

He points toward a clearing farther ahead. I ready myself, inhaling deeply. Toushana reawakens, buckling in my chest like a block of ice cracking open. Suddenly I can hear a bird assembling a nest, tiny branches scraping against one another as they're fitted together. Earthiness from yesterday's rain grows more intense and I can smell it, stronger than anything else. Octos's heart beats calmly next to me. My heart thuds against my ribs.

"How are you so calm?"

"Calmness lends itself to a clear mind. You should try it."

"I'm perfectly calm," I lie.

He gives me a knowing look. *The trace.* He's worried Jordan will sense me and find us. Before my life fell apart at Chateau Soleil, before we fell apart, Jordan broke off a piece of his kor and put it in my chest, connecting us forever. It allows him to sense any intense emotions that I feel and see where I am so that he can come to me. At the time, the trace was to protect me.

If he found me now, he'd kill me.

Jordan is a fully fledged Dragun.

And his one job is to execute toushana-users, like me.

Jordan. My fingers snap to the lump in my inside pocket, where there's an old *Debs Daily* clipping from early fall commemorating a new flock of Draguns. Jordan was spotlighted. He glared at the camera; a round coin minted with a talon was pinned at his throat. Even in black-and-white print, his eyes were depthless, and his edges were more razor-sharp than I've ever seen them. Regret tugs at a knot in my chest. I never imagined we'd end up this way. Octos watches me with interest. My toushana is volatile and dangerous, yet somehow it's easier to control than my feelings for Jordan Wexton.

"Just up ahead," he says.

"I'm not so sure the trace works the way it's supposed to anymore."

I have had a roller coaster of emotions these last few months, and Jordan hasn't shown up once.

"Maybe." He walks faster, reshouldering his bag, and I hustle to keep up. When he finally stops, he pulls a silver vial out of his coat pocket.

"You're going to use your toushana to sun track the location of the Sphere."

I blink. "What?"

"Sun tracking is the most demanding way to use your magic. Your binding to toushana gives you a unique relationship with the Sphere."

"So I'm not destroying anything?"

Something shades his expression. "Yes and no. Let me demonstrate."

He takes the vial and spills a tiny hill of glowing yellow dust into his hand.

"Sun Dust. Ground from ancient sun stones, the source of magic itself. Watch." His mouth hardens and his complexion flushes, but before I can ask if he's okay, shadows ribbon through the air and spool in his free hand. I don't blink, watching as he draws toushana from outside his body to himself. He tosses up the fistful of Dust, and a hazy cloud forms in the air around us, obscuring everything. I blink to clear my vision, but it doesn't help. Octos's eyes roll in their sockets. When he opens them, his pupils are small as pinpoints. I gasp.

The toushana in his grip suddenly dissolves and the cloud of dust around us vanishes. He grunts, exasperated.

"The few times I've been successful at it took me many tries."

"So you've sun tracked the Sphere before?"

His throat bobs. "There's no greater test of your handle on dark magic. You will be able to do it much easier if your grasp of toushana is strong enough."

"It's strong enough."

"Suspend. Count. Flare. Cloak. Say it."

I do, and he checks the journal where he was taking notes earlier before handing me the vial. "Sunrise was four minutes ago. It'll crest these trees shortly. When it does, start. Say it again."

"Suspend. Count. Flare. Cloak."

"You'll have one chance. If you miss the flare, it could be weeks before we spot another."

I tighten my fist on the vial.

"When the Sun Dust suspends in the air, pull on your toushana until it feels like cold needles are pushing behind your eyes. When you open them, your toushana will tear through the haze of Dust to allow you to look directly at the sun. Count every spot you see." He glances at his journal again. "High number of sunspots these last several days indicate a flare is imminent. When you see a burst of light, it means the Sphere is on the move. Cloak immediately and command your magic to take you to wherever the light goes." He clamps a hand on my shoulder and stands with his feet shoulder-width apart.

"Then what?"

"Then we will gaze on the majesty of the Sphere with our own eyes."

My heart knocks into my ribs. "Then I've mastered my toushana?"

"*Mastered* is a strong word. I'd say you've mastered not hurting yourself."

"Good enough. How many minutes?"

He points at a cluster of maple trees in warm oranges and bright yellows, tinged by the shifting season. An ember of sunlight glows behind their branches. "Any moment now."

I pour a hill of Dust into my clammy palm and ready my magic. Threads of cold pulse through me. There isn't even a whisper of the warmth of the magic my grandmother used to anoint me. Toushana is the only magic I have now.

Toushana is who I am now.

Sunlight winks between the trees against the soft blue sky. I roll the fine grains of Dust in my hand and toss them up. They hang in the air. Cold scraps through me, wrapping around my heart. The sharp chill claws its way up my chest, rib by rib. Pressure builds in my throat, then releases in a ripple as an icy feeling wraps around my head. Icicles prick behind my eyes. I open them and the world is black

"*That's it.*" Octos's grip on me tightens.

A piercing dot of light appears, my toushana tearing through the darkness. One spot at first, then a rush of several.

"Ten, eleven, twelve."

They flash faster, lighting up my vision like an empty night sky hand-dotted with stars.

"Twenty-seven, twenty-eight, twenty-nine."

I count silently, numbers rolling through my mind, faster than my words can keep up. When I manage words again, I blurt, "Fifty-seven, fifty-eight."

"It's coming," he says, breathless, his grip on me trembling. "Don't look away. Not even for a second."

The dots stop appearing. The blackness bleeds to soft blue. Then a swatch of morning colors. And I realize I'm staring at the actual sky again. Panic takes flight in my chest. Suspend. Count. *Flare.* Cloak. Where's the flare? But before I can get the question out, the morning sky shifts, brightening.

"Something's happening."

"A flare," he says.

The sky ripples orange, then purple. A bright light flashes and streaks across the sky.

"Cloak, now!" He locks both arms around me.

I steady my feet and twist into the coldest depths of myself, willing my toushana to transfigure us into fragments of matter. Cold magic seeps from my pores, swallowing us in shadows, disintegrating every part of me until I'm nothing but a floating feeling, a dark cloud of air. Weightless, I can still feel Octos attached to me. The flare sticks in my mind's eye. *Follow the light.* The world darkens and my stomach drops as if the floor has gone from beneath me. *Take me to the Sphere!*

Pressure builds, and my magic thrums. For several moments that's all I feel. Then thick, salty air fills my nostrils. My feet thud onto the earth, and I barrel into Octos but catch myself before face-planting. I gape at the back of my hands, then my palms. No purple, no pain.

"No bruising!" I stumble up.

But Octos's head swivels in every direction. "The Sphere. It should be here."

There's only night sky and rocky grasslands. The glowing orb that holds the magic of the Order together is nowhere in sight.

"Suspend. Count. Flare. Cloak. I did what you said."

"You did," he says, still searching. I hold up my hands for him to see. But Octos looks right past them before storming off toward the coastline. "We should at least be closer."

"Octos!" I hustle to keep up with him. The ground ends abruptly at a stretch of ocean. Below, waves batter the rocky mountainside, bathed in moonlight. "I don't know why the Sphere isn't here, but that can't be my fault."

He faces me with a slouch of disappointment. "No, it's not. Sun tracking is an imprecise science. The steps, though, you performed beautifully."

I stand straighter and show him my hands again, which finally he studies. He flips them to either side.

"Any pain?"

"None."

"Very good work, but we're going to have to try again."

My heart stops. "What do you mean, *try again*?"

"We're going to sun track again, another night or so. Maybe a month."

Something hot turns in my chest. "I don't have a month."

"We gain nothing by rushing your training." He pats my shoulder. "Come on, at sunrise we can try again."

"No, Octos." I ball my fists.

"What do you mean, *no*?"

"I'm done training. I have to find my mom."

"You know you can't do that. Draguns will expect that. Abby will be more successful without you with her."

"I'm not afraid of them."

"Then you're arrogant. You overestimate your own power, something else our training can address." He walks away. I don't follow.

He stops, sliding his chin over his shoulder to glare at me. "Come. Along."

"I said, we're done training."

"Quell, you have to trust me."

"I have. And now you have to trust me. I've mastered not hurting myself, you said it yourself. I passed the last test." I offer Octos his Sun Dust vial back and tighten my bag on my shoulders. "I'm going back to the safe house to see if there's been word from Abby. From there I'll figure out what to do next."

"Quell, please. A few more nights."

"For all I know, *Draguns* could have found my mother by now! Do you have any idea what they'd do for information on me? Because it's all I think about when I lie awake at night!"

"You *must* stay calm."

"I'm as calm as I can be!"

"The trace," he whispers, as if the words alone will summon Jordan.

"He's not coming." I hold my chest, remembering the silver flame that burns inside it. Jordan's flame. "I've experienced a whirlwind of emotions these last several weeks, but Jordan hasn't found me. Either binding with my toushana ruined the trace or he's choosing not to respond. If and when I see Jordan Wexton, I will be ready to end him before he ends me." I unleash my toushana and it swallows us in a dark fog. My fingers throb with a pain I thought was behind me.

Octos tries to step closer to me but my shadows push him back. He won't stop me this time. At first, he told me to stay at the safe house until he got there. A month I waited, with the person in charge, Knox, and her helper, Willam, side-eyeing my every move. I didn't know what lies Octos told them to let me stay there. I didn't know what to say or not say. Every night I worried they'd try to strangle me in my sleep. Then he showed up and finally began training me. But that took several weeks. I am done waiting. I need to find my mom, with his help or not. I pull my shadows back into myself with a big breath, and Octos gapes at my growing bruises.

"I can handle it." I walk away.

"*Quell!*" The unfamiliar lilt of anger in his voice stops me dead in my tracks. He catches up to me and shoves the vial back into my hand. "*One. More. Night!*"

Then his eyes widen.

He turns pale.

"We both have to go *now.*" He grabs me by the sleeve.

"Stop telling me what to do and listen for once!" I shove away and push the vial back to him, but his hands fumble the metal. He gasps. I watch as the vial of Sun Dust plummets toward the ground. He grabs for it, but it lands with a smash. Sun Dust bursts from the top, spilling all over the grass, dusting it in a bright glow.

"No, no, no." Octos whimpers, trying and failing to grab handfuls of fine Dust before it disappears into the ground.

"Maybe now you'll start listening to me."

His eyes widen.

"I'm leaving. Now."

He follows without a word.

TWO

⸺✳⸺

Jordan

Unmarked tourists crowd Yaäuper Rea like fleas.

What was once a university at the heart of the Order's operations now masquerades as a museum. My insides swim with nerves; raiding here feels like sacrilege. Still, I put another step forward and gesture for my team to gather. The Dragunhead intends to name me second-in-command, but if I fail at something this big, in a place this important, I'll never see a raid again, let alone lead one. Everything I've been working toward, all I've sacrificed, all I've lost, will be for nothing.

I twist a ruby ring on my finger, recalling the notes on the target. He's described as young, tall, and slender, with dark brown hair, wearing jeans, a windbreaker, and a red baseball cap. He was first spotted exchanging goods with a Trader in New Jersey using toushana, which put him on the brotherhood's radar. From there we trailed him to London: he was carrying liquid kor in quantities large enough to level a block of small buildings.

We followed him here to Wales. He landed early this morning, but didn't show his face outside his hotel until midday, when he took a train to Yaäuper—coincidentally, the busiest time of day for the museum. I'm not entirely sure what he's planning, but I have my suspicions. If I'm right, the blood of hundreds could be on my hands.

"It's a shame what they've let come to this place," Charlie says beside me. He is the most seasoned in today's flock of Draguns. His short black beard has peppered significantly since I saw him a month ago. His usual stocky stature has slendered, his meaty arms hardly noticeable in his sleeved top. Before I finished at House of Perl, Charlie guided me on upholding Beaulah's rules. Since I've left, we've only butted heads. But this time, I don't disagree with him.

"A damned shame."

Loitering bystanders bottleneck nearby, drunk with the sight of Yaäuper's ornately carved architecture, endless arched windows, and flying buttresses. Charlie's thumb runs back and forth across his commissioning coin, its silver minted with a cracked column. My jaw clenches. *It should be a talon*. He notices my glare and smirks, amused.

"Is he working alone?" Charlie asks, slipping the coin into his pocket.

"Appears so. But we need to follow him, let his plans start to unfold, to know." The team surrounds me and I count heads. Five here, plus one at the entrance scoping out the scene. Far too many for a raid in broad daylight, but the Dragunhead wouldn't be argued with. I had grabbed a few familiar faces: my former mentor and Yaniselle, my first of many things, both from Hartsboro, the seat of House of Perl. Both Draguns with extraordinary skill. Despite our pasts, they're unarguably the best. I selected a few others with impressive raiding records who had finished from various Houses.

The shortest tagalong, who isn't taller than my elbow, has dark scruffy hair, pale ruddy cheeks, and big hazel eyes. The Dragunhead insisted he join.

"How old are you?" I ask when I spot the boy, his collar pinned by a cracked column, magically changing the shape of his nose in the reflection of a puddle.

"Too young," says one of the others as he runs his nails back and forth over the tally marks tattooed prominently on his bald head—marks of his achievements. Boastful like a typical 'Roser. "It isn't the way it's done."

Charlie pulls out his coin and flips it before blowing Tally Mark a kiss.

"He's a *kid*," I say.

"He's a spawn of Perl perversion. Another training to wear the talon as a costume."

The boy's eyes widen.

"You sound jealous." Charlie smirks.

"Enough," I say.

"You *Perls* think you're above the way of things."

I flinch at the surname I was born with. A stain on everything I stand for. My father lost our family name when I was younger. The only thing he's ever done that I've wanted to thank him for.

"That boy's a Wexton," Charlie says.

I step closer to Tally Mark, and the pounding organ in his chest batters his ribs.

"Another word of division on my raid and—"

Tally Mark crosses his meaty arms. I can feel the hatred and judgment rolling off him: for the House that bred me, for the privilege that I have as a Headmistress's nephew to rise in position so swiftly. A crater vibrates in my chest. Words move through me like bile that needs to come out. I *hate* my House, but I can't say that. I can't shout how deep my aunt's obsession with power has become, how there are no rules she won't bend and few she won't break. She and my father were cut from the same cloth.

The Dragunhead is the only one who actually cares about protecting magic. *But some things are too destructive to admit out loud.* The face of the girl I have to kill comes to mind like a summoned ghost. *Many things.*

I allow some distance between Tally Mark and I.

"Regardless of your disaffinity for my name, you will do what I say, as I say it. And I've said *enough*." I don't need his approval. I need to finish this raid, apprehend the target, and ensure no Unmarkeds are harmed. That puts me a step closer toward having the reputation and influence I'll need to flush the corruption out of this Order.

The boy stares at me with fear in his eyes. I lower myself to his level.

"You were saying?"

"You asked my age, sir. I'm nine."

Beaulah's sending them younger and younger.

"Mother says I have a better shot of being invited to join the brother-hood if I've got raid practice under my belt." It's true. I'd done so many raids by the time I was seventeen, an invitation from the brotherhood had seemed like a given. Perl débutants who become Draguns outnum-ber other Houses ten to one. My aunt is as subtle as she is strategic.

"Target spotted, but he's a ways off from the doors," Yani says over the speakerphone in my hand. "Stand by."

"Aye."

The team's conversations move on but the boy is frozen, his gaze stuck on Tally Mark.

"Ignore him." I squeeze the boy's shoulder. "Remind me of your name?"

"Stryker, sir. But my friends call me Stryk."

"I'm not a sir."

"You're raid leader. Mother says we're supposed to obey on raids with-out question. So nobody gets hurt."

"Look at the young'un." Charlie slugs him in the arm playfully. "Knows *all* the rules."

"Well, your first order of business is to stop calling me *sir*," I say.

Stryk nods, then bites his lip. I look to the rest and dole out assign-ments before turning to Tally Mark, who's still fuming.

"What personas can you pull off today?" I ask.

"A restaurateur or a bum musician."

"Use the musician, loiter near the door."

"Do we have execution orders?" he asks, slipping on a hat to cover his tally-tattooed head.

"Today, your ears are your greatest weapon, Tally Mark." I clap him on the back.

His jaw clenches at the nickname.

"Focus on what matters: the raid. Keep magic use discreet. This whole place will end up a bloody mess if we're exposed. No one needs that kind of death on their conscience."

Tally Mark motions for the others who also finished at House of Ambrose, and together they mutter in prayer. "The Sovereign, point out the darkness. The Sage, bless our hands with skill. The Wielder, blow the winds of fate our way."

"You better hope those fake gods hear you, boys." Charlie jostles Tally Mark by the neck before tossing his bag to Stryk to carry.

"Target is approaching the doors," Yani says from the speakerphone. "Coming up the south side of the building. Repeat, Red Ball Cap is in play."

I grab Charlie by the sleeve before turning to Stryk. "Your second order is to stick with this guy. And no magic, just watch."

Stryk's posture deflates.

"Mother says—"

"Stop worrying about everything Mother says." Craters dent the boy's cheeks. Charlie's mouth hardens but he remains silent like a good Dragun. I tug my coat tighter around myself and push more insistently through the crowd of paying trespassers. My team disappears into the throng as well. The line at the entrance to Yaäuper is slow, but I spot the target stepping through its doors and follow at a distance. When we're inside, I present the shifted tickets, and in minutes we're past the entrance ropes.

"Garden courtyard tours this way," someone yells, and I signal to Charlie. He and the boy head that way.

"History tour starting this way," says another. Red Ball Cap moves toward the history guide and I do the same, careful to stick to the perimeter of people.

"Now, if you'll stand in the center there and look straight up, you'll notice a dome of colored glass." Gasps erupt from the crowd as our tour guide pulls at his high-waisted khakis. "Most assume these are just random pictures. But these are *stories*, legends of magic that thirteenth-century artisans worked tirelessly to capture."

I shift my feet in irritation and keep an eye on Red Ball Cap. He hangs back on the perimeter of the crowd, looking around more than he looks up. The tour guide calls our attention to a particular story: a window of flames surrounding a village.

"That one there is one of my favorite tales, about dragons roaming the earth, burning villages, determined to eradicate the human race and claim the planet for themselves."

"Utterly ridiculous," I huff, and heads swivel in my direction. I force my lips to smile.

"The legend goes that villagers could hear screams and smell burning flesh for miles," the tour guide goes on. "Until Elopheus, a humble farmer of no special gift or talent, managed to slay one of these beasts. Then he dressed himself in the dragon's skin and found he could suddenly breathe fire, too. He flew from village to village, protecting the people and chasing away the dragons forever."

Cameras raise and I groan. Elopheus is probably rolling over in his grave hearing this warped version of history. Red Ball Cap and I meet eyes, and I bite down my annoyance, hoping my scorn hasn't given me away. I grab my phone and take a picture of the windows, trying my best to appear impressed.

Outside, the sky flickers an odd orange, then purple, before flashing bright white.

My brother comes to mind unbidden for some reason. He is a traitor in more ways than one. First, he tries to shatter the Sphere, then he runs off with . . . *her.* Red Ball Cap breaks from the edge of the crowd, clears a roped-off area, and disappears down a stairway. I shove thoughts of Yagrin away and follow him.

The basement is silent and dim, but light streams in from the ground-level windows overhead. "Into the basement," I whisper into my phone, but the signal flickers. The beat of Red Ball Cap's footsteps quickens as it grows fainter. I follow him deeper into the bowels of the museum, when I turn down a familiar dead-end corridor packed with storage crates and RESTRICTED AREA signage. The last time I was here was the evening before my Cotillion. Yani and the rest of my Perl peers threw me a surprise celebration in this palace of magical history. The Dragunhead had to sign off on the approval, and security was strict. The others spent the night drowning themselves in dancing, drinking, and hanging from the ripped ceilings. But I spent it down here, in a secret library, home to a legendary collection of magical texts, at the end of this corridor.

I speed up. The inner workings of the Sphere, original writings from Dysiis—the founding father of toushana—dangerous information that should have never been left behind with only a doorless stone room to conceal it.

When the target reaches the end of the corridor, he presses his hands against the walls. I hide around a corner, stealing a glimpse at him. Shadows bleed from his palms and the brick blackens, disintegrating beneath his touch. He destroys enough of the wall to step through.

Once he's inside, I hurry to the opening he's just created and look inside. Thousands of texts cover every inch of wall. A single candle with a tiny wick burns on a table. *He isn't working alone.* Someone else was here. He grabs the light and rushes to the shelves. His fingers trail several spines before pulling a book off a shelf. But he quickly closes it and moves to another. He parts the next one, flipping furiously. When he tears a page out, my heart seizes in my chest. I step over the crumbled opening and join him inside.

"I'm pretty sure we're supposed to stick to the rooms along the tour."

His pulse picks up. He wears a bit of jewelry. He has no visible tattoo marks.

"Those guides are always so boring, don't you think?" His hand holding the torn page moves to his pocket. I close the distance between us.

"The rules are the rules. Stealing pages from ancient texts is also probably a no-go."

"I've never been much for the rules." His palm opens and shadows seep through his skin, spooling in his fist. Not rippling through the air as toushana does for me and my brethren. His seems to appear in his palm *out of nowhere.* I blink, hard, but tighten my fists, glaring at his magic to discern for certain if the magic is indeed coming from *inside* him. He hesitates, clumsily pulling at the toushana, and my certainty abandons me. As he fumbles with it, I command the chill of death to my hands and dark magic rushes to me in an instant. He reaches for me, but I'm faster. My hand hooks around the base of his skull. Before he has a chance to react, my wrist pushes against his windpipe. The black dancing on his fingertips dissolves, leaving a nasty bruise behind.

"What's happening, please, I can't feel my—" His body straightens like a board in my grip as the Dragun choke takes him.

"Do you have any idea how *not* smart it is to call on toushana when you don't know how to control it?" I tighten my grip; his eyes widen. "Right now, toushana is moving into you at such a high rate, it feels like freezing water is replacing your blood. Like you're slowly being turned to ice. Soon you'll pass out from a lack of oxygen to your brain. Then your heart will give out. Unless you tell me very quickly who ordered you here." I loosen my grip to free up his tongue.

"Like I said," he chokes out. "I'm not much for rules."

"I—" Suddenly my heart twinges, stuttering in my chest. For a moment I can't breathe. Confusion clenches my brow as anger burns deep in my belly, swelling and strong. The feeling, its place and intensity, nudges me with unfamiliarity.

It's not mine.

It's hers.

Quell.

Heat roils through me, my own frustration rising as the image of her freckled skin, head of long curls, brown eyes, somehow both fiery and tender, form in my memory. I wait for some visual of her location, but it doesn't come. The trace I have on her has not shown me her location since she bound to toushana. Binding to dark magic destroyed that part of the tracer magic.

A rocky ache turns deep in my chest. My grip tightens on my captive. Her name sits on my tongue. Her face lingers in my mind. The way her nose would crinkle when she was uncomfortable. The way she'd hide her laughs when we first met, as if she hadn't given herself permission to feel things like that freely. That changed drastically. As if part of her came alive at Chateau Soleil right in front of me. I remember the last time I saw her, when I *truly* saw her, when the glimpses of her desperate determination finally made sense. She is a raging storm when she wants something: forceful, unyielding, uncontainable. She would not be possessed by anyone or anything. *That* Quell is whose anger I feel now, and a tangle of emotions wrestles in my chest.

My feelings for her can't be real. She played a game with me, using me to get better at magic, concealing her secret the entire time. The look in her eyes when I pleaded with her to not bind with toushana and seal her fate deepens the throbbing ache. I confessed that I loved her—and she turned her back on me. A feeling of revulsion rises so viscerally in my throat that I try to gather it in my mouth to spit it out.

She was *right* under my nose! What she did at House of Marionne's Cotillion, and what she's done with her toushana, makes a mockery of this Order.

When I find her, she's dead.

Not by my orders. By my hand.

I force myself back to the present, waiting for Quell's anger to pass, separating it from my own frustration. When it dissolves, my insides uncinch.

Then my chest pangs again.

This time with frigid fear. My arm trembles and nervousness thrashes in my stomach. I close my eyes and suddenly Yagrin's harried face appears: the trace I put on my brother, working like a trace is supposed to. Behind him is a stretch of rocky grassland and an ocean.

She's angry.

He's scared.

The urge to go to them gnaws at me. My hand slacks and Red Ball Cap wriggles from my grip. His fist slams into my nose and the world spins.

"Slick, are we," someone behind me shouts as I blink the world back into focus. Yani whips past me in a blur of smooth black hair and deep brown skin.

Red Ball Cap darts to the doorway, but Yani is faster, grabbing him in the choke.

"I'll hold him," I say, finally coming to. "Grab Charlie. He'll help you take him in."

"You grab Charlie," she says, refusing to release her hold. Her dark eyes glitter with ambition, shinier than the cracked-column coin at her throat. Yani's lethal and sharp. But she's also stubbornly fiery. Always on the edge of flirting with her demise. "I don't need a babysitter to bring a Dark-bearer descendant in." The jewel in her nose twitches with her smirk.

I blink. *Darkbearers* . . .

There are toushana-users. But long ago there were toushana *worship-pers* who terrorized, pillaged, and slaughtered their way across kingdoms for hundreds of years, just for the hell of it. That's who Elopheus *actually* spent his life fighting.

Darkbearers have been gone for centuries, but magical bloodlines rarely just die out. There are rumors some still congregate in secret. Beaulah always said rumors are born from a seed of truth. She's wrong about a lot, but maybe she's right about this.

I wrestle with Ball Cap's collar. On the back of the target's neck is a circle of angry red flesh in the shape of a sun with a shaded center. A mark I've only ever seen on the pages of a history book.

"You will burn for your traitorous life," I spit.

"You know nothing about me or my life," he says.

I snatch the page he'd managed to shove in his pocket. It's a diagram of the Sphere with hand-drawn annotations, torn from the book *The Unbreakable Pact.* "I know that if you had any regard for your life, you wouldn't be here."

"Have you heard what's happened to the Sphere? You must know what's coming, and yet you're here, more concerned about me."

I watch him closely. His pupils are relaxed; the thud of his heart has eased some. *Is this a game, a warning, a threat?* I turn to Yani. "*Wait* for Charlie."

She purses her lips but doesn't mutter another word. I send another message, this one asking Charlie to meet us in the library and bring a Retentor. To my great relief, it sends. Thankfully, he, Tally Mark, and Stryker are here in minutes. Charlie takes over restraining the target so that I can pull Yani aside.

"How'd you know what he was?"

"How bad do you want to know?" Her teeth pull at her lip.

I ignore her. "When you get back to Headquarters, write your report. Any other intel you have needs to be included."

"Wait, don't burn him!" Stryk rushes over and tugs at my arm. "Mother says—"

"What did I tell you about listening to Mother?"

A question glints in the boy's amber eyes, but he skips off.

"You shouldn't poison that boy's mind like that," Charlie says. "Whatever your grievances with Beaulah, that is his House mother."

"We're not under the Houses anymore, Charlie. I'm not your boy to shape and prune. Get the captive back to Headquarters. Book him. If he burns, we do it quickly. I have no doubt he's working with someone much smarter."

Charlie's lips thin as he and the captive head out the door.

"Yani, get Stryk back to Hartsboro."

She takes the boy by the hand and staggers her feet, preparing to cloak. "You know, I almost thought you'd lost the nerve. That that girl broke you . . . permanently."

"Concern yourself less with your thoughts of me and more with my orders." I turn to the boy. "Stryk, you did great today."

"Can I use magic next time?"

"Probably not."

"But *why?*" His eyes well with tears. "I'm *really* good, I promise. I can shift my whole face! Been practicing since I was eight."

"And I could at six."

His mouth falls open. His unruly hair covers his brow in bangs, and he wiggles one of his front teeth every few moments as if it's some nervous habit. He just wants to do a good job. Make his House proud. Beaulah has indoctrinated him well.

"In an ideal world, you could use magic anywhere and anytime you want. But the world doesn't work that way, Stryk. It can. But it doesn't. Not yet. We've got to fix our reputation first." I move his bangs aside to see him better. "That's why you're going to be such a good Dragun. You'll help restore magic's good name, keeping it away from the people who want to use it to do bad things. You think you could help me with that?"

"I *know* I can."

"Then the future is bright."

The boy blushes, and Yani pulls him to her.

When the library is empty, I feel for my brother again. These raids the Dragunhead insists I focus on are only so helpful when the future of magic hangs in the balance because of my brother, Yagrin.

And *her.*

But now this? Darkbearer descendants, organized and on the move. The Sphere's condition is emboldening people. I tighten my core, close my eyes, and feel for him. But there is no fear churning in my gut, no sense of anything from her or him. The whiff of his location is gone. How close have they gotten to finding the Sphere these last few months? My hope has been that, if they were close, I'd feel it through my brother's trace. I summon the cold, preparing to cloak. *To Headquarters.* I need to speak with the Dragunhead.

I must find Yagrin and Quell *now.*

Or soon there won't be any magic to protect.

THREE

——✳——

Quell

"This is a mistake," Octos whispers as he watches every corner of the forest behind the safe house.

"She's written *four* times, Octos!" I shake a fistful of Abby's letters that I'd missed at him and keep going. *"Four!"*

Crisp autumn air whips by as if it's irritated, too. The truth is none of Abby's letters have been very descriptive, and each was a little more confusing than the one before it. But the point of each was to ask me to meet her at the spot we'd arranged: a secluded patch of trees south of the safe house where Octos and I have been staying. Thankfully, the most recent letter suggested we meet up tonight.

"We'll be back before Knox and Willam return. If you're scared, go back." I expect him to turn around. It isn't his mom out there somewhere. But Octos shoulders his backpack, slipping both straps on his arms, and hurries to keep up. Afternoon sun weaves through the canopy, and all I can think about is my mom, where she is, if she heard about what happened at Cotillion, if she's worried. If she could see how strong my magic thrums through me now, she'd see I made the right choice. She'd pinch my arm, smirk, and wink. *She'd do that. She would.* I blink to clear the tears forming in my eyes.

"If they find out you've shared their location, we'll be looking for somewhere else to sleep tonight."

"It wouldn't be my first time." I stomp ahead, keeping an eye out for a break in the trees where a small stream intersects with a slumped oak tree. *Follow the water three hundred paces west. Then another one hundred south. Don't lose count!* My feet rush over the damp earthen floor, skilled at moving swiftly and quietly from years on the run, making myself invisible. Octos takes another strained look around but follows when I skip over the tree and turn in the direction of sunset.

"We really need to reconsider sun tracking the Sphere," he urges.

I don't respond. The moment passes and a babbling rush of water pulls us south, deeper into the forest. At one hundred paces, we stop. The air is still; the branches don't move. Something shifts in the distance. A sudden twist of light sends a shiver up my arms.

"You've gone pale," Octos says.

"I'm fine." My insides are lead. "She'll show." After a few minutes, I knock two sticks together three times and wait.

Knock. Knock. Knock.

Three knocks in return. *She's here.* I tighten at my center, and a trickle of cold slides down the crown of my head. I feel for my diadem but there's only hair. Abby doesn't know I bound with toushana at Cotillion. She wasn't there. When I saw her afterward, I hid my diadem and told her that I'd outed my grandmother's secret to everyone. That's why I was running.

I slip out from the shadows. "Abby?"

"Quell?" She steps into the light alone. Her dress is a deep purple with capped sleeves. Her cropped dark hair has grown out some, and she wears it tidy and pulled back in a low bun. Her diadem sparkles in the sunlight overhead. I race toward her with a hug. "I didn't think you were going to show tonight either."

"I'm so sorry I didn't respond to your last letters."

"It's alright. Are you okay?"

"Don't worry about me. I'm fine." I squeeze her, hugging her again. "You look really good, Abby. You're taking good care of yourself."

"It's been a lot going from town to town. Making excuses at my internship." She flips open her compact. "Almost out of transport powder. But Mynick has been helping me get more. He's good to me."

"I'm glad to hear it."

She eyes Octos. "Is everything . . . with practicing your magic going okay?"

I look away, unable to lie to Abby's face. "It's going alright. Thanks for coming alone."

"Of course."

I try to exhale when Abby sighs, exasperated. "I couldn't bring Mynick if I wanted to. He failed his Dragun exams on purpose, but it only got him snatched from his bed to spend two nights in the dunker." She folds her arms. "The Dragunhead intends for him to see it through."

Octos grunts. If Mynick's not able to get out of becoming a Dragun, that could be a problem.

"Have you found out anything about my mom?"

"I wish I had better news. But, Quell," Abby says as she gives my hand a squeeze, "I can't find anything about her. I thought maybe her hair or something could have changed from the picture you gave me. But she's gone. A ghost." She sighs. "It's too bad you skipped your Cotillion, because what if she was there? Like, what if she came to see you debut?"

I cock my head to the side. "Abby, what are you talking about? I didn't miss my Cotillion. You did. I wrote and told you to meet me afterward."

"No I didn't. That's ridiculous. I remember the black dahlia arrangements in the crystal vases. And the plum sashes you did as an accent to the House colors. I was there and didn't see you anywhere." Abby plants a hand on her hip. "What's come over you? Everybody knows you ditched your Cotillion."

Octos and I share a glance. He steps closer to her.

"Abby, we met afterward in the Secret Wood. If you were inside the ball, you'd recall the cloud of black fog enveloping the stage."

Abby gapes at me, shaking her head in disbelief.

"In the forest I told you that I exposed Grandmom's tether and asked you to look for her," I say. "Remember?"

Now it's Abby whose forehead creases in confusion. "What do you mean by *tether*?"

I remind Abby of how Grandmom used tracer magic to tether débutants as they bound to her House at Third Rite. How I didn't complete Third Rite and instead revealed her secret to everyone. I leave out my toushana.

"If that happened, I'd remember. *I* was at House of Marionne's end of season Cotillion. *You* were not. You didn't finish!" Abby's stare is lucid, but a crater dents between her brows. "Quell, what kind of game are you playing?"

She's forgotten.

"Your grandmother's behind this," Octos whispers beside me.

"When was the last time you visited Chateau Soleil?" I ask, my throat thickening as the pieces of what's going on click into place.

"A month ago. After we met here the last time."

"Did she send you an invitation?"

"Yes, I . . . actually, I don't remember an invitation, exactly. But somehow I knew about it and went." Her tongue pokes her cheek.

"And what did you do there?" I ask.

"It was a reception. Everyone was there. She wanted to speak about the rumors circulating about the House."

Refreshments. Food. Drinks.

Elixirs.

Poisons.

"She used the tether to summon you. Then she gave you something to alter the memory." The truth is a knife between my ribs. "So that everyone in House Marionne has fake memories of my Cotillion." My world dents at its edges. My grandmother could have planted literally anything in her mind. And not just Abby—anyone tethered to her House. Octos stares at me with a brow raised, and I realize he's worried about the same thing.

"Guys, what are you—"

"Abby, listen to me. My grandmother can summon you to her any moment. Don't take any food or drink from her. Don't even breathe the air in that place."

"Replacing memories for all those tethered to House of Marionne doesn't get rid of the talk about what happened," Octos says. "There had to be others at the ball, from other Houses, who saw?"

"They'll be written off as gossips. See?" I gesture at Abby. "My grandmother's as clever as she's evil. And always ten steps ahead."

Abby's gaze darts between us. "I did hear some things about—*terrible* lies, Quell, about how you accused your grandmother of enslaving her House. How you unleashed dark magic at the party to ruin it because you were denied participation. Someone even said you and Shelby Duncan were conspiring together. And that you killed her!"

Something shifts in my bones. "People think I *killed* Shelby?"

"I don't believe any of it." She grabs my hands.

"Oh, Abby. I'm so sorry." I hug her and she sinks into my hold.

"You're saying . . . Did Headmistress really—" She begins to sob quietly.

"Abby, it's going to be okay. Just trust me, okay?" I tell her everything that happened again and detail the plan of why *she* was looking for my mom—because *I* can't, not if Draguns or my grandmother are after me, because that's the first thing they would expect me to do. I'm careful to leave out how I bound to toushana. I need to shield my own truth. She nods, a few tears still in her eyes. By the end, the afternoon sky has dimmed. Knox and Willam will be back before dark. We're running out of time.

"Where exactly have you looked for my mom?"

Abby pulls out a notepad and hands it to me. It's filled with addresses from cities all over.

"I did find out that, at one point, she wasn't traveling alone. But no one I asked knew who she was with. And that was a long time ago, back when you were at the Chateau."

"Where was she when she was traveling with someone?"

"Chicago."

There's no House near there. "What was she doing?" I mutter, more to myself than anyone. I search Octos for understanding, but he only shrugs.

"We should hurry back," he says.

"There's still light left," I assure him. "Even if we get back a few minutes after them, they won't miss us." Safe house grocery days were an all-day affair. Keeping a houseful of people fed while living off the Order's radar was no quick job.

"If they see us coming out of the woods from this direction . . ."

"They won't." I'm less worried about not having a place to stay if they kick us out and more worried about what they'll do if they find out Octos lied to them about who we are and why we're there. Octos sets down his backpack and digs through it for something that he doesn't find.

"I'm going to get a glimpse of the house from the edge of the trees." His cloak takes him, and I turn back to Abby, who is staring in the distance.

"Did I remember everything the last time we met here?" She rubs her arms.

I nod. "We had no idea she was going to use the tether that way, and so soon. Does Mynick know all this?"

"He does. So he should remember." She exhales, and I consider urging her to keep Mynick in the dark about all this until I'm sure I can trust him. But this isn't the time to stress her out more.

"Where exactly are you staying?" Abby asks.

I'm not sure what to say, but I try my best. "The people we're staying with are very"—I search for the right word—"private."

"Are they in the Order?"

I don't answer her.

"I'm doing everything I can to help you. Please don't keep secrets, Quell."

"We're staying at a safe house," I whisper, hesitant to say any more.

Her eyes widen. "Those still exist?"

"Quell, the truck," Octos shouts, his voice coming from somewhere in the distance. "I'll try to stall them."

"I have to go." An idea nudges me but I immediately slouch in disappointment. If I had my key chain, I could give it to her. But Grandmom turned it to dust.

Abby throws her arms around me and I hug her close. "I'm done training. But he's right, I should probably keep my distance. I'm going to stick to the shadows and look around, too." I squeeze her once more. "Next time, we won't meet like this. I miss you."

"I miss you!"

"Remember, stay away from my grandmother's territory. As best as you can."

Abby nods, and I show her the way the stream curves through the forest to the south. "Follow that, it'll get you out of here unseen." I watch until Abby's out of sight before shouldering my bag and grabbing Octos's. Something beneath its leather flap flashes on and off.

My heart stutters.

I open his bag and gasp.

The pulsing glow is my mother's key chain.

FOUR

✳

Nore

The dead hovered near the doors of the ballroom.

"They're here," Nore said to her brother, wondering if he smelled their sour stench.

"Of course they are. You're of age to debut. They're waiting. And watching." He held out his arm as they stood at the entrance to the Gala. The room burst with floods of guests wearing fine clothes, boasting every style of diadem or mask, ornate and simple ones. Marked balls made her especially queasy. She preferred the public ones where unmarked were welcome, where magic was hidden and fewer people knew who she was. Across the grand room's entrance was a wall of windows that looked out across the snow-capped Rocky Mountains.

Her brother was dressed finely in a drab gray tuxedo that appeared threadbare, but she recognized the careful pattern of its stitching. These clothes were handmade. He jingled gold coins in his pockets before offering her one. "If you're nervous."

Nore wasn't going to let the dead make her superstitious. She tugged at her gray shawl before hooking her arm onto his. She'd been the presumed heir of House of Ambrose since birth. But she'd seen the disembodied shadows of her ancestors more often since she stopped using Red's persona than she had in her entire life before. Something was up. "They couldn't find me as Red, I suspect."

Her brother's expression lit up. "Actually, I think you're right."

Now they didn't want her out of their sight. *But why . . .*

"Good evening!" An usher in a teal suit and iridescent mask bowed at them before pulling the grand arched doors open. "You're first of the great House families to arrive. It's an honor to greet you."

Nore gave him a nod.

"My research has taken a turn, sister." Her brother leaned in for a whisper. "There's a link between the ancestors and our magic."

"What kind of link?"

"Haven't figured that out yet."

The usher eyed them, his foot tapping softly as a reminder to them to keep moving forward. Ellery took a step, but Nore's feet anchored them in place.

"We have to go in, Nore."

She couldn't move. But it wasn't the ancestors. She was growing accustomed to ignoring their brooding presence. It was the feel of the dress against her skin. The music sifting between the doors and the people swaying to it. The last time she was at a fancy ball, a different escort was on her arm. With Red's face and Yagrin beside her, she was fearless. It felt *good* not being the only one who wanted nothing to do with the Houses.

Dread coiled in her stomach. She didn't want to go in there and play the role of heiress. She hated the Order, and all she wanted was the one person in the entire world who understood that on her arm. She looked up, hardening every part of her that she could feel. It would be easier to pretend Yagrin was dead. It'd still hurt, but hope cut deeper. She drew in a sharp breath and let it out slowly. Life with the surname Ambrose had well acquainted her with doing what she didn't want to do.

"And you're sure Mother will be here?"

"I saw her maids preparing her dress before I left. She'll be here."

The usher cleared his throat.

Ellery turned to him. "If the door is too heavy, I can hold it for you."

He reddened. "Please, sir, take your time."

Her brother's lips split in a smile that didn't reach his eyes.

"Whenever you're ready," he said to Nore. She closed her eyes and realized her hand was trembling. She hadn't felt this nervous since she attended the Summer Bloom Tea this past summer at Chateau Soleil in order to get face time with Headmistress Darragh Marionne.

"Say the word and we'll leave," he said.

Ellery was on her side no matter what. Yagrin had been on her side, too. The days he'd steal away to spend with Red at the farm made her feel like there was no Order at all. She bit the smile at her lips, thinking of the way he would press her to tell him *everything* he missed since they last saw each other. He listened intently to every single detail, enthralled, and none of it was about magic. They would wander the meadows barefoot for hours, then lie down, their limbs tangled around each other, watching the clouds in silence. Doing nothing in particular. She didn't want to be anywhere else or with anyone else.

She forced herself to step forward, inside the Fall Harvest Gala ballroom.

Nore clenched her teeth and looked for her mother. Garlands and swags in deep rusts, warm browns, and golden yellow rimmed windows, doors, and chairs around the ballroom. Textured fabrics swallowed the tables, spilling over their edges and puddling on the floor like blooming flowers. The scent of pumpkin spice and cinnamon assaulted her. The holidays used to make Nore nostalgic, reminding her of being with the ones she loved most. Now the smell sickened her.

She refocused. Her mother *would be* confronted that evening. She wiggled in her plain gray dress, and the blade, hidden in her corset, dipped in toushana, rubbed her ribs. A fire dagger, the Trader called it. Carried by Draguns. A weapon so deadly it could kill death itself. She wouldn't need to use it. Possessing it alone would show her mother she meant business.

"Nore Ambrose, tenth of her blood, Cultivator candidate and heir of House Ambrose," the usher announced. "Escorted by Ellery Ambrose." He went on with Ellery's titles, but she wasn't listening. Her breath was a rock in her chest. She skimmed the ballroom, and when she spotted a tall dark-suited fellow with a coin at his throat, her heart leapt. *Yagrin.* He turned. It wasn't him.

Dead. Yagrin was dead to her. She had to remember that.

Ellery covered her hand with his. Her nails dug into his arm. She hadn't been anywhere as Nore since her mother announced publicly that she'd gone on sabbatical. She tightened her lips. When she got what she wanted from her mother, she'd never have to be in a place like this again.

"One second." She left her brother's side and cornered the usher by the door.

"Madam, I'm very sorry if you felt I was rush—"

"When my mother arrives, come find me. Do you understand?"

"Yes, ma'am."

"The *minute* she arrives." Nore reset her focus straight ahead and rejoined her brother's side.

The deeper they went into the room, the more heads turned their way. The stares clawed at her insides. When she was at the Tidwell, dancing with Yagrin, her persona let her be free. Here she had a family reputation and oppressive expectations. She might as well be hooked to strings from the ceiling. Her chest squeezed, but she blew out even breaths. All she had to do was endure this wretched place until her mother arrived.

A busty woman in a heather-gray dress with capped sleeves and a simple bone corset strode toward them, waving. *Mrs. Hargrove.* She was dressed in classic Ambrosian style, in which the plainer the outside was, the richer the inside was. The Hargrove surname was almost as old as hers.

Her brother groaned.

"The Hargroves aren't the worst choice."

"Traitor," he teased.

"Alright, alright. I have an idea," Nore whispered to him. "If either of us needs to be rescued, dust off your shoulder, and we'll make whatever excuse we need to come to each other. Deal?"

"You're brilliant," he said just as Mrs. Hargrove smothered him in a hug, smooshing his face against her overly sprayed hair. His mouth puckered as if he'd swallowed something rotten, and Nore hid a snort behind her gloved hand.

"Dear, it's Ellery," Mrs. Hargrove shouted at a stocky gentleman in a plain gray suit. He was absorbed in a conversation with a statue of a man whose tuxedo trimmed in golden fleurs made Mr. Hargrove look like a servant by comparison. The man listened intently but kept an eye on his pocket watch. "Darling," she shouted more insistently across the crowded ballroom. "Tell Ellery about the stones you found on your Egyptian excursion this summer." She squeezed Nore's arm. "We all know how your brother loves a good adventure."

"He certainly does," Nore said, watching the doors to the ballroom.

Mrs. Hargrove lugged her husband from his conversation without apology. "He's *dying* to talk to you. Aren't you, Darren?"

"Yes, yes, Ellery," Mr. Hargrove said, tipping his hat. "How have you been?"

"Cigar?" Mrs. Hargrove pulled a silver smoking case from somewhere in her giant bosom and offered Ellery one.

"Thank you, madam, but I am fine."

She didn't offer Nore one, which annoyed her even though she didn't smoke.

"And while we're at it . . ." Mrs. Hargrove gestured at a group of girls huddled around drinks, whispering giggles behind thin gloves. "Daphne, Regina, Sara Kate, get your sisters. Ellery is here!"

Nore squeezed her brother's hand once more in consolation before he disappeared in a flock of grinning Hargroves. She spun on her heels, relieved to not be the center of conversation, and glimpsed the doorway again. No sign of her mother. Then she nearly slammed into someone.

"Nore Emilie Ambrose, is that really you?"

"Mrs. Efferton!" Nore's heart ticked faster. She curtsied at the familiar face, muscle memory taking over. Nettie Efferton was an elbow-rubbing gossip from House Marionne. Someone you wanted to keep on your good side.

"Mrs. Efferton, how are you and Judge Efferton?" The polite greeting spilled from her lips effortlessly. "I regret I missed your Serenade this summer." The woman responded, but Nore gazed past her, looking around the ballroom for her mother, just in case.

Mrs. Efferton checked her hair and sparkling red-and-silver diadem in a passing mirror before hooking her arm with Nore's. She resisted, and Mrs. Efferton looked at her curiously. Nore took a small step, and the judge's wife dragged her toward a table of members dripping in jewels, shellacked in pounds of makeup, and swallowed by rich fabrics. House sigils everywhere. Tiny fleurs barely noticeable on handkerchiefs, a cracked-column charm dangling from a bracelet, a scale with a darkened sun etched on a ring. Diadems in gold or silver arced over the members' heads, their woven hairstyles equally ornate to complement their diadems' shape and color.

Nore couldn't breathe. She closed her eyes briefly and thought of her wheat fields kissed by evening sun, the way her toes felt in the dirt, how time moved so slowly at her farm. Her heart thudded a little easier.

"You know, I almost took your absence personally," Mrs. Efferton said. "But when you didn't show up at the Chrysanthemum either, I asked around and heard you have been on sabbatical?"

"Yes," she forced out, trying to calm her raging panic. Eyes everywhere stared at her. She could practically hear their thoughts: Nore, the heiress who no one's ever seen do magic. Nore, the heiress her mother keeps hidden. Nore, the girl if they really knew, they'd *hate*. Nore, *Nore*. Nore!

"Did you hear me, dear?"

"Sorry, what?"

"I said I'm sure Isla is glad you're back. A House needs a strong show of leadership, and the heir . . ." Mrs. Efferton pinched Nore's cheek.

Her sloshing insides quieted and instead her jaw ticked. She wasn't a child.

"Being visible is an inspiring nod to the future. And with the grave news about the Sphere, hope matters more than ever. Don't you agree?"

Nore scowled. House Ambrose had survived hundreds of years without her. She didn't care one bit if people saw or were inspired by seeing her. She wanted to find a place in the valley of a mountain to start another farm. She wanted to wake up to roosters crowing and eat cake for breakfast and swim in the lake for a bath if she felt like it. She wanted to *live,* instead of holding her breath in a world that felt like a corset tied too tight.

"You do agree, don't you?"

"Of course."

"Join me at my table for a drink, would you?" It wasn't a real request. Nore was already being dragged that way. Mrs. Efferton would flaunt her to the judge's friends as if to say, *Look at me, I am friends with Head-mistress blood.* But this was the way the Order worked. Mrs. Efferton wasn't the least bit interested in how Nore's sabbatical was or why she needed a sabbatical in the first place. Nor were the Hargroves interested in anything more than marrying into the House bloodline in the hopes a granddaughter might fall in the line of succession one day. The Order was a bunch of peacocks flashing their tail feathers at each other. Nore wanted no part of it.

"What did you do during sabbatical?" an elderly woman asked as she sat at the table. "One hears things, you know."

"Verna," Mrs. Efferton chastised.

Verna shrugged and sipped from her drink.

Nore's irritation thrummed. But her eyes were fixed on the doorman in the distance.

"You know, Nore," said a girl who couldn't be much older than her. The neckline of her red gown slashed across her chest and hooked over one shoulder. Rubies sparkled from her ears and a gold dot ornamented her nose. Her dark, sweeping eyelashes curled and seemed to wave. "Some blush on those cheeks and perhaps highlights in your hair would really be nice on you. You're so beautiful, and gray is such a drab color."

Nore took a fluted glass from a passing tray and gulped it down.

"Your dress would be simply unforgettable with a bit of brocade," someone cut in. "You'd have all the eligible suitors looking your way." The one who spoke wore teal feathers in her swept-back hair. Her face was ornately painted and sequined with jewels that matched her diadem. House of Oralia prided itself on freedom of expression in every way.

Nore surveyed the circle, and oddly found herself wishing someone from her House were there beside her to sit through this public interrogation.

"Blue would do so much for your eyes."

The walls felt like they were closing in. This was mind-numbing. She hastily dusted her shoulder, roving the crowd for some sight of her brother's long hair. Ellery met her eyes across the room and her heart skipped a beat. She dusted her shoulder harder and he nodded as if to say *I'm coming*.

"In fact, if I could just—" The girl in the red dress reached for Nore's dress straps, and the pressure building in her chest burst. Nore slapped her hand away, hard. The girl jumped.

"Forgive me, I must have missed these fashion and beauty lessons when I was preoccupied with analyzing the anatomical structure of complex elixirs. That research was the groundwork for figuring out how to shift *others'* faces, not just our own. An art only us *drably dressed* Ambrosers have been able to pull off. But do go on, what season is best to wear silk again?"

No one spoke. A few tugged at their jewels and avoided her gaze. Nore pled wordlessly with her brother, who was still watching her as an army of Hargroves held on to him. The usher still hovered at the door. He caught Nore's eyes and shook his head. *Where are you, Mother?!*

"Mable, did you see the Hargrove girls at the Chrysanthemum?" Mrs. Efferton asked. "Howling like that and calling it singing?"

"And what about the rumors from your House, Nettie?"

Mrs. Efferton, a House of Marionne loyalist through and through, pulled at her pearls.

"Yes, I'd heard some concerning things," Nore said, stirring the pot. *See how it feels to be poked.* Truly she hadn't heard much—only that Darragh Marionne's granddaughter caused some trouble and ruined her ball.

"I've heard that Darragh can control her members with a magic tie she has on them. Her granddaughter apparently outed the news at Cotillion."

Mrs. Efferton guffawed.

"Oh please," another said. "I heard Darragh *killed* that daughter of hers, and that's why she's been missing all these years. The granddaughter was after vengeance at that Cotillion, I bet you."

"Yep, I heard that too," Nore said. If ridiculous rumors kept her out of the hot seat, she'd fan the flames in that direction.

"I actually heard something far more sinister," said the Oralia girl, picking at one of her face sequins.

"You all are ridiculous." Mrs. Efferton took an aggressive gulp from her glass. "This entire conspiracy is no more than a ploy by the Duncans to destroy our great House."

Nore spotted the usher hustling his way through the crowd toward her. "Excuse me, ladies, my mother has arrived." She dashed away before anyone could stop her, working the blade from beneath her clothes.

"Where is she?" Nore asked.

"She came in a rush, but I overheard her say she'd only be here a few minutes. And by the time I got to you, she left."

"What!"

He eyed the blade in her hand. She huffed and stuffed it into the sleeve of her glove.

"Thanks for nothing."

An Audior sang into a microphone, playing the music accompaniment magically with nothing more than her fingers. Nore sifted through the crowd for her iron-faced mother, just to be sure, when the entire room seemed to still. Every head swiveled to the door, where Darragh Marionne stood in the entryway. The usher opened his mouth to announce her arrival, but she grabbed his wrist and he snapped his mouth shut. Whispers swarmed.

A knot twisted in Nore's chest. The last time she'd seen Darragh Marionne, Nore had been sobbing, filthy, alone, and terrified, hiding in the fields, watching the barn she used to call home be razed. Weeks earlier, at the Summer Bloom Tea, Nore had vaguely appealed to Darragh for help with a toushana problem because she'd heard a rumor that Darragh Marionne was the person to see for questions about the illicit magic. But the Headmistress feigned ignorance. But her granddaughter, Quell, seemed to be onto her secret. When Nore reached out asking to meet her in the Secret Wood, the House's security ran her off before she could see if Quell ever showed. She hadn't heard anything good about that girl since.

But after her farm was destroyed, as Nore hid, rumors spread that the heir to House of Ambrose was missing. That's when Darragh came looking and found her. She had offered Nore help under strict, confidential instructions.

Regret cinched in Nore's chest. Darragh moved through the room, dripping with nonchalance, and an idea struck her: She didn't need her mother's help if she could win Darragh's. Again. She followed.

"Headmistress Marionne, do you have a moment?"

"Nore." Darragh's lips thinned. She adjusted her dress.

"I wasn't sure you'd be here."

"And why wouldn't I?" Darragh met her eyes.

"I—I thought you'd be busy. Season just ended."

"Get to it, Nore."

"I'm sorry."

They'd had an agreement and Nore backed out. She sent a bouquet of black roses hoping to soften the blow. But nothing in Darragh's face said she'd forgiven Nore as her gaze moved on.

"I should have listened. I should have—"

"How desperate are you? Talking about this *here*?" She walked away, eyeing Nore over her shoulder as if to say, *Come along.*

She followed Darragh at a distance, through a waitstaff entrance to the ballroom, down a long corridor, and into a service elevator. She rehearsed what she was going to say over and over in her head. She had to get the

Headmistress to look past her betrayal. Darragh slammed a red button and the elevator doors locked with a click.

"Out with it. What do you want?"

"I'm ready to follow through on my part of our agreement. I wasn't then, but I am now."

"I can't help you anymore." Darragh adjusted the rings on her fingers.

"Can't or won't?" Her chest quaked.

"What difference does that make?" Darragh had told Nore the first step to getting rid of her toushana was to die. She had to let go of every person who knew her. Nore had agreed—and at the time she'd meant it. But every time she worked up the courage to break up with Yagrin, to tell Ellery goodbye, the words would not come.

"I couldn't let go. But now I have nothing to lose."

Silence grew between them.

"I can't help you."

"Why not?" Nore snapped. Her fingers moved to the imprint of the blade in her sleeve. She would not be this close to help and lose it again. Darragh smirked.

"Your audacity is impressive. But the answer is no." She slammed the button on the elevator, and the doors opened to a panicked Ellery. Darragh shoved past them.

"*What are you doing?*"

"Ellery, she has a way out for me. And if she's willing to give it to me, I'm going to take it."

"*Stay away* from Darragh Marionne."

Nore sighed, unconvinced.

"Mother was here," he said. "But she's gone now."

"I heard. I can't believe you let her leave."

"I could hardly get away from the Hargroves."

"I hate this place."

"Do you? Or do you just hate what it's done to you?"

"Are those different?"

He sighed and opened his arms for a hug. She tucked her head underneath his chin, listening to the calm thump of his heart. It was steady and strong and reliable, like him. If the Order were made up of Ellery and Yagrin, she wouldn't mind it. Really, if Mother were gone, then maybe she'd have an entirely different view. But those were foolish, impossible dreams.

"I can't stay here."

"Where else are you going to go? Back to the farm?"

She hadn't yet told her brother about the razing, because he could get a bit too insistent about what she could and couldn't do. "No, it's not safe there."

"So where have you been staying?"

"Here and there. Wherever I can find."

Her brother made her face him. "You can run from the Order, Nore, but that's not the same as escaping it. Come home and make your case to Mother. I will back you up." There was an earnestness in his eyes. "Remember, she *wants* something from you."

"Yes, an heir." She felt sick.

"We can use that as leverage."

We. She elbowed him affectionately. He was such an idealist. He didn't know the harshness of their mother's love the way she did. He hadn't been held down for days without food, without water, as Sun Dust was rubbed into his skin until he felt like he was on fire. He was the Ambrose son who'd discovered six new uses for enhancers before he was fifteen. He commanded awe from their House like a star performer onstage. But he didn't realize that beyond the stage lights everyone else was sitting in darkness.

He *was* onto something, however.

Nore's mind whirred. The key to getting what she wanted was showing the other person she had what they needed. She knew *exactly* what Darragh needed.

And Nore was the only person who could give it to her.

FIVE

⋅⋅——✳——⋅⋅

Quell

My toushana rages in me with each step. I hold Mom's key chain tight in my fist. There is no explanation for Octos to have this, unless . . . The thought lodges in my throat, urging each foot faster until I'm running through the forest. *He will answer for this.*

When I reach the edge of the forest, I can see the safe house on the hillcrest in the distance. With scraps of wood nailed to the windows, it's a fortress in the middle of nowhere, surrounded by farming fields. Knox's van and Willam's truck are parked side by side, and Heeler, their mutt, is tethered to a tree, yapping. I creep close to the house. The side door creaks open and I hide, pressing into the whitewashed siding. Octos and Willam make a beeline for the truck. The two of them lug crates of grains and frozen bags of meat inside the house.

"Attaboy." Knox hangs by the open door and tosses Heeler something before taking a stern glance around. I lean into my hiding place, easing out a slow breath. Heeler sniffs the bone, then barks harder in my direction. Knox grabs the last bag of groceries from the truck.

"Where's the girl?" she asks Octos as they head inside.

"She was outside in the field, reading," Octos says, covering for me. My jaw ticks.

Knox glances at the faint glimmer of sun. Once the locks on the house are closed for the night, no one's allowed in until morning.

Shadows can't hide when Sola Sfenti's watching, Knox had told me once before.

Shadows . . . Draguns, she meant.

Though no one has outright told me, safe houses seem to be for people on the run from the Order. I watch as Octos casually answers more of Knox's questions, his hand tucked in his pocket. But none of his covering for me does anything to calm the burning anger simmering beneath my skin. I turn Mom's key chain in my hand. *How long has he had this?* Toushana tugs in my chest; the cold bleeds into my core, spreading through my limbs, and wraps all over me like an icy blanket. *He's going to tell me why he has this. Or I will make him.*

When they disappear inside, I walk to the front door and twist the knob as I was taught. It resists. *Locked. Always locked.* Then I twist it five more times in snappy succession to signal those inside that I'm not an intruder. I race around the back to the kitchen door. On the way, I make sure to kick up some dirt on my pants' legs and bottom so it appears I was actually doing what Octos said. Lace curtains flutter before the door swings open.

"Octos said you were reading. Where's your book?" Knox asks, holding the door open just so, lodged against the wheelchair she always sits in. Her legs, amputated at the knee, are folded underneath her.

"I was reading the clouds . . . not a book." I slip Mom's key chain into my pocket. "Got all dusty, lying out there." I smile.

"You shouldn't be out there alone." She peers past me before widening the door just enough that I can slip inside. Knox runs things here. Nothing happens without her say. Even her trips to get groceries are meticulously planned, never the same market twice in a row. Sometimes she and Willam, her main helper around here, will drive an entire day to find a place to shop. And they always buy *so much*, enough for that month and plenty extra to store.

Inside, Knox corners me with her wheelchair. The pendant she always wears around her neck gleams. Her kinky white hair is in thick knots down her back. She studies me with glacial blue eyes, stark against her lush, dark skin. Her gaze snags on my heart. Always on my heart.

The first night I showed up, I said exactly what Octos told me to say: that I was a friend of his and had nowhere else to go. I said nothing of my magic. And she didn't ask. She locked me in a room with a small bed and sat outside the door. For ten days and ten nights. I was fed, given water. No one was unkind. Eventually, Willam came and laid out the rules of the house. Gradually, I was allowed freedom to roam during certain hours. I was assigned chores, and by the one-month mark, when Octos finally showed up, I was as free as the dozen or so others living in the house. This safe house is actually one of the few places in my life I've felt safe.

I clear my throat and she moves out of the way. The kitchen swells with bodies helping to unload the groceries. Knox watches me, so I pitch in, but I can't get Octos's betrayal out of my head. I put away a sack of potatoes and slam the cabinet door too hard. Everyone in the kitchen freezes, watching me.

"Sorry." I shove the last bag of dry beans into a trapdoor in the back of the top cabinet and leave. Down the hall are two small sitting rooms, one bedroom, and a bath.

Octos is nowhere in sight.

I climb the stairs, each footstep heavier than the one before it. There are four rooms upstairs and an attic with a slew of beds. I stop on the second landing and poke my head into the first bedroom at the top of the stairs.

"Octos?"

"He's in there." Dimara, the only other in the house about my age, exits the upstairs bath. She wrinkles her nose. "That smell, girl." Mirth plays on her lips. "You've got to work on that smell."

I shift awkwardly as we pass each other. Being out for weeks of training doesn't really allow for daily showers. She points to the study at the end of the hall, which is more like a very large, doorless closet with a bunch of bookshelves and a chair.

Octos is reading a book by lamplight.

"Quell, I think I found—"

My hand is at his throat, magic rolling through me in an icy wave. Black coils of mist bleed from my fingers, twisting around his neck. I dangle Mom's key chain in front of him, and his eyes widen.

"I can explain," he chokes out. "Quell, please . . ."

How could he possibly explain this in any way other than outright betrayal? At best he's a liar. I press harder, and he groans. Then, as my magic grazes his chin, something odd happens. His jaw shifts, jutting out. His cheeks sink in, defining his cheekbones. The trickle of black at my fingers rises, blowing across his entire face, and Octos's beady dark eyes and deep-set brows morph into someone else. My stomach drops. It feels like I'm standing on the edge of a cliff, about to be pushed off.

Show me, I tell my magic, fanning my toushana across all of him in one smooth motion. His whole body shortens. His stringy hair darkens to jet black. It rises above his shoulders while long bangs sprout across his forehead. My heart knocks in my chest, but I can't look away. The brown in his eyes lightens ever so slightly as the rest of his disguise dissolves.

"Who are you?" I stare. Then my gut twists as I recognize that familiar, determined stare. I stumble backward and he frees himself from my grip. "You're . . . *him.*"

The guy from the gas station in New Orleans. His face had changed into the person standing in front of me. The same guy I saw at the Tidwell Ball in a disagreement with those other Draguns.

"You're—the Dragun who has been hunting me." Black dents the edges of my vision. I can't breathe.

"I can explain everything." His mouth moves, but I don't hear the words. Cold tangles in my chest, then cinches in a knot. I force out a tight breath. Then another. And another. Remembering I'm not the scared girl on the run from him anymore. My magic unleashes like a whip. My bones ache at the rush of toushana, but I thrust it against him even harder. Magic slams into his body, knocking him backward. He hits the shelves, sending books tumbling everywhere. He drops to the floor, cowering.

"Quell, please." A fear like I've never seen glazes his eyes.

"Who. Are. You?"

"My name—my name is Yagrin. Dragun, twelfth of my blood, House of Perl." His chin falls.

Everyone I trust betrays me.

"Quell, please, we can't do this here." His eyes dart to the stairs just past me. *The safe house. Knox.* As I do the same, my eyes cut past a mirror; the girl in its reflection is seething, swallowed in a black fog of rage. A girl I don't recognize. I step back. My throbbing hand blackens, deepening the bruises that were already there. I draw in a long breath, my toushana retreats, and the fog in the tiny office space clears.

Inside, my toushana bites at my bones.

Strike, it says.

I hook my hands together. "Talk. Fast."

"I did not hurt Rhea, I promise you."

"Don't say her name like you knew her."

His throat bobs. "When I cornered you—early summer, before you ran to your grandmother's—at that motel, remember?"

"The first time I learned you were a liar. Yes."

"I took your mother from the motel. She was kept for questioning, that's protocol. My order from Mother was to bring you in, not her. So I knew she'd be questioned and let go."

"You took her to Beaulah Perl's House?"

"I did. Mother calls in favors from time to time, under the Dragunhead's nose. And this was one of them."

"Go on."

"When I found you at the Tavern, you were different than what I expected."

I raise my chin.

"So I took on my oldest persona to get to know more about the target Mother wanted me to bring in. Octos was a very close friend of mine. My only friend, really, for a long time. We met as kids. He's dead now." Yagrin swallows, and I don't know if I should be disgusted or moved that he plays dress-up as his dead best friend. "Anyway, you were in the Order, an heiress from a high family, but not willing to cheat your way to success. It struck me with an odd sense of hope, and I'm not a person who's very hopeful. Not much longer after that, you found me again. You saw me—well, Octos—a grimy Order reject, as someone worthy of trust. That's when I decided I'd stop hunting you for Mother. The Order needs people like you, Quell."

I shift on my feet.

"I returned to House Perl and visited your mom, who was still there, to tell her I wasn't going to hunt you anymore. I visited her more than once and we talked a lot. Eventually, she opened up about how you both used to live. How she has no love for the Order either." His eyes dart away. "I'm ashamed to admit that I worried it might have been a trap. That Mother convinced her to lure me into admitting how much *I* hated the Order so she can finally have me killed like I know she wants. So I didn't go back for a long time. When I came to my senses, I went back to see your mother, and I promised to do all I could to protect your life."

"She was there," I mutter, more to myself than him. "For how long? Abby said she saw her in Chicago months ago. And my mother wrote me a letter."

"That was me." He sighs. "Watch. Please don't be afraid." He slides his hand down the bridge of his nose, and Yagrin's face shifts with my mother's dark eyes and warm brown skin.

"No!" Words stick in my throat. I steady myself on the furniture beside me as I stare at a *lie* of my mother's face. *It's not her.* I snatch at his face, my toushana ripping the mask away. "*Never* take her face again! *Never.*"

He throws up his hands. "I'm sorry. I just wanted you to see. That was me in Chicago wearing her persona. I delivered the letters to you, too."

I can't breathe. The world spins. *When was the last time anyone saw my mom?*

"Your mother gave me a bit of her blood. That's how Anatomer magic works, for most of us, anyway."

I clench my fists. "You could have killed her and took it."

"Your mother agreed to let me impersonate her to help you. She thought the safest place for you was to keep you at Chateau Soleil. Look me in my eyes, Quell. You know I'm not lying."

"You were wrong," I say. "About me being safe at my grandmother's."

"I didn't know all Darragh Marionne was doing. Your mother didn't either."

"Is my mother still at House Perl?"

"I went back the day before your Cotillion and she was gone. I was given no information. My House, the Draguns, my own family, they all keep me at arm's length. Quell, I hate to say this, but she's probably d—"

I shake my head. *No.* I try to picture Mom broken and battered, the life gone from her body, but the pieces don't come together. She is a survivor. She's the one who taught *me* how to stick to the shadows, how to fool those with their eyes wide open. How to *not* exist in order *to* exist. "Did you see her body with your own eyes?"

"No. But Beaulah discards everything that isn't of use to her."

"What *facts* do you know?"

"Quell." He steps toward me. "I looked for her name on the Sphere, where all the members' names who have bound are. It wasn't there."

My mother never bound to magic. Binding requires plunging a honed magical dagger into the heart, meshing blood and magic together forever. It absorbs the whole blade. But my mother gave me her dagger before we separated, which meant she never completed Third Rite.

"I also checked the Book of Names, where inductees' names go once they're anointed. Not there either."

She may have never been anointed. I don't know that she was ever inducted. I just know that she had a fancy dagger.

"You would say anything to keep me from killing you."

Yagrin sighs. "You're wasting your time hoping for any other outcome. Your mother is—"

I hold up a hand, thrashing with shadows.

Yagrin stiffens against the shelf at his back. "Quell, the Order is the enemy. Not me. Look how they've ostracized you. Look how they force the people who don't fit their rules, like Knox and Willam, to live. If we work together and find the Sphere, we could destroy it all. Take their power from them. Then no one has to live this way anymore."

The last few months suddenly make so much sense. "You've been . . . *using* me," I snap, charging at him. He chokes on the darkness bleeding from my hands. The bruising on my fingers stretches across my skin, up my wrists, clawing its way up my arms. Rage burns through me, colder than my magic has ever felt.

"Easy, Quell," he wheezes, and I can taste the fear on his breath. "Try to calm. Breathe."

"Shut up. How do you expect me to believe a word you say?"

"I could have killed you in an instant these last months." His eyes deaden, and I see someone in him that I've only seen in the boy I used to love. *A killer.* "I've lied to you, but I've never hurt you. The Order ruined my life." His voice cracks. For a moment Yagrin is far, far away. Sadness sinks his shoulders. "I hate them all." He looks away. "Except my brother," he mutters under his breath. "I won't apologize for any of it. This is what the Order deserves. And if you don't agree with that, you haven't seen how monstrous it is yet." Yagrin slides to the floor, hugging his knees. "If I don't find it, she died for nothing. Everything I've put up with was for nothing. *You* can track the Sphere better and faster than anyone. *Please* help me. Help us all."

He says *us*, but he means *him*. If Knox and Willam saw my condition as freedom for themselves, Yagrin never would have lied about why we came in the first place.

"You're so good at manipulating people, you've forgotten how to tell the truth."

My mother is not dead. She may be held against her will somewhere, or running deep off the grid, but she is alive. I know it in my gut.

Someone clears their throat.

Knox.

Shit.

"Dinner's ready." Her glare travels from Yagrin, to me, and back to him.

I walk to the stairs, unsure how much Knox heard. Yagrin follows. At the foot of the stairs, the front door is open. Willam stands there; his gaze moves past me, to Yagrin behind me—and I realize the open door is for him.

"Your business is yours, but we can't live with someone we don't trust. Be on your way, sir," Willam says to Yagrin.

"Come with me, please, Quell," Yagrin pleads. Willam tosses his bag at him. I expect him to beg them to let him explain himself. But he picks it up quickly, suddenly in a hurry.

"Your choice, girl." Willam indicates my bag nearby on the floor as well. Knox folds her arms. A crowd of curious eyes watch from the dining area, silent.

I can leave too, if I want. They won't stop me. Or punish me for lying about why we were here. A clean break.

I grab the door, and Yagrin's gaze widens in anticipation.

SIX

—✳—

Jordan

The entire way back to Headquarters, the fate of the Order hangs over me like a guillotine blade.

As the glass doors of Wexton MidCenter Hotel swish open, I hurry inside. If the Sphere bleeds out, magic as we know it is done. *Then what was it all for?* The years enduring my father, surviving Beaulah. The raids, the body counts. It's all meaningless if our world ceases to exist. My fingers find the commissioning coin in the slip of fabric at my collar, and I hold it tight in my fist.

"Afternoon, Mr. Wexton," says the concierge. "Can I prepare the penthouse for you?"

"No need, Joel, but thank you." I unfurl the scarf that wound around my neck thanks to the overly chummy Chicago wind. I summon an elevator going down, but one going up arrives instead. Guests shimmy out, then more fill it back up, and I wedge myself in a corner, unable to scrub the Darkbearer descendant's boldness from my mind. Our world is in danger.

She did this. The girl with the perfect poise and soft brown eyes. Who spent her short time near the Order defying every rule that holds it together. So much power and yet so disloyal and reckless. If she'd never bound with toushana, my brother wouldn't have anyone to use to exact his revenge.

"Which floor?" someone asks.

"Eighty." I turn the talon-shaped key in my pocket. The elevator climbs, and with each stop, it empties. Thinking of Quell summons memories I'd like to forget. The way she effortlessly commanded the attention of every room she entered, her crooked smile and her mouth tipped to the side, especially when she was nervous. The feel of her hair tangled around my fingers. The way I wanted that long night we spent practicing for Second Rite to last forever. We'd stayed up until morning, swapping stories and joking about how the maezres all seemed a bit too uptight.

I let the wall hold me up; my neck flushes with heat, and shame burns my chest. That sugary grin she wore the first time I let her have a green candy, all it took for me to share that seemingly small part of myself. Despite all my insistence she be perfect, the thrilling moments she allowed herself to *not care* about the Order, her last name, or any of it. When we danced. When we stayed out past curfew. When she'd discovered whatever crimes she believed her grandmother had done, all she wanted was to run away from everything *with me*.

My heart turns like a stone in my chest. Nothing seemed to matter to me either when I held her. Not the Order. Not my family. Not my magic. Not my past. The thought sickens me.

And now she's out there with my brother. Roughing it together, relying on one another to survive, learning more about each other, trusting each other for *months* while trying to destroy the Sphere. My jaw clenches. They're both going to pay for their decisions, but especially him. Hunting them down is the only thing that matters now. The Dragunhead has to reassign me.

Once the car is completely empty, I press my talon key to the button panel, and a black button with a talon sigil appears. I slip my key in and the elevator plummets.

Its doors open and the glass entrance to Headquarters gleams in front of me. I skim past the security barriers with a flash of my talon coin, my mask seeping through and hardening on my skin. The center of Dragun

operations is an underground maze of offices and tunnels that run beneath the city. The sterile lobby is sparsely dotted with furniture and
people. Draguns, readying for the day's assignments, hustle in every
direction, daggers at their belts, file folders in their hands, coins at their
throats. I wave to a choice few. There's a single desk in the lobby: a second security barrier of sorts that my talon key won't get me past. I march
toward it. My shoes clack against the glossed floor, but each step feels like
a quake in my chest. He *is going to* listen to me.

Even though I've worked for the Dragunhead for only a few months,
I've done what he's asked of me exactly how he's asked it, exceeding his
expectations. My second raid I flushed out a safe house suspected to house
Darkbearers in Oralia territory and found a basement full of enhancer
stones and boxes of compacts full of transport powder. I confiscated it all
and then I found their supplier and brought him in, too. I've proven myself quickly. My stomach sinks and my pace slows as I realize that doesn't
always matter . . . It wasn't until I could perform certain magic flawlessly
that my own father was willing to have a conversation with me one-on-
one. And it took even longer before he would bring me around anyone he
knew. But the Dragunhead strikes me as much more reasonable.

At the desk, Maei, the Dragunhead's secretary, signs for a crate of fire
daggers, clicking the pen on her clipboard before standing to greet me.

"Unload in the warehouse?" the shipper asks. She sends him off with
a nod. The Dragunhead's grand office doors, ornately carved with each
House's sigil, loom behind her.

"Morning, Mr. Wexton." She hooks and rehooks a button on her
sweater between fidgeting with the amber brooch on her scarf. Hot or
cold, she always wears the same long blue skirt, a button-up, and some
variety of sweater, its pearl buttons a complement to her silver-studded
diadem. I eye the clock hanging high on the wall. Maei eyes me. *Something happened earlier.* They're probably out there hunting the Sphere as
we speak.

"I need to see him, Maei." I step around the desk.

"I'm sorry, he's in a meeting that cannot be interrupted." She places herself between me and the door. That pen of hers may as well be a sword, the way she stands sentry. "We don't burst in on the Dragunhead without notice."

"How much longer?" I ask.

"It shouldn't be much longer, sir. If you want to wait at your desk, I can come get you." Her gaze darts to the doors behind her. *This is a meeting I'm not supposed to overhear.*

"Thank you."

She smiles, but her pointed features only make her look more severe. "We don't burst in on the Dragunhead," she mutters over and over, more to herself than me.

The immediate corridor off the lobby opens to a glass-encased room with rows of desks. Plaques line a back wall. I shed my sweatshirt from the raid onto my desk and slip on my House coat. I pace, watching Maei through the windows; she's still muttering to herself.

Minutes pass, but it feels like hours. A few stragglers wander in but leave with no more than a head nod. The trace on Quell and Yagrin is quiet. *Where are they now? How much closer?* Maei's pen clicks faster as she shuffles and reshuffles papers on her desk. An hour passes. There is still no twinge in my chest from them.

I return to the lobby. "Maei, this can't wait." I shove past her and push open the doors.

"Please, sir, we can't just burst in," Maei's voice pecks at me, but I'm already inside. The Headmistresses of the Houses sit around the Dragunhead's desk. All but one: Darragh Marionne. Beaulah clears her throat. I avoid her gaze. Litze Oralia offers a tight smile while Isla Ambrose stares stoically. My father fills a chair in the corner of the room. The knot in my shoulders squeezes. He should be taking his mandated hiatus for his health—or whatever reason I told the Dragunhead as an excuse to get rid of him. As if he can read my mind, he uncrosses and recrosses his legs. *He doesn't matter.* None of them do. Not if the Sphere shatters and magic is lost.

"Jordan?" The Dragunhead's brows cinch.

"I'm sorry, but it's urgent."

"I apologize, sir," a frazzled Maei says, clicking her pen nonstop. "I—I asked him to stay put."

"She did. But this shouldn't wait."

"How urgent?"

"We have days, I would guess, at best. We need to reprioritize."

"Well, Council, I'm afraid we'll have to pick this up later," he says to the Headmistresses. Then he tucks his lip in thought. "Jordan, give me a moment to close this up."

I nod.

"A private moment."

I glance at my father, who's staring smugly for some stupid reason, before backing out of the room and parking myself beside the doors. Maei doesn't even try to woo me away from them this time.

"Sorry, Maei."

"He doesn't like that." Her brows draw together over watery eyes.

"I'll make sure he knows it's not your fault."

"I've heard your concerns and made notes of everything." The Dragunhead's voice is low and a bit muffled. I lean in to make out the rest of his words. "*If* the rumors of the tether are true, we will not be rash. Dissolving a House must be done carefully."

House of Marionne. It's unfortunate. I'd had such high hopes Marionne would be different when I arrived there as Ward. But I saw Darragh's true colors this summer when she wanted to hide Quell's secret. The tethering rumors don't help her seem any more innocent.

"We don't *need* you, Sal," says a voice I know all too well. Beaulah. "The Council has the authority to make this move on our own."

"You need *Draguns,* unless you want war between the Houses; therefore, you need me."

"She must be stopped," Beaulah urges.

The irony of Beaulah pushing for this. I trace the six gold virtue pins—valor, discretion, honor, sacrifice, duty, and loyalty—that trail down my lapel, and a nauseating earthy scent hits me. A tradition unique to House Perl, and yet Beaulah defies half the virtues with the secrets she keeps. My thoughts move to my cousin Adola, and my heart sinks.

My father exits first, and I straighten, suddenly realizing my wrist-watch needs a good polish.

"Have a good day, Mr. Wexton," Maei says, offering my father his coat and hat. He snatches his things, says nothing to her, and instead turns to me.

"So this is how we interact now?"

Dirt has somehow wedged itself in the rimmed crevice of my watch, and no manner of picking is getting it out.

"You've changed," he goes on. "Since going to Chateau Soleil as Ward. I hardly noticed it at first, but it's glaring now that Darragh Marionne's poisoned you with *weak* values."

Anger flickers in me. I count the incomplete set of pins at his chest. *Five, not six.* I stroke my loyalty pin—the one he doesn't have—and his nostrils flare. He isn't worth a response.

"Or is this new attitude about that girl?"

I whip out the fire dagger wedged in my waist belt and my father flinches. Then I keep picking at the stubborn dirt in the seam of my watch. "You should say thank you to Maei for your coat and hat."

He scowls. "You will need me one day, son."

"Yes, to follow orders. Get back to your hiatus and be sure to notify Maei when you arrive home."

Before he can fire off a response, the Headmistresses exit in a barrage of chatter. I slip inside the office and shut the door. The Dragunhead is a spindly, thin man with long gray hair in fraying waves down his back. He sits at his desk, bony hands steepled. The fine trim of his coat, bearing colors and symbols from each House, and the gleam of the stone in his brotherhood ring sharply contrast with his glum posture. With the Headmistresses gone, the sternness of the Dragunhead's dark gray eyes softens.

"A day of grave news, I'm afraid." He meets my eyes. "But what about you, son? Is everything alright? You've mentioned before that you and your father didn't get along, but . . ." He lights a roll of peckle leaf and takes a puff. "Are things getting out of hand?"

The knot in me tightens. *I'm not here to talk about my father.* "He is a leech in our Order. He just happens to have a powerful sister." I sit in one of the open chairs at the Dragunhead's desk.

"He is also your father. He's served the brotherhood for decades. Some might say he paved the way for you to rise quickly and shine so much. He, not your aunt, gave you your endorsement."

"Because I was the best candidate."

The corner of the Dragunhead's lip curls up. He takes another puff.

"And it makes him look good. I'm not going to pretend to condone his self-interested behavior. He doesn't serve this Order; he serves himself. And that doesn't work for me." Admitting the truth unravels the knot I've become, and I sit up taller. "I had his endorsement, but if I were bad at the job, you wouldn't have me here, giving me more responsibility. I've shown you time and again who I am. That is why you keep me here. Sir."

He considers me; his crooked smile unfurls something warm in my chest. He pulls out a small velvet box from his desk. "Before we go on, let me hear this urgent news."

I tell him everything: how during the raid I felt my brother and Quell, but when it was finished, the remnants of the trace were gone. "They are tracking the Sphere aggressively. And I'm worried that they're very close."

"Why her?"

I swallow. "What do you mean?"

"Why is your brother tracking the Sphere with Darragh Marionne's granddaughter?"

Because she has bound to toushana.

I shift in my seat, and the memory of Quell's dagger slamming into her ribs plays on repeat like a broken record in my head. It's stolen my sleep for months. And yet . . . I haven't been able to form the words. To say what she's done aloud to anyone. Rumors swarming about Darragh

Marionne's most recent Cotillion have made their way to the Dragun-head's ears, but he's dismissed them as just that, because the stories are conflicting. And I haven't said anything to the contrary. My neck breaks out in a cold sweat.

"Jordan?"

"I'm not sure." The lie stings and the shame burns. Maybe I am my father's son.

"If the Council is right about their suspicions," he goes on, "Darragh Marionne has attached her graduates to her House with a tether."

"That's what Quell wanted everyone at Cotillion to believe."

"Some old, perverted strain of dark tracer magic, sounds like."

"Darragh Marionne is squarely Sfentian, sir. That House doesn't know the first thing about dark magic."

"If the rumors are true, perhaps her beliefs have shifted from what you once thought. And I'm hearing from the Council she's erased the recent Cotillion from the memory of all those in her House."

"I wouldn't put much past her, but that is hard to believe."

"You're saying Darragh is innocent of tethering her graduates? Amassing an army?"

"I'm saying I'll believe it when it comes from someone who is not a habitual liar. Or someone who doesn't have a vested interest in seeing the fall of that House."

"Beaulah."

I incline my head. "However, I will admit that Darragh Marionne and Beaulah Perl have both shown me that they see the rules of this great Order as flexible."

"Do you support dissolving the House?"

My heart squeezes, pumping faster. We're already down one House since House of Duncan dissolved. *Replacing Darragh seems to be the best option.* But there are no easy answers for a House without heirs.

"That is not a decision I'm prepared to make, sir."

"Perhaps not now. But—" He parts open the velvet box, and inside is a heart pendant on a silver chain made of the brightest red gem I've ever seen. It's encased in silver and inscribed with each House sigil. *The Dragunheart's lavaliere.*

"It's more beautiful than described," I breathe. The stone was forged into a heart shape and given to the Dragunhead's second-in-command. The last Dragunheart died over a decade ago. The Dragunhead hasn't selected a new one since.

He twists the pendant in the light and its red hues ripple, deepening and shimmering beneath its glassy surface.

"Stand, Jordan." He rises, too. His gunmetal mask, trimmed in black, bleeds through his skin. "I've been waiting for the right moment. And I see no better time."

Breath sticks in my chest and I can't feel my knees. I force myself out of the seat and stand still, my mask hardening on my face.

"Your raid went flawlessly. The target was Kix Vorgsiv, a descendant of a Darkbearer line we didn't have on our radar. But with some convincing interrogation, we've uncovered an entire nest of them, hunkered down together at a safe house near Sacramento. I am very proud of you—not just for this raid, but your leadership these last few months."

"Duty doesn't require credit."

"And that is precisely why you're getting it."

I don't have words, so I nod.

"It's odd, isn't it?" he says, detaching the necklace from its box. "For generations, we've protected thousands from being hurt by those with toushana. But our nickname comes from the killing we do, not the saving. It's the burning that people remember."

I ponder a moment, thinking of the guy we apprehended at Yaäuper. "*Is it* that strange?"

The Dragunhead listens intently.

"Our power is not in our command of toushana, but in the fear we strike into others. We *want them* to remember it. It's the only thing that keeps them from banding together and trying to overthrow this place." My thoughts move to the girl, the outlier, who fears nothing.

His mouth slides into a satisfied smile as he gestures for me to stand in front of him. "It is my job to be of sharp intellect, sage wisdom, and swift decision. But I am not perfect." He cups my shoulder and it feels like the weight of the world. He ropes the heart necklace over my head. "This fourth day of November, I hereby name you Dragunheart of the Prestigious Order of Highest Mysteries."

I steady myself on the desk as the world blurs through my tears. *I've done it.*

"Nothing compares to this honor, sir."

He dusts off my shoulders, pulls out a handkerchief embroidered with intertwined leaves, and polishes each one of my pins. "One day you will rise to the Head and have to find a new Heart. Keep your eyes"—he taps my chest—"and your heart open. Can you do that?"

"Yes, sir. I can do whatever needs to be done." I blink and see a freckle-faced girl with eyes brighter than the sun on the back of my eyelids. Then I picture my magic closing them forever.

The seconds tick past like hours as I sign a few papers Maei needs to formally announce my position. An interview with *Debs Daily* is set up, and before I realize it, it's late. The Dragunhead settles at his desk and spills brown liquid into a short glass.

"Sir," I say as he offers me a drink. "I would like to locate Quell and Yagrin personally."

"Protecting the Sphere is more important than bringing a pair of rogues to justice."

"It took my brother months, but he's found the Sphere before. I saw him crack it with my own eyes."

The Dragunhead stills. "Your *brother* did this? You hadn't mentioned that before."

"My apologies. It was in the report. I assumed you knew."

"And the girl?"

"She wasn't with him then. But she's with him now." My heart knocks against my ribs. "I will assemble a team immediately and find them."

"No. You will focus on the Sphere. I will get you a record of coordinates of its last dozen sightings, some Sun Dust, and my best brains on sun tracking. We will put everything we have behind you on this."

It's not enough. We're not equipped. Yagrin can track the Sphere so well because he studied it intensely for years. Quell is *bound* to toushana. She will be able to track the Sphere faster than any of us here. If I tell him that, he'll know I've kept something from him. The ruby pendant shines on my necklace. *I allowed her betrayal. He's my brother. It should be me.*

"Sir, trust me on this. If the Sphere cracks, magic is *gone.*"

"I'm well aware of what's at stake. But Jordan, you are my new Dragunheart and *this* is of the utmost importance." He leans forward. "The balance of power in this Order is hanging on by a thread. I need *you,* my best Dragun, on this. Not tracking your brother and some girl." His mouth quirks. "I know you will always put honor and duty above family, but not everyone does." He rears back in his seat, clasping his hands. "You will protect the Sphere by finding its location. I'm assembling a team of engineers who can hopefully enhance its existing defensive mechanisms."

"But—"

The Dragunhead picks up the pendant on my chain, and I can feel the Order, our future, *Quell,* slipping between my fingers. "Make finding the Sphere your one and only mission. I will put a team on hunting down your brother and the girl. But I need my best man protecting the Sphere. Find it, keep it safe at any cost, while I prep the engineers and sort out this House of Marionne mess. Are we understood?"

"Yes, s—"

My heart squeezes as a wave of fear—fear that is not mine—skips through me. I sink into my seat, feeling for the source of the tightness. The Dragunhead's talking, but the world in front of my eyes shifts. I can see Yagrin running furiously, looking over his shoulder. I stand.

"Jordan? Are we clear?"

"I—yes, sir. I need to go."

His brows dent. "Very well, then."

I thank him again, exit his office, and barrel my way into the elevator and up to the hotel lobby. I hold the sense of Yagrin's location tightly in my mind until I'm in an alley. *It's not disobeying orders, not technically.* If the Dragunhead knew Quell was bound to toushana, he'd understand. This *is* how I protect the Sphere. I have no choice.

"To Yagrin," I whisper, and Headquarters disappears.

My feet slam the hard ground, and I inhale the cold night air. The dark thicket of trees rings with the patter of footsteps. I hold still, listening. *They are here somewhere.* Chills scratch all over my bones as I cloak, the toushana disintegrating my body into shadowed pieces. Gusting through the trees, I hover along as a cloud of darkness until I spot him. Yagrin runs as if he's almost out of steam. His long dark hair is slick on his head, and his rain-soaked clothes stick to his body. My head begins to throb as the cloaking magic begs to be released. I hold on tighter, scanning the forest for long brown curls. But there is no sight of Quell.

Yagrin suddenly halts and glares in my direction, his red mask sloped across his face. I urge my weight to the ground until my feet are firmly planted and I am whole again.

He pales. "Brother."

"Where is she?"

"She's not here, Jordan. I'm at this alone."

Yagrin's racing heart simmers beneath my skin.

"You were never a good liar," I say, looking around again, careful to not take my eye off him for too long. "I'm here under orders from the Dragunhead. For the sake of the Sphere and the integrity of this Order, I demand the truth. *Where* is she hiding?" I scan every shadowed crevice of the thicket of trees around us.

He clutches his chest, where the light of my kor disappeared so many years ago. "You'd sense her if she was."

I look around again. The night is as silent as death. He's right. She's not here.

"Where is she?"

Yagrin folds his arms in that way he used to do when we were little, whenever he was determined to be as stubborn as a mule.

"Does she know what you are? *Who* you are? That you're a manipulative, lying snake?"

"She knows what I tell her. And I tell her whatever I want."

Anger licks my spine. "You backstabbing bastard."

"Mad she ran off with me?" My brother throws his head back in laughter. "Of course she did. She wants to be around someone who's not auditioning for Daddy's approval."

"I don't give two shits about our father," I spit.

"Who said anything about our father?"

"She's smart. She'll figure out that you're lying to her."

My brother flinches.

"She already has . . ." A smile tugs at my lips. "And she let you live?"

"You think she's a killer."

"Everyone is, under the right circumstances. She's bound to poison. You've read the books. You know what they say. It's only a matter of time."

"She has more heart than you realize."

"You don't know the first thing about her."

"I know she likes the cold. Her favorite thing is dancing. Though she pretends it's not."

I see red. "Shut up."

"Her favorite color is blue. For the ocean. And one day she hopes to settle there with her mother. In a small house, with—"

I charge at Yagrin, knocking him to the ground. His mask bleeds back into his skin as I land on top of him. I pummel him in the ribs until he arches his back, rolls to the side, and throws me off. I slam the ground hard; my side is throbbing. *Yags was never much of a fighter.* But his fist connects with my gut and knocks the wind out of me. I manage to wrap my legs around his waist, tug him onto his back, and return the favor, straight to his jaw.

"Your left hook was always so weak." He spits blood. "This isn't about the Sphere at all. You want revenge on the girl who reminded you that you have a heart."

I pound him with my right hook and he yowls in pain. "Better?" I pull him up and unclip the restraints from my waist.

He smooths the blood off his face with the back of his hand. "So you're here to, what? Kill us?"

"By authority of the Dragunheart, second to the Dragunhead—" My side aches.

Yagrin's gaze falls to the shiny ruby pinned to my chest and he sucks in a breath.

"You're going to kill the girl you love, Jordan? And me, your brother?"

I clip the restraints on his wrists. *Time in the Shadow Cells will do him some good.*

"Enough of this. *Listen* to me." He wriggles in their hold. "Like I listened to you all those years. The Order can't be what it should. It can't even be what it used to be."

"If you want to *make* it to Headquarters at all, shut your mouth."

"This is not us, brother. We protect each other."

My grip slacks as I stare at those wide brown eyes that used to sparkle with mischief. *When our father was the only villain we wanted to outrun.* I can practically see the scrawny little boy he was—his tidy blazer, Mother straightening his bow tie *just so*—staring back at me.

"*I protected you,* you mean. But you've gone too far this time, Yags. I can't anymore." As I carefully place my hand on his neck to hold in the choke, an apology lodges in my throat. But the time for reconciling is behind us. My brother gets to choose his path. He won't choose mine or anyone else's. And I know my path.

"By the authority of the Dragunheart, second in the brotherhood—"

"Father and Beaulah couldn't care less about you. They love *what* you do, not who you are. That's never going to change. Quell is not your enemy. Letting yourself love her is the only hope you have to make it out of this with your humanity. The Order is broken, brother. Learn to face the truth for once in your life."

His words lasso something violent that thrashes deep in my chest, and I grab him firmly in the choke. "Learn when to shut up. You're under capture, to be delivered to the brotherhood for fair judgment."

He doesn't resist. With my free hand, I fire off a message to Yaniselle and Charlie.

Meet at dawn for your next assignment.

One criminal down, one to go.

SEVEN

————✳————

Nore

Nore eyed the driver loitering beside the shiny town car. Outside the hotel hosting the Fall Harvest Gala, Marked and Unmarked bustled in every direction. She slid a stick of gum in her mouth and elbowed Ellery, who crouched beside her.

"It's him," she said, pointing at the driver. Her plan had two parts, and the first was the most risky: if she were caught trying to impersonate a Headmistress, she'd be arrested—and her last name, for once, wouldn't matter. "Do it now."

"Nore—"

"Ell!"

He groaned. "You swear to me, after this, you will come home."

"I swear." *On my own terms.*

They pressed deeper into the wall of shrubbery that ran along the outside of the hotel and kept an eye on the valet line of cars and waiting drivers. Hotel staff buzzed in and out of the building, but in their corner of the landscaping, they were well shielded and out of sight. Her brother sighed and Nore braced for the warmth of his magic. Taking a persona didn't require the same length of study as it did for Anatomers in other Houses. Their House had pushed past that limitation of magic. Their House had pushed past a lot of things. Though the effect didn't last as long as mastered study of a persona, an Anatomer from House Ambrose could change their face, or someone else's, to the appearance of anyone they laid their eyes on. *Without* using their blood.

Ell's fingers ran down her face. A sneeze tingled her nose as her pale skin bronzed, then deepened to the color of rich earth. Her red hair shortened and coiled, graying at her roots. In moments, Nore stood taller; her body was heavier, her hips wider. Her knees felt a bit weak and her back hunched ever so slightly.

She was Darragh Marionne.

He moved his magic toward her clothes and she stopped him.

"Just try to change the color of my dress. That should be simpler." Her brother's Shifter magic wasn't as refined. He'd hoped to master three strands and garner a brotherhood invite, but he barely had two. Gradually, the gray of her linen turned blotchy pink. She cinched her long coat tightly around herself. It was dark outside. *That would have to do.*

"You have the brush?" he asked.

Nore squeezed the stone in her hand and nodded. When the hustling throng of people outside the hotel died down, she slipped out of their hiding spot. Her heart knocked against her ribs. *Please let this work,* she prayed to the Wielder. The real Darragh Marionne was still inside at the ball. But the evening was wearing down and she wouldn't be there much longer. When the real Darragh left the party, Nore intended to be in her private car, where Nore would force her to listen to an offer she *couldn't* turn down.

Nore strode over to the car, mustering as much confidence as she could, and dipped her chin at the driver. She wasn't enthusiastic about going back to Dlaminaugh as she had promised Ellery, but if she was successful in getting what she wanted from Darragh, she wouldn't be at Dlaminaugh for long.

"Ready to leave, Headmistress?" the driver asked.

Nore shook her head no, careful to not utter a sound. Even House Ambrose could only push Anatomer magic so far. The best she had was her outer appearance.

The driver opened the door, and Nore white-knuckled her coat's lapel, the first part of her plan executed flawlessly. She looked for her brother as she slipped inside the car. He strolled up right on cue.

"I'm Ellery Ambrose, tenth of my blood, Anatomer, and firstborn of Headmistress Isla Ambrose. And you are?" He stuck out his hand to the driver, who shook it tentatively.

"John."

"Nice to meet you, John." He stuffed his hands in his pockets, careful to angle his body to block John's line of sight to the town car's tinted windows. "What do you say about this weather, eh?"

The weather, really?! Ell had to do better than that if they were going to keep him distracted enough to *not* notice when the real Darragh Marionne exited the hotel.

Nore pulled out the Retentor brush. There was no time to let the magic wear off naturally. The smooth, flat stone fit perfectly in the palm of her hand. She rubbed it in slow circles across her skin, and the tingle of Anatomer magic leaving her body prickled her all over. In a moment, her body shortened, her back straightened, and she was Nore again. She perked up her ears to her brother's conversation. Her heart thumped harder with every passing minute; John and her brother went on and on about the first snow coming so early in the year. Nore craned for a view of the hotel's entrance, biting her lip.

When Darragh Marionne appeared, Nore pressed back in her seat. She couldn't chicken out now.

The Headmistress stood outside the glass sliding doors of the hotel, finishing a chat with an elderly man with a fancy fleur-de-lis suit and antique timepiece. They ended their conversation with an odd gesture: a hug. Nore never took the hard woman for a hugger. She also didn't realize Darragh Marionne still had friends in the Order. Darragh strode to the car.

"Madam?" The driver's muffled voice streamed through the windows. A crease cut between his brows. "But she was just—"

Nore held her breath.

"She went back inside a while ago," her brother explained. "Said she'd forgotten something. She walked right past us."

Nore bit the inside of her cheek.

The driver gaped.

"You must have missed it," Ell said.

"You look like a confused puppy, John. Fix your face," Darragh snapped. "And open my door."

"I apologize," Ellery chuckled, offering Darragh a hand. "We were caught up in conversation."

Darragh eyed her brother's hand, then looked right through the car window before getting inside. Nore sat up tall and tried to imagine how Red would handle this. She could be Red on the inside, if not on the outside. In truth, Red was *her:* the person Nore was when she wasn't worried about her last name, or what her mother and the Order might think.

She swallowed as Darragh joined her inside and closed the door. The Headmistress reared back in her seat and folded her arms when she saw Nore. *Not the least bit surprised.*

"I'll be brief." Nore's throat thickened. *Be Red.* "You're drowning in rumors about your House. Some of which, I suspect, are true."

Darragh's stare was iron, but in her lap, she held her handbag in a tight grip.

"In no time, the Council will be calling for the dissolution of your House, if they haven't already." *A bluff.* But if the rumors *were* true, that was the Council's only logical next move. And judging by Darragh's nervousness, Nore was at least close to the truth. "You're going to have to pay up for your alleged crimes."

"Make your point," Darragh shoved out through her clenched jaw.

"You need my help." She measured her tone just so. Red was confident. *She* was confident. "Headmistress terms are for life. Death is knocking at your door."

Darragh flinched.

"But House of Marionne can thrive with my help. You can escape all the consequences the Order would try to bring down on your head, and rule as the Four-Hundred-Year King once did, if you wanted."

Darragh's gaze narrowed. *The first gesture she didn't try to hide.*

"You can be immortal." Speaking it out loud made Nore's chest seize. Most believed immortality wasn't possible. But her House was notorious for discovering the impossible.

And possessing the legendary Immortality Scroll was their most revered public "secret." Their inaugural Headmistress had discovered it and changed her surname to make sure everyone knew it. House of Ambrose. *House of the Immortal.* "I will trade you the deepest secret of our House in exchange for you freeing me from this poison before it has a chance to grow."

Darragh was as still as stone.

"Ma'am!" A knock at the window made her jump. "Are we ready?" The driver pressed his eyes to the window and gaped at Nore. Darragh didn't move, her stare fixed on Nore.

"How do I know you have access to the Scroll?" she asked.

"I don't. My mother does. It's in the family vault. I will return to Dlaminaugh and steal it."

Darragh's gaze moved to the window. She tightened her folded arms. "I had your name erased from the Book of Names. Do you have *any* idea how difficult that was? Then you back out on our agreement."

"I know there's no reason for you to trust me again," Nore said.

"Absolutely *none.*"

"But you have no other choice."

Darragh's jaw clenched. She knew Nore was right.

"Up front, I only ask for you to agree. Once I've delivered the Scroll, then you can help me with my toushana. That is fair. You have nothing to lose." Nore clenched her fists as if she could hold the outcome of her request in her hands.

"And how do you know you can trust *me?*" Darragh met her eyes.

Nore stewed on her words. The Order was made of monsters. But Darragh had proven to be a worthy ally before.

"Because you've never shown me any reason that I can't." A silence followed as Darragh's jaw worked. Nore didn't dare say another word.

"You have a deal. If you tell a soul, including that brother of yours, the deal is off. And you'll find out that there are fates much worse than death, Miss Ambrose. Now, get out of my car."

Nore had a plan. It *would* work. She knew where the family vault was. She just had no idea how the heck to get inside it.

EIGHT

—✳—

Quell

The look in Yagrin's eyes when I shut the door on him still haunts me as I sit, waiting, at the dinner table. *He really thinks he's doing the right thing.* Boiled potatoes, rice, and roasted meat are laid out. Every face at the table, all dozen or so of us, is tight-lipped and wide-eyed. But it's Willam whose attention sends a shiver down my spine.

The gentle giant doesn't say much, but he's hard to miss. His skin is drier than leather, the plaid shirt he always wears is buttoned all the way to the tip-top, and usually a straw hat covers his head. But this evening he sits across the table, staring right at me with narrowed eyes. The top button of his shirt is undone, and an angry, circular red burn scar is on his throat. Someone passes him a plate and his broad frame rotates away to grab it. But when he hands it off, his eyes settle back on me.

"Aren't you hungry?" Knox asks, and the events of the last half hour send goose bumps up my arms. *She heard everything.*

"Why did you do that?" I ask, reconsidering the glass of water in my hand. "Offer to let me stay but make him leave."

Willam and Knox meet eyes.

"Because I know your mother," she says, and my glass slips from my hand.

"I—"

She shakes her head. "When we're alone."

I'm frozen. Kedd, one of the younger men here, nudges me with an empty plate and I take it, my body and mind out of sync. My mother never mentioned anything about a safe house or anyone named Knox. Someone else passes me a tray of something and I go through the motions. Dimara, across the table, hands me a warm bowl of potatoes. A question glints in her eyes, but the scrape of Willam's chair as he gets up from the table grabs my attention. As he passes, the scar at his neck is easier to see. Faint lines for a column, cracked in half, are as red as if they were dug right into his neck. The symbol reminds me of the coin Yagrin wore when he was after me.

"Are you a Dragun?" I blurt.

"I'm just Willam," he says as he leaves the dining room with Knox on his heels.

My stomach gurgles but I force a bite into my mouth. I lean in and listen, my hearing senses keenly sharpened since binding with my toushana.

"I'm going to make preparations," Knox says. "You leave by midnight."

"Rein is almost full-term, and the twins are sick." Willam's voice is pinched with frustration. Knox sighs.

I don't know how they ended up here, or how they know each other, but Willam and Knox run this house like a well-oiled machine, always in step with one another. I've never seen them disagree.

"This is *hasty*," Willam says, and I imagine his domineering frame hovering over Knox insistently. "Yagrin isn't stirring up trouble. He's running from it."

"We follow protocol," Knox says. "Always."

"He's not like the rest of them. You can see the heart better than anyone, Knox. You know I'm right about this."

"I'll start a search for a new nest," she says. "Midnight."

For a moment, there is only dining room chatter, the others oblivious to the way all their lives are about to change. Then Willam blows out a heavy breath. "And the girl?"

"We'll talk about that when she's not eavesdropping."

I straighten in my seat. Willam and Knox rejoin us. He looms at the edge of the dining table like a tree with heavy branches.

"After dinner, everyone will prepare their things. We begin roaming protocol tonight." He wipes his mouth with a napkin, then leaves.

Dimara slaps her fork down on her plate and glares at me. "What have you done?"

I'm sorry, I try to say, but the words come out as a crack. *This is their home*. I know how much that means. The two bites of food I did eat reappear in my throat. I wish I could put Knox at ease and promise that Yagrin would never do anything to jeopardize their location. But I don't know where Octos's mask ends and Yagrin's begins. There's no way to know how much of the person I trusted the last few months was real. I push my plate away.

"May I be excused?"

"No. You need to eat." *Because who knows the next time I will be able to eat this well*... Knox doesn't have to say. I look for her eyes, but she won't meet mine. Guilt tugs at me like an anchor.

"Who are you *really*?" Dimara has a fistful of tablecloth. Rein's lip quivers and her hand strokes her swollen belly. Everyone stares in my direction.

"I'm exactly who I said I was: Quell. I fled from House of Marionne. It was the other guy who lied."

"*Your* friend."

Someone sucks their teeth. Another *tsks*.

"How long have you been here, Dimara?" I ask, refusing to take the bait. Arguing will accomplish nothing.

"I was born here. Like most of us."

My next bite halts at my mouth. I'd envisioned Dimara finding her way here like Yagrin had.

"You didn't flee from a House." I'd assumed this was a welcome safe space for anyone fleeing from the Order. But the way Dimara looks at me makes me shift in my seat, and I realize they function like a tight-knit family here. Outsiders must not be welcome . . . which means Knox and

Willam made an exception for me. I meet Knox's eyes, trying to think of something to say, when Dimara slams her knife into the table.

"I could smell it on you, you know?" Her top lip curls. "*Magic.* I tried to warn you."

Knox clears her throat, and Dimara fills her mouth with a hunk of bread. "Finish in silence."

Other than the twins' hacking coughs at the end of the table, the tension in the room for the rest of the meal is sharper than our dinner knives. My brain won't stop whirring through questions about my mother and wondering what I should do next.

"Knox, may we speak alone now?"

She tugs at her necklace. "Clean up and meet me in the mudroom."

I open the door to the mudroom and Knox joins me inside.

"How do you know my mother?"

She pauses to close the door before rolling closer to me.

"Are you going to be okay, child?"

"I will. My mother?"

"Everyone knows about the prodigal daughter of Darragh Marionne."

"You made it sound like you *knew* her."

She pulls at the end of one of her white locs. "She used to live here. Both of you did." Before I realize it, Knox has grabbed a pack of matches from a shelf and strikes one.

I jump back, my heart stuttering at the sight of even a small flame.

"Still scared." Knox blows out the match and flicks the whole thing in a bucket of water.

"I don't remember."

"You wouldn't. You were very small. And it wasn't for long."

"What happened to Willam?"

"A lifetime of people-watching has made you very perceptive. He was a Dragun. But he found himself stuck between loyalty to the brotherhood and loyalty to his Headmistress. Years ago, I found him nearly lifeless in a ditch."

Branded. The red scar at his neck. "Draguns are awful. That's terrible."

Jordan's warning the last time I saw him runs through my mind. When he said it would be *him* to come after me. I wonder who he's told, how many Draguns are out there looking for me. My toushana churns. *I'll be ready.* I wait for Knox to tell me more, but she starts unclipping dried laundry from lines.

"So that's what you and Willam do here? Keep *certain* people running from the Order safe? Visitors aren't welcome, it sounds like."

"Safe houses are descendants of families who've escaped the Order's worst evils. And you're correct. No visitors."

"But Octos . . . Yagrin."

"A fellow named Octos used to live here a long time ago. But he left suddenly. That happens from time to time. We don't take others in, but on occasion we'll lose one who thinks they have a better chance at life on their own. Yagrin must have known him. I don't believe your friend wishes us harm. But someone could pry information out of him and that's not a risk I'm willing to take."

"He's not my friend. I hardly knew him. He was just the only person besides my mother that I thought I could trust."

"I would imagine that list has grown tonight."

I shift on my feet and eye Knox's legs.

"Dragun attack when I was a child."

I gasp. "The world is cruel."

"The world is what those in power make it, Quell. My mother and I were coming home from the store when she was attacked by Draguns. If I were smart, I'd have run. But instead, I ran to her. When they realized I was her child, the descendant of a—" Her chin slides over her shoulder as if the word to finish that sentence would bring up her dinner. "They finished her. Then they came after me. I was seven."

"I'm so sorry." An image of my mother dead on some sidewalk tears its way into my mind. My heart thuds. "So, you have toushana?"

"Not exactly, no. But they thought I did. I managed to get away and a

Shifter, Healer type, amputated my legs before the magic could kill me. My father was a Shifter, really good with metals. He made me this fancy chair."

"It's magnificent."

She blinks and the blue in her eyes deepens. Then her gaze cuts to my heart. "The Great Sorting was a bloodbath."

I swallow. "I'm not familiar?"

"In Misa—the ancient magical city—all manifested magic was welcome. My ancestors only had toushana then. But they had a reputation among the citizens of Misa for responsible moral character and trustworthiness. Toushana was powerful, but they did not abuse it. When the magic city fell, none of that mattered. The Upper Cabinet had carefully placed members in Washington by then. They'd discovered rumors of Misa's existence and immediately ordered that the magic city be razed to the ground. From then on, Marked members would need to blend in to the Unmarked world through a House system. House of Perl was founded. Decades later, Marionne. Then Duncan, and so on. But those who manifested toushana were ordered to be killed during the Sorting because they posed too great a risk to the Order's power. The Houses would not be equipped to train the use of toushana, and it was too volatile to risk. The Order only saw who my ancestors *could* be, Quell. The horrible things they *could* do. They ordered my family to be burned."

My nails dig into my arms.

She shrugs. "Magic is dangerous, and safer to just be left alone. My great-great, many-*greats*-grandmother created the first of what became a network of safe houses for Misa refugees. But she still lived every single day of her life in fear. I refuse to. That is why there is no magic used here, and if you do stay, you may never, ever use it again."

"Stay? I—"

"So you're going to help your friend, then? Tear down the Order?"

"He's not my— Look, I have to know what's going on with my mother."

"Mine died on a sidewalk. My great-grandmother was killed by Draguns as well. My grandfather burned alive. I have cousins I've never met, but I hear they're doing fine. Living without magic on the West Coast. I know, and how does that help me thrive now?"

"You can't expect me to ignore that she's out there somewhere." Toushana pulls at my bones as my frustration rises.

"My expectations aren't what matter, Quell. Yours do." She squeezes my arm affectionately. "Make your decision quickly. We leave at midnight." The calm confidence of her expression makes me feel like it's possible. That if I go with them, the Order will never catch us. That they have a trustable safe haven and I could be happy. *Why didn't we stay here, Mom?* So many questions.

But my mother's out there somewhere . . .

And giving up my toushana?

Cold shudders through me. "I'm not like you. My magic is who I am." I sigh. "Thank you for offering me a place and for not judging me. Other than my mother, no one has ever made me feel . . . Anyway, I can't go with you. I have to find her."

"Willam expected that to be your decision." She parts the door wider, rolling aside to hold it open for me.

"I think what you're both doing here is really important. And I'm sorry about everything. I didn't want it to go this way."

"I hope you find what you're truly looking for, Quell."

I grab my bag from the door and leave. I *will* find my mother *and* master this toushana inside me, whatever it takes.

When the fall wind hits my face, I pull a slip of paper out of my pocket, stewing over Knox's words. The paper Beaulah shoved into my hand as I fled my Cotillion has faded a lot. My path is mine to choose. And I've made my decision. I'm not sure what the future holds, but it includes my mother and my magic. No one will take that from me. I summon the comforting chill in my blood to cloak.

I have to go to the last place my mom was seen: House of Perl.

PART TWO

NINE

∗

Quell

The sharp night wind blows my cloak away, and the feeling of being watched snakes its way around my throat. On either side of the winding street are trees with thick trunks and sprawling branches draped with rusty golden leaves. The crisp, cold air hums with a distant thrash of water. I walk, but I'm unsure which direction to go. *Why here?* The magic is never wrong: when it's told a location, it takes you there. But there isn't a rooftop or paved drive cutting through the trees.

Lights glow in the distance, and suddenly a horn rips through the air. An old car, polished brand new, swerves around me, and my heart thuds in my chest. It skids past, then screeches to a stop, and the driver window comes down.

"Get out of the street, crazy lady!" The man's middle-aged with salt-and-pepper slicked-back hair, dressed in fine pants and a fancy bow tie. His passenger leans out her window, wrapped like a present in a tight red dress. Pearls dangle at her chest and long gloves cover her arms.

"Are you alright?" she asks.

I bite my lip. "I had a flat tire down the road. I was almost home."

He and his date share a glance, then his expression darkens. *"Fratis fortunam."*

They're from House Perl. I could have guessed by the colors they're wearing. I feel for the slip of paper Beaulah gave me with her address. She invited me at the end of my Cotillion, but I don't exactly trust her. Jordan never had anything good to say about this woman. *It's better if she doesn't know I'm coming.* No time to hide anything.

"I'm sorry?" I feign ignorance. "I'm not very good with Latin."

"Good enough to recognize it's Latin." He steps out.

"Charles, come on," his date pleads. "We're already late."

"Where's that car?" He looks around, closing his door. "How long have you been on foot?" He cocks his head, walking closer. Silver glints at his throat, and gold buttons trail down the lapel of his jacket. *A Dragun.* "If you're looking for Old Greenwich, you need to head that way." He points. "Back here is private property." The night shifts slightly as something dark ripples through the air.

Toushana curls in my bones. I clear my throat.

"I don't want to cause any problems." *I just want to find my mom.*

"Then you should repay the greeting." A mask of black, trimmed in gold, bleeds through his skin. I swallow. Ice creeps into my veins, trailing into my wrists and through my fingertips. I can expose myself or get rid of them some other way . . . Magic prickles my fingers, but I tighten my fist. I'm not hurting anyone. My only way out of this is the truth. As little as I can share.

"I have an invitation from the lady of the House." I pull out the slip of paper and show him.

"You should've said something sooner!" He lugs an arm over my shoulder and drags me along.

Moments later, I'm in the back of their car, flying down the road until we abruptly slow and turn down a narrow gravel inlet to the nest of trees. We hit a jarring bump.

"Ow!" his date yowls.

"Sorry, doll. The DB5 wasn't made to go off-road." He draws circles on her knee. "I keep telling Mother to pave this entrance. How do you know Mother?"

The question is for me. I sink deeper into the seat. They haven't asked my name. Nor have they offered theirs. His is Charles, because I heard her say it. "I met her at a ball once." That feels like a decently convincing lie. Charles is about to ask another question when we come to a sudden stop in the middle of the woods, with no sign of a house anywhere. We get out and my magic picks at me like an itch, fearing I've made a mistake.

"Where are we?"

"First time visiting Hartsboro." He smirks. The girl ropes her arm around his, and they disappear into the trees. I race after them and realize there are all manner of fancy cars parked in and around this forest. We walk long enough for the girl to begin complaining about her heels sticking in the ground. He scoops her up in his arms, and she giggles as he nuzzles her neck. It makes my stomach turn. We pass several signs, all with the same warning.

100 ACRES OF PRIVATE HUNTING GROUNDS
ENTER AT YOUR OWN RISK

"It's there." He points to a ditch full of a dark, sludgy substance.

"I don't understand."

He sets her on her feet, and she flips a blade out so fast I miss where it comes from. In a flash, silver scrapes against her skin, then its sharpened tip drips with blood. She holds the spot where she just nicked herself over the depthless ground. The ripples slope into precise angles until the thick substance shifts into a set of steep stone stairs cut into the ground. *Beaulah requires a blood offering to get inside.*

The woman tosses the blade in the air and I catch it.

"See you in there," she says as the pool re-forms and the glimpse of stairway disappears.

"I take it she doesn't like surprise visitors." I swallow.

"Blood from an invited guest is all it needs." He pricks himself, re-opens the passageway, and disappears down the steps. I study the knife, the girl's blood still wet on its tip. *If it notifies her who is crossing the threshold into her property, she'll know I'm coming. Will the magic know if my blood is bound to toushana?*

I twist the blade, its metal gleaming in the moonlight, and an idea strikes me. He never said a person couldn't enter twice. Without enough blood on the metal to drip, I dip the blade into the pool and wait. *Please work.* If I lose this knife, that's it—I'm not getting in here. And this was the last place my mom was seen. The black pool thins, then shifts, bending in steady rhythm until there are stairs once again. I tuck the weapon in my sleeve and descend.

The ground closes above me. Ahead is a stone passageway. I follow it to an intersection, keep straight, and then listen for the footsteps. I reach a set of stairs to the ground above. I climb but freeze when I hear voices.

"I'm cold. She'll be fine. Maybe she chickened out." *The girl from the car.* I press against the stone. Her beau agrees. When the world aboveground is silent, I emerge from the tunnel beside a lush, winding water garden so tall I can't see beyond it. Beaulah is either very paranoid or extremely clever. The path through the garden meanders through a maze of low-lying pools wreathed in bursts of colorful foliage. When I clear them, the grounds finally open up. And there is Hartsboro, the training ground for House of Perl, tucked away like a secret.

The old mansion's brick is the color of midnight. It sits on a small hill, reached by an expanse of steps like I imagine I'd find at a fancy government building or museum. Black Roman-style Corinthian columns line the front, but I'm still too far away to read the words etched into the stone. Two levels form the central house; wings branch off to either side and wrap around a center courtyard, where gardens are arranged in the shape of a sun. The house's farthest ends disappear into the surrounding trees. Sparkling lights, grand balconies, sweeping windows, and lush manicured lawn—it's as magnificent as Chateau Soleil, but in its own way.

I bristle with irritation. Jordan grew up here. And he is the last person I should be thinking about.

I scrub the boy I used to love from my mind and step aside, tucking my chin down, as another couple in nice clothes passes. They hustle toward the estate but veer from the grand carved doors and instead detour around the building and disappear.

The main entrance gates are manned by Draguns. I have to find another way in. I hurry in the opposite direction, determined to avoid any more of Beaulah's guests. I follow the stone walls on the perimeter of the grounds, careful to stay in the pockets of dark. But I stop when I notice, beyond Hartsboro, a blackness of thick, dark woods. The chill in the air deepens and my toushana coils fast, ready to strike. *You're alright. Calm down.*

I round the estate's wing. I'm skimming the side of it for some kind of entrance when laughter cuts through the silence. A voice is coming from beyond a wall of shrubbery. Laughter rings again, louder, closer. *Rumors of what's happened at Chateau Soleil are everywhere.* Getting caught could mean death. Ice seizes in my chest, but I keep my hands loose. I won't be easy prey.

I spot an iron gate in the wall of green when I hear the voice again. This time its familiarity turns my arms to gooseflesh. I lift the gate's latch silently and ease myself through. Inside is an amphitheater trimmed in what must be a million roses. On a dais crowned in wrought iron is a pair of lovers tangled around each other. The girl rears her head back, hair spun up in an elegant bun at the crown of her head, the silks of her dress puddling on the floor, as a gentleman kisses up and down her neck. It's too dark to make out either of them well, but I don't recognize them. Maybe I misheard. I'm sliding a quiet foot backward toward the gate when her diadem glints in the moonlight. Radiant dark jewels intricately worked with gold metal sparkle. I *know* that showing. I move closer. A twig snaps under my foot.

The girl fumbles with her dress to cover herself, and I step closer for a better look. Her complexion is warm brown and hardly dusted with makeup. As if she'd need it. Her skin is smoother than velvet, and high cheekbones slope around her angular face, making her wide eyes pop. Her back is straight, her neck long, and her shoulders are pressed back, effortlessly elegant, poised despite the compromising moment I've found her in. If she wasn't scrambling to cover herself, I wouldn't know she was shaken at all. I recognize the sharpness of her jaw and aquiline nose and realize where I know her from. Why her diadem looks so familiar.

"Adola?"

Beaulah's niece and heir to this House. Jordan's cousin.

She leans into the light to see me, then gasps. I hold a finger to my lips in warning, darkness dripping from them. Adola gapes at the magic in my grasp, then her shock hardens into something else. Her lover fiddles with the buttons of the pants he just slipped on. That's when I notice he is in plain clothes. No mask bleeds through his skin. There's no House color in his wardrobe. This guy has no magic.

"How scandalous." I join them on the dais to get a better look at the girl I last saw at the Summer Bloom Tea I hosted in my grandmother's rose garden. She was so measured and poised. Now she's struggling to re-dress, her earthy complexion pale with embarrassment.

"Quell, how are you?" She slips her arms into her dress, and the fellow with her hastily zips her up. "I've heard all kinds of things. I was worried." She turns to him. "Go," she urges. "Don't speak of this to anyone." His eyes snap to my magic. *"Now."*

He darts off.

She smooths her skirt, but she hardly breathes. "Well?"

We're alone. I could press my magic to her throat and force her to lead me inside. But if there's another way . . . The Order wouldn't bat an eye at getting rid of her little non-magical boyfriend. I stretch my fingers, then tighten them into a fist, calling my toushana back into myself.

"An Unmarked cannot look upon magic and live."

She swallows.

"Take me to your aunt. I want to talk to Beaulah privately. If you do that, your secret is safe with me."

For a moment, Adola only blinks. She tosses me her long hooded coat to put on. Then she releases a ragged breath and says, "Fine. Follow me."

TEN

——*——

Quell

Adola leads me out of the amphitheater to a servant's entrance down a set of steep steps.

"We're just going to walk in? That's your plan?"

"The staff was given the night off. This is how I got out."

I study her for some hint of dishonesty, but there's no scheme in her eye. Still, this *is* the House of Perl heir. The same heir who played a humiliating joke on me the first time we met.

"I can cloak," I insist. "Just tell me where she is on-site."

"*Tutum et perspicuum.*"

My brows cinch.

"Cloaking isn't possible on the grounds. People don't pop up on Mother," she says.

"Your aunt, you mean?"

"I didn't misspeak." She offers me a hand down the stairs. I follow her inside Hartsboro.

Hartsboro's grand rooms and tall coffered ceilings remind me of Chateau Soleil. Where my grandmother's estate glistened with gold and ornately carved accents, the inside of House of Perl has an understated grandness. A confidence. As if it doesn't need to prove itself. It is statuesque without being overwhelmingly spacious. Luxurious, without being gaudy or glamorous, with sleek fixtures and accents that aren't gilded or frilly. There is wood, stone, and brick instead of porcelain and marble. Suits of armor instead of sculptures. Plaques of history and portraits of prior Headmistresses line the paneled walls. And beside them is an engraved list of never forgotten names.

My heart knocks into my ribs when I spot the names of the two girls who were killed this past summer: Brooke Hamilton and Alison Blakewell. All thanks to my grandmother. My gut swims.

A hall of portraits portraying distinguished members of the House is the fanciest, with an impressive display of diadems, masks, and tiny gold pins. Being in a House again unsteadies me. *I did the right thing at my Cotillion.* I told the truth. Still, I can't move, flooded with memories of walking the halls of my old home, certain a different life was on the horizon. Only to realize the little house on the beach, the life Mom and I imagined for ourselves, would be harder to grab hold of than I thought. Adola urges me to keep going.

That's when I spot it.

A painting of Jordan, an enlarged version of that photo of him from *Debs Daily.* My fingers feel for the lump in my coat where the copy of the article sits tucked against my chest. His prim suit, cinched at the collar with his coin. His devilishly gorgeous face despite his hollow stare. His green eyes were a sunlit meadow, now they're a field of ashes. Beneath the frame is a title: DRAGUNHEART OF THE BROTHERHOOD, followed by a starting year—this year—without an end date. I back away and bump into Adola. She grabs me by the arm, pulling me along. I go with her, but I swear I feel the portrait staring at me, squeezing my throat. My heart races. Every corner we turn sends a cold shiver up my arms, and I have to remind myself why I'm here. My mother was *here.* At Hartsboro. She could have stood in this very hall. I walk faster.

"Where is your aunt?"

"Her office, usually." She creeps along, holding her arms tight to her body. "It is in the Dysiis Wing. We can't risk taking the direct route."

We pass through a formal dining area that's longer than any room I've ever seen; its chandeliers are made of carved bones that are eerily realistic. Past it, the foyer opens up to a lounge, its furniture arranged around a projection of the Sphere. The matter inside the orb undulates, still blackened like the last time I saw it at Chateau Soleil, but its glassy surface is cracked like a shattered eggshell.

"What happened to the Sphere?" I gathered from skimming issues of the *Daily* that the Sphere had been attacked, and things in the Order are shaky. But the Order has never done anything but make my life a nightmare. I couldn't care less what happens to it. The Sphere, on the other hand . . . I had no idea it'd become so fragile.

"Is it true what they say about if it bleeds out?" I ask.

Adola's chin slides over her shoulder. "It's worse."

"Worse?" But she doesn't elaborate. Magic *gone* for lifetimes. I nudge my toushana, and the coldness shifts against my ribs as I try to picture myself without toushana to keep me safe.

Yagrin used me to track the Sphere. He said he'd located it before. No one I know hates the Order more. Suddenly, I know who is responsible for the attack.

We turn down another long corridor and arrive at a room that smells like stale smoke and fresh leather. It is filled with chairs, a bar, and crystal game tables; bookshelves line the walls.

"Are they onto him—um, the person who cracked it?" Could more than Jordan know she had been on the run with him?

"I don't know." She runs her hand down the side of a bookcase before her fingers disappear in the seam. "But my cousin will find whoever did it. He's the sharpest Dragun alive. And he was just promoted to second-in-command of the entire brotherhood."

"*Jordan?*" I spit. "I *cannot stand* your cousin."

"That's not what I heard." Adola pulls and the bookcase swings forward. A sassy retort bites at my lips. I've given Jordan Wexton enough of my time. He won't dominate my thoughts, too.

We step into a secret corridor and pull the fake shelf closed. *Jordan.*

This is where he lived. He walked these halls. He navigated its secret corridors. Nausea rises in my throat. This place made him into an Order-obsessed, backstabbing betrayer. I *hate* him. But I think I hate myself more for hoping that he would be different than everyone else in the Order. That he actually cared about me. That the girl he shared green candy with was worthy of love.

Dusty air prickles my nose, and I smooth my leaking eyes to focus on the light from tiny peepholes that cuts through the darkness in every direction.

"Each bookcase in the House leads to a different part of the estate. No one uses these but family and . . ." She tugs at the skirt of her dress. "*Please* don't say anything."

I nod and urge her forward. The hidden interior hallways of Beaulah's house are a maze of corridors. Adola halts suddenly and I slam into her back. She presses a finger to her lips and points to a tiny hole in the wall. Peeping through it, I see a grand study room sparsely furnished with a fireplace, bookshelves, a desk strewn with papers, and a few pieces of leather furniture. The narrow hole makes it impossible to see the full room.

"She's in there?"

"Should be."

I grip Adola's wrist as she tries to leave, and lean against the trick wall to open it. It swings forward, opening into Beaulah's office. Everything is glossed wood and dark colors. And suns, so many engraved suns, on every surface, carved into the shutters, on the windows, on ornamented fixtures, on the lamp, and etched into the hard floor. But Beaulah isn't here.

"You said she'd be here."

"This was my best guess."

I circle Beaulah's desk, checking beneath documents, going through her drawers—looking for what, I'm not sure. "Take me to her bedroom."

She pales. "I can't do that."

"You knew she wasn't in here." Toushana thrashes in my chest. "You're wasting my time." No one is trustworthy. Everyone is in it for themselves. "What game are you playing?"

"I did what you asked! You *agreed* you wouldn't tell if I took you to find her, which I did. It's not my fault she's not here." Adola fidgets.

I march up to her, letting the cold brimming beneath my skin bleed through. Adola's eyes widen. "You're lying. *Take me* to her."

Adola's mouth hardens.

"There's a party or something going on tonight. I saw people dressed up. Is she there?"

Adola blinks one too many times. I pace, considering my options. Then I inhale deeply, awakening my toushana. *Maybe I don't need her.* Magic flows through me, and I tighten my center. Blood rushes to my head. My ears are cold, flooded with a symphony of sounds. The faint chatter and clinking of glasses, along with a low melody of music, urge me into motion. I'm back behind the bookcase, tracking a heartbeat until it's louder, clearer. Until there are many hearts beating at once in a concentrated area. A crowd of people.

"Quell! Please, you can't—" But Adola's words are hardly audible as she hustles to keep up with me. Following the sounds of people takes me to a different section of the estate, past rooms full of desks, more than one sprawling ballroom, a honing lab, endless halls of dormitories, and a strange wing of the house with scorched walls and windowless session rooms, empty of tables or chairs. I finally hear the clink of champagne glasses; soft cheers and low music roll around in my head with a chorus of dozens of heartbeats. When I stop, the thudding is a thousand hammers in my head. I peer through a peephole and find a finely dressed crowd. I glare at Adola.

"*Please* don't go in there, I'm *begging* you! Mother will kill me." Tears well in her eyes at the sight of my arm wedged against the door, ready to shove it open.

"Everyone knows Perls are liars. Should have known you'd be no different." I push the bookcase forward. We spill out of the corridor into a swanky reception in a dimly lit, windowless room. A chill washes over me, and it takes me a minute to realize it's not my toushana. It's a cold hovering in the air like a cloud of death. The music stops. The conversations quiet as every head in the room swivels in our direction. My palms sweat, biting iciness clawing at them. Beaulah moves among the frozen crowd, clutching a fluted glass, her red, shimmery gown dangling over her feet. At first she watches me in confusion, before her narrowed gaze widens in understanding.

"Quell Marionne."

Low whispers swarm the crowd. My heart knocks into my ribs. Everyone waits for her reaction. I let toushana seep through my skin but hold my hands in tight fists to conceal my secret. Fear got the best of me with Adola, but I don't need all these people to know. Beaulah strides toward me and the cold slithers around my bones.

"Headmistress Perl, I need to speak with you," I shout.

But the room suddenly grows colder as familiar dark ripples move through the air. And it startles me. *Toushana.* I check my own hands to be sure I'm not hallucinating. But the toushana moving through the air isn't coming toward me at all. It's disappearing among the crowd. *Draguns.* I skim for coins at throats, and many are wearing ones with cracked columns. Several do not have coins at all.

I blink, watching dark whiffs of magic coil around wrists of people who have no business drawing on toushana. Several curious gazes move to me as if they can sense my nervousness. I keep staring, waiting for the scene to change. Waiting for any of this to make some bit of sense. When Beaulah Perl reaches me, I am barely breathing. The amber stones in her diadem gleam, a complement to the fur wrapped around her shoulders, pinned with a glittering brooch in the shape of a cracked column. I take all of her in—the dark gems on her knuckles, the pearls pressed to her ears—reading every line in her stoic expression, noticing the way she is the only person in this entire room completely at ease. And though she tries to hide it, there is the slightest glint of satisfaction in her eyes. She studies me up and down, drinking me in, and then reaches for my hand.

"What is this?" I nearly choke on the words. The magic that's been a death sentence over my head since I was a child is here, in this room. "I— I mean, I *asked* if there's somewhere we can speak?"

Her mouth bows into a smile. Then she fans a hand in the air. "Please, guests, join me in welcoming the heiress to House of Marionne." She faces the crowd and the cautious stares morph to curious ones. Several raise their glasses and return to their conversations, the music jumping back in motion. But one pair of eyes doesn't leave me: Charles's. Reclined on a slick piano, he sips his drink, watching me.

Beaulah notices. "Charlie is a good boy. That girl on his arm, Penelope, was never my choice for him. But you have to loosen the leash on some things or they'll tug hard all the time. Now the mood's a bit lighter—shall we?" She holds out her elbow.

"Mother, she *made* me bring her here!" Adola, who I'd almost forgotten about, shoves her way through the crowd toward us. "She threatened to *kill* me."

"Hush your mouth, girl, before you embarrass yourself." Beaulah turns to me, and under her breath, she asks, "Is this true?"

Not exactly, but she needs to know I'm serious. "Yes."

She pets my hand. "Next time you want to coerce someone, it is much safer to use your toushana to destroy their memory of helping you. It's painful for them, but only for a moment."

I swallow hard, unsure what to say.

"I was told you weren't feeling well this evening," she says to Adola, whose gaze darts to me. But I keep my mouth shut. "Calm yourself down, dear. Quell won't bat an eye at anything she sees here." She watches for my reaction before smoothing Adola's cheeks. "You're a Perl. Everyone expects you to shine. Mingle. In a bit, I might have you demonstrate some of your own shadow magic for us."

Adola's heart speeds up. "Please, not tonight." She smiles plastically.

Curious . . . Beaulah's heir is intimidated by the use of dark magic or something.

"She can be so shy sometimes," Beaulah says to me. "Some other time."

"Thank you, Mother." Adola curtsies and rushes away.

We walk and I lose sight of Adola among the festive crowd dancing and nibbling hors d'ouvres being passed around on trays.

"There is toushana in this room," I say, unable to resist. "Are others here . . . bound to it like me?"

"Oh, no, no one here was born with toushana. We haven't been that fortunate. But we do dabble." She winks and it unsettles me. I spent my entire life running from the Order because of who I am. None of this makes any sense.

I study the crowd, my eyes adjusting to the dim light. A gentleman in a corner streams blackness to something small until it's a pile of ash. Then he sweeps the ash into his palm and tosses it into his mouth.

"Is that going to hurt him?"

"Taylor has an eccentric appetite. Don't mind him."

Across the room, a lady throws her head back in laughter while massaging a fist of thrashing shadows. The air buzzes with dark magic. I skim faces for scorn, fidgety hands, raised brows, discomfort, or judgment, but there are only jazzed smiles and a festive atmosphere. Beaulah's beside me, standing tall, her shoulders pulled back. A smile spreads across her face.

She's *proud* . . .

I let my arms hang loose at my sides but hesitate to release my tight fists.

"You don't fear toushana."

"I only fear one thing: the unknown."

I look for some hint of dishonesty in her, but she doesn't even flinch.

"Not even with the Sphere's condition?" She must fear for the Order.

She tidies the fur sloped across her shoulders. "That will all be in hand soon. The Dragunhead is quite competent." She turns a gemless gold ring on her finger.

"Does he know you openly allow toushana use here?" An odd feeling wraps around my ribs just hearing myself say the words aloud.

"*Openly?* Who's watching?"

There isn't a single window in this room, and it wasn't exactly easy to find. Getting onto the grounds was nearly impossible. Adola fought me to come here because she didn't want to be responsible for outing her aunt's secret. I watch faint whiffs of darkness hanging in the air. The cold lurking beneath my skin quiets, and my fists finally come undone. The toushana they use is called *to* themselves. It's not inside them, like mine is, as she said. None of them are bound. But still. I blow out a shaky breath.

"What kind of party is this?"

"We miss the business of the Season's Rites and Cotillions, so we use the *off*-Season time to host our Virtue Pin Trials. It's a Perl tradition. I like to recognize distinguished accomplishment. A House thrives on the dedication of its members. And nothing breeds dedication more than pride."

Beaulah wears six gold pins, like the ones Jordan had, nestled in her shawl.

"There are many Draguns here." Only Draguns are allowed to draw toushana from outside of themselves, to use it. She must train the others how to do it.

"You're quite observant. Every House has its secrets, Quell. Ambrose's immortality. Darragh's garden of black roses."

"But they're *here*. Not at Dragun Headquarters."

"I've given them a safe place to explore the things they're naturally good at. They love their Mother. Can you blame them?"

Mother. The word ricochets like a bullet through my chest as Beaulah leads me into a quaint lounge separate from the reception. We settle into a pair of leather armchairs, and she pours brown liquid into a glass.

"How did you find Hartsboro's entrance? I'd have known if the blood of a Marionne was offered at my gates."

I explain how I ran into Charles and how I used his date's dirty knife.

"Powerful, observant, *and* clever." She swishes the liquid in her glass. "A débutante, bound to toushana, in this day and age. I never thought I'd see the day." Her gaze traces me, pausing at my head. I'd almost forgotten. I tighten from my center and shove my magic up through me until my black diadem shows itself, brilliant and defiant.

"It's a spectacle."

I shift in my seat. But I can't stop watching the gleam of awe in her eyes.

"You have nothing to fear here, Quell." Her gaze falls to the tiny scar on my chest where my dagger disappeared. "People are gifted in different ways. Who are we to judge those gifts?"

"I've lived my entire life on the run. The Order judges me."

"Yes, I suppose history proves they are very hard on people like you."

"I was speaking for myself, personally." There were others like me. Bound to the toushana they were born with. *But they did horrific things!* They *earned* that name: Darkbearers. "I'm nothing like those the Order judged."

She crosses and recrosses her legs. "The Order did make a point to get rid of known bloodlines with dark magic after Misa fell."

I think of Knox. *Not all of them.*

She smirks knowingly, as if she can read my mind. "And the Dragunhead remains committed to sniffing out any remaining, of course. This makes your predicament curious, to say the least."

"I won't apologize for what I did."

"And no one in this close circle of my friends will ask you to." Beaulah raises her glass and offers me one. I wave away her offer. She flinches ever so slightly, trying to hide it by taking a sip of her glass. But I don't miss it.

"To be clear, you and I, we're not friends."

"I hear my nephew is looking for you." She smooths her skirt.

I stiffen, and a smile tugs at her lips. And I feel like that's the first glimpse of the Beaulah I've heard about. Delighting in making others uncomfortable. But I'm not the scared little girl at Chateau Soleil anymore. I'm also not one of the others here who appear to tiptoe on eggshells around her.

"I didn't come here to answer your questions. I want to know where my mother is."

"Ah, yes." Warm light glints in the amber stones arced above her head. She has a confident yet ominous presence, like the rest of this place. "Rhea was here recently. What do you want to know?"

"Is she still here?"

"No. I'd have mentioned that right away."

"Why did she come here? Did you help her?"

"One of my Draguns brought her in. I'd originally asked him to bring *you* to me because I'd heard rumors that you were different. I wanted to see and assess for myself—without telling your grandmother, of course. Darragh would run you off like she does everyone else in her life."

She heard of my toushana and *wanted me* here? I push my hair behind my shoulder and hook my hands onto my knee, listening. It occurs to me that my grandmother and this woman have known each other a very long time.

"I wouldn't put anything past Darragh Marionne. This Sphere business is no accident. Someone wants to take down our great Houses, and who has better motive than someone with no allies?"

"You think my grandmother was behind the Sphere cracking?"

"You seem surprised."

"She's a terror. I'm not surprised; I just happen to know you're wrong."

She waits for me to volunteer more information.

"At any rate, it was smart of you to get out of there," she says. She strokes one of her six gold pins. *Discretion*, if I remember correctly. She pours another glass but keeps her eyes on me. "What was it like under her care? And how has your toushana done since binding?"

"Answer *my* questions. That's why I'm here."

"Knowing what you want and being clear about it is a great strength, Quell. I respect that. What is it you want to know *exactly*?" She rears back in her seat.

"What did you do when my mother came here? Be specific."

"I welcomed her and sent her to the guesthouse." She glances over her shoulder at the reception. "I'm sure you understand why we like to keep regular guest access . . . contained. I inquired about you. But she wouldn't tell me anything, which didn't surprise me, of course. And one day she was just gone." She steeples her hands.

I fold my arms. *There's more to that story.* She doesn't lie, exactly; instead she withholds important details—which is slimier, I think. I can feel my chance at truth slipping away. She plays it cool, sipping her drink. But I know that spark in her eye. I saw it in Yagrin. She's fascinated that I've bound to toushana. She's *dying* to ask me more questions. But she won't volunteer more information. I could search these grounds myself, figure out what Beaulah's *not* telling me. What did my mother do here? What exactly made her leave? That should give me an idea of where she went.

Beaulah isn't the only one who can get what she wants from people.

"Fine." I pause a beat to sell this act. "Thank you for giving her a place to stay." I pop up from my chair, and for the first time, Beaulah appears unsettled.

"You're not leaving, are you?"

"You're enamored of toushana."

She doesn't move.

"Study me. Learn all you want about what it means to be bound to it. Consider me your science experiment."

Her grip on her glass tightens.

"In exchange, I need"—*to figure out what you're not telling me about my mother's time here*—"a place to stay, off the radar. I don't trust you." I stick out a hand. "But perhaps I can come to."

Not a moment passes before her hand is in mine. "Welcome to Hartsboro."

We shake. But she doesn't let go.

"Integrity says a lot about a person, Quell. Keep your word and my nephew will never know you're here."

Betray her and he will, she doesn't have to say.

"This place can be a haven for you or a dungeon of shadows."

I snatch my hand away and smooth my dress. "We have a deal, then."

She smiles, and I hurry back to the party, trying to forget the look of triumph on her face.

ELEVEN

Jordan

I can't remember the last time I got such wretched sleep. My brother's in jail. *And I put him there.* The trace on Quell is silent and the Dragunhead wouldn't be argued with, even after I brought Yagrin in. Thankfully he wasn't too furious. I told the Dragunhead I ran into my brother while out doing my job. My stomach still sloshes at lying to him. Again.

I tuck the vial of Sun Dust he gave me into my shirt and double-check the image Maei messaged me late last night. She's buzzed me for updates on the hour, every hour, since. The image is blurry, but the blackened orb is hard to miss, hovering over a sandy expanse of desert. The last I saw it, it was covered in webs of cracks. Now each crack has spread into a million tiny ones, and it's a miracle the Sphere is still holding together at all. We're running out of time.

The tip came from a member who spotted it while vacationing, but by the time Draguns got there in the morning, the Sphere was gone. So the Dragunhead sent me here instead to get answers from a Sphere expert. Two days of cloaking to get here has my magic stiff. I flex my fingers and tuck the photo away, but my heart seizes in my chest as I imagine the Sphere's matter bleeding out. And all that would mean.

Me without magic.

The Order in shambles.

Memento sumptus. If it's all lost, then what was any of the sacrifice ever for? My fingers find the jagged scar on my chest as I walk toward a concrete box of a house up ahead. It's nestled in a field beside a natural spring and looks just like its description in the report. The smooth slate walls, without windows or doors, blend in with the cloudy sky. An overgrown garden eclipses most of the house from view. Blink when passing and you could miss it. Francis Clemon Hughes III, the oldest living Dragun, lives inside. And he's the best at sun tracking the brotherhood has ever known. Better than my brother, and that's high praise. Sun tracking was the only thing Yagrin ever did right.

"Are you sure someone lives in there?" Yani asks.

"He's a 'Roser," Charlie says. "This is some trick."

I listen with all my senses. "He's in there." *If this guy knows anything, he's going to help us.*

"When did he retire? And *why*?" Most Draguns serve until death.

I check the file again. "It doesn't say. Check the surrounding area for evidence of anyone else here," I tell them.

"We're literally in the middle of nowhere," Yani says, feeling for her blade. "You were always *so* cautious." Halfway around the world. Two hundred miles from the closest village and a half day's walk from the nearest road.

"We follow protocol. I'll look for a way inside." Circling the perimeter, I find every side of the building is covered in sprawling vines and wild plants. There is no break in the foliage or indication that Francis has left this cube at all.

Charlie rejoins me. "Nothing."

"Same." Yani unclips the fire dagger at her waist and slices at the tangled weeds that crawl up the sides of the residence. We're going to have to get more aggressive.

"Form up. We attack on my say." I signal for the ready, on my count. And summon the chilled shadows. Cold rushes at me and I grab hold of it, a fistful of toushana. We unleash the destructive magic on the structure all at once, darkness slamming into its hard walls.

Nothing happens.

"Again!"

We pull magic to our bodies, harder, and the world darkens around us. We thrust a cannon of thrashing darkness to assault the block of cement. Shadows slam into the slate surface and vanish. Few things can withstand toushana's deadly touch. We try again. And again, until my vision blurs and iciness creeps from the tips of my fingers into the bones in my hand. But nothing changes.

"Enough." When I release the toushana and push it far away, it takes me several blinks before my head feels right again. I walk the perimeter again, surveying for any damage I might have missed. There is no time for delays; every second we're behind is another second Quell gets ahead.

"Persons and purpose?" A voice from nowhere unsettles the birds in the trees. Charlie and Yani meet eyes. She falls back to figure out where the Audior magic is coming from. "Name your persons, state your purpose."

"I am Jordan Wexton, Dragunheart of the Prestigious Order of Highest Mysteries. We are here on official business and mean you no harm. I summon you out of your house by order of the Dragunhead. Refuse to comply and you will be charged."

Silence.

Yani elbows me, then clears her throat and raises her voice. "Sir, pardon my companion. He is new on the job and a bit too eager."

I glare at her.

"What he means to say is, we've come to visit from Headquarters," she says in a honeyed tone. "We have a few questions for you about the Sphere." She finishes with a gentle inflection and a kindness in her voice that is the furthest thing from genuine. It's sickening to be reminded of how I believed the best about her, when we were younger and she had fooled me. And how I didn't learn my lesson with Quell.

A single wall of the house shifts. Tiny beads of condensation form on its solid surface until the cement barrier on one side of the house vanishes, melting into swelling droplets before morphing into a hazy mist. A withered hand cuts through it.

"Inside, quickly," he says, stretching his veiny fingers.

His heart beats calmly, and through the haze, his expression gleams with earnestness. I take his hand and he pulls me through a wall oscillating between states of matter. I shiver at the feeling of slimy tentacles slithering all over me. Yani enters next, and after a moment, Charlie dashes through, tucking his phone away. Once we're all inside, the wall hardens.

"Francis." He offers his hand again, this time to shake. But I'm stilled, taking all of him in. A bone mask, tinged yellow and eroding at its edges, seeps back into his skin. He waits, hunched, his back bowed with age, but his stare sharply lucid. His gaze moves to my pendant.

"Jordan."

Yani whispers, "What is he, like, five hundred?"

"He's probably one of those immortality-obsessed 'Roser weirdos," Charlie whispers back, loud enough for me to hear.

Thankfully, Francis only blinks, not seeming to notice. "Sal finally picked someone." He holds on, still shaking my hand, drinking in every inch of me. I can't help but notice that his frayed long-sleeved shirt and threadbare pants do not conceal his concerningly spare frame. Fading tattoos cover the backs of his hands. There's a simple kitchen: no mirrors, decorative tile, or painted walls. In true Ambrosian style, it is as gray as the floor and ceiling. The most colorful part of the house is the mantel lined with urns, each with their own style of markings. Beside it is a kneeler for praying.

Francis drags over a stool and an overturned pail. As I sit on the stool, my foot unsettles crushed plants wreathed around a blanket on the floor. After his career, why would he choose to spend his life alone, here, like this? He offers Yani his bed as a seat.

"I'll stand," she says.

"To what do I owe the pleasure of a visit from Headquarters?" He smiles, but there is only weariness in his expression. His pallid skin barely holds on to his bones.

"Wait, wait." Francis rushes to the kitchen to hastily fill a few cups with water, and another with yellow liquid from a separate pitcher. He returns with a tray. "Forgive me. I haven't seen another person in more years than you would believe."

"By choice," I say, perplexed by this legendary Dragun I've read, studied, so much about, for years.

"Still so green." He offers us the tray of drinks. I take the glass to be polite but run a finger along my jawline. Charlie and Yani catch it, lowering their cups. Never can be too careful.

"We're here about sun tracking," I say.

Francis's smile fades. "I thought Headquarters had questions about my work on the Sphere. My tracking days are done."

I try to not let my surprise show. Francis's reputation precedes him. I check my notes a third time. Son of a war vet. His family was very poor before the war, and worse after. Magic was his ticket to a new life. They immigrated to the States and rose swiftly in the ranks of Ambrose. He was recruited by the Dragunhead before he finished Third Rite. He discovered House of Duncan's illicit toushana practices and single-handedly brought the House down, exposing the truth: that Headmistress Duncan was trying to use toushana to mine gold. He is a legend. Sun tracking extraordinaire. There is no note about him ever working on the Sphere.

"What sort of work?"

"My great-great-papa and his men designed the Sphere's casing. Natural talent for certain types of magic tends to run in a bloodline. So the Dragunhead brought me in once or twice to locate it." He shakes his head. "Never again."

I slide to the end of my seat.

"The Sphere has grown dark, Francis."

Francis furrows his brow. "Dark how?"

"The matter inside is blackened and the casing has cracked."

He shoots up from his seat. "Impossible."

"You think we'd be here if we were lying?" Yani scoffs, rubbing the handle of her dagger. Charlie watches.

"Come back with us. You have to help save it."

"Save it? You don't want to be anywhere near that thing if it bleeds out." He straightens an urn on his mantel. "Papa and his whole team died to make that Sphere. Creating a casing to hold the magic of so many took a *precise* balance of hardness, density, and elasticity. The freshest minerals, the proper number and type of bones, barrels of blood stored at a precise temperature for a set number of days during a certain phase of the moon." His gaze darts between us, then away. "They had to use *strong* magic to break these ingredients down."

"They used toushana."

He nods.

Yani and Charlie share a glance.

I suspected that from the color the Sphere's taken. "But how?"

"They drew on the shadows, all at once, and shut their collective proper magic inside the Sphere. But toushana touched the ingredients, you see, infecting them. So dark magic ended up inside the Sphere, too. All is fine when the matter is clear. The proper magic is balanced."

"But that's all changed."

"Think about it. *All* that magic has been held inside the Sphere, churning, refining its concentrated power, for hundreds of years. It's blackened now. The toushana is winning. The Sphere *cannot* break. It will wreak havoc on not just the Headmistresses but the world as we know it." He grabs my wrist tightly. "Whatever you do, green boy, the matter inside the orb *must* be contained."

"Come with us. Let's track it down. The Dragunhead has plans to fortify it."

He gets up and paces. "That I can't do. I'm sorry."

"I don't understand," I say roughly. "The situation is dire and you know how to help, but you're going to turn your back? What would your papa think of you?"

"If his affections were that fickle, I'm not sure I would care what he said." Francis sighs. "Your passion *is* inspiring. The Order leadership hasn't had that fire in some time." He stops walking and looks around the room, patting his pockets. "If you'll excuse me just a minute." He exits through the wall.

After all the years he's given to the Order, the years his parents and theirs gave to magic, he would dishonor all of it with a single decision. Someone with his expertise would shirk the blatant call to duty. If I have any say, he is going to help. Magic is on the line.

"I don't like this," Charlie says.

Yani doesn't say anything, looking at me with unease.

We wait for some time, but Francis still doesn't return.

"Grab some of that stuff he's drinking. I want to test it and some of these crushed plants around his bed. Both of you, wait here." I approach the wall, and it shimmers translucent, when Yani grabs my wrist. Then she eyes her hold on me before snatching it away. "Sorry."

"Stay here." I step through the wall, round the house, and find Francis's body face down in the dirt, bleeding from a singed gash in his back. And ice cold.

TWELVE

Quell

Adola is silent as she escorts me from Beaulah's private quarters. We pass a series of paintings, a few with an artistic take on a starry night sky over a sandy beach. The nights when my mom and I were in bed at the same time, we'd whisper about living close enough to the ocean to hear it and feel its salty, cool air on our skin. Did she remember that, too, when she walked this hall? The familiar ache pulses with an acute new pain. It's one thing to imagine where she was. It's another to walk the places she did, see what she saw, breathe the air she did, and know that she stood here and thought of me, too. I speed up to keep with Adola. We stop at a bedroom inside the main house.

"I want to stay in the guesthouse your aunt mentioned." *Where my mom stayed. That's the first place I want to look around.*

"Mother said to find an available room in the family's private wing." She dangles a brass key. Beaulah wants to keep me close. I swallow.

"Well, tomorrow I need you to show me where the guesthouse is."

"Whatever you're up to, keep me out of it." She shoves the key in the door.

I'd hoped to be done twisting her arm.

"I wasn't asking." Part of me crumbles at the way her nostrils flare. She doesn't want to get in trouble; I remember feeling like that. Wanting to please my Headmistress. But I saw the fear of death in her eyes when we crashed Beaulah's party.

"Whatever your real reasons are for being here," she says, "Mother is very perceptive. You won't fool her for long. And I can't afford to be caught up in any schemes."

I feel sorry for Adola, but if she won't cooperate, I'll bury the knife deeper. "I saw how nervous you were when your aunt told you to perform in front of everyone."

She hesitates.

I knew it. Either she can't do dark magic or she can't do it well. And her aunt has no idea. I turn to walk back toward the party.

"Wait! Quell, *please*. Where are you going?"

"I thought I'd tell Beaulah how we met tonight. And maybe mention that you might not be the heir she thinks you are." It says a lot that Beaulah hasn't already figured it out. Adola's skilled at wearing masks. So was I, at Chateau Soleil. It's exhausting to constantly look over your shoulder. Guilt cinches my stomach. Adola could probably use a friend who knows what that pressure feels like. But I bury the feeling with thoughts of my mother.

She balls her fists. "Please just come inside the room. I'll get you a map of the grounds and show you to the guesthouse tomorrow."

Adola's very helpful under duress. But as I follow her back to my room, her sullenness bites at me. She closes us inside.

"Mother will probably send you attendants in the morning." She won't meet my eyes, and I'm reminded of a girl desperate to hide a black diadem. Returning guilt nicks me in the ribs. And this time I can't ignore it. I sigh.

"Adola, I don't have to be your enemy. Is it that you don't know how to draw toushana to yourself or that you aren't good at it? Whatever it is, I can probably help you."

"No." She puts more distance between us, but I can see her hands start to shake.

I whisper, "How bad is it? Do you not have magic at all?"

"*Of course* I have proper magic," she spits. She raises her chin, her diadem gleaming.

"But you're not good at drawing the dark kind?"

She huffs.

"Let me help you." I cross my arms, waiting for her to fold.

"I would *never* accept help from someone like you." She tosses the room key at me. I've never seen someone look at me with such disgust. "I'll meet you here after breakfast to go to the guesthouse."

She rushes out.

Abby was so nice to me when we met. I lied to her, kept secrets from her. *And I still do.* My only friend who hasn't betrayed me. And now I'm blackmailing Adola. *Ugh.* Maybe I am a terrible person. My toushana rolls around in my chest. I flip a switch, and sconces flicker to life alongside a fire that is already burning. The room is huge, trimmed in dark colors with red and black accents. An oversized four-poster bed is painted with faux cracks. There is a sitting area, a vanity, and several wardrobes. Moonlight streams through wide windows over an antique tub in a connecting bathroom.

Cologne sits beside the sink. It smells of sandalwood and vanilla, and the hair on my skin rises. Thoughts of Jordan come to me in a rush and I drop the bottle. It shatters on the floor, filling the whole room with the scent of *him*. Without my thinking of it, toushana pours out of me, and I smooth shadows across the glossed floor until the mess is gone and all that's left are a few scorch marks on the marble. *No, there's no way.* I back out of there and close the bathroom doors, searching the rest of the room for proof that I'm wrong.

But a photograph in a tiny frame on the fireplace mantel crushes my hopes. It's Jordan, riband slung across his chest, arms roped around others beside him. This *is* his room. Adola did this on purpose. There is no way I'm sleeping in that bed, even if Jordan hasn't slept in it for years. It's the principle of the matter. I consider sleeping in the armchair beside the roaring fire; my limbs yearn for a night of proper rest. *Too cramped.*

So I peel back the covers begrudgingly. His sheets are the softest silk linen. And the bed makes me think of him in ways I wished it didn't. I climb inside, unable to resist. Nothing about this place or the people here is completely as it seems. I need to remember that with Beaulah. And Adola, too. I should have learned that lesson with Jordan already.

I toss and turn, but despite my exhaustion, sleep doesn't come. Every square inch of this room is like staring into a nightmare. I close my eyes but see him, so I keep them open until my eyelids become heavy. By the middle of the night, I can't stand it and I get up. Somehow the scrap of *Debs Daily* announcing Jordan's promotion finds its way into my hands. I hold it up to the framed portrait on the mantel. A younger, smiling Jordan poses in front of an old historic building. Deep creases hug his bright green eyes and a smile. Joy, frozen in time.

Something fractures inside me, and it feels like there's a gaping hole in my chest. A hole I'd thought my toushana had filled.

That *Jordan . . . I miss him.*

The framed picture is a sharp contrast to the one of Jordan in the newspaper where, even in black and white, shadows wrap around his eyes. There is no happiness in his expression, only anger. Which, because I know him, is caused by pain. *How did we end up here?* I never let myself cry over him after everything went down. Yagrin and I left right away. Then there was the safe house, a million things to busy my mind. But here . . . his scent is still faintly here. It breaks me.

It was never supposed to be this way.

I can hardly breathe between sobs. I blink quickly, hoping to push the tears away, but it doesn't help. I miss the boy I glimpsed behind the mask. When we snuck through the kitchens and stole cake. The care he took when he transfigured an entire beach just so I could study. When he looked at me and saw something that only my mom ever has: worthiness. *It felt so real.* He felt so real. So safe.

I sit and let the wall hold me up, hugging my knees until my chest aches. Then I curl up right there on the floor and cry until my eyes are dry and sleep finally takes me.

I'M DISTURBED BY rapid knocking at my door. I unfurl myself from my covers on the floor. Morning sun shines through the windows. I smooth my puffy, swollen eyes in a mirror before unlatching the door. Adola hurries inside wearing a dark, breathy frock, diadem shining as if it's been freshly polished.

"Are you ready?"

"This is your idea of a joke, putting me in Jordan's bedroom?" I manage, voice heavy from the night before and such little sleep.

Adola flashes a surly grin.

"If you want to keep me on your good side, you won't mention him. Ever." I throw the key at her. "And get me a different room." I retreat to the bathroom to scrub the pain of Jordan Wexton and me off my face for good.

THE GROUNDS OF Hartsboro are alive. Off Season for the Order runs from fall through late spring, when everyone is usually back at home, attending regular school. But the halls of House of Perl are full of débutants and maezres hurrying in every direction, dressed for lessons in simple black dresses or pants, robust diadems arced over their heads and masks sloped across the top halves of their faces. I even spot a few Electus who haven't emerged.

"The off Season is busy at Hartsboro," I say to Adola. I hadn't imagined so many eyes around. That will make sneaking to the guesthouse trickier than I expected.

"It's Trials week. And we're a close-knit House."

"Are there classes in session?"

"Trials are at night. So maezres offer a few enrichment sessions to busy guests during daylight hours."

"I'll get a copy of the schedule from Beaulah." And assuage any concerns she might have about my being here and give myself an idea of when the halls will be empty. House of Perl has its fidelity on display, with more tapestries, House crests, Latin inscriptions, and plaques filled with original writings from people whose names I don't recognize. Somewhere I hear a chorus of recitations of House history.

"We'll cut through the Instruction Wing," she says, taking a sharp right at the hall ahead. We pass beneath a banner boasting the House slogan: *Memento sumptus.* Remember the cost. "The guesthouse is behind the main house."

I stuff my hands in the pockets of my dress, remembering the gaping nothingness I saw in the wall of trees behind the estate last night. Adola leads me down a long corridor of classrooms; one has a heavily bolted door.

"The forge." She indicates the room at the end of the hall.

"A forge for?"

"Magical armor."

I shake my head. I've never heard of magical armor. But she doesn't offer more information. We walk the length of the estate, passing the study and common areas before finally slipping outside. A manicured lawn stretches out before us, ending abruptly at a line of trees. Workers are setting up a series of raised platforms. With them is a Dragun, checking his Order-issued phone.

"More festivities tonight?" I ask.

"Sure, you can call it that." Adola's arm moves across her body, and she grimaces as if she's sick to her stomach. Beyond the tree line are wooded acres so thick, it may as well be nighttime inside them. The Dragun breaks from the crowd and jogs with a slight limp toward us. I recognize him: Charles. Fatigue shades his heavy eyes, as if he didn't sleep a wink last night either. Adola greets him, but he watches me with curiosity.

"You're much feistier than I expected."

The Dragun coin at his throat taunts me. *Jordan.*

"Charlie, please let my aunt know that the platforms for Trials are the wrong size."

His expression softens when he looks at Adola, before his brows furrow. "She won't be happy about that."

"Tell her quickly, please."

His eyes find me again, lingering for a moment on my diadem, and he flashes a satisfied smirk before he hustles back toward the main house.

"That should buy us some time. I love Charlie like an uncle, but he is Mother's pet through and through. He can't get a whiff of what we're doing." Adola picks up the pace.

"What are these Trials I keep hearing about?"

"Would you walk faster? We've already been seen once." She hurries across the field before slipping beneath the wooded canopy. When I join her, the sun hides from us and the woods become a cone of silence. No hint of a guesthouse. We follow a well-worn path deeper into the forest.

"Trials are how we earn virtue pins," she finally says. "Accolades specific to our House. Perls are ambitious, if nothing else, and the easiest way to garner favor with my aunt is to have a decorated collar. A complete set is six, and earning all is very rare. My cousin—"

"I know."

She smirks.

"And the heir to House of Perl has how many?"

That wipes the smile off her face. I don't suppose Beaulah Perl is happy about that either.

"The guesthouse is just up ahead," she says.

The hidden abode is two stories, with a steeply pitched roof and the same number of small windows on each side. Its navy-blue painted siding would be hard to see in the shady forest if it weren't for the overgrown greenery clawing its way up. The wide porch creaks as I hurry up the steps, relieved to be closer to some answers. *My mother was just here.* The thought tightens a knot between my shoulders. I hold the door open but Adola's taken off, back toward the estate.

Inside is a cozy living room, and beyond it a kitchen and another sitting room.

"Hello?" I give the common areas a quick walk and listen for any hum of heartbeats, but the guesthouse is quiet. I hurry down the hall of bedrooms and check the first room, twisting its knob, but it doesn't give. Toushana seeps through my skin, disintegrating the door handle. Beaulah may know I did it, but if I find a clue to where Mom could have gone, I'll be out of here before Beaulah can question me. I give the door a firm push and it opens.

The room is filled with personal belongings. The bed is unmade and a pile of dirty clothes are on the floor. I close the door quickly and try the next room. And the next. Each locked room is filled with things and reasonably disheveled. None of the items belong to my mother, from what I can tell. Still, I carefully check every single room.

When I twist the knob on the last one, it opens easily. The room is bright and inviting, with a sprawling rug; a large, freshly made bed; and an empty closet. There is a layer of undisturbed dust on the dresser. My heart squeezes. *This could have been hers.*

I rummage through the dresser but the drawers are empty. *Where are you, Mom? Dead,* I can almost hear Yagrin saying, again, in my head. I slam the drawer shut. *My mother is a survivor!* I pull back the covers on the bed and feel beneath the mattresses. Nothing. I sift through linens in a trunk. Still nothing. I remove all the folded blankets, but the bottom of the trunk is empty. I'm tossing them back inside when a stack of crinkled papers tumble to the floor. Each item is a different color, and stained, with ripped edges. I faintly make out faded calligraphy and an envelope to match. *The Ditmore. The Caldwell. Harvest Fest.* Invitations to various balls. Addressed to various people whose names I don't know. These were collected. Probably stolen. But who—

The door bursts open, and I shove the stack of invites down the bust of my dress.

"Hello there again." Charlie smiles. Beside him is a portly fellow with flushed cheeks in a nice suit.

"You can't be in here, madam," he says. "All the guests are in sessions at the big house, so I stepped away. I'm sorry I missed you. I would have told you as much."

I press my palm against myself to hold the invites in place. "I'm just looking around."

"You're a special guest," Charlie says. "Mother wants you in the main house."

"I wasn't quite finished."

Charlie doesn't move. The suited man's gaze darts between us. I swallow the urge to protest and escalate this, risking giving up what I did find. But as I leave, I turn to the suited man and ask, "How long has the guesthouse been so full?"

"With the prep for Trials, I haven't had any open rooms for *weeks*." He stares, apparently bewildered by my inquisitiveness.

That was my mother's room. I follow Charlie out the door. I should've expected Beaulah would have eyes on me everywhere I go. She's cautious to a fault.

When we're outside, I stop Charlie, annoyed that my plans have been thwarted.

"You're in charge of security on the grounds?"

"Not exactly."

"Then who are you?"

"A trusted confidant."

"Do you live here?"

"I do, most of the time. In the north wing. And all this matters to you because . . . ?"

"Because I want to know who you are and why you have the authority to pull me away. Nothing I was doing concerned you. It was a vacant room."

"Mother's House. Mother's rules. And *your* mother, Rhea . . ."

Hearing her name knocks the wind out of me.

"She's no longer here. You could have just asked."

"Is it wrong to want to see where she stayed?"

"Not wrong." We start walking. "But it makes it look like you don't trust us."

"I don't trust anyone."

We walk in silence until we're out of the forest.

"I met your mom," he says. "She was real nice."

I press the invitations hidden against me, digging my nails into my skin.

"I was bummed I didn't get a chance to see her off. I was in bed sick as a dog, all day, the day she left. If there's anything else you want to know, just ask."

We don't talk the entire way back to my room, Adola's warning about Charlie fresh in my mind. I don't trust Charlie or Adola, but if I had to pick, I'd pick her. I understand the pressure on her shoulders. I don't know anything about this man or what drives him.

"Mother wants to see you at dinnertime in the cigar lounge," he says.

I agreed to be her science experiment, so I don't see a way around coming when she calls.

"If you want me to escort—"

"I can find it." I offer a tight smile before disappearing inside my room. *I didn't even get a chance to look in the closet, under the bed, or in the bathroom.* Who knows what I missed? I have to get back to that guesthouse when everyone, including Charlie, is distracted. I slip out of my shoes before pulling the invites out of my bust. Each is hard and well worn.

My mother never mentioned the balls she attended before she had me. She never talked much about life with Grandmom. But the one thing I do know is that my mom is careful: she only takes calculated risks. Collecting so many invitations from various people would not have been easy. Why would she do that? I flip through the invites again, looking for some kind of message or written note. But there's nothing. Just papers that have long been trash.

I sigh and shove them back under my mattress. Then I sit and wonder: *What are you up to, Mother? Where are you? What did you think of this strange place? Of Beaulah's secret circle? Her penchant for toushana?*

Did it scare her? What will she think of me?

The more I think of my mom, about the last few months, and the room I'm now forced to stay in, the heavier everything feels. I try to pic-ture her kind eyes and summon some memories of her voice. And in my mind I hear what she always used to say: *There's good in you, Quell. You're going to be okay.* I lie down and close my eyes, but the tenderness of those words is drowned out by the events of the evening.

At least for a few hours I won't have to feel anything.

THIRTEEN

Jordan

*D*inner still swims in my tummy. My father looms over me, his hand firmly on my shoulder, staring at the hunting grounds in front of us. My aunt signals to a small audience watching from the big house behind us. My brother stands in the window. When he sees me looking, he puts his palm on the glass.

"Over here, come along." She leads me to a wooden platform between two others, where boys much bigger than me are guzzling down water and taping their wrists and ribs. My father follows, but Headmistress Perl stops him with a hand.

"You'll make him nervous, Richard. Get back upstairs. It's going to be a long night."

My father's lips thin as he departs, but my breath doesn't come easier.

"Don't worry about him," my aunt says. "Just focus on the now." She gestures to the thicket of trees, their tops glowing in the moonlight. "Master your focus, nephew. It is a weapon."

"Yes, ma'am." My hands shake in my pockets. She reaches in and grabs them. She holds them, and I try hard to be still.

"Everything that happens in the forest tonight is just making you into the person you were destined to be. Like the heroes in the stories. You get to be a warrior. Would you like that?" She pats my hand.

I can't nod fast enough.

"This test is usually reserved for peers five or six grades above you. But you and Yagrin are in the family line: you should be able to handle it."

I watch the other boys for confidence in their posture, some assurance that whatever we're doing is going to be okay. But neither looks my way.

"Jordan, have you ever worked really hard to earn something but then lost it?" she goes on.

"Yes. A toy I'd earned from doing really well on my Latin lessons. But I haven't been able to find it in a long time. I think my brother stole it."

"And how does that make you feel?" she asks.

"Sad."

"You are a bit angry with your brother about it, aren't you?" She strokes my hair, and the gesture reminds me of my mother.

"I guess so."

"It's okay to be mad. Let yourself feel that. Use it to fuel your magic. That's how the Order feels about magic. We've worked very hard to shepherd magic through the years so that it wouldn't be lost. Our forefathers gave their lives to guard it. But there are people who would try to rob us of it or exploit it and control how we use it."

Her eyes burn like a firestorm and I straighten. This is serious.

"Today's test is like a game. A way to show us you can help protect what's ours. That's what your father does, what your grandpa did, what all Draguns do. Do you think you can do that?"

"I think so."

She pinches my cheek, and I kind of hate it. But, I kind of don't. "At the heart of the forest, near the old oak, you'll find a bunch of things. One is an old family relic. Bring it—and only it—to me in one piece. You may use any magic that occurs to you freely; no one will stop you. You have until sunrise."

A shiver finger-walks up my spine. That's a long time to be out here alone.

"And one last thing." The Headmistress checks her watch. "You will have to make choices along the way. But, Jordan, there are no perfect choices. Only ones that will help you retrieve the relic and those that will not. Choose properly."

A howl splits the night air. "What's out there?" I can't stop fidgeting.

"Wolves and other things," she says, her gentle hand on my back urging me forward. "But you have no reason to be scared."

She taps my chest.

"Because they fear the darkness. And we fear no one."

A horn blows, and she eases me off the platform. My feet thud on the ground and I feel the impact in my chest. The others sprint off, their legs twice as long as mine. I look back. Yagrin's still watching. As I walk, my heart ticks like a timed bomb. How will my brother know how to find the oak tomorrow, or how to defeat the terrors that wait for us in the forest, if I don't survive this first? I tighten my fists and close my eyes, imagining my face on the bodies of those glorious warriors in the stories I've read, with their fire broadswords and magical armor.

I open my eyes and dash into the forest at full speed. The old oak, I know: I can see it from my bedroom window. I head straight for it, at the heart of the forest. As I approach the clearing, something somewhere howls again.

I scan the woods but don't see anything. I run faster. I should've found the oak by now, but everything is beginning to look the same. I switch directions, scaling sprawling tree roots. A coppery smell burns my nose, but I run and run until my lungs ache. I stop for a breath.

And spot glowing eyes in the brush.

I BLINK AWAY the memory, and Headquarters bleeds to full color. I exhale and straighten in my chair. It's been two days since I turned in my brother, and I still haven't been able to sleep more than a few minutes at a time. Across the lobby, the Dragunhead's office door is ajar, and Maei is still not there. It's ridiculously early, but I had known the pile of reports on my desk would grow while I was away hunting answers about the Sphere. When I arrived this morning, on top was a note from the Dragunhead: *Officium est honor volentis.*

Duty is the honor of the willing. In other words, *hurry up.* The pressure to clear my workload before he arrives beats like a drum in my head.

I'm usually always ahead on things, and he doesn't need any reason to question the pendant that hangs from my neck. As swiftly as he gave it, he could rip it away.

Francis's file is missing several pages. The samples I brought in to be tested are nowhere to be found. So I escalated his death to murder, but the Dragunhead hasn't yet signed off on a formal investigation. I set the file aside, strumming my fingers across my desk, imagining I can hear the song they would play. But I pound an angry fist on my desk. With the Sphere's worsened condition, any defenses it has will be weakened. I have to find Quell or get to the Sphere before she does. Not in a month's time. Not in a week. *Today.*

But with no whispers of her anywhere, my only option—the second-best sun tracker in the brotherhood—is in a cell that I put him in.

I try to review a few raid reports, but a glimpse of the gold on my lapel drags my thoughts back to the night I earned my first virtue pin. We broke into the family Healer's stores and had Yagrin ingest some dark stone to make him vomit, so he appeared too sick to go first. I took his spot and earned my pin, the youngest in Perl history to do so, then briefed Yagrin on everything to ensure he could do the same. But he failed.

I can still feel the lashing Father gave me afterward, but what I remember most is the way he looked at me. Like I didn't deserve the duty pin on my chest. Like my very existence disgusted him because I couldn't do the task he assigned me: *ensure* his precious firstborn pass with flying colors.

I stand and pace as I try to read another report. But no manner of distraction can smother the burning in my belly as the past nags my conscience. When we had showed up at Hartsboro's doors with a tuxedoed Yagrin, he was ten, and I was eight. Though I've always been expected to behave as if I'm oldest. Expected to compensate for his childishness. That day he was supposed to be tested on what forms of magic he could show. But I knew he hadn't unearthed any. I had unearthed two. And then my aunt stumbled upon me doing magic and begged my father to leave me with her at Hartsboro.

My mother cried. My father fumed. He told my aunt how I was a troublemaker, always getting into things that didn't concern me. But she waved his warning away, and it was the first time I saw someone shut my father up. My aunt's insistence felt like a warm hug back then; I wanted nothing more than to leave my father's domineering shadow and become everything my aunt saw in me.

He agreed, only on the condition that I keep Yagrin on track: passing his Rites, earning his virtue pins, and securing the position of House of Perl Ward. But I quickly realized how impossible that was. Yagrin didn't have any interest in magic, or the Order, or any of it. I did all I could to help him study: preparing all his note cards, reciting with him, giving up my own liberty time to ensure he was ready for his tests. I read texts aloud to him because he refused to do it himself. Sometimes my own performance suffered, but it didn't matter to Father. Yagrin was the one who needed to succeed.

Perhaps I ruined him.

Memories of our childhood linger like a hungry ghost. I find myself at Maei's desk and pick up the sentencing roster. How much time, exactly, does Yagrin have left? I open the folder to a long list of names, and Yagrin's is somehow already close to the top. Ice skids down my spine. I flip the pages backward, trying to understand. These are endorsed executions, one after another.

The brotherhood took in more Draguns this past Season than it has in years. More Draguns means moving through the sentencing lists even *faster*. Over and over, I count how few names precede my brother's, but the number doesn't change. In the time I was gone to meet with Francis, there have been nine burnings. Sickness moves from my gut to my throat. Yagrin's life hangs in the balance. *Days* . . . if he's lucky. I close the papers on Maei's desk and stare across the lobby at the pile of work I need to get back to. My brother is a sorry excuse for a Dragun. This is his own fault.

But I can't move.

He never wanted this life. He did everything he could to avoid it.

"It is his duty!" I kick the nearby trash bin before raking a hand through my hair, grateful no one is in here to witness my petulance. I've done my duty. I've watched the light leave a person's eyes; I've racked up a handful of bodies in the last two months. And yet my heart thunders harder now than it ever has. I thought he'd have more time. To think. To change his mind and cooperate.

If I do nothing and abandon him to his consequences . . .

By week's end my brother will be a body on some other Dragun's list.

I storm past Maei's desk and slam the down button on the elevator. I can't help him if he refuses to be helped. But if I ruined my brother, perhaps saving him is worth one more shot.

THE UNDERGROUND FLOOR where captives are kept stirs when the elevator dings open. The basement floor of Headquarters is a sweltering tomb of stone, and within a few steps I'm already sweating. I slip out of my House coat, the room's elevated temperature burning my skin. I hate coming down here. Rows of cells run in either direction. Light from street-level windows slices through the darkness.

Each cell is closed by a veil of writhing shadows. Dark magic clings to a thin, translucent barrier made from some of the same material as the Sphere's casing, creating a door that is impassable. The Shadow Cells are probably the Order's most innovative and deadly use of toushana. I think of Francis's papa. *People probably died to make these, too . . .*

My skin is slick with sweat. The prison is kept abnormally warm to keep captives from easily using toushana. I arranged for my brother to be in a well-lit area—a small kindness I hope he recognizes. I find him crouched on the ground, drawing circles in the dirt floor. The same motion, stroke after stroke. The trail of dirt forms tiny piles, and suddenly I can feel it all over my skin. I fill my lungs with air and hold it, shoving off the panic. *I'm okay. I am not that boy anymore.* When my brother looks at me, it anchors me to the present. He slips into Octos's skin, the persona he used to trick Quell into trusting him.

"Yagrin."

He doesn't respond.

"I've come to talk to you."

He still doesn't move. Everything with him is a fight, I swear.

"Have it your way." I unsheathe the fire dagger from the pocket inside my jacket and slice the door down the middle. The flames on the blade rip through the dark mist, parting it like a curtain, and I step through. I pull my brother to his feet. Octos stands a whole head shorter than me in ratty clothes. He smooths his greasy hair behind him. *What did Quell see in him?* A kindred spirit?

Quell. Her stare was like a dagger to my soul. She made a mockery of me then by lying about everything. And she makes a mockery of me now by evading capture. The sooner she's gone, the better. The safer the Order will be.

"Your real face, Yagrin."

"You look terrible," he says. "Not sleeping again?"

"Enough of your games. I need you to show me how to track the Sphere."

"My answer hasn't changed," he says, rubbing the tattoo marks on Octos's skin.

"I'm trying to reason with you."

The blue in Octos's slanted eyes darkens to brown as a glimmer of Yagrin bleeds through.

"But it was you, dear brother, who brought me here."

"For your treason. I'm done covering for you."

"Then what would you call this request for help?"

"A chance for you to help *yourself* for once. Agree to help me track the Sphere so that I can—"

"Beg the Dragunhead for my life? I can practically hear him fawning over you now. Jordan, the best Dragun to ever live. *Jordan,* the epitome of honor. *Jordan. Jordan. Jordan!*"

"After everything I've done for you, that's what you think of me?"

"What are you after if not the Dragunhead's approval?"

I can't believe my ears. There was a time when my brother, even in his ambivalence, believed magic itself was deserving. That it was so special, and such a gift, that we should do all we could to ensure no innocent person had a reason to fear it. He'd still go through the motions when things got hard. But ever since they killed Red, he doesn't seem to care about anything anymore.

"Deep down, you know that the Order should matter. And people like—" I drop to a whisper. "Our aunt needs to be dealt with."

"The difference between us is you think it's still possible."

I shake him by the shoulders.

"You can't eat a plum once it's rotted from the inside." A cocked smile splits his lips. "Quell was tickled when I told her that. She asked how I knew what a rotted plum tasted like. She did that laugh—you know the one, where she barrels over and snorts."

I shove him.

"You feel braver in Octos's skin. Being yourself reminds you that you're still a scared little boy who never got Daddy's approval?"

He shoves me and my back hits the wall hard. "No, that's your job."

Anger rises in me, for the years of standing in for him without recognition, or even matched effort, doing everything to keep him from his own fate. But I loosen my fists.

"You're not going to destroy everything the Order built. I won't allow it. You're also not going to destroy yourself if I can help it."

"The irony." He sits on the hard floor, back against the wall. He traces the same marks from before into the dirt, and I dig a nail into my skin to pin me in the present. Closer now, I see it's a letter. *R.* I sit beside him and his body shifts; Octos's hunched shoulders narrow. My heart squeezes, hoping he's come to his senses, hoping he'll look me in the eye *as himself,* and gird up for what I'm asking him to do—*care* whether he lives.

But my brother's face and body only shift to another persona in his repertoire: Liam, a childhood friend Yags had before we lived at Hartsboro. The only other time I've seen Liam's persona was when our mother was ill and Healers were out of hope that she'd pull through. She did, but those were dreary days in the Wexton household. Even for my awful father.

Liam hooks his elbow up, dangling his arm and wiggling his fingers, pretending to play an air guitar. "I used to mess around on a real one of these with her." He smiles. "She liked them."

Red.

Quell.

It's not quite the same, but I understand the acute pain of losing some-one.

"I'm sorry. About Red." I don't know where the words come from, but I immediately want to shove them back down my throat. "Life has not been kind to you," I add for reasons I cannot comprehend. "I wasn't pleased to hear what they did." Her body was never found—not in one piece, that is. If it had been, there would have been a report. I looked. There wasn't one.

His smile is gone.

"I didn't come here to fight. I came here to talk," I continue.

He rests his head on the wall and hums some somber ballad. I don't know how to get through to him when he's this way, determined to avoid anything difficult. Then the song takes me, its melody familiar.

"I know this one." A tune our mother used to sing. Liam hums louder. I listen as he finishes the bridge, and it takes me to a simpler time when, no matter how vicious our fights were, he was still my brother. Now it feels like there's an entire world between us, a divide that cannot be closed. His choices brought him here, but I can practically see the blood on my hands. He's my brother. The same brother who pulled out my first wiggly tooth because I was too chicken to do it myself. The same brother who stood with me in front of our mother when my father's temper was bullish. The same brother who also survived our childhood.

"Yags. The Dragunhead will call you for sentencing any day now. It would be foolish to expect anything other than a death sentence. *Help me* sun track."

He squints Liam's small eyes. "You've aged a decade since the last time I saw you. Is it nightmares again? Have they changed since—"

"You're as stubborn as Father." I stare down at him and suddenly see little Yagrin, with his big eyes, the first time he saw Hartsboro and learned that *he* would be following in Father's footsteps. He had trembled. I'd stood beside him. Together we had walked into my aunt's house. If he could just follow me again now, maybe I could find a way through this mess.

"Maybe. But you're as lost as he is."

"Give me something I can use," I urge him. "Either help me with tracking or tell me something about your time with Quell so I can make a case to the Dragunhead that you're valuable alive."

His eyes suddenly light up, his mouth bowing in a sugary grin. "You remember that time we got lost in the bowels of Hartsboro? When that old batty butler almost peed his pants explaining to our aunt why he couldn't find us. Oh, Brisby." He looks right at me, and it hurts to think that hope is so painful that he must run from it this determinedly.

A voice cuts through the darkness. I didn't even hear the elevator open. The Dragunhead is outside the cell with a few others.

"Sir."

"Jordan? I assumed I'd find you at your desk. Your brother's sentencing meeting is this morning. Is that why you're down here?"

The world dents at its edges. *Today? I thought there would be more time . . .*

My brother, still wearing Liam's disguise, pales. He looks at me and we may as well be kids again.

"I need this prisoner's sentencing delayed. I require more time with him, sir."

Yagrin's heart rams in both our chests.

The Dragunhead's gaze widens in surprise.

"He is going to help me protect the Sphere with knowledge only he has," I add. "Which he's now willing to share." I hold still. "When I'm done with him, we can revisit the sentencing."

For several moments there is only silence. "If you're sure he is of critical use," the Dragunhead says.

"I am, sir. He is cooperating. Which makes him valuable right now."

"The Heart has spoken," the Dragunhead tells the others with him. "Yagrin lives. For now." He taps his watch before departing.

FOURTEEN

✳

Quell

I awake to darkness and panic. Night has fallen. *Beaulah!* I'm supposed to meet her. When I pull the door open, a petite woman is standing there; I can hardly see her face over the stack of dresses across her arms.

"I'm Della, your attendant while you're here. Pleased to meet you." She curtsies before coming inside. More attendants pile into the room, loaded down with jewelry boxes, shoes, bags, and garments.

"Uh, I'm perfectly capable of dressing myself, thanks." I reach for a dress, but Della doesn't let it go.

"Mother insists."

She's determined to watch me at every turn. I eye the spot where I shoved my invitations, and thankfully they're out of sight. I concede, and Della and the other attendants busy themselves all over my room. By the time I'm dressed, I've been scrubbed with lavender-infused water and waxed; my hair's been washed, styled, and coiffed; and a set of jewels heavier than any I've ever held lies across my neck. I'm breathless when Della and her crew leave, but I hurry to the mirror.

Every part of me sparkles with darkness. From the black sequin gown that hugs my waist, then flares; to the glamorous smoky eye makeup; to the obsidian earrings pulling at my lobes. I pull my belly button in toward my spine and feel the stirring of my magic deep inside. Cold rushes through my head, and black metal emerges from my sprayed hair until my full diadem arcs above my head. Its rose-colored stones shine. The girl in the mirror is a far cry from the one who hid from her grand-mother so many months ago. I hold my chin up, eyeing my diadem once again. I don't have to hide it here. For the first time in forever, I can be proud of who I am. *The time.* I should go. But I could stare at this girl in the mirror until the sun rises.

Two steps out my door, I think of Abby. I need to update her the first chance I get.

Using the map Adola left me, I hurry to the cigar lounge, late to meet Beaulah. When I arrive, a smoky sweetness reaches my nose. Adola is waiting outside the doors.

"Aren't you supposed to be getting me a new room?"

"It's Trials week. Guests are traveling in from all over. You're stuck with the room you have."

I glare at her. "I'm sure you tried your best."

The doors open and someone who I don't recall seeing at last night's party exits. He doesn't bat an eye in my direction. "Shouldn't you be at the platforms?" he asks Adola.

"I'm going at the end of the week." She glances at me.

"Fratis fortunam." He holds the door for us to enter.

"The heir has *days* until her own Trials," I say.

She cuts me an angry look.

"You could let me help you and all would be well."

"I'd rather fail."

"You don't mean that."

Beaulah waves me over as Adola pushes past me. I make my way around the lively audience; they shimmy to peppy music in fine tuxedos, sparkling dresses, and decadent furs, their necks and knuckles swallowed in jewels. Drinks or cigars are in every hand, and there's chumminess to everyone's demeanor. It's like walking into a room where everyone's in on the same joke. People compliment my dress as I pass. Several eye my diadem, and the attention covers my skin in prickles.

I keep to the perimeter of the room, and I smile politely at the next string of compliments. Beaulah is seated beside a wall of windows overlooking a balcony and the lawn below. I join her. The open field we crossed earlier is empty except for three raised platforms. Adola doesn't join us. Instead she gives plastic greetings to everyone and isolates in a corner. I swear, the girl is determined to hate me.

"I hope you weren't alarmed earlier at the guesthouse," Beaulah says. "When I couldn't find you, I was concerned, so I sent Charlie to look for you. You should stay out of the woods. As a precaution."

"I'm perfectly capable of protecting myself."

"No one doubts that." She squeezes my shoulder. "You're here just in time for the finish." Beaulah turns her attention to the grandiose view of the grounds below. The commotion in the room settles as more people gather around the window. A bottle of champagne is passed around and glasses fill. One is shoved into my hand as I notice a dark-robed person below, holding up five fingers.

"Five minutes," someone says.

Beaulah grabs a cigar from a tray. "Watch the tree line."

Another few minutes pass. The robed figure holds up two fingers.

"What's happening?" I ask, but Beaulah only leans forward in her seat.

"Gather around," she announces. "Any moment!"

The dancing music shifts to a soft melody as the crush of bodies bubbling with excitement tightens even more around us. I slide to the edge of my chair—watching for what, I'm not sure.

A horn blares. The robed figure holds his arms in an X overhead.

"*And . . .*" Beaulah mutters.

Three people emerge from the forest, each collapsing at the finish line. The room explodes in applause. However, Beaulah doesn't move.

"*Georgie?* Where is he, Headmistress?" The woman speaking holds her handkerchief tightly to her chest.

"He's a strong boy, May. He's got one more horn."

"He's down to *seconds.*"

A long wail from the horn blares right as someone dashes out of the forest. Barefoot, shirtless, and covered in filth. His long blond hair is wild and his expression feral. His skin is coated in red. I straighten, realizing that it is not paint. Beaulah and the boy's mother embrace in a tight hug. She catches me staring, and a thousand questions swirl in my head.

"I'm sorry," I say. "Congratulations to your son. I'm sure you must be very proud for the, um, pin he is earning."

Beaulah pulls off a shelf an ornate box like one I'd seen in Jordan's room at Chateau Soleil. The one he refused to let me touch. She passes it into the woman's hands. "This is Miss Marionne's first time visiting Hartsboro."

"Ah. The Trials are our favorite tradition. I didn't get to say hello last night." She says the last part under her breath. "I'm Maybel Kinsley, of the original Kinsleys. Nice to meet you in person, Miss Marionne."

"Pleased to meet you."

"And just in time," Beaulah says as the four candidates from the grounds below enter the room. Each is slick with sweat, their bloodied clothes hanging in shreds. Georgie is the worst off, with a puffed eye that's swelling shut. Raw slashes cut into his pale chest and he stares into space, hardly breathing. The room greets them with raucous applause, chanting, "*Memento sumptus.*" The revelry finishes with a collective growl and a firm fist to the chest. The four candidates are bleary-eyed and jumpy as they watch the crowd close around them. Champagne sloshes in glasses, and the music picks up. The room pops with celebratory giggles.

"Let's get them pinned," Beaulah shouts, with four boxes in her hand.

Mrs. Kinsley appears beside me with Georgie roped onto her arm. I try to meet his gaze, but it's vacant, as he stares at nothing. His fingers are badly bruised and remind me of my own hands. *What on earth happened in that forest?*

"Mom—they put us"—his voice cracks—"in holes. And—" His hand trembles on his mother's arm.

"Listen to you. You sound delirious. You're okay."

He sways.

"*A chair.* Can someone get him a chair?" I take him by the arm and sit him down.

"What's happened to you?" I ask, but Beaulah steps between us as a fine tailored coat with red stitching and gold buttons is slung over Georgie's shoulders, uncaring of the blood beneath. A garment I know well. The buzz of idle chatter and clinking glasses quiets as an audience of bright eyes and wide smiles swells around Georgie. She helps him stand and the beautiful jacket hides his battered body.

She opens the box and a gold pin gleams inside.

"George Kinsley, Marked son of House of Perl, you've earned this distinct honor for valor. Pin number one hundred sixty-three. You join the ranks of one hundred sixty-two others in our great House who've been bestowed such an honor. If you receive this honor, say *I accept*."

His mother elbows him.

"I accept," he whispers.

Beaulah presses the valor pin to his coat. The longer he stands there, the more lucid he becomes. His mother dabs her face, teary-eyed, as Beaulah moves on to the next candidate across the room.

"Thank you." He perks up. "My magic was faster this time, Mom," he says. "The details are fuzzy, but I just know my magic was way faster. *That*, I remember."

"You're sure you're alright?" I ask.

"I've never been better." He flexes his bruised fingers, which don't appear to be hurting him anymore. "Tore right through the earth when they buried me."

I titter but realize no one else is laughing. "You don't mean *literally* . . ." Guests swirl around us, dancing. Georgie smooshes his brows and turns his wrist, examining a deep gash in his flesh. *He absolutely does mean* literally.

I swallow a dry breath.

And blink.

Then blink again.

"*Valor*, Miss Marionne, is difficult to breed," Beaulah says. "I have my methods."

The air crackles with laughter. Glasses clink, and cheering shouts blare in my ears as the world spins. I tighten my grip on my chair but it doesn't help. Georgie pulled himself from a *grave*. How?

But the answer hits me. Not everyone in Perl knows Beaulah's dark secret.

"You used toushana," I whisper. His eyes widen. I touch my diadem. "You can tell me."

He nods. "She told me I could if it answered to me."

My skin turns to gooseflesh. He *fought* his way out of pounds of dirt piled on top of his body before it suffocated him. With only his will and toushana at his fingertips. The cold in my bones unfurls, screaming, begging to get out of here.

"You learned this in your sessions?"

He glances over his shoulder, then leans in. "She picks some of us for special classes." *The children of those in her inner circle.*

"Is everything okay here?" Mrs. Kinsley barges in.

"Everything's fine, Mom. I was speaking with Miss Marionne about how good my Trials went. Actually"—he shifts—"my bones are still hurting."

"Give it a few hours, dear. It'll all be a lot better in the morning, from what I recall. You'll hardly remember your time in that forest. What you'll remember most is"—she pokes the valor pin on his chest—"*this.*" She kisses him despite his best effort to dodge it.

They depart and I stand, unable to stomach the nausea.

"I'm going to bed," I tell Beaulah. Her fingers lasso my wrist.

"I'm sending along some light reading to prepare you for our time together tomorrow."

"Right." *Experiments.* I rush out of there, and once the lounge is completely out of earshot, I take off to a run. Burying people alive? As a test! Bile climbs up and out of my mouth before I can stop it, and I hurl on her polished floors, Georgie's deranged expression burned into my mind.

I have to get what I need from this place and get out of here.

FIFTEEN

⸺✳⸺

Nore

Nore stared up at the gargoyles perched along the roof of Dlaminaugh Estate and shivered. Their elongated bodies sloped down the sides of the building and their claws dug into the stone. As a girl, Nore had pictured them as an army keeping watch while she slept, like soldiers on the battlements of a fancy castle. Now they seemed to be glaring at her audacity to return. But she had to find that Scroll, which meant figuring out how to get into her family's vault.

The gates parted up ahead and the estate came into full view, drowned in a blanket of snow. Dlaminaugh was built to inspire envy, much like the students who studied within its walls. It boasted broader buttresses and hundreds more windows than even Yaäuper Rea. Stuck to a steep mountainside, it was a masterpiece of multiple buildings constructed in Gothic stonework but modernized with tall peaks, sharp angles, concrete, and long stretches of glass walls. Its pitched roof touched the clouds, pushing the bounds of architecture beyond its natural limits.

When she crossed the gate's threshold, the dead waited for her.

She avoided their sunken, shadowed eyes. As she passed through the courtyard, she kept her gaze on the grand glass doors ahead. Flat headstones paved the cobbled entryway, each with the surname *Ambrose*. She hated the way it felt when she walked across someone's grave, like she was stirring up buried secrets. The ancestors pressed in closer: they didn't seem to like it much either. Nore strode faster, keeping her chin tucked tight into the hood of her sapphire House robe. But no matter how fast she moved, her heart rammed faster. She gulped a big breath of icy air as the Dragun on guard approached.

"Miss Ambrose?" His wide eyes were outdone only by the grin on his face. "How was your sabbatical? It's so nice to see you out and about." *Finally*, he didn't have to say.

Her hands trembled. She shoved them into the pockets of her dress. He bowed, keeping his eyes to the ground. A silly but effective rule Mother had made. If they didn't look at her too long, or too hard, they wouldn't notice the way her diadem was in a slightly different place each day.

"Good morning." She walked right past.

"Should I call Headmistress?"

"You will do nothing. That is all."

He nodded. She nodded back and her diadem slipped. Her heart leapt. He wasn't looking, so she pushed it back in place. Nore hurried, skirting the main doors and darting around the estate's exterior, past the Mortuarri Observatory, beneath the Hall of Discovery bridge (which linked two of its buildings), and around the Electus and Primus quads. She used to roam the grounds dreaming of stowing her stuff in her Electus bunk, exploring the mysterious family vault, and studying until the wee hours of morning in the Caelum, the library in the clouds—*with millions of books*. She used to lie awake for hours imagining what her diadem would look like, who her roommate would be, and what a Cultivator ring's magic would feel like. But none of that ever happened. She had no magic. Her eyes stung, and she told herself it was the cold.

When her boots hit grass, she picked up to a run and left the ancestors behind. They stayed outside and didn't wander too far from the courtyard, usually roaming one of their many graveyards.

The gravel path that snaked to the farthest corner of the property dead-ended at her private cottage. Her fingers and toes were numb by the time she climbed the steps of her rickety porch. The rustic residence was an

anomaly on the sterile grounds. Like she was. But when her mother had
the cottage built, Nore had insisted on one thing: that it felt like *hers*. Her
hanging and potted plants were watered and the windows were shuttered,
but the light inside was on. The welcome mat had been dusted clean.
Her mother probably had that done regularly to suggest that she could
be there.

Nore grabbed the doorknob and her heart seized. She was twelve when
she moved into the cottage for private lessons. Or that was the cover
story Isla Ambrose told everyone. By that point, Nore already knew to
not let anyone ever know that the heir to House of Ambrose had shown
absolutely zero propensity for magic. Nore had once asked what would
happen if others found out; all Isla said was *I don't want to give you nightmares.* She made Nore get ready in locked rooms without windows. She
didn't let her socialize with anyone on the grounds unless she, Nore's
brother, or her private maezre were present.

Mother's reasoning sounded like fluff. Her mother was embarrassed
that she had birthed an Unmarked heir. Nore would make a habit of exas-
perating her mother, playfully threatening to announce it over the House
intercoms. Her mother was already so severe, getting under her skin was
irresistible and easy. Until one day, when she was eleven, Nore overheard
a Dragun say, *An Unmarked cannot look upon magic and live.* She never
played games with her secret again.

For two years in that cottage, her mother left her alone, and it was
glorious.

She rode Daring every day, exploring all parts of the Pacific Northwest,
where Dlaminaugh was tucked away. She leaned into her love of working
with her hands: sculpting, painting, sketching—you name it, she tried it.
Ellery even taught her how to fish, hunt, and make a fire with nothing
but wood. He was gifted magically, but he indulged all her Unmarked
curiosities.

Until one dark evening when her mother told Nore she was prepared
to try again and dragged her to the basement of the estate. Night after

night, Isla Ambrose tried every method she could think of to cultivate magic in Nore. The experimentation was mild at first: using rings to try to stir something. But that's when Isla's tactics changed: elixirs that burned Nore's skin raw, a facial shift that left her unable to see for a week. The last time her mother tried something, Nore bled a whiff of dark, cold magic from her fingers. She had gathered her things, run to Ellery, and insisted they leave that night. That was the last time she saw this place.

The cottage was Nore's safe place, but holding the knob felt different now. She'd made a home somewhere else. *With* someone else. And now both were gone. Nore backed away from the cottage door. Then she paced the length of the porch before forcing down the lump in her throat and pushing her way inside.

Her quaint abode was a collage of memories. Her home was very minimalist, its walls the color of stone. There were only a few modest pieces of furniture. A book she loved to read lay open on the chair. Her favorite heather-gray blanket was in a pile on the floor next to her metal-framed bed with its paper-thin mattress. Nothing inside had been disturbed, which in and of itself was a bit unsettling. Her mother tried to control everything. But Nore was the one thing she would no longer control. Perhaps she'd realized that and left Nore's stuff alone.

She couldn't cook, so she stored her favorite books in her stove. She padded over and checked. They were still in there. Her skin prickled as if she'd stepped back in time. She pulled out baskets of thick, colorful yarn from beneath her study desk. She'd tried knitting, since studying magic went nowhere. She'd managed to make a few small things, which she strung up on the walls for color. She sifted through the threads and her hand hit something hard: an old film camera.

Yagrin. She felt sorrow well in her again. She'd always told him she was going to teach him to take really cool photographs. The old kind with grainy texture. Nore hugged around herself, remembering the way she showed him how to shuck corn and pluck a chicken. He was so tickled that he'd chased her once, dancing like a bird, begging her to pluck him. There was no House, no toushana, and no mother who loathed her. When they'd lie together under the stars, the only sound was the slow thud of his heart, and it lulled her into an illusion of a world that was her own.

They'd stay for hours. He would twist his fingers in her hair, and sometimes he ran his touch along the slope of her nose. She'd almost come clean with him once about who she really was. But he stared at her as if she was a daydream. She couldn't take that away from him. Her life was the lie they both needed.

Nore let out a heavy breath and felt her pockets. The only thing she'd kept from the farm was a pair of earrings he'd gifted her. It was Yagrin's idea to get her ears pierced in the first place. He made an entire ordeal of it, taking her to celebrate afterward at some fancy nightclub in a city with way too many lights. That night they didn't sleep until the sun rose. She pulled the earrings out and hooked them into her ears. Her stomach knotted. She'd never worn something so frivolous in her own skin, as Nore. But she loved the way having them on made her feel.

Oh, Yagrin. She ached with longing and wondered if he felt the same. She grabbed a pillow and squeezed it. He would think she was a horrible person for pretending to be someone she wasn't. Someone she *can't* be. Nore shoved the pillow away as the weight in her chest grew. She had enough things to deal with. Sadness wasn't going to be one of them.

She pulled out a journal to jot down her thoughts. Where would her mother keep something as important as the family vault key? The only thing she knew about that vault was that on Nore's coronation day, her mother would hand over access to her. She tapped her lip. *Sometimes the most astute solution was the simplest one.* Would she keep it in her office? Her bedroom? Those were too expected. Nore paced and thought. She thought and paced. But no matter how much she tried to focus on her plan, her cottage was too quiet and too empty.

She rummaged through cabinets for a canvas but only found paint. So she grabbed a brush, sloshed it in a dollop of red paint, and streaked a bright red stroke across the wall. She bit her lip and looked over her shoulder—for what, she wasn't sure. Then she arced another red stroke across the drab gray. She drew another, and another, until she could see the red barn of her farm, its slanted roof, the glowing wheat fields surrounding it, and the winding dirt path leading to it. When she finished, the mural on her wall was a masterpiece only she could appreciate. She stepped back and savored the bubbly way looking at art made her feel. Her fingers were covered in paint, her gray dress, too. Mother would be livid. She giggled and touched up the portrait before realizing her brother was leaning in the doorway, his smile tugged sideways. He had an armful of her moss roses, which apparently didn't make it.

"Ellery!" She clutched her chest. "You can wipe that smile off your face. I'm here for one reason and one reason only."

"It will be different this time, you'll see." He joined her inside, dumping the remains of her plants. "You have a future here, Nore."

"A past and a present. That is all."

He shakes his head. "Have you seen Mother?"

"No."

"And how long do you think that'll last?"

"I wish it could last as long as possible." Her mother was going to be shocked she was back.

He laughed. Heat rushed to her cheeks. She couldn't tell him why she really wanted to get inside the vault. He would never go along with her plan and she couldn't risk this failing. She wanted out of the Order. And her deal with Darragh Marionne was her only hope.

"Don't mention anything about me being back to Mother yet."

"She's going to know, Nore."

"I know. But I want her to think you're on my side." She grinned, and despite how hard he tried to hide it, Ellery grinned, too.

"Oh and I brought you this, too." He pulled a book from his bag and handed it to her. "I was, uh, going to try to resuscitate this one for you. But it didn't go so well."

She took the book and thumbed through it. "Oh my goodness, Ell, that's it!" Ambrosers were bookish to a fault. She knew where to look for the key to the vault. The only place Ambrose revered was a room full of books. It was so special that their priests were buried there, in the walls and floors, right among the shelves. Even Headmistresses were buried outside, but the intercessors for the Wielder, the Sovereign, and the Sage were held above the rest.

As if he could read Nore's mind, Ellery asked, "How can I help?"

"The priests' bodies are still buried in the Caelum?"

"You're suddenly sentimental about House piety?"

She unstuck her tongue from the roof of her mouth, wondering how much she could say. "I just want to see them."

His eyes narrowed in mirth. "I'm watching you, Emilie."

She elbowed him for calling her by her middle name. She wanted to pull back the veil on her plan, but it was a risk. "There is one other thing you can help me with."

"Yes?"

"Could you steal me some of those orange chocolate bars Crafter Kendor makes?"

THE CAELUM DOORS were locked. A sign that hung from the door read CLOSED FOR RENOVATIONS. PRIEST OFFICES TEMPORARILY RELOCATED TO THE TEMPLE GARDEN. Nore peered through the glass at an endless sea of books and jerked the handle again. But it didn't budge.

Ellery tapped on the glass, two books to return in hand. Her brother shrugged.

She grumbled. "Oh, come on. Don't you need to swap out your books?"

"Just doing a bit of research. It's fine." He nudged her with his shoulder. "I'm just *really* glad you're home."

"Don't get used to it." Nore peered through the glass again. "There has to be a way to get in there without breaking in or alarming security. Isn't there some kind of magic you can use?"

"I'm an Anatomer, Nore, and a fair Shifter on a good day. Not a genie."

She moved him out of her way and inspected the doorframes. If there was a way in, she was going to find it. But the more she thought about it, the more the Caelum didn't make sense. Would her mother keep a key she may want to use frequently in a busy workplace? Winkel, priest to the Sage, spent half the moon's cycle in prayers with students in and out of his office all day. Nore sighed.

"Even the furthest ends of possibility have their limits. Some things are finite."

Yes, but library access wasn't one of them. "That's what the Order believes about toushana. But I'm going to get rid of it."

"Only further proving that you belong in this House."

"Does she?" Her mother's voice panged through her.

When she turned, the air in Nore's lungs froze. Isla Ambrose stood about her height, with dark gray hair pulled straight back in a tight pony-tail that stopped just past her shoulders. Nore tugged at her own hair, making sure it covered her earrings. Her mother wore a Cultivator's ring, and a thin silver diadem hovered above her head. She wore a plain gray wool dress, a simple but regal gown that had been drained of life and color, like an overcast sky that had never seen sunshine.

"What are you doing here, Nore?"

She watched for some hint of relief in her mother's surprise, but she was a blank slate.

"In less than five years, on my twenty-second birthday, I'm your re-placement, the House laws say. Where else should I be?"

"I've given up on you. I know you certainly have given up on yourself."

Engaging her mother was like lying down to sleep in anticipation of a recurring nightmare. Nore stiffened but mustered the best inflection she could and said, "Well, you're wrong. I haven't. I've decided to come home and make those twenty years of trying to produce an heir worth it."

"Twenty-*six*," her brother corrected. "She had me after twenty. A son. A grave disappointment."

She wasn't sure what to make of the droll undertone to her brother's words, but she liked that he seemed to have her back in front of their mother, at least.

Her mother stared with the knowing of a dead Ambrose. "You've always been a bad liar, Nore." Her expression was unreadable. Nore had never seen the woman smile, let alone been hugged by her. "Do not embarrass the family or I will donate your body to the ancestors."

"Mother." The sharpness in her brother's tone arched their mother's brow.

"Only a joke. Calm down, Ellery." Her steel-gray stare slid to Nore. "You will continue your studies with your tutor at dawn. Remain as unseen as possible on the grounds until—"

"Until *you* get this poison out of me."

Isla snatched the embroidered blue House fabric from Nore's shoulders. She worked her hands together, the Cultivator ring on her finger glowing, until the robe shifted into a heap of threads that fell to the floor.

Her mother turned to her brother. "Ellery, we're finally getting that case of Sun Dust from the Dragunhead that you've been working on. Be there to receive it at seven, bring it to the Hall of Discovery, and send for me immediately." She reached up to his broad shoulders and a crack broke her thin mouth. "And Elena Hargrove is in the receiving room for tea. Exciting."

Her mother stepped over the mound of threads on the ground. "Welcome home, Nore," she said, then strode away. It shouldn't matter to Nore at all. She didn't even want to wear the heir robe. But if there was a little girl dying an excruciating death inside her, her mother just ripped apart whatever piece of her there was left.

SIXTEEN

―――*―――

Quell

A stack of books waits for me at the foot of Jordan's bed. I grab one and cold writhes in my bones.

Darkbearers—A Misunderstood History

Darkbearers. Toushana-bound magic users known for pillaging, stealing, and killing. I've never called on my magic to purposely hurt anyone. *Yagrin.* A lump rises in my throat and panic flares in my chest. I shove the book away, scooting back in my bed. But black seeps from my fingers, connecting with the leather cover. The book crumbles into a bed of ash. I slow my breath and hook my shaky hands together until they are warm. Beaulah has me all wrong. They all have me wrong if that's what they see in me.

When my heart slows, I peel myself out of the covers. I could hardly sleep, haunted by the way Georgie and the others had looked coming out of that forest. Maybe the reason Adola has been so on edge is because her own Trials are this week. There's no way she's prepared. I can help her draw on toushana. And she can cover for me to get back to that guesthouse. There's no reason we should be at odds. I need to talk to her.

When light breaks, I throw on clothes and skirt past Della, who's waiting outside my door with an armful of fresh linens.

"Didn't want to wake you." She tugs at my arm, trying to lead me back inside. "Can I run a bath?"

"I'm on my way out." I pull away.

"To?"

Beaulah intends to have me watched every second of every day. "*To* take a stroll around the water gardens."

"Please take a few attendants with you! In case—"

But I dash off before Della can finish. I stop by the House manager's office with a letter for Abby tight in my fist, discreetly letting her know that I'm no longer at the safe house and we can't meet up until I find a new spot. But in the meantime, she should send me anything and everything she's heard about my mom. No matter how seemingly small. The outbox is on a desk filled with papers and packages; I drop in the note with Abby's full name on the front. It vanishes.

The halls of Hartsboro are crowded. I skip over to the Instruction Wing and casually stroll past a series of open doors, where lessons are in progress. But there's no sign of Adola. The dining atrium is filled with people eating. Charlie is there, talking with his hands in a passionate debate with Mrs. Kinsley over something. I hurry along, about to detour to Adola's room and wait there, when I spot a gleaming red diadem and long jet-black hair.

"Adola!"

She walks faster before cutting a sharp left back toward the Instruction Wing and disappearing into one of the classrooms. *How* is she going to survive being buried alive if she doesn't let me help her? I have to make her understand; I know what it's like to be in a place like this, hiding what you really feel and think.

I smooth my clothes and grab the knob. Scorch marks mar the stone walls. A stale odor hangs in the air. Débutants in dark robes work by candlelight in various groups around the room, so focused that not a single head turns my way. Adola maneuvers around a maezre with a giant green-stoned ring on her knuckle, and I follow her.

"Can't you take a hint?" she snaps at me.

"I can help you." I pull up a chair and sit.

"I don't care." She retreats to the cabinetry at the back of the room, where she finds a wooden box. A set of thick rings with various colored gems are inside, and I recognize them immediately: Cultivator rings. Dexler taught me how each holds a type of magic. Green for Audior magic, purple for Shifting, and so on, enabling the Cultivator to channel each type of proper magic. But Adola doesn't seem to realize I can help her in ways these rings can't.

"Can we talk?"

The metal ring Adola slides on is dull, well used. Another in the box has the stone missing completely. She studies its empty gold prongs, which fold over each other like a bird's nest, and I wonder how long she's been going at this, trying and failing to get her magic to work the way she wants it to. I could hardly do it for the time I was at my grandmother's. But everything about Adola's desperate ambition suggests she *wants* to be here. For a time I fought to be in a prison, too.

Her nostrils flare. "No."

"*Now,* Majorie!" the maezre shouts at a girl behind us, and the whole room tightens around them.

I move my seat beside Adola to whisper, "I need to get back to the guesthouse."

She's about to respond when the maezre shouts, "*Transform* it!" The room fills with hamster squeaks that rip into throaty screams, followed by a loud bang. "Off we go, straight to the Healer. Everybody out."

Adola snatches off her ring and repacks her bag.

"I'm trying to help you!"

"You're not helping. You're interrupting." She tosses her remaining things in her bag and returns the ring to its box before hurrying to the door. I stand in the way.

"Miss Marionne?" It's Beaulah, standing in the hall just outside the doorway. Adola curtsies, and we all step into the hall. "Shouldn't you be in the etiquette refreshers this morning?" Beaulah eyes the bag Adola is dangling behind her legs, and I can feel Adola clam up beside me.

"She was showing me some of the morning's sessions."

Beaulah's whole expression brightens. "I won't keep you two, then. Quell, I'll see you shortly."

My heart hammers, but I smile.

When she leaves, Adola cuts me a look that could kill. "Why are you covering for me?"

"Isn't it obvious? Because I want to help you."

"I was covering for myself just fine until you showed up." She storms off and I let her go, torn between throwing her a life raft and leaving her to her fate. She finds a table in a deserted corner of the dining atrium, and I keep my distance. She pulls out a stack of note cards and studies them before emptying the contents of a pouch onto the table. She glances around before rubbing her fingers together, and the faintest whiff of darkness streams through the air toward her, forming tendrils of black in her hand. She works her magic on the items, but the thread of toushana dissolves as quickly as it came. I cringe. It's worse than I thought. Her stream of magic is far too weak. She is going to suffocate in that grave, and she knows it. She bangs the table before burying her face in her hands.

I join her.

"You're scared of it; that's why it's not obeying you. It isn't like proper magic. It has an appetite of its own."

"Would you just *leave me be.*"

"No, I'm not leaving. I still need your help."

She shoulders her packed bag. "*Don't* follow me this time."

"Adola, I'm not your enemy."

"Aren't you, though? Isn't that exactly who you decided to be when you arrived here? I know what your kind are like. Ambitious, incensed with self-importance, vengeful, *cruel.*" Her words cut in a way they shouldn't. I don't know this girl. Not really. And yet sometimes it feels like staring at a mirror.

My *kind*? "A toushana-user?"

She raises a brow. "Toushana-*obsessed,* more like."

But her aunt . . .

Now I get it. Adola doesn't just fear her aunt. She hates everything about her. After seeing Trials, I can't say it surprises me.

"Adola, you don't even know me."

"Maybe not, but I know what you will become."

A chill skitters up my arms. "A Darkbearer," I whisper. Adola narrows her eyes.

"You have me all wrong. I'm sorry, alright? I shouldn't have black-mailed you to help me. I should have been honest with you from the beginning."

Adola huffs, but she also doesn't move, so I keep going.

"Look, I am just here trying to find out the truth. My mother . . ." I glance over my shoulder before leaning closer to her. "Had a stack of ball invitations people'd thrown away. I found them hidden in her room in the guesthouse. I think it means something. Only, I'm not sure what." The release feels like a long exhale. "This place unsettles me, too, Adola. At Trials the other night—" But I can't find the words to rehash what I witnessed. The revelry and horror. "I felt sick to my stomach when I left."

"It's revolting," she says, reclining in her seat.

I let out a big breath. "I won't ever twist your arm to help me again. I'm really sorry."

Adola doesn't respond for several moments. She twists the ends of her long hair around her fingers before saying, "I hope you're being honest. Time will tell."

"I mean every word."

She meets my eyes, and there is a patience there I haven't seen before. As if she sees *me* and not the monster everyone's convinced I am becom-ing. So I tell her about my mother. How expertly good she is at hiding and covering her tracks. And how much I miss her, how I need to see her, especially after so much has changed these last few months. Once I start, the words won't stop. And it feels good to just talk and be myself.

By the time I'm done, Adola's hands are braided on the table. "I don't remember my mother." She tucks her chin down.

"You know," I go on, "when I was at Chateau Soleil, I was terrified people would find out I couldn't do magic like them. I lived every day worried someone would find out and kill me. But someone helped me." I leave out her cousin's name. "He ended up being awful, but without his help, I wouldn't have survived."

She swallows. "I lie in bed at night thinking about what it will feel like when the dirt hits my face. Sometimes I wake up gasping for air." Her voice cracks. "I've tried everything. And all this time spent, I'm behind on Second Rite. My aunt is breathing down my neck to debut at the start of next Season."

"I know what that's like."

We share a beat of silence, and it's nice. I hadn't realized just how much we have in common.

"The next time you pull on toushana, use your feelings from deeper inside. Channel that scary feeling you have when you lie awake. It'll strengthen your ability to pull on the darkness. And when it touches you, hold on to the cold; let it spool itself up, allow it to get close, pretend it's a part of you, let it linger—"

She stands. "I should go." But before she turns to leave, she stops. "Thanks, Quell."

"Sure." This time I don't follow her. Instead I check the clock and realize it's time to meet Beaulah.

SEVENTEEN

Quell

Beaulah is waiting for me in the main corridor of the Instruction Wing, holding a box of rings. I fill with dread.

"This way." She leads me into a windowless room with scorched walls and no tables or chairs. In a dim corner is a tall, narrow shelf stacked with bins. Beaulah slides a ring onto her finger, and its stone glows purple. Beside her are manacles welded to the wall. She smooths her palms over them. They flatten, lengthening before Shifting into leather straps.

"These are a bit gentler, I think."

I swallow. "What exactly are we doing?"

She holds up my hands, showing me fading bruises. "You're hurting yourself when you use toushana."

"Oh, those are nothing."

"Don't be ridiculous." She presses on an injury, and it feels like the bones in my fingers are breaking.

"You were going to study me," I say, wincing.

"We'll get there. But this should be dealt with."

I *had* started to better control the toushana so that it didn't hurt me, but when I used it on Yagrin, these bruises happened. I bite my lip and hold my hands out to her again. She inspects them closely.

"So wary of trusting people. I can't say I blame you." Beaulah lights a few long-tapered candles, fitting them into sconces. "Have you ever seen your kor, Quell?"

I recall the flickering red flame, the source that lives inside me, that energizes my own magic. The flame that Jordan pulled from his chest, unlike mine, was silver. "I have."

"When toushana binds to a person, it alters their magical body chemistry. Your flame may be stronger, but it can be unwieldy, taking on a sickly shape or color. I'd like to examine your kor. Just to be sure it's thriving."

"You can, but you're not strapping me down."

"Very well. Come closer, back flat against the wall."

I do as she says. She selects the golden ring without a stone from the box and slips it onto a free finger. "Deep breath in." She lays a palm flat on my chest. "This will hurt."

I hope trusting this woman isn't a mistake. When I inhale, my chest feels like an iron hook is fastened to my ribs. Beaulah draws her hand away from me slowly, and it feels like a million threads of barbed wire are being pulled out of my chest. I writhe, pain quaking through my body.

"Still, now."

I grab a fistful of my clothes, and Beaulah stretches the space between her hand and my chest. Air is being sucked from my lungs. I wheeze, trying to hold still as a flame grows in her hand, shiny like metal, with a dark black center. The silver fire flickers. She *tsks*.

"What's wrong?"

"Relax, child." She cups the flame. The air in the room thickens, and condensation drips down the walls. The metal of her empty golden ring brightens. Then she presses the flame back inside me in one smooth motion. My ribs ache, shifting aside as the cold fire disappears into my chest. I feel it snaking through my insides, all the way to my limbs, and the pain finally stops.

My hands! Both sides. "The bruises are gone!"

"Your kor was a bit withered. I shifted some oxygen from the air to freshen it up. You must have used it intensely recently."

Sun tracking with Yagrin. Then attacking him when I found my mother's key chain.

"It's important to prepare your toushana before using it heavily. And afterward, to let it rest."

"How do you know all this?"

"'We cannot honor the integrity of the furthest bounds of known magic until we've contemplated its darkest capacities.' That's from *Dysiis: Original Writings*, volume one, section four."

Dysiis. The name is vaguely familiar.

"My kor was red. Now it's silver." *Like Jordan's.* "Is that okay?"

"Red's fresh. Silver's best. Once a Marked plunges their dagger into their heart, their kor takes on the color of the metal, giving it a silver hue. Your grandmother really didn't teach you any of this?"

I don't answer, which is answer enough.

"What a shame." Beaulah smiles. "There's much you don't know. I mentioned mementaurs when you arrived. Memory magic is a fickle thing, but with practice, you can press your toushana to the temples." She demonstrates. "Feel around for the threads of thoughts and pluck the one you want to destroy."

"I've never heard of that type of magic."

"You probably haven't heard of tracer magic either. Draguns have a rich archive of magic specific to their vocation. Any other curiosities?"

There is one, but it sticks in my throat. She's been open. Maybe there is room for me to be open, too. "I would like to search my mother's room."

"Because you believe I'm lying."

"Because there could be lingering pieces of her there."

She straightens. "Jordan made you out to sound conniving."

I grind my teeth at the name and his judgment.

"I assumed his broken heart tainted his vision." She folds her arms. "I'd hoped you and I would establish a bit of trust, Quell. Given how freely you move here." She thinks I'm hiding out here while the commotion of House of Marionne is sorted out. I intend to keep it that way.

"I thought we did." I sit up sharply.

"Have we?"

"My grandmother has toushana. The rumors about her binding students to her house with Third Rite are true. She's wiped the memories of all her members. I've seen it with my own eyes. Would I tell you that if I didn't trust you?"

Beaulah's palm flattens on her chest. And the corner of her mouth curls up.

"Fair enough. Now that we've bonded." She winks. "Ready for a bit of experimenting, I think." There are a series of bins on a shelf. She grabs a blue one from the tip-top. Inside are various stones.

"Draw your toushana."

Waves of cold rush beneath my skin. Shadows push like sharp needles through my fist. Beaulah rummages through her bin of rocks. She tosses a gleaming yellow one at the magic thrashing in my grip. The shadows devour it, and her jaw ticks. She drops another stone in my hand, but it disappears immediately.

Her tongue pokes her cheek. "I'll have to think on this more." She replaces the bin on a top shelf, precisely where it was. "I'll see you tonight."

I grimace.

"Don't you want to be there?"

"I watched you have your debs *buried alive*." The truth slips out and I can't force it back in. "*No.* I don't have the slightest desire to go. Or to read the books you've sent to my room, if we're being completely honest."

"You act like his mother wasn't *right* there. As if my Draguns weren't all over that forest. We would *never* let any harm come to anyone. I watched Georgie take his first steps. I *love* that boy." She pokes me in the chest, and it's the first time I've ever seen Beaulah truly upset. "You won't imply that I don't."

"It's cruel."

She puts the bin of rocks back on the top shelf and returns the straps to manacles. When she faces me again, her expression is kind.

"Do you know how many people live their entire lives trying to find the courage to face their fear? There's *nothing* Georgie will hesitate at now." She pets the ends of my hair. "After all the time you spent at your grandmother's, you cannot tell me you don't wish you could have stood up for yourself sooner."

I can't meet her eyes. There's some truth to that I can't deny.

She opens my palm. I know what she wants. I fill it with shadows—swirling, dark, angry shadows. "All this power, Quell, is useless if fear controls you. And if you want honesty, you're desperate for your mother because you're scared of the girl in the mirror."

My heart hammers. "I love my mother and miss her."

"Even now, fear erects walls around your conscience."

I don't believe my ears. "You want me to agree that burying débutants alive is a proper way to teach them bravery."

"I *want you* to trust your magical instincts, Miss Marionne. Which are telling you that Georgie *is* more prepared to survive this Order today than he was yesterday. He will not be among the threatened, he will be *the threat*. And that is a *good* place to be in a world like ours. In your gut, *you know* that's true."

For minutes, we don't speak. Then Beaulah sets a gentle hand on my shoulder.

"A good Mother trains the children she loves for their later benefit."

"My mother loves me."

"And yet your grandmother and your mother both left you so unprepared." She dusts off my clothes and I let her. "You'll be running forever until you look at that girl in the mirror and, without anyone's approval, *unleash* her." She walks toward the door.

"I am not a Darkbearer," I mutter.

She marches back toward me. "What is a Darkbearer but a person who knows what they are capable of? A person who is not controlled by fear, or by an institution, but exists on their own terms? Tell me, Quell, if you made the rules, would other little girls like you have lived their entire childhood *running for their lives?*"

I can almost feel the ratty blanket Mom and I slept on in our first apartment before we had any furniture.

"*Scavenging* what you can?"

I can still feel the ache of my stomach and the often bare fridge.

"*Moving* around like some vagrant?"

I see the looks people gave, that time we had to ask strangers for change.

"Of course not."

"Darkbearers of the ancient days are dead. And so are their crimes. Call yourself what you want, Quell." She purses her lips in thought before continuing. "But the Order needs someone like you. Everyone has a role to play." She gestures at the shelf. "Take advantage of all my years of research. Get acquainted, get comfortable. If you cannot be yourself around people, then are they your people?" She waits for a response.

I think of Abby and pull at a thread on my clothes, unsure what to say.

"You are *not* worthless; you are a gift."

Beaulah's words are a warm blanket in a blustery world that confuses me more the longer I encounter it. My toushana is who I am, but if I let myself give in to it fully, who am I then? Where does that lead me? The history books say one thing. Beaulah says another. *Trust myself,* she'd say.

She watches me go, and her words replay in my mind like a song. And I'm not sure if it's stuck in my head or if I've put it on repeat. I've never heard anyone talk about me or my toushana that way. Embracing it at my grandmother's was the epitome of defiance. And I worry every day whether my mother will even look at me the same way.

I don't speak the entire walk back to my room, my mind whirring. Georgie did seem alright after he calmed down. But his fear wasn't the only thing left in that grave. A piece of his humanity stayed buried. *But if it makes him safer, allows him to have a life that's his own, how can it be entirely wrong?* I can't pretend that part of me doesn't wonder what it would have been like to grow up proud of my magic . . . instead of scared that its existence would get me killed.

I sit on Jordan's bed. He endured these Trials. He has all six pins. His deft command of his magic, the confident way he draws on toushana, his saturated mind of Order history, even his perfect etiquette—Beaulah carved, designed, and carefully sculpted every part of him.

No wonder he is so rigid. There were moments when he would let me peek behind the mask just enough to deceive me into thinking that the Dragun in him is breakable. He isn't. Beaulah made him that way. That will be Georgie in a few years.

I don't love her methods. But there is something disgustingly admirable about that woman's ability to breed resilience.

There is a letter with Abby's handwriting on the nightstand waiting for me. I rip it open.

Here's everything I have. I hope you're okay!

She's written a long list of locations, from Chicago to New Orleans, where my mom has supposedly been spotted. There are annotations underneath the locations explaining where she obtained the intel. In some cases it's secondhand through word of mouth. Other times it is someone she trusts or, in the case of Chicago, video evidence that my mother was in fact there at some point. *But Chicago was Yagrin impersonating her.* I sit back, wondering which sightings were her and which could have been him. Abby's list includes two balls: one in National Harbor and another in Manhattan.

An idea strikes me. I grab the invitations from between my mattresses and skim them again, looking for any similarities. On Abby's list is:

October 17—Minneapolis

When Season was in, there was a ball in Minneapolis. I flip through the invites until I spot one in Minneapolis: *the Foshay.* The date on the invite is also in October. *The dates!* I hadn't looked at the dates on any of these because they're all so worn and old.

September 3
May 12

These are all dates when Season was in; I was at my grandmother's. These invites aren't random. The truth knocks the wind out of me. My mother collected them because she thought I'd be there. *She's looking for me.* I keep flipping. *January 23*: a save-the-date for a spring tea next Season. And—my heart hiccups.

VEIL OF MUMS BALL
November 20

That's in three days. My heart races as I review them all again and find one other that hasn't happened yet, but it's months from now.

This is my chance. My mother will be at the Veil of Mums Ball, hoping to find me, in a matter of days. I grab a note to write Abby.

Meet at the coffee shop across from a library in Fairfield
(off Old Post) November 20 at 6 pm
Dress formal. I'll explain when I see you.

EIGHTEEN

·‹══════›·*

Jordan

L iam's face lights up, and the sight tugs at my lips. He spins the guitar
I just gave him, smoothing his hands along its glossed surface. I
check my watch. The Dragunhead is away, finally investigating Francis's
death: ruled a murder, but expecting me in his office with an update on
my progress in two hours. In that time, I need my brother's guard down
so he can open up.

"I thought you forgot me in that cell," he says, resting against a bench
on the rooftop of Wexton MidCenter Hotel.

"Uh, hardly." I had sent Yagrin extra meals and an actual bed while I
caught up on the stack of work at my desk and avoided the Dragunhead's
persistent questions about how Sphere tracking is going. I busied myself
with papers while he spoke to me, unable to look him in the eye. He stressed
that I shouldn't be worried about Quell. I told him I haven't been. *Partly
true. There are no signs of that girl anywhere. I have no leads to worry about.*

But Yagrin is going to help me in more ways than one today. I need
him to start teaching me how to sun track *and* tell me more about his
time with Quell. My jaw clenches. How far did their friendship go?

"I wasn't sure," he goes on, and I put thoughts of him and Quell to
rest. I need his help. "Especially after you *lied* about me helping—"

"Hush." I cut a cautious glance around. A Dragun is inside, guarding
each entrance to ensure we're not interrupted.

"It was more wishful thinking, I'd say." I watch for an eye roll or shoulder shrug, but my brother only strolls, stroking the guitar's strings. I follow at a distance, careful not to push too hard.

"It's impressive how you've mastered holding your Anatomer magic so well. I avoid it. Hate the way it feels."

He doesn't respond.

"Will I get to see my brother's actual face today?" I ask, checking the sun's position overhead. High noon is supposed to be a great time to sun track.

No response and no change.

Yags stops at a pair of lounge chairs near a glistening bed of rocks full of dancing flames. I sit beside him, and Liam's blue eyes find me.

"Thanks for this. And the bed."

I nod, trying to find the right way to phrase what I want to say next. Yagrin's brown eyes bleed through Liam's and stay. I stare at the glimpse of the brother I know. The slant in his eyes has tilted more over the years. He plays his strings and I let him, listening in silence. When the song finishes, he plays two more. By the time that's done, I gather the words I've been tossing around in my head, none of which feel quite right, and force them out of my mouth.

"It's a perfect day for sun tracking."

"Indeed it is," he says without any bite in his tone. I move closer to him, and my hand moves to the vial in my pocket. But just as it feels like the chasm between us is closing, his gaze falls to the virtue pins on my lapel. He sneers.

"I don't get how you can stand her."

Beaulah.

"I hate her as much as you do. But I won't apologize for my accomplishments."

"There's more than accomplishment that comes with those pins." The blue of Liam's eyes hasn't returned. Yagrin still stares back at me. I shift in my seat. Beaulah *is* very insistent about virtue pins and what they mean in her House. When she pins them on, asking the receiver to accept them, it always feels a bit like swallowing an eel. But my brother only ever earned a single pin, for discretion. And not because he couldn't earn more. By the time his magic showed strongly, he had already grown apathetic, refusing to practice anything but sun tracking. He loathed the pressure. So he slacked in every way.

I adjust my coat, the sun catching the gleaming line of gold on my chest. My brother turns the pegs on the headstock of his guitar. He has nothing to show for his life but bitterness. All things considered, he's probably, in some small way, jealous of me.

The next time he looks at me, the brown in his eyes has returned to Liam's blue. *Walls back up.* I prop my leg on my knee and settle into my seat, hoping I look more chill than I feel.

"I was thinking about that ordeal with the butler you reminded me about," I say. "It was quite ridiculous. But I liked old Brisby. He smelled a little weird."

"It was that tonic he used in his hair, I think." My brother smirks.

"Remember when we swapped it with Father's aftershave?" The picture forms in my mind: my father's red face, his greasy beard, and the stale-smelling liquid dripping over his face and clothes. A guffaw bubbles up and bursts from my lips. It feels foreign and jagged, almost painful, like a hammer hitting a brittle piece of concrete. Yags chuckles, too. When our laughter settles, I feel lighter.

"What an awful waste of space that man is," he says. "Not Brisby."

"Father," we both say at the same time.

"You know, as much as I loathe the brotherhood and how you are sliding further into its clutches—" He glances at the ruby heart pendant. "The best thing you've ever done was tell the Dragunhead about Father's health so he *had* to be sent away."

"That was good, wasn't it?"

"Absolutely brilliant. It's almost like we're related."

I slip the vial of Sun Dust from my pocket. But I hold it in a closed fist, realizing how bringing it out right now will look to him. Talking with him like this is . . . nice.

Yags glances at my closed fist. "Sometimes I think you forget I know you better than you know yourself."

I open my hand, my cheeks flushed.

"You were awful at sun tracking last time I saw you." Yagrin learned to sun track during a session Beaulah offered for her inner circle of pupils. He'd try to talk to me about it, but I was busy trying to attend as many raids as possible. I would give anything to go back to those conversations now.

"I was *fourteen*, Yags."

"You probably still can't do it."

My heart skips a beat. "Try me."

"You know who *is* really good at sun tracking?" He smiles and the answer mocks me. *Quell.* Between gritted teeth, I force out, "Oh, because she is bound?"

"She can suspend Dust like you wouldn't believe." He's practically giddy. "I would bet anything she feels the Sphere's magic in her bones, like those old stories Nana used to talk about."

Heat thrashes in my chest as I think of my brother and the girl I stupidly used to love colluding to destroy magic. Rage is a snake inside me, ready to strike. But as my brother turns to face me fully, his posture slacks. I ask, "How did you two evade us so long?"

I don't breathe.

His hands glide along his guitar before he meets my eyes again. Familiar brown is back. He waits several beats, and I force myself to take a deliberate breath. Eventually, he glances over his shoulder before leaning in. "There are entire communities who are very good at evading your brotherhood."

Communities . . .

Safe houses.

They're notoriously wary of outsiders. Once they've gelled as a unit, they don't usually let anyone in. I hadn't even considered them. How did he convince them to let them stay there? I have so many questions. But I feel like the mountain between us is starting to move, and I don't want to destroy it. If I find Quell because of intel Yagrin gives, that could save his life. *I want my big brother to live.* I swallow my questions and instead say, "That is clever. Truly."

"Thank you." He snatches the vial from me, but I can't stop thinking about the safe house network. I wonder if any recent raids have turned up any hints of her. I'm going to pull those files. My brother spills a tiny hill of Dust in his hand, and I tighten my grip on the seat, not believing this moment could get any better. His mask bleeds through his skin.

"Suspend. Count. Flare. Cloak." He tosses it up in the air, when the door to the rooftop bursts open. Maei runs toward us, as pale as a ghost.

"Mr. Wexton!" She looks at Yagrin. "*This* Wexton, I meant." She pulls me aside, her hand trembling. "There's been an urgent security breach. The Dragunhead's out until your meeting! A whole flock of Draguns left this morning on raids." She reddens. "Territory deployments are shifting this week, so plenty of folks are gone for that."

"Maei."

Her heart flutters like a bird.

"Slow down."

She shoves a file folder in my hand. Each highlighted point rends my heart.

Marked person has taken control of an Unmarked residential building in Boston.

There are thirty residents; six are elderly, seven are children.

Unmarked law enforcement is there, bewildered and unable to even get into the building.

Only demand he's made is to be left alone; the hostages are not coming out.

"I need two teams."

"That's what I meant, sir. We just sent out so many, I don't have many easily reachable."

My brother watches us from a distance, no longer wearing Liam's persona. I wave him over, and Maei chews her nails off as I share the privileged details of the situation with him. Technically, he is still a Dragun. He lets me finish without a word, but the etch of his brow deepens.

"That's awful," he mutters.

"Will you come with me?" I hang on my brother's response. At this chance for him to meet me halfway on whatever we're doing here. He sighs, and I know his answer before he says it.

"I can't betray my conscience and stand with the brotherhood anymore."

"Yagrin, there are *lives* of innocent people on the line. The brotherhood *does* good things. You have to concede that."

He holds out his wrists to Maei.

"Take him back to his cell."

"Sir, there's one more thing," she says, fiddling with his restraints. "The perpetrator says he is from House of Duncan."

NINETEEN

⸺✳⸺

Quell

For two days I pass the time. Beaulah studies me, and I dip into one of the books she sent as I wait to hear from Abby. Trials weren't as hard to watch the third time. I'm not sure if it's because I knew what was going to happen or because Georgie was there, strutting around exuberantly.

And at night, I lie in bed thinking of Jordan, wondering what he made of this place. He was always hesitant to say much about it.

When the morning of the Mums Ball comes, I pack up in anticipation of seeing my mom. Everything, including the books Beaulah gave me. Maybe I do have some things to learn. It would be vastly easier if Adola could cover for me. She thinks I'm a monster, but she'll see that's not true. I find her room and slip a note underneath the door, wishing her luck on Trials.

The door opens. "Quell? What are you doing here?" She grabs the note. "You're leaving?"

"Can I come in?"

She grumbles, parting the door wider. Adola's room is nothing like Jordan's: it is cluttered, and every surface is covered in open books or journals full of handwritten notes. There is no floor in her room. There are only more books. Old-looking ones with gold pages and others thicker than a dictionary. There are more half-empty coffee mugs around the room than I can count. And above her desk hangs an oiled portrait of a half-naked man being forced by a riled-up crowd to drink poison. I study it closer, perplexed. I see a date: *1787.*

"Quell, why are you here?"

"Your Trials are tomorrow. Did you try the thing I mentioned?"

She folds her arms.

"I really am here to check on you. And say goodbye." In a low voice, I explain I'm meeting my mom.

"You're really leaving?" She shifts on her feet. I set down my bag.

"I really do hope you do well at Trials."

She sits on the edge of her bed and gestures for me to join. "The thing you told me did help. Thanks."

"What else goes on in the forest? Is it just the burial?"

"*Please* stop talking about it. I'd prefer to do Third Rite a thousand times than a virtue pin trial once."

I eye the time as I sit beside her, thinking of centuries ago—when Darian, twin of a Sunbringer, chose toushana over his proper magic to stop a magical poison rotting their mother from the inside out. And just several decades ago, some say Darkbearers were on the ground in eastern Europe before Allied bombers helped destroy the oppressive regime's oil refineries, which led to its eventual downfall. Even if I were what Adola fears, from what I've been reading, some Darkbearers did incredible things. She's pushing me away for no reason.

"Have you ever talked to your aunt about your magic?"

"Of course not!" She stands and paces.

Her walls are up with Beaulah, and I wonder if they've ever had an actual vulnerable conversation of any kind. Beaulah Perl may be many terrible things, but she is passionate about dark magic. I bet she would *help* Adola, not tear her down. I consider telling her that, but I keep my mouth shut as she gazes into the distance, not wanting to shake her up anymore.

"I'm scared, too," I say. Something inside me uncinches.

"What?"

"To see my mom. I know it doesn't make sense, but I keep thinking: What if she doesn't recognize me? Or what if she thinks I've made a colossal mess of things?" *What if she isn't okay going back on the run again?* I let out a heavy breath. "The pressure to not be a disappointment, you know?"

"I don't care what my aunt thinks anymore. I just want to survive." Adola tugs at the end of her hair. "I still think about *her*."

"Beaulah?"

"Brooke," Adola whispers. "She was one of my aunt's favorites, a rising star. She left with a friend to run an errand for Beaulah one day. Now they're both gone. Dead. I don't know what happened, but I know my aunt's obsession with toushana didn't help."

The girls my grandmother killed. "That wasn't your aunt."

"You're defending her?"

"No, I—I'm sorry. What I meant to say was you'll be heir one day. Maybe you can change things."

"You would not believe how far away that feels. Living in a House where your aunt worships darkness." Her gaze falls to my hands. I stick them in my pockets so she can see me, not my magic. Maybe that will crack the walls she's built.

"Dark magic is part of me. I can't change that. But it's not all of me; I'm not evil. The best I can do, what I'm *trying* to do, is figure out who I am. And hold on to that person."

"And finding your mother will help you with that?"

"All we used to have was each other." Mom speaks a language only I can understand—she understands how to be invisible, how to survive. "I have to find her. I stood up for myself. I hope she'll be proud of me somehow."

"And if she's not?" Adola watches me.

The thought makes my knees weak. "I have to get going. You have a chance to *make* this a House you want to be a part of."

Adola tucks her lower lip. I make my way to the door, flexing my fingers, which are covered in smooth skin, not bruises. Yesterday, Beaulah had me destroy a dozen enhancer stones. Then she brought me pieces of magical armor to unleash toushana on. Those were much harder to decompose, but after a few hours, I managed to turn the metal to a pile of broken shards. And my hands still haven't purpled.

"I'm still figuring out your aunt. But she's not as awful as she seems."

Adola's head cocks.

I shrug.

"It was nice of you to come by." She crosses her bedroom, then opens the door.

"Maybe I'll see you around," I say.

"Maybe."

The door closes, and I slip behind one of the trick bookcases. If Beaulah finds out I'm leaving, I don't think she'll be happy about it. In the bowels of the estate, I hurry until I find an exit. Cold night air hits me as I dash toward the water gardens. Once I clear the walls of the estate, I pull at my cloak. *To Fairfield.*

Goodbye, Hartsboro. Hopefully for good.

THE QUAINT EATERY is one of many in a shopping strip in Fairfield, about an hour from Hartsboro. Or, in my case, the breath of time it takes to cloak. Across the street is the luxurious hotel where the ball will be held. I arrive early and watch the nearby streets for loiterers to make sure I haven't been followed—and keep an eye out for Order members. The coffee shop swells with patrons for the lunch rush, only to empty again. No one lingers too long.

Once the sky begins to dim, I enter and find a booth in a corner. I hold up the menu; it covers my face well. A waitress asks me what I'd like to order, twice, before the bell chimes and the door to the coffee shop swings open. Abby enters, wrapped in a long, dark dress and a shawl that complements her bright eyes. My grip on my chair slacks, and it takes every ounce of my self-control to not run and hug her. She is skirting between tables when the door chimes again. Her boyfriend, Mynick, enters in a dark suit; his greasy bangs are unmistakable. I shift in my seat.

Abby joins me at the booth tucked far in the corner. I put my back to the door and keep the collar of my coat up.

"Quell!" she squeals, reaching across the table for my hands.

"It's so good to see you." I squeeze back and try to exhale. I need to tell Abby the truth about my toushana someday soon. But today is not that day. "Thank you for coming, Abs, really. Juggling this with everything else you have going on."

"My internship's been pretty flexible." She turns a yellow-gemmed bracelet around her wrist. "Getting time away isn't ruffling too many feathers."

"Are you still finishing by next Season?"

"Yes." She pats her backpack beside her on the seat. "As long as the world doesn't fall apart first."

Mynick slides into the booth beside Abs. And I recall how much Jordan didn't like him that one time they talked.

"Hi, Mynick." I hold on to the lip of the bench. Last I remember, he promised Abby he was going to try to get out of becoming a Dragun. *Why* would she bring him?! My eyes snap to the slit of fabric at his throat, and my heart patters faster. No coin there.

"How have you been?" I ask him.

He fidgets. "Oh, you know, studying, research, practicing all kinds of things." He smiles darkly. "And trying to keep this one out of trouble."

Abby looks between us, her fingers stroking the Third Rite scar inches below her clavicle.

"Has my grandmother tried to summon you again with the trace?"

"No. And I haven't gone south at all."

"So you're doing okay?"

"A little sore. My scar started throbbing."

"I'm having it looked into by a Healer friend," Mynick says. "The Dragunhead's aware of the rumors about your grandmother tethering graduates to her House, you know?"

Chills skitter up my arms.

He goes on. "I heard the Council is pushing for her to be beheaded and her House to be shut down. Like Duncan's."

"What would happen to everyone in the House?" I ask.

"They'd be removed from the Order permanently."

"Everyone?"

"The House no longer has an heir," he adds, giving me a knowing look. I feel sick. At one point in time this would have all been my responsibility. "It's all rumors, who knows." He hooks an arm over Abby's shoulder and she sniffles. As much as I don't want Abby's career to dissolve, my grandmother has to be dealt with.

I squeeze her hand. "Well, if the truth comes to light, we have to fight for a solution that's fair. You don't deserve that."

She chews the inside of her lip.

An elderly couple has come in and sits at a table by the window, far enough out of earshot. After another careful look around the coffee shop, I pull out the invitations.

"Abby, could I show you what I found?" I ask, hoping Mynick takes the hint. But he's dressed as if he's in on this. She takes the invites, flipping through them.

"Where are you staying?" Mynick asks, his elbows on the table.

"I'm on the go, not staying in one place too long."

"Where did you get these?" she asks, flipping through the invites.

"My mom was looking for places I'd be. And she still is." I move the Veil of Mums Ball invite to the top. "This one is across the street. It starts in a half hour. I was thinking you could go and find her. I'll wait here." They don't respond, so I keep going: "She'll be trying to blend in, in plain sight." I slide to the edge of my seat. "She taught me that becoming part of my surroundings was the key to going unnoticed when in public."

"Wait, why would you have to go unnoticed in public?" Abby asks.

I swallow. She'd never believe a blatant lie.

"She didn't want anyone from the Order to find me."

Abby raises an eyebrow and sits back. "That's . . . weird."

"I think she must have known about the tether and never wanted my grandmother anywhere near me."

"Why didn't you say something before?"

"I'm sorry." I exhale sharply.

Mynick strokes his bangs.

"Oh, have I mentioned that my mom is very wary of heights? She also doesn't do elevators. Always stairs. It's a fear she's had since childhood, she told me. Should you write this down?"

"Quell, we've been doing this for months."

When I meet Mynick's gaze, his eyes pan away.

"Something to say?" I ask.

"I'm just here to support Abby. Ignore me."

"What are you thinking? Please share."

He sighs. "Look, sometimes I wonder if your mother's better at hiding than Abby is at searching. No offense, babe."

Her fingers drum on the table. "I do always seem to be two steps behind her."

My nails dig into my seat. Are they trying to back out at the last minute? "This is different, Mynick. If she thinks I could be there, she's going to come out of the shadows to look for me."

He rests his elbows on the table and leans in. "Finding your mom would be easier if you came with us to the Ball."

I sit back in my seat. "But that's impossible."

His brows bounce. "It isn't."

"Ah, that's brilliant," Abby squeals. "Why hadn't I thought of that before?" She squishes his face between her palms and kisses him.

"Slow down. Thought of what?"

"I can change your face." His smirk curls darkly. "Anatomer magic is one of my strands."

"You can use it on someone else? You can make *me* look different?"

He nods. The Ambrose motto. *Intellect cuts the sharpest.* It almost makes their pride palatable. Almost. If Mynick is willing to get his hands dirty, then maybe he is worth trusting.

"I'll need a dress."

"Happens to be my favorite hobby," Abby says. "I can still come with you, if you'd like. Mynick?"

"Sure, the Veil of Mums is always a rad time," he says sardonically.

"Then it's settled," I say. "Let's get out of here."

TWENTY

———✳———

Quell

Mynick's hand shakes as it moves down the slope of my nose. Every muscle in my face squeezes, then tingles, as my mouth shrinks and my lips plump. New hairs sprout, thickening my brows and changing my hairline. My eyes are suddenly heavy in their sockets, and I can feel them widening. The slopes of my cheeks fill in, and my long hair darkens to the color of night, shortening into very tight coils that hang above my shoulders.

"Someone's coming." Abby ducks her head into the bathroom we're using inside the lavish hotel.

"Almost," he says. His magic trickles down my back like a rush of warm water; my body widens in some places and narrows in others. My skin tone warms, deepening from golden brown to a bronze hue.

"How long will this last?"

"It will wear off gradually over time. An hour, maybe two. But sometimes personas can dissolve spontaneously. "

"So I am walking in here and my disguise could wear off any second, without notice?"

"You'll feel some tingling. Just try to keep calm."

Talking with lips that don't feel like mine makes each word out of my mouth sound a little funny. Then I realize . . .

"My voice!" My heart knocks into my ribs as the pieces of the plan feel like they're coming undone.

"I can't help you with your voice in a time crunch, I'm sorry."

"This is a terrible plan. Maybe you and Abby should just go and I stay in here."

Mynick smooths his hands over the dress Abby put together for me, and my body fills it like it was made for me. "You can't back out now. You're almost there."

He's right: finding my mom will be much easier for me, if I can just keep calm. He surveys his work before stepping out of the way so I can see myself in a mirror. A lackluster diadem sits on my head. I glare at it before moving my arms and rotating my head. Sure enough, the stranger staring back at me does the same.

"What was she like? In case I'm seen by someone who knows her."

"She's been dead a long time. So you're all good."

My breath hitches. *A dead girl.* How fitting. I get a closer look. "You didn't change my eyes."

"Those have always given me trouble." He smooths a thumb over my eyelid once more, then *tsks* when I reopen them. "I'm sorry. But maybe that'll help your mother know it's you."

This will have to do.

"Are you guys done yet?" Abby says, ducking her head inside the bathroom again. "I'm not sure how much longer I can keep telling people it's broken before one of them insists on fixing it with magic." Abby sees me and gasps. "Oh, Mynick, you've outdone yourself."

"Are you sure it's good enough?" I stare right at her, wondering if my eyes give me away.

She spins me twice. "If I passed you, I wouldn't have a clue who you are."

Mynick checks his watch. Then he holds out an arm to Abby. She ropes around it. "We'll see you inside."

I hide my bag, with everything that means anything to me, behind the commode in the biggest stall and lock the stall door. Then I pull the icy chill to my fingers and smooth it on the top door hinge. It corrodes on contact. The door dislodges, and the whole thing juts forward, dangling from its one working hinge. At least the stall appears out of service.

This will work.

The ballroom's doors are wide open, and sweet, cheerful music welcomes me inside as I approach. An attendant waits at the door, greeting and announcing guests.

"Unescorted, madam?"

My heart thumps. "Yes, sir." I curtsy. *A name. I hadn't thought of a name.* "Miss Lark Marie Doumont. House of Perl." I dip again in a perfect curtsy, the red taffeta of my gown brushing the floor.

He announces my arrival, and I blow out a tight breath, stepping inside.

The ballroom is a palace of mums bursting in full bloom, in every autumn hue. A swath of finely dressed guests move around decadent tables overflowing with rich fall-colored fabrics, shiny plates, gold flatware, and dainty glasses. The walls are plastered with scenic wallpapers of moody landscapes between tall, slender windows. There's a crowded dance floor large enough to be a room of its own. I gather the skirt of my dress in my fists. Every House is here celebrating the year-end off-Season fall ball.

The music reminds me of the Tidwell, a ball I attended with the boy I'd like to forget. Still, the glamour of this event unfurls something warm in my chest. This whole place dazzles. I hold my shawl tighter around my shoulders, remembering the way it felt to move to music, to be held close to him. Back when I believed his touch meant something and hoped there could be a life for me that sparkles like this.

It hurt to love him. And yet it hurts to miss him.

I'm not sure which is worse.

I move through the clusters of people immersed in chatter, their fine clothes showcasing a tapestry of House colors, with one person on my mind—*my mother.* I slip past, mostly unnoticed. Occasionally someone looks my way, but I offer a polite smile and keep moving, searching for some glimpse of anyone who looks like my mom. She would blend in with the backdrop, determined to not be seen. I scan the room. Waiters pass trays between the tables, and I study each of their faces for any hint of familiarity. *Where are you, Mom?*

The music changes and a rush of bodies brush past me, swarming the dance floor.

"Madam, might I have this—" someone says.

I walk away from the dance floor even faster, going to mingle with the servers. But as I approach, they scatter. It's poor etiquette for servers to crowd the guests. I sigh, exasperated, when I spot someone removing appetizer plates.

"Excuse me!" I flag them as they try to scamper off.

"Madam?"

"I have a question about . . . about a server who . . ."

His brow knits in confusion.

"Who left their, um, *glasses* at my table."

"Eyeglasses? They took them off and left them?"

"*Yes*. And so I just wondered if you might point me in her direction. She's about my height, deep brown skin, and dark eyes. She has long hair, but it's mostly gray. She sometimes walks with a limp because her feet hurt. And—"

"Your server spoke to you about her feet?"

I tug my ear. "I could tell by how she walked. I tend to notice small details."

"I sincerely apologize that you were troubled from your evening with such carelessness."

"No, I didn't mean to—"

"It's no problem, madam. If you'll hand them to me, I'll find who they belong to." He holds out his gloved hand.

"But my description, it matches one of your servers?"

"My shift just started, so I'm not sure who is all here, but I can find out."

I grimace. "Thanks. I'll get them from my purse and find you."

He departs, and I snatch a glass of champagne from a passing tray. Mynick patrols the perimeter of the dance floor. I look for Abby but don't see her. I wonder if she's having more luck. I toss the flute back and tug on my gloves. *Think.*

"Your dress is just exquisite," a woman in a simple gray gown with a well-pushed-up bust says, blocking my way. *If I appear approachable, I've been standing in one place too long.* I start toward the dance floor to get a better look at some of the couples. I can't imagine my mom blending in as a guest. Still, I cannot afford to leave any rock unturned. Dancers spin past me, and not even one looks a thing like Mom. If she had friends in the Houses, maybe she could be disguised, as I am?

Mynick loiters near the entrance to the ballroom before slipping out the door. I spot Abby, roped into a waltz with someone. A sweet, high thrum of a fiddle skips through the air, followed by the patter of a drum and the ting of a triangle. The crowd roars, and the few filled seats that had remained now empty.

A pair rushes past me, practically knocking me over.

"*Watch where you're go—*"

Three Draguns enter the ballroom.

My pulse picks up.

They go in opposite directions, surveying the crowd, occasionally stopping a person to ask questions. I have a fistful of my skirts when I notice my hands. They aren't mine. I blow out a slow breath.

Draguns . . .

Could Jordan be here?

As if the thought has a magic of its own, my gaze snaps to him as he enters the ballroom with a hardened, scanning glare. An usher lets him through without a word, and suddenly I can't move. Jordan adjusts his coat, his jaw clenched tight. He is taller than I remember. His top lip curls in disgust as he scans the room. His usual suave swagger is stilted, his steps heavy. Angry or frustrated or something. My gut swims. *He's here, right in front of me.* I stumble backward into a chair.

I'm frozen, remembering the last time I saw him with my own eyes. The night I fled Chateau Soleil. "I need you," he'd cried, begging me to stay in this caged world with him. He gave up on us. On me. It tore me to pieces to hear words I'd longed for him to admit, only for them to not matter anymore.

And there he is. Standing across the room.

My magic startles awake, icing my bones.

My knees are weak, but I move through the crowded room, watching him, careful to keep the commotion of the dancing between us. There's no warmth in his expression, no mask of politeness that people usually hide behind in public. Instead, hard lines chisel his face in places where they hadn't before. As if he's aged years in a matter of months. I dig for anger, but my throat thickens. Looking at him feels like a knife cutting into a nearly healed wound. *He said he loved me.* What kind of love was it if it could be so easily broken? What did those moments mean between us if he could so easily throw them away? Everything in me wants to march up to him and throw one of these abandoned drinks in his face.

My eyes prick with tears, and I clench my fists, my pain churning into anger. *I hate him.*

Someone's hip bumps into me and I move aside, unable to take my eyes off Jordan as he makes his way around the room.

"Are you alright?" the person says, lingering. But I can't manage a sensible word.

He holds out his hand. "Might I have this dance?" He takes me before I can come to my senses. And before I know it, I'm whirling around with some tuxedoed fellow on the dance floor. The room spins, but with every turn, I keep my gaze fixed on Jordan Wexton.

"How did you spend your summer?" my dancing partner asks. He is quite handsome, with golden eyes, a low-shaved beard, and a teal bow tie. House Oralia. He touches me gently at the waist and ushers me into a spin underneath his arm, and I lose sight of Jordan.

"You look quite lovely tonight."

I manage to smile and realize he's not wearing a ring. He isn't just being polite. He's flirting. His voice drones on in a fuzzy lump of nothingness, saying something I don't hear.

When the music shifts, his hand at my waist pulls me closer, and we sway side to side for the next eight counts. He stares at me expectantly.

"What did you say? I missed it."

"I gathered you didn't want to talk about summer. So I asked if you had any plans for the holidays."

"The holidays," I repeat, scanning to find Jordan again. The number of Draguns in the room has doubled. And Jordan is not near the bar or at any of the tables. "Look, I don't want to date you."

"*Ow.*" My partner winces, and I realize my nails are dug into his arm. "My family and I like to spend ours in Aspen," he goes on.

"Please, shut up."

To my relief, the tempo of the chorus picks up, and he lets go of me. I turn twice and lock hands with a new partner. This one wears a red vest and wedding ring. Still no sight of Jordan. I blink hard. Maybe I imagined it. Maybe he's not actually here. With my free hand, I run my fingers across the features of my face and force out a breath.

"Is everything okay?" my new partner asks.

"We're not talking. Just dance."

We promenade, moving in step with each other, side by side, our hands linked, when I spot Abby. She and a partner dance toward us as all the dancing couples split into two lines.

"No luck on my end so far. How about you?" I say as she comes close enough to hear me.

"Unless she's wearing a different face, she isn't on this dance floor," she says, stepping backward, the distance between our lines growing. The dance switches; we circle and my partner turns me.

"What about Mynick?" I ask, but she's already too far to hear me without shouting.

My hand slips from my partner's, and I search for an opening in the crowd to escape this prison. But I spin and end up back-to-back with my next partner. The music takes on a peppier lilt as it ushers in the final stanza, thank goodness.

Our hands lock behind our backs with an ease that feels familiar. I kick, tapping my feet, left first then right, executing the dance perfectly but still keeping an eye on every server that passes through. Back-to-back, we sidestep, when I spot Mynick returning with another pair of Draguns. My grip tightens on my partner. They're looking for me. They *have* to be. *That snake!* The cry of a violin signals the next move. My partner spins me around to face him. I gaze up into green eyes.

Jordan pulls me tight to his chest.

TWENTY-ONE

✳

Jordan

Fear burns in the girl's eyes. But their shade of brown seems to silence the sounds in the ballroom. Their uncanny familiarity. She yanks her chin down sharply, watching her feet. I'm not sure what has her frazzled: the pendant on my chest or her worry that she isn't a good dancer. But she's quite good. I reach for her chin, to pull her gaze back up, before closing my hand in a fist. I don't know this girl. I hold her gently against me, following the steps of the music, my body familiar with its rhythm.

The last thing I want to be doing is dancing, but I need to blend in. The song plays on, and the chaos that has wound me in a knot over the last few days eases with each step. It's been endless: Searching for intel on safe houses that mention anyone who could possibly look like Quell. Combing through Yagrin's instructions on sun tracking. He really left me high and dry, bailing on that Duncan raid. By the time I got there, one of the residents of the building had been killed. Wearing one of my personas and a stolen law enforcement badge, I cornered the guy inside and managed to bury my dagger in his gut before he hurt anyone else. He was deranged, shouting about all kinds of things: his House's resurgence, the revenge to be had for all the wrongs done to their House, and how he intended to find Sola Sfenti's bones and unearth new magic. The Dragunhead's investigating what exactly the hostages saw before I arrived. The world is unraveling at its seams.

I tried to tell Yagrin about it, but he just wanted to hear more stories of when we were young. Stories I've buried. The sleepless nights also don't help. And Charlie and Yani have been quiet since someone murdered Francis. So tonight, I'm hunting down a suspected financier of safe houses. If Quell's been in or around them, Audubon would know.

He sits alone in a corner of the ballroom with a briefcase beneath his seat. He is supposedly meeting here tonight with someone. The music peps up, and the next dance is an eight count. My dancing partner executes the moves perfectly, demanding my full attention. I smile. Dancing with someone skilled is so much better . . . She twirls effortlessly, then folds into my arms for a sway from side to side. She stiffens against me, so I put some distance between us, hoping that will help her relax. But she sticks close, pressing her face against my chest for the next move, and I swallow hard.

"Are you alright?"

She smiles and glances at me for a second; her eyes make me completely forget what I was going to say next. Her arms climb up my shoulders, hooking behind my neck. I hold her waist gently. *I haven't been this close to someone since . . .* I can see her, almost smell her. The music bumps faster, and I skip to it, remembering being tangled like this with Quell, how we wound around to the music with a magnetic synergy as if the song was written for us, each note composed by our beating hearts. Her eyes were the same brown as my partner's, more breathtaking than a field kissed by sunset and sweeter than honey.

I dance backward a few steps, both of us holding our flat palms one on top of the other behind our backs. And when I look at the girl on the dance floor with me, for a second, I pretend she is someone else.

We rotate, touch elbows, and rotate the other way. Memories of Quell haunt each dance step and shift into the melody. The sounds remind me of her. My dancing partner feels like her. And I let all of it take me until my memories and I are alone in that ballroom. I move faster, beside myself, and miss the next step. It knocks me back to my senses.

My cheeks flush with shame, my heart races. And I can hardly look at the girl. As the music approaches its crescendo, she spins in my grasp one last time, pressing her back against my chest. I hug around her for the final four count before the first dip. She steals a glimpse at me, eyes the color of a satyr butterfly. But as I bring her up, I spot a pair from House of Oralia with artsy painted faces wearing bright teal dresses follow a woman in a dark red suit out a side door, then glance over their shoulders. Perl thinks Oralia is a joke of a House. Now they're having private meetings? My insides twist. Audubon hasn't moved. But the ballroom has changed. It's more crowded. *It's like ambu*— I spot coins on throats everywhere. Draguns. All over this place.

The hair on my arms stands up. No one knew I was raiding here tonight. Charlie hovers near the ballroom entrance. He's hunched over, as if the bones in his back hurt to move. He's visibly more frail than the last time I saw him. He scans the room. When he looks in my direction, I can tell he hasn't been sleeping well either. He is pale and his stare is weary. He takes another look around before ducking out. Is he looking for me? Beaulah? I look for Yani but don't see her.

The shrill of violins races to the song's end, and I turn the girl in my arms swiftly, looping her under my arm before bending her backward for the finish. The music ends. The dance floor bursts into applause. She doesn't breathe, watching me as I set her right on her feet.

"Your eyes, they're—" But my words are cut off when several things happen at once.

Draguns form up around the dance floor, led by someone I recognize but can't quite place. The girl, now behind me, is swallowed by the crowd.

Every corner of the room fills with shadows. Dancing turns to scattering. Lights flicker as people dash in every direction, away from the cloaked Draguns swarming the dance floor. People crash into tables, vases shatter, candelabras hit the ground. Shouting drowns out the music. Chaos erupts as Draguns attack—*who* or *what*, I'm not sure. I bite the inside of my cheek, my anger boiling as party guests flee to the fringes of the ballroom, the dance floor now a storm of shadows.

Gazing through the haze, I spot her.

Quell.

Wavy ringlets of hair drape over her narrow shoulders, freckles cover her face, trailing down her smooth skin and disappearing into the neckline of her dress. Her deep brown eyes are an abyss. One I used to long to drown in. The gentle curves of her face. The fullness of her lips. *That mole near her jawline.* It is her. I can't move, afraid to shatter this moment, if this is actually happening.

She stands in the midst of the chaos and time ceases to exist. She wears the fine red gown of the girl I just danced with. It punches the wind out of me. She stares and it has a hold on me. My throat is dry; the mayhem is silent, and all I can hear is my thudding heart. All I can feel is hers, too. *It was her.* The truth unsteadies me. The Draguns are after . . . her. They're here for Quell! I clench my fists. But before I can summon my toushana or say something, she vanishes in a dark mist.

Bodies jostle around me. The world is hollow of sound. I danced with her. I *danced* with her! She was right there. In my arms. My heart squeezes so tight I fear it might shatter my ribs. I storm up to the ringleader of this disruption.

"How did you know it was her?!"

"Jordan. I—I mean, sir." He struggles to tear his gaze from the mayhem on the dance floor. "The target . . ." His head swivels, brows dented. "Where did—"

Someone nearby gasps, hands cupped over her face.

"Abby?" I say. It's been months since I've seen or even thought about Quell's old Housemate. Abby chokes on her tears and runs off, scared to death, like half the people in this place.

"You're Abby's guy," I say to him, realizing why I know his face. Last I saw him he wore a stitched talon at his throat.

"Mynick." He flashes me a silver coin before pressing it to his collar. And I shove him.

"Right now, your name is *imbecile*." I drag him aside for a private word. "*Why* didn't I know about this raid? Her disguise? Any of it?" The ballroom is a field of wreckage. "This is *not* how we do things." I shove him. Not only was I kept in the dark, Quell slipped right through their hands! The Draguns in the room re-form around us. *"Fall back."*

Mynick is too stunned to respond. On my periphery, Audubon slips out the door, his suitcase tucked under his arm. *She came here tonight for a reason.* He could be working with her . . .

"Shut whatever this is down," I tell Mynick. "Get to my office and wait there before I rip that coin from your throat and brand it into your skin."

I hustle out the door after Audubon, the stain of disappointment on Quell's face as she took in the chaos seared into my mind. I'm firing off a message to Charlie when I spot a closed door at a stairwell exit. *Help me on the south stairway.* I shove my phone in my pocket, grab the icy magic from the air, and cloak. Audubon flees at full speed. The world shifts, darkening at its edges as I nose-dive through the stairwell from the penthouse floor. I re-form in front of a panting Audubon.

Sweat rains from his brow. His arms are empty. "Who'd you give the money to?" I ask.

His eyes dart to the entry door of the second level of the hotel: it's propped open by the suitcase. As swiftly as I turn to snatch the suitcase, it is gone. The door swings closed.

I dash through the door to the second floor but find the hotel hall empty—except for a woman in a fancy wheelchair, warming herself under a blanket, waiting for an elevator. I search the halls in both directions, as well as the fire escape outside the window. Nothing. No one.

The woman rolls herself to the elevator. My mind whirring, I walk over to the call buttons and request a car going down.

"Very kind," she says, tugging her blanket tighter over her lap, pushing her white knotted hair off her shoulders before resting her hands on her wheels.

I send a message to the others as the elevator doors open. The woman rolls forward, catching the corner of her blanket under the wheel of her chair. It slides half off her lap, revealing . . . the corner of a suitcase.

Her heart races and I feel it, my senses awakening. Her icy blue eyes meet mine.

"You!" I grab her by the throat before she can respond.

ONCE MY CAPTIVE is securely off to Headquarters, I duck my head back into the ballroom to ensure the Draguns are gone. Thankful that at least this happened at an Order-exclusive ball. If this were a public ball, with Unmarked, this place would be a bloodbath. Still, the relief doesn't allay my thoughts of Quell. She knew she was dancing with me. *Why would she come here?* She's working with someone. She has to be. The crowd has thinned considerably, but the place hasn't been completely cleaned up. The Dragunhead won't be happy about this.

"Mr. Wexton, hold it right there!" Mr. Cartier, host of the Veil of Mums Ball and the mayor of Fairfield, marches toward me.

"Sir, I'm very sorry for the disruption tonight."

"Is *this* what the Dragunhead had in mind when he put you in charge? You have any idea how much time and funding goes into this annual ball?" His thick mustache twitches. "Not to mention the fundraising we're doing. All that money for kids—*lost*."

All that money to ensure his reelection, he means.

"A person never laid their eyes on a Dragun in my day," he goes on. "This running raids out in the open, the way you young boys like to do, is no good. I'm going to have a word with the Council about this."

"You do what you need to do, sir. Again, I apologize. I will get to the bottom of how this happened."

He wags a finger at me. "This would never have happened on your father's watch. If he would've been appointed, we'd be better for it."

My jaw tics. "If there's nothing else, I should be getting back."

He huffs and stalks off. I blow out a breath, but it doesn't help. Was Audubon helping Quell? And what about the woman in the chair? She is going to give me answers!

TWENTY-TWO

—✳—

Quell

The chaos of Draguns flooding the ball, looking for *me,* precisely where I was looking for my mother, plays like a horror reel on repeat in my head as I escape. I could have been killed. Charlie pulls me along, running with a limp, looking more withered than the last time I saw him, just days ago.

My Anatomer disguise had dissolved the minute Draguns swallowed the dance floor. So I cloaked in the middle of the commotion and re-formed outside the hotel, watching the doors in case my mother fled as well. When Charlie ran out of the hotel and spotted me, he said Draguns were coming down the elevator behind him. He had urged me to follow him and stick close.

"Did you see her anywhere?" I ask, hurrying to keep up with him as he leads me down the alleyway behind the hotel.

"She's not here, Quell," he says, fiddling with his phone. "I've been patrolling for hours, waiting for you. Your mother didn't show."

My pace slows. My chest is heavy.

"Come on," he says. "Almost there."

The truth hits me. *This was a trap.* Did Abby know? She watched the dance floor flood with Draguns. She watched as Mynick gave the signal for them to surround me. And she just stood there and did *nothing* before running off! "Mynick set me up. He suggested I go to the ball, then ambushed me."

"Don't know the guy. But he didn't want to try to capture you one on one. That isn't a bad thing."

That may be true, but it doesn't make me feel any better. Rage burns in me, frigidly cold. There's really no one left I can trust. Abby is as good as dead to me. How *dare* she and Mynick play me like that! Charlie's head swivels as we cross an intersection to put more distance between us and the hotel.

"How'd you even know I'd be at the ball?"

He looks at me, bewildered. "Mother sent me to make sure you got out of there safely, of course."

"How'd she know my plans?"

"Mother knows everything." Charlie holds his side, wincing, before narrowly skirting a car laying on the horn as we cross another street.

"You don't look so good. Are you sure you're alright?"

"I'm fine." He tugs his jacket tight across his chest.

"Did you know the brotherhood would be here tonight?"

"Mother told me. It must have been a quiet raid. The guy leading it is as green as an Electus finding their kor the first time. He made a mess of that place. What an idiot." Charlie laughs and it grates against my skin. How could anything be funny right now?

"I was almost *killed.*"

"Sorry." He clears his throat.

The scent of Jordan lingers from the dance. Once my nerves wore off and I realized he wouldn't know who I was, the music took us. For a breath, it felt like we were in on the same secret. Admitting that I enjoyed the dance sets my teeth on edge. Was he in on the raid? Did he know it was me all along? The chaos seemed to catch him off guard. My bones twitch with an ache, my toushana in a frenzy. Finally, we stop running; we rope arms on the back side of a convenience store, preparing to cloak.

I exhale, oddly relieved to be going back to Hartsboro.

THE THRUM OF my heart is steady when I return to House of Perl. Beaulah is probably furious that I left without a word to her, but at least here

I know I won't be ambushed. Charlie escorts me to my room. When I enter, Beaulah is sitting in the armchair. A dog that looks too large to be a dog but too small to be a wolf is curled up by the fire. It rises when I enter, and my toushana unfurls, bleeding through my hands. The wolf pup growls.

"There's no need for that, Irish wolfhounds are complete pushovers," Beaulah says. "Please sit. I've asked Della to have my personal Healer visit you tomorrow, after you've had some rest, to make sure you are truly alright."

I hesitate, unsure how to respond. I was expecting her to greet me with anger . . . But the lines carved into her expression are relief, not irritation. I may have been wrong to judge her so harshly.

I sit on the edge of the bed, the last hours whirring like a hurricane in my head. And now I'm back here, no closer to finding my mother than I was before. I pull a blanket over my legs and resist the urge to curl into a ball. *Maybe Charlie missed her.* Abby said she didn't see her either, but how can I trust anything she's told me now? The more I ponder, the more I spiral. And I realize Beaulah's still staring at me.

"Did you find her?" She strokes her pet.

"What?"

"At the Veil of Mums. You were so determined to get there, it wasn't hard to figure out what you must have been after." She holds up the stack of invitations that I left under my mattress. "A little digging confirmed my suspicion." She crosses her legs. "Was she there?"

"You're smart enough to know the answer to that question."

"Quell, I want to keep you safe."

"I told you, I don't need you to protect me." I get up from the bed, kick off my shoes, and remove my earrings and bracelet at the vanity. But the necklace won't unhook.

"Don't you, though?" She rises from her chair and gestures for me to turn. She works at the hook of my necklace. "Had I not sent Charlie, would you have gotten out of there unscathed, without making a mess of things?" She sighs. "Quell, I knew your plan before you left. And I admit

I was upset by it. Because it tells me that you still do not understand that I wish you no harm."

"Not wishing me harm isn't the same as wishing me help."

"How have I refused to help you?"

"You're keeping details from me about my mother's time here."

"I am just focused on what really matters. You're at a critical stage of development."

She isn't going to convince me that reuniting with my mother is a bad idea. "Tell me about the day she left again. Did she even hint at where she might be going?"

"There's not much to tell. I was traveling." She circles me. "Your focus on your magic right now is a much better use of your time. The first several months after binding with toushana are vitally important if you're to reach your full potential."

My full potential. My whole life, I've only been a girl with the wrong kind of magic. Beaulah sees something in me beyond who I was, or who I am now—some fugitive in hiding. And the thought unsteadies me.

Everyone focuses on my toushana. Yagrin wanted me to train. Adola can't separate who I am from what I can do. Beaulah wants me reading her old books. My mother wants me to live as if I don't exist at all. But what if I want to be more than my magic?

The truth cuts: I am my toushana and I always will be. And I've been trying to separate it from who I am, trying to be something else.

Beaulah pulls out the vanity's cushioned seat. "If I may?"

I sit, and her dog finally settles on its paws and lies down. She takes my hair down and pulls a wide comb through it. Her gentleness surprises me. Perhaps Beaulah is more misunderstood than anything.

"You're distracted."

"I've never been more sure of what I really want in my entire life." *My mom and I, back together.*

"That's what you tell yourself. But it's obvious you haven't even taken a moment to consider what *you* want from life, Quell. Who *you* are." She parts my hair into three pieces and starts braiding it.

"You mean a Darkbearer."

"That label has such a negative connotation. But yes, Darkbearers embraced their dark magic. And lived in full command of it. That didn't make them evil. Why did you bind with your toushana, Quell?"

"Because I wasn't willing to erase part of who I am."

"And what was your plan after that? You find your mother and then what?"

A house near the beach. A life away from this madness, from the Order, from magic. My stomach twists. But *is* that what I really want? To have my magic but keep it in a box as I have been? To leave this world of possibility behind? I hated wearing that fake diadem tonight. I hated the way I had to walk into that ball as someone else to survive.

I refused to live a life at my grandmother's without my toushana.

A shiver scrapes up my arms.

I stare at my hands; the faintest whispers of toushana dance on my skin. I remember how Mom and I would hide, how she would be riddled with fear at even the chance of anyone seeing my magic. How she would chastise me for even *thinking* about using it. It's only been a few days, but something in this place calls to me, despite my misgivings.

I don't want to live a life hiding it either.

If Beaulah can actually show me how to fully step into all that I am—the girl who everyone else already has decided I am—why fight it anymore?

I play with a tendril of toushana and touch a leaf on a small plant on the vanity. It blackens, coiling into itself, then crumbles into dust. I bite my lip and glance up at Beaulah to apologize for destroying her pretty plant. But she beams with an affection I've never seen before or felt from anyone. And I can't look away from her.

Everyone wants to *kill me* for what I am. This woman, despite her secrets and her half-truths, *saved my life* because of what I am. She sent Charlie to find me, despite my determination to write her off as a monster. Who else has ever pushed me to consider myself? To think of what *I* want? My own mother never said those words. Beaulah has only accepted and helped me. That matters.

Maybe it matters more than anything.

Everyone believes I'm a Darkbearer, no matter what I say or do. So maybe I am one. I'm done running from the name. Beaulah ties my braid and lays it over my shoulder.

"I'd like to do a full day of experiments with you tomorrow, but *my* way. There are some parts of my toushana I'd like to explore," I tell her.

A smile spreads across her face.

"Do you have time tomorrow? I realize it's the day before Adola's Trials."

"I will make time, dear." Her wolf pup stretches, then laps my hand with its slimy tongue. I grimace. Beaulah shoos him away.

"Rest tonight. We will work tomorrow. We have quite the celebration planned for Adola. It will be a long, but rewarding, end to a busy week. You'll have fun. That I'm sure of." She walks to the door and pauses at the doorknob, her dog at her feet. "Quell, I am proud of you for realizing there are people who will never understand you. Not the Order. Not Jordan. And not your mother."

You're wrong, I wish I could say, but I can't stop thinking about how desperately my mom and I hid. How buttoned-up she was about anything about the Order. How she never told me there were other people with magic like mine.

"I don't care about the Order. It never served me anyway."

"Good."

"And Jordan and I aren't a thing."

Beaulah's brows widen in surprise. "I hope that's true about you and my nephew. He will kill you, dear, and not lose a wink of sleep. I know because I bred him to be that way myself." She tosses the invitations in the fire before closing the door behind her. I stare at the hungry flames, stewing on Beaulah and how differently she regards me versus almost everyone else in my life. My mother is out there somewhere. And I will find her eventually. But maybe it's okay to do something for myself for a change.

I take out a notepad from the bedside table and settle at a desk with a Darkbearer book.

TWENTY-THREE

---*---

Jordan

Mynick is waiting at my desk, his glossed green mask on his face, when I enter Headquarters. He uncrosses his legs and straightens when he spots me.

"Sir, I thought you knew—"

I hold up a hand to shut him up and indicate one of the private meeting rooms.

"Signatures on all these, sir." Maei follows us inside, handing me a clipboard and pen.

"How upset is he?" I ask her.

"He's pretty mad. The mayor called him in the middle of the night. He's been here ever since, waiting on you to come in."

I sigh. "I'll see him in a moment."

Inside the conference room, Mynick opens his mouth before I shut the door, and the frustration of the last several days boils over. I grab him by the throat.

"From now on, you need my permission to take a piss. Am I understood?"

I release him. He rubs his throat and sits. I slide him the report detailing the fallout from his raid: the costs to repair damages, the Retentors pulled off their jobs to remove traces of toushana in that ballroom, the scathing remarks by the mayor, and a dozen irate members questioning the Dragunhead's methods. My name is mentioned more than a few times. But the worst of it: the three people injured trying to escape and Quell wasn't even apprehended! He starts signing, slouched in shame. What was the Dragunhead thinking, commissioning this guy?

I scrub a palm down my face. "You're too new to be running raids. Who authorized you to assemble a team without my sign-off?"

"The Dragunhead. He assigned me to find Quell." The Dragunhead *had* told me plainly that he would put someone on finding her.

I stiffen.

"How did you know it was her?

"I'm sixth of my blood. A Retentor, Shifter, and *Anatomer*, sir, from the House of Ambrose."

"You *helped* her?"

"Quell and Abby met up. I came with her. There wasn't much time to put something together, but when I saw the opportunity I seized it."

"What else do you know about Quell's whereabouts?"

"They met up before in some rural spot in Virginia a couple of times. Then she moved from there. Abby didn't know where."

I rear back in my seat. *Hopping from safe house to safe house.*

"Is it true? All that stuff she supposedly did at House of Marionne while you were there?"

"Stop talking." I stand, the walls closing in on me. "Leave. Just get out."

AFTER SURVIVING AN hour's lecture from the Dragunhead, my boots clack on the hard floor of the Shadow Cells. This captive I apprehended with Audubon's briefcase also lived in Virginia, according to her driver's license. She and Quell were both at the ball. Not a coincidence.

The prisoner is kept on the isolation row as a precaution. When I arrive, she's in her chair. A thin sleeping mat is on the dirt floor, same as the other cells. My jaw clenches. I *told* them to ensure she was given a raised bed at the precise height of her chair.

I clear my throat.

She doesn't even turn her head in my direction.

I open her cell, slicing through the veil to step through. The scent of dirt hits me and my heart skips a beat. I wait for my pulse to simmer down. "Someone is going to fix your bed. This is not how things are done. I apologize for that."

She rotates to face me, her blue eyes combing me from head to toe. But she still says nothing.

I dig the thin silver case out of my pocket. "Gold bars, a ton of unmarked bills, and this. Sun Dust. What did you need so much money for?" I prefer a confession, even though I know exactly who she is now that I've checked her prints. Knox Molaudi, of the West Coast Molaudis. Her family is ancient. Before the Great Sorting, before the Houses, her ancestors were known toushana-users in Misa.

She rolls away, turning her back to me again. I step into her path.

"Are you affiliated with any House?"

I need something to show the Dragunhead. I'm running out of excuses. There's no record of a Molaudi ever enrolling in a House. Living in secret for generations hardens a person. This won't be easy. I walk the length of her cell and let a few moments roll by. Her cold eyes are fixed on me, unblinking.

"How did you come by such a fancy chair?" It's decked out in tiny details only noticeable up close. There are spikes on the wheels, engraved vines along the armrests, and the tiniest gems embedded in the handles. The wheels appear to be coated in a thick layer of ruklemint, the same magical ingredient used on dagger blades to help enhancer stones melt in more easily. "Very skilled Shifting magic made this. The attention to detail is exquisite."

"Minting coins was my father's favorite hobby, so he learned a bit of Shifting that way. But I'm sure you already know that."

"It's a shame he wasn't more suited for a House."

She flinches, and I can feel her roiling anger. Maybe she'll talk now. But she meets my eyes for the first time, and my heart tightens. Then she stares right at my chest. A probing coldness scrapes across my ribs, and I grab my blade.

"What are you doing?"

"Just looking." Her head cocks. "And what I'm seeing is *very* interesting."

I hold the dagger at her throat. "You're connected with a network of illegal safe houses that harbor crimin—"

"*Refugees.*"

"*Most* of whom have toushana—"

"Which they're *forbidden* to use. And as you know, Mr. Wexton—yes, I know who you are. I know a bit about your family, too." She doesn't balk, despite the blade at her neck. "Magic strengthens with use. So their *not* using whatever they *could* be capable of is a moot point. Because after a time, they have no magic at all."

"It is not that simple, and you know that is unproven. Toushana in the body is a *deadly* risk. They are still a threat to the Order!"

"Am I the threat in this cell? Was I the threat in that hotel?"

I yank my blade from her neck and pace.

"It frustrates you because what I'm saying makes sense. What the brotherhood does is inhumane. Senseless violence on harmless people."

I storm up to her. "Draguns protect people from those who would harm them! Have you *seen* the history books? Darkbearers would peel the skin off bones *for fun*. Toushana insidiously infects people, giving them an appetite for power at any cost." I blink and see my father's face when Beaulah knocked his loyalty pin off his chest. The only thing she's ever done that I still agree with.

He'd become incensed for a stronger grasp of toushana. He relished the power toushana gave him over people. I don't know where his ambition began and the toxic magic warping his brain ended. He was practically dead to me before then.

"Do you know the name Quell Marionne?"

Hearing her name from my own lips brings those moments in the ballroom back to mind. Knox grabs my chest, her hands lightning fast. I try to get away, but icy tendrils dig into my skin around my ribs, hooking onto my heart. I can't move. The blue in her eyes darkens as she stares right at my center. My heart squeezes, my whole body growing colder.

"Mmm. Yes." She shoves me away with such force I stumble back. "I've seen a lot of books. But I've lived a lot of life, too. And I spent most of it protecting the people I care about. That says more about me than anything else. It seems you and I are the same that way."

"I am nothing like you."

"Your kor tells a different story. It's been split *twice*. Playful curiosity could make a person split it once, perhaps. But only desperate love would make a person do it a second time. Who do you love enough to give your kor to, Jordan?"

The world drains of color. I put more distance between us. Being reminded of my feelings for Quell, feelings *I should not have,* is like being stabbed over and over.

"I can guess."

I feel for my fire dagger, but she grabs my wrist. I try to snatch away from her, but her hold on me is a manacle. "You put on a good mask." She whispers, "*But I see you.*"

My heart lodges in my throat. I try to argue back, but no words come.

"And because I see you, I will tell you that I knew her briefly. Finding her would be a good thing." She releases me and I scramble to the door, ripping my fire dagger through the shadowy barrier. In the corridor, I try to slow my raging heart.

"Does my cooperation buy my people any mercy?" She rolls to the gate, peering through the translucent door, her stare still piercing. "It should. That's fair."

"Fair?" I manage, still breathless. "What is fairness?" I leave her there, my mind spiraling. I've tethered myself to a girl I used to love, who I now have to kill because duty demands it. Fairness isn't a thing in this world. At every step, I'm haunted by regret that I allowed myself to love her. I jab the elevator button. I take a ride up to the main floor, and I'm at my desk before I can no longer feel Knox's unnatural touch on my skin.

Quell has to be dead to me, or our history will always be a weapon. I've got to double down on our efforts to find safe houses. Gathering my notes on suspected locations, I split the pile into thirds and fire off a message to Charlie and Yani. I need them both back in, stat. We will lead three separate teams and raid these spots at the same time.

I will find you, Quell.
And when I do, you're dead.

TWENTY-FOUR

··——✷——··

Quell

Beaulah's Healer hovers over me, her yellow-gemmed bracelet dangling. She is an older woman with a stubborn bottom lip that wouldn't smile if she glued it in place. She works her magic, wiping a hand along my body, occasionally jerking her wrist or drumming her fingers.

"I assure you I'm fine," I say, unsure what exactly she's doing. But I can feel her Shifting magic moving things around inside me. "I have a session with Headmistress."

"Just another moment."

She slips a ring on her finger: a gold one without a stone, like I've seen before. "Your body temperature is a bit warm." She hooks her fingers in the air above my ribs, on the side of my body where my toushana usually slumbers. Something near my hip shifts. Shadows seep from that side of me. She catches some of them midair in a fist. Then fans the dark mist away.

"Everything feels normal now. I think that should do it. A bath would be good to cool you down. Come see me again if you have any pain. The Healer ward is in the Dysiis Wing."

"Thank you."

She leaves, and my body is a bit sore where my magic moved. But I grab my books and hustle to meet Beaulah.

I was up late, learning how Darkbearers first discovered they could bind with toushana. There were no Houses or Cotillions or Third Rites back then. But someone, somehow, figured out that if you took the blood from a person born with dark magic and used toushana on it, the toushana didn't destroy the blood. It actually healed any abnormalities in it. And if you boiled it to concentrate the magic even further, then froze it into a blade, you could plunge it into your heart to bind yourself. Third Rite was modeled after this practice. And no one gives Darkbearers credit for that. They all hate Darkbearers, but their very magic is based on Darkbearer knowledge . . .

Beaulah is waiting for me when I reach the session room. Adola is there, too, getting a talking-to.

"That's all, niece." She pats her shoulder. "One more day."

"Quell?" Adola lingers in the doorway. "I'm heading to the atrium, if you want to come?"

I hate that we've found ourselves at odds like this. But if she's determined to see the world one way, there's only so much I can do. And I'm done making excuses for wanting to understand all I can do. It's time to put myself first. "I'm actually meeting your aunt."

"Oh, sorry. Right." She shifts. "After?"

"We'll probably be here for a while, but I'll see you at Trials tonight. And tomorrow."

She gazes between us before leaving.

"So what are we working on today?" Beaulah's bin of rocks is on the top shelf. The manacles haven't been moved. I'm taking the lead, and she's prepared to follow.

"You mentioned preparing my toushana before I use it intensely. I want to understand how to do that."

"Alright."

"*And*—I want to see how intense it can get."

Beaulah steeples her hands, then cracks her knuckles. "I'm glad you met my Healer today. You do understand you may need to visit her again?"

"I've run from people my entire life. If I'm going to stop running and start living, I need to understand how safe I am in my own skin."

"Latch yourself into the manacles." She puts distance between us. "There is a reason the Order fears Darkbearers, Quell."

"I want to *feel* the power they fear."

She starts by having me summon my toushana. I call to my magic, letting it build in me slowly. Cold hums through me at an easy pace.

"Don't hold back. Enliven as *much* as you can without releasing it."

I don't breathe, letting pressure swell in my chest. Magic coats my lungs, claws up my ribs, wraps around me. The weight tugs, pulling me down. Metal digs into my wrists, and I bite down, trying to not scream.

"More."

Magic grows in me as I tighten and strain. Pain ripples through my body, then it melts into a wave, an unrelenting aching. My bones throb with an icy sensation until my arms no longer have feeling. The burning chill of magic gathering in my body scrapes my bones, scratching like the prick of a thousand needles under my skin, demanding to be released. *"Please!"*

Beaulah doesn't respond. She fumbles through her bin for something.

My temples pulse, my heart rocks, my lungs burn like they might explode.

"When I step outside and bolt the door, release. Let every particle of it flow through you. Hold back *nothing*. And when you get scared, let yourself feel the fear."

Fear. My insides quiver with nerves as a wave of memories flash through my mind: a burning room and me on a bed in the center of it, sprouting black metal from my head, staring into the face of Yagrin the first time I found out he was after me, the moment I said goodbye to my mom, and the time Jordan felt my blood turn cold. The most terrifying moments of my life and she wants me to lean into it? "Wait! What if I can't do it?"

"Remember your Cotillion. All that resilience is who you are. The darkness fears no one."

I swallow. "What if—what if my magic is too strong?"

She smiles dotingly. "Hartsboro was the first House and original

Headquarters for the Order. The Cabinet, the brotherhood, it all used to operate from here." She runs a hand along the wall on her way to the door. "These were fortified with an ingredient used to make the Sphere's casing. They should hold up." She opens the door. "*Trust* your instincts. They'll know."

The door clanks shut. My chest is still a pressure chamber, clawing for release. I count myself down and ease out a long exhale.

But air shoots out of my lungs. And my magic explodes. It feels like a hundred daggers are being pushed through my skin at once. The room swells with shadows, blackness pooling out of me. Toushana tugs at my heart. Like an ice pick lives in my chest. My lungs beg for breath, but it feels like filling my lungs again will snap me in half. The world rumbles, unloosing debris as more darkness, thicker shadows, and biting cold magic seep out of me.

Toushana licks the walls, and cracks rip through the stone from floor to ceiling. Blackness gathers around the metal bracelets holding me up, like hungry leeches. My hand is swallowed in shadow. Then the hold on my wrist buckles. And I fall, slamming my knees to the ground. I wait for the pain to ripple up my side, but it's like my toushana devours that, too. The thick bolts that held me dislodge from the wall, rotted and rusted, and clang on the ground, missing me by an inch.

I gulp down a desperate breath. The room is an abyss of an impenetrable fog. I try to stand, but my bones ache.

"Help!"

But there is no one here to hear me scream. A cough scratches my dry throat, the dusty air choking me. Toushana scrapes itself along the ceiling, where cracks are starting to appear. *No!* I hug my knees and close my eyes. This place is going to come down on top of me.

Trust your instincts.

Think. My heart slows. The magic in the air stills.

I released it. *I* control it. I drag myself up to my feet, remembering how I've drawn my magic into myself before, and fill my lungs. At first, very little happens, but I inhale deeply again.

"*Back inside*," I command it.

The mist in the air shifts, like a storm cloud parted by sun. My heart leaps. I open my palms and breathe deeply, in and out. Release-release-rest, but in reverse. The shadows stir, but then, slowly, darkness ribbons through the air, siphoning back into me. Gradually the haze in the air clears. The room is a charred mess but I can plainly see the door. I heave my limbs toward it, banging on it until Beaulah opens it.

I collapse at her feet.

It takes a while, but with Beaulah's Retentor ring and odd-looking brush, she cleans up most of the damage. She returns the room to its unaffected state, repairing the shelves and reattaching the manacles to the wall. I help, as much as I can, by sweeping up the ash on the floor.

"How did it feel?"

"Impossible. I've never felt so much magic in my body before. It felt like I was going to bring this whole place down on top of me."

"It may have, had you held it long enough."

I hug around myself, shaking a bit from the soreness I feel all over. My hands are covered in bruises; my arms and body, too. But deep in my chest a flicker of warmth like I've never felt burns. As deep and as special as magic. Pride bows my lips in a timid smile before I burst into a gleeful laugh.

"Did you prove anything to yourself?"

I can still hear the rumbling walls. "I am a force."

She pushes the restored shelf back in place. "You know, you remind me of myself when I was younger. You do what's necessary to get things done. I had an appetite only an upbringing like yours could breed. It is a powerful weapon. You are wise to use it."

I furrow my brow and stare at her quizzically. "Don't take this the wrong way, but I find it hard to believe you could possibly know about my life growing up."

She takes the broom from me and sets it aside. Then exhales. "The first time I scavenged for food, I had to drag over a log to be tall enough to reach into a dumpster." Beaulah angles her face away. "My older siblings were so malnourished their magic wasn't answering. Six of us, and only two still use magic. I wasn't willing to risk that. So I gorged myself on whatever I could find. Richard was the only one who ate the scraps I found." She turns her back to me. "I remember being most worried that people would smell the trash on me. We didn't have running water. This grand house, and we didn't even have that. So I'd bathe in the water from the water gardens. Just grateful I could scrub myself until my skin was red." She gazes off in the distance. "No one could know our secret. That the first House in the Order had lost all its wealth, thanks to my squandering mother. We always had an excuse to miss out on parties. And we never hosted any. Débutants were kept to very small classes in one wing of the House. They were given the little food we did have to keep up appearances. We had no staff and only two maezres, citing the excuse that we had very selective standards."

She breathes a laugh. "I grew to not mind the smell because it meant I would sleep on a full stomach. My siblings only whined and complained. When one of my sisters starved to death, my father died of a heart attack. The shock killed him, I think. I told my mother I would tell the papers she murdered both of them. Unless she made me heir. I never saw her again. I found a whole closet of frozen meals in my mother's suite. She'd been eating *just fine* all those years."

I gasp.

"I learned very young that there are those who have power because it is given to them, and others because they take it."

"What happened to the rest of your family?"

"I raised my siblings like they were my own. With everything in my hands, I set out to make this House be what it should again. All they had to do was toughen up, play their part, do their duty. And *stop crying* about it. Some didn't agree with my methods and left. One tried to usurp me. Adola's mother. Stupid girl. But her daughter will be better than she ever was." She unstraps the manacles, eyeing the time. "I rebuilt our name. Now, forgive me. I've gone on for too long."

I haven't moved. Beaulah pulls nervously at her sleeves, and I don't know what to say. She meets my eyes, and beneath their sternness is a glimmer of uncertainty, worried she's shared too much. I realize now that when I showed up at Chateau Soleil, all I really wanted was someone to look at me and *see* me and for that to be okay. I step closer to her. "You must have lived those years terrified. I'm so sorry."

"The path to breakthrough is paved in fear. Don't be sorry. I'm certainly not."

It's strange to think how much Beaulah and I have in common. To see how, to an extent, her rougher edges make sense. No one understands what growing up cost her.

"Did you ever do things that you worried were wrong?"

"Sometimes people think they know more than they do. And talk too much. Their ignorance can get in the way. You can't hesitate to cut people out of your circle, Quell." She tidies my clothes. "Look around. I regret nothing." She studies my purpled arms. "We have to soak you first next time."

"Thank you for showing me all this."

"It's refreshing to welcome another into my circle. Something tells me you won't disappoint." She pinches my arm.

"Also, thank you for helping me with my magic."

"It is an honor to watch your talents flourish, Quell. You may find that soon those talents are needed." She raises a brow.

"The Sphere, you mean."

"If it bleeds out, all that power you have will be gone."

"That can't happen," I say.

"I agree. But we will save that plotting for another day. Get some rest. Give my Healer a visit ASAP. We have much to do together."

I leave feeling a lot of things, but the strongest one—that thrums in my veins and puts a bounce in my step—is pride. I've never felt more powerful in my entire life.

TWENTY-FIVE

＊

Nore

Nore fiddled with the earrings beneath her curtain of hair. It'd been days yet she was no closer to figuring out where her mother would keep the key to the family vault. Darragh had already written to check in. Nore didn't have any updates, so she hadn't responded, which left her feeling like a fish was wriggling in her insides at all times. She had one idea of a place to look, but getting away from her lessons with Maezre Bessie Tutom was proving difficult. Nore watched the clock as Maezre Tutom stewed over a text, waiting for her to answer a question she'd already forgotten.

"Well? Are you going to answer?" She tapped her foot. They'd been at this for hours, memorizing House history and a month's worth of Latin vocabulary she'd missed. "Let's switch gears." Maezre Tutom slapped the book closed and popped open a box of rings. "Get up, let's get some blood flowing." She slipped on a green one and dangled her hand to grip Nore's shoulder.

Nore sighed. The burn of the maezre's magic seared her shoulder. Her arm shuddered in pain, and the whole thing went numb from shoulder to wrist. She winced.

"It's just been a while since you've tried."

"Not to be disrespectful, Maezre, but according to *Cultivating Finesse*, the art of Cultivating works best when amplifying magic that is already there. As you know, there is no Audior magic in me to amplify. That ring can glow all it wants; it won't help. I don't have magic. And I'm fine with that."

Maezre Tutom turned her to look her right in the eye. "You will not talk that way, young lady. Do you hear me?" She slipped on a different ring. In moments Nore's shoulder was burning again and her arm was numb.

This must be what lab rats feel like, Nore thought.

They went on for an hour or more, before Nore's stomach rumbled so loudly that it made a convincing appeal for a lunch break.

"It's been quite some time since I've tutored you, but your memory is keen. Your mother told me your sabbatical went well and you'd come back sharper."

"She said that?"

"She did. Still, we are quite behind." Maezre Tutom patted a stack of books she still wanted to get through. "Heirs shouldn't need more than one Season to debut; it makes a House look weak. Adola Perl will be finishing at the start of next Season. Drew Oralia finished in a single Season. The Marionne girl, if the rumors are true, finished in mere weeks. How much sharper should your intellect be, *Ambrose*? It's already been *years*, multiple Seasons. You would disgrace yourself, this House, further?"

Nore groaned.

"*Intellectus* . . ." She gestured for Nore to finish.

"*Secat acutissimum.*" Her stomach churned again, as if on cue.

The maezre sighed. Then she tapped Nore on the head, pressing the diadem—that kept slipping—into her scalp. "We really should glue that down."

"You're not putting glue on my hair. That is where I draw the line."

Tutom held her arms open, but Nore wasn't quite sure what to make of the gesture. Her own mother didn't hug her. She tipped forward on her toes, folding at the waist ever so slightly, and her maezre did the rest. The burly woman squeezed her tight and patted her cheek.

"We're going to get you sorted. Never met an Ambrose I couldn't Cultivate. You won't be the first." When the maezre let herself out, Nore dashed out of the cottage on her heels. When she entered the courtyard, the ancestors rose to meet her. A shadow blew close, grazing her skin, and it felt like fingertips of ice.

"Away!" She kept her gaze to the ground and picked up to a run. When she crossed the threshold of the estate and left the ancestors behind, she exhaled. She'd stolen Sun Dust once from her mother's desk, where the maid had set a vial while she cleaned the vault. The woman at least knew where the vault was. Maybe she'd seen the key? It was a risk. But the maid doted on Nore, and she hadn't seen in her *so long*. And if Nore approached it casually enough, she'd never suspect a thing.

Nore moved through the corridors, pretending not to hear the whispers or see the scornful stares of her peers. She held her head perfectly level, but she thought she might vomit the whole time. Dlaminaugh was a place where you earned everything, including your bed. So she was *born* hated. She followed the main stair to the private wing. At one point she heard Priest Kimper's booming voice and walked faster. The last thing she needed was to be chastised about skipping her prayers to the Wielder. When she reached the landing, she steadied herself on the rail and checked her diadem. Once she'd caught her breath, she smoothed her clothes and roved the halls for one of the family's maids. When she spotted one coming out of her brother's room, she rushed up to her. Maura's mouth fell open. She wiped her hands. "Is that really little Emilie?"

Nore blushed. She couldn't help it.

"Well, I said you'd never show your face here again, and I have been made a liar." She pulled Nore over, spinning her around. "Let me get a look at you, girlie."

She gushed and Nore let her. *It is nice to be missed by someone*, she supposed. Maura doted on her and went on about all she had missed: the passing of Priest Brosm, the maezres who had resigned for unknown reasons, and all the balls, which were intellectual competitions in their House; Ellery's drama with suitors; and her mother's increasing aloofness.

Maura spoke a million miles a minute. People like that dizzied Nore. When Maura paused for a breath, she jumped in. "I have a question, Maura."

"Go on."

"Where would I store something very personal and valuable?"

"The family vault." She held out her hand. "Did you have something you need me to pass along to your mother?"

"No, I was actually thinking I'd stick it in there myself. Could you remind me where Mother keeps her key? She told me, but I forgot." Nore hooked her hands behind her back, digging a nail into her palm.

Maura closed her lips and tapped them. And after several moments, she finally said, "I'm sorry, little Emilie, I cannot betray your mother's trust like that."

"So you know and you're just *not* going to tell me?" Nore's irritation rose.

Maura hesitated. "I should be getting back."

"Maura."

But the maid kept walking.

"Maura!" She didn't turn around. Nore really only had one ally here. She could search her mother's bedroom, maybe, but she'd have to sneak in there after lunch, during her lab hours. Her stomach rumbled again, and this time it wouldn't take no for an answer. She was late to meet Ell. She wasn't facing her mother at lunch alone. Someone had to run interference.

When she crossed the bridge into the Hall of Discovery, she eyed the trick wall where the family vault hid. She *tsked*, no closer to knowing how to get inside. Her brother appeared, setting a stack of crates against the wall beside several others, before wiping his hands on his pants.

"Ready for lunch?" he asked.

"Are all brothers gross? Or is it just you?"

He flipped his hair, running his fingers through it. "The girls don't seem to mind."

"Now I've lost my appetite. Thanks."

The parlor where their mother ate was only for family and house staff. She and her brother entered, and all but the final course had been served. She could feel her mother's eyes following her. On the way to her chair, she grabbed a copy of *Debs Daily* to busy her hands. Maybe she could try prying for information on the key with her mother.

"Good afternoon," Nore said to no one in particular. If she was going to pry, she had to at least pretend to be polite. Ellery pulled out her chair. She thanked him and sat down. She was trying to think of a conversation topic to lead with, when the front-page headline of the paper knocked her heart into her ribs.

DARRAGH MARIONNE, HEADMISTRESS AT HOUSE OF MARIONNE, TO ANSWER FOR ALLEGED CRIMES

Nore's eyes raced across the article.

"Nore? You've gone pale."

It took her a moment to realize her brother was talking to her.

"I'm fine." She folded the paper and shoved it under the table. If Darragh Marionne burned, Nore was stuck with toushana. She was stuck attached to this Order forever. She had to write to her and soon. A server set a creamy coffee in front of her, and she glared at the cup. She had to pull it together or she would be trapped in this prison—and eventually she'd be dead. Nore cleared her throat and forced herself to look around the table and greet each person. Beside her brother were several of her distant cousins, who apparently were visiting from Alaska. Mother sat at the head of the table all by herself.

"Mother," Nore said, taking a sip of coffee, trying to blink away an image of Darragh Marionne on fire. "How was your morning?"

Her mother's brows dipped. Nore realized her hair was behind her shoulders, exposing her earrings. She fixed it and took another sip. "What about you, Ell?"

"All fine. I'll be out at the stables today to help with the shoveling."

"There are people who take care of that," one cousin asserted.

"Yes, and today I'm one of them."

"Mother, when the ancestors are buried in the courtyard and they're stripped of their few material possessions, do those things go in the family vault? Or are they disposed of?" Nore may as well go for the kill.

"What do you think?" her mother said, working her teaspoon back and forth in her cup. It was a trick question to engage her in conversation: Nore knew the answer.

"The ancestors believe that the material worth of a thing is not its monetary value but what it represents. And on that spectrum, intellect is something that cannot be bartered. Because it is wholly possessed, intellect will always have more merit than mere possessions. So, I think they burn them."

Her mother let the silence stretch, but Nore didn't miss the gleam of satisfaction in Ellery's eyes. Even her cousin leaned forward at the table to get the full sight of her.

"You happen to be correct," her mother conceded. "Though on occasion a special item might make it into the family vault. Speaking of which—Ellery, I saw the stuff you left for me today in the Hall."

Nore leaned over in her chair. "Has she ever let you put those crates inside the vault yourself?"

"Whispering at a table is poor manners, or did you miss that day of etiquette?" Her mother shoved a bite in her mouth. "I'm very sorry, cousins. Forgive their manners."

Her eldest cousin cleared his throat.

In her most level voice, Nore said, "I'd love to see the vault someday."

Ellery stared, head cocked.

"You reach above your station quite boldly this morning, Nore."

Nore bit down the sassy retort that came to mind. She couldn't back down now. Not when her mother was talking. "I am curious. And curiosity is the seed of intellect. You should be pleased."

To that, her mother only took another sip, which felt a bit like a win.

"I could go see it on my own if you're too busy. I'm sure Ellery could assist, as long as you don't mind giving him the key."

Her mother chewed silently for a long time before saying, "*Claves secretum reginarum.*"

The key's secret is the queen's, or the secret keys are the queens, or something like that.

"I *am* the key, child. There is no getting into the vault without me. That access is blood-granted."

"So then, you'll take me?" Nore pressed.

Ellery's spoon clattered on his plate. He silently pleaded with her to stop this before the whole meal imploded. Nore's mother dabbed the sides of her mouth with a napkin, sighing through her nostrils.

"What is the first consideration when augmenting the density of magic in a person?"

"Knowing their precise bone density before *and after* Binding." Nore sat straighter.

"And what would you say was the most impactful development in the postmodernist era of magical innovation?"

"Well, it depends on whether you're examining that through a Sfentian or Dysiian lens. The latter is probably medicinal uses of toushana. And the former is unarguably the evolution of anointing, allowing a more inclusive Order membership. Not everyone wants to don a crown."

Her mother smiled cheekily. "And I suppose you also know the elemental composition of each enhancer, along with its prerequisites."

"I do. Should I list them for you?"

"Did you also know that coming in here *late,* and dressed so ostentatiously, is a flagrant show of disrespect for the station you *presume* to hold?" Her mother glared, and something in Nore snapped.

"I answer your condescending questions and you attack my accessories?" She was *done* tiptoeing around this woman. She pulled her hair back and wound it into a messy bun. She turned her head, touching her earrings, making sure everyone saw them. Her brother watched, his spoon frozen on the way to his mouth.

"I'm looking for a necklace to match." She sipped her drink. "If anyone has any jeweler recommendations, do let me know."

"*Nore,*" her brother muttered.

She leaned across the table. "You know, my first plan was to burn your eyes out of their sockets with Sun Dust, but my brother talked me out of it."

"And your second plan?" her mother asked, unfazed. "The real reason you're at my table."

"For now, it's to enjoy wearing my earrings."

Her mother rose from the table. "Ellery, don't delay."

"Where are you going?" Nore muttered. "I need your help."

"I'm proposing to Elena Hargrove today."

"You're *what?*"

A smile curled her mother's lips.

"You find her boring and—how did you put it? *An intellectual dud.* You don't even like the way she smells!"

"It keeps the peace."

Nore stood so suddenly that her cousins at the end of the table jumped. She glared right at her mother. No one ever told Isla Ambrose the truth. And that was part of the problem.

"You're a terrible person, Mother."

Her mother froze.

"You ruin everyone around you. Especially those who should be closest to you."

Her cousins excused themselves from the table. Her mother did not move or blink. Nore's heart pounded in her chest. *There.* She'd told her mother what she really thought of her. What *everyone* probably thought of her.

"Thank you, dear, for your perceptive assessment of my maternal duties. We can only hope to the Sovereign that, one day, your intellect will match your reckless mouth." Her mother was about to say more when someone entered and whispered something in her ear. She held her chest. Her mouth thinned. "If you'll excuse me." She tossed her napkin on the table. "Oh, and one more thing. You will be at the ball we are hosting this weekend."

"I will not!"

"You will. Your brother will be announcing his engagement, and you will not be an embarrassment."

Anger burned in her chest. The audacity of her mother to take away her freedom *and* her brother's, when he deserved nothing but the best.

Her mother turned to leave.

"On your list of ways to ruin others' lives, could you add finding a way to get rid of this t—"

"Mind your tongue."

The servers froze.

Nore's mouth snapped shut. Once her mother was gone, she turned to Ellery, who rubbed circles into his temples.

"Letting you kill her would have probably been easier to watch, honestly." He sighed and pulled out her chair, then kissed her forehead and turned to go. But she grabbed his wrist.

"The night of the ball, can you change me?" she whispered in his ear.

"If this is about the vault, Mother's the key—which means the vault is not going to open unless it thinks you're her. She said *blood-granted*. That means DNA. Anatomer magic doesn't alter DNA."

There were other ways to get her DNA. She patted her pockets, and then tried to remember where Maezre Tutom said she could find more enhancer stones and elixir ingredients. "Understood. I think I still have a plan."

"What are you imagining? You don't have—" He stopped himself.

"Don't need it. Never have." She winked.

"Please don't do anything dangerous." He squeezed her shoulders before leaving.

She bit into her knuckle. It wasn't a perfect plan. But it was a start.

TWENTY-SIX

❋

Jordan

Nothing about this raid feels right.

The territory's border town is more suburban than rural, with few trees. Very little cover. The houses crowded onto the narrow street have decorated porches offering seasonal greetings. Welcoming visitors. An uneasiness slithers up my spine.

"You're sure this is the place?" I ask Kieran. He shows me the file on the suspected safe house once more. I check the notes again. About a year ago, Knox visited with someone in a park near here who returned to this house. Kieran filed the report. And this morning, Audubon was spotted in that same park.

Quell, are you in there?

"Yes." Kieran huddles with me behind a large truck in the driveway. "Blue siding and a wraparound porch."

I scan the perimeter. One of our flock, disguised in overalls, leans over the open hood of a truck down the block. Another is playing the concerned neighbor and repairing a lawn mower. A few others have slipped inside cars parked on the street.

"I don't like this," I say to Kieran. "You?"

"It does seem a little unusual."

I squeeze the side button of my phone to get a message to the team. "Give me a clear perimeter every thirty degrees. And keep your eyes on the entry and exit points."

Shadows shift in the glimmer of the fading night sky as my men adjust the cordon.

"You're with me," I tell Kieran as we slip around the side of the house. "Time?"

"Sunrise. Fifty-eight minutes."

With a neighborhood this populated, this raid could get messy *fast*. Neighbors know each other. And there are a bunch of us. An Unmarked person cannot look upon magic and live. The protocol is rigid.

"We have to be out of here by sunrise. We can't risk daylight in a place like this."

Even in the early-morning light, I can tell Kieran's color has faded.

I squeeze his shoulder. "It's going to be fine."

"My last two raids ended badly. Public burnings." He meets my eyes, and a scared little boy looks back at me.

"You'll need to cloak to get inside. Anything else could set off alarms."

"Alarms, right."

I grab his wrist. "If you see anyone who fits the description of Quell Marionne, notify me before you take your next breath."

He nods.

"Time?"

"Fifty-two until sunrise."

"Meet you around back. I'm going in."

Kieran darts off, and I summon the deathly cold to my fingertips. I fold into it until every part of me shifts into a dark mist. Up through the air, past the windows, I rise, slipping between the metal grates of the air shaft beneath the dormers. I hold still as the world comes back in focus. The attic is warm compared to the lingering chill from my cloak.

I hurry down the attic stairs and ease the door to the second floor open. The hallway is silent. As I move down it, counting the rooms, faint snores slow my steps. There are three bedrooms and two bathrooms. I creep down the stairs to the first floor. But when I reach the living room, I freeze. It's filled with coordinated furniture and framed family portraits.

I study the smiling faces, and my pulse picks up. In the kitchen there's a full sink of dishes. The pantry is sparsely filled, not stocked full. I peek in a few closets and it's full of storage bins. No grab bags. The hair on my neck rises.

People in safe houses don't live like this. Unless . . . it's a new cover?

I signal for Kieran. He slips through the seams of the back door.

"Are you absolutely sure this is the right place?"

"I saw him in that park, just down the road, with my own eyes. This is the only suspected safe house for hundreds of miles. Why else would he have been near here?"

I quiet him, listening for any indication that we've been too loud.

Safe houses are like a crime scene without fingerprints. They are shells of a home, easily wiped clean. And never personalized. I think of Knox, what she said about people in safe houses losing their ability to touch dark magic because they don't use it. How that fact technically opens the argument that they're no longer a threat. It unsteadies me.

"Sir, are you alright?"

"I'm fine. We need hard evidence that they are Marked."

Kieran follows me up the stairs; the glow of night-lights dot down the hall. I summon the cold, ready with thrashing shadows in one hand, just in case. Kieran does the same. We approach one of the bedroom doors, and I cup the knob gently.

Behind me, a child's shrill cry scratches my ears.

I turn. Kieran's as pale as a ghost, a child, who is no taller than my waist, standing in the middle of the hall gaping at the darkness in our fists. They stare up at us with red-rimmed eyes and a sleep-tousled head of hair, their little features scrunching in curiosity. They point at the shadows before shoving a thumb in their mouth. Realizing we've been seen by a *child* feels like a knife sticking me in the ribs. Voices stir beyond the door nearest me.

"Back away slowly," I say.

But the moment Kieran moves, the child wails again. The knob in my hand twists, but it is not my own doing. I shove Kieran forward, swing open the door to a nearby closet, and conceal ourselves inside.

"Baby boy, oh, it's okay," a sweet voice hums in the hall. I watch through the slightly parted door. The child's eyes are fixated on the closet door that we disappeared behind.

He points in our direction.

My heart stops.

"Back to bed, sweet one." The mother walks away, toward the room at the far end of the hall.

"The notes don't mention any kids!"

"I watched the house for days!" Kieran drains of color. "Never saw one."

"Are you *sure* these are Marked people?" I shake him by the collar.

"I saw a woman who . . ." His brows smoosh. "Come to think of it, she doesn't look anything like her. But I saw a woman use toushana to get through a locked gate at the park. I followed her home, *here*. Maybe they moved?"

I rest my head back on the wall for a moment to stifle the urge to strangle him. Perhaps I took his tip about Audubon in haste, trusting he'd done his damned job. If he had, he'd have casually talked to neighbors. Asked questions. Visited their friends. Created a rock-solid information loop so this does not happen. We are *not* reckless killers.

"I'm not convinced these people are magical," I say. "And *if they aren't,* you just condemned them to die."

His eyes widen with something heavier than regret: fear.

"Stay here." There is one clear way to tell. I cloak and move through the second floor as a shadow, looking for the mother. I find her tucking the child in bed. The room darkens as I slip inside. She stiffens, her brow furrowed in confusion, gaze darting to the window. Then in my general direction.

"Honey!" she shouts.

A man rushes in. "What is it?"

"I don't know. I just feel . . . there's something."

I move closer, letting the edges of my shadow graze her arm.

"Call the police," she screeches. "Something isn't right. Someone is here. I—"

"Calm down—"

She hands him the child and dashes out. I follow her before rejoining Kieran in the closet.

"They're calling the police." I can't believe the words I'm saying. "This isn't a safe house. These people are not magical. Your lead is wrong."

"Dear," the husband chimes, "he was just scared. He's back in bed now." Their bedroom door creaks open, then clicks closed. Their stirrings settle and the house is again silent.

"The child saw our faces," Kieran whispers, his expression scrunched in horror at what must come next. "And the parents felt your cloak." He releases a shaky breath, and it takes me back to the nightmare of cleaning up my first raid gone wrong, when I was still a deb at Hartsboro. We set the house on fire. And there were actual toushana-users inside. I couldn't eat for a week.

"I can do it, sir," he whispers, but he can't even look at me. It reminds me of Yagrin. Our work *should* make us sick to our stomach. Taking lives should never be easy. But this . . . this is an acute kind of discomfort. It's not just Kieran. I feel sick, too. But he's not wearing a gleaming red pendant.

"You will do nothing else but leave. I can't let you mess this up, too." I open the closet door wider. "Take a day. I'll file the report. After that, you'll be reassigned to desk duty for a while, until you're able to sleep again."

He nods, forlorn. I squeeze my phone. "Abandon target. We've been compromised. Head back. I'll finish up here."

From the second-floor landing I can see shadows shifting past the windows as my men depart. I sit on the top stair, waiting for my hands to stop shaking, and Knox's words tear at my conscience. *We are not inhumane. We are not senseless killers.* I cannot believe I'm allowing her treasonous accusations to still ring in my head.

There are principles to uphold for a reason. The sun is more beautiful after a season of rain. Forests grow back stronger after a burn. How can the Order be what it was created to be if no one will do the despicable things needed to keep its existence secret until it's safe to be out in the open? If the Dragunhead were here, he would not balk at what's required. I stiffen my chin, sickness thickening in my insides.

The child is so young. He'll forget my face.

But the mother saw my cloak. She felt my touch.

She only saw shadows.

Protocol is rigid. It has to be.

I grab a fistful of carpet, just to do something with the frustration burning its way through me. I blow out a breath and force myself to stand. The soft blues of morning glow outside, streaming through the windows. I stand there for what feels like an eternity before entering the child's room. He's fast asleep, tucked under covers, his little hand dangling off the edge of the bed. I move closer to him, my heart ramming my ribs, as I draw the cold blackness to my fingertips. My foot nudges a stuffed bunny that's fallen out of his crib. I stare at it. The child's chest rises and falls in a steady rhythm. And I envy him. *What I wouldn't give to sleep like that.* The admission burns my cheeks.

Protocol.

My heart ticks faster.

I stand there until the room has noticeably brightened. A sharp heaviness like I've never felt twists inside my chest, like a broken bridge with jagged edges trying to weld itself together.

We are not inhumane.

I am not inhumane.

Protocol.

I feel for magic and tighten my fist.

TWENTY-SEVEN

·· ———✳——— ··

Jordan

"I *need* a timeline!" The Dragunhead tosses a copy of *Debs Daily* at me. A photo of his unmasked face is on the front, under the headline: *Has the Dragunhead Lost His Touch?* "When will you find the Sphere?"

"I'm working on it, sir, with my brother." I shift in my seat. He shakes a folder at me and my chin hits my chest.

"This report includes details of a raid you were on recently. *Raiding* is not what I told you to do, Jordan."

Shame over the failed raid, and what I did two nights ago, has burrowed a hole in my chest. I don't think it'll ever go away. I don't deserve to be Dragunheart.

"And you didn't come in at all yesterday, Maei says?"

"I . . . was sick. The raid took a lot out of me."

He throws the file on the desk. "Yes, it sounds like it was a hot mess."

I glare at the folder, remembering how I stayed up most of the day yesterday, furiously filling it in with all kinds of details.

"Look at me, son."

I can't look at anything but my pendant.

"Alright." He draws in a long breath and lets out an even longer one. Then he closes the door to his office. "What is it? Come on, now. You're the Heart. I'm the Head." He sits on the edge of his desk, beckoning me to meet his eyes. "Out with it."

I'm silent for a long time. There are some things I can't ever say aloud. "Sir, have you ever . . . On these raids, there are things we must do, but it doesn't feel right sometimes, if I can be honest." My grip on my seat tightens.

"You can always be honest with me. And I will always give it to you straight."

The commissioning ceremony when I was awarded my Dragun coin comes to mind. Then the day I debuted, by plunging my dagger into my chest. And when I accepted my sixth virtue pin, completing the set. And the moment the Dragunhead hung this stone from my neck.

"How do you know for sure the brotherhood is making a difference?"

He traces the lines of his face before pouring me a drink.

"Like, I've wondered about mementaurs. Maybe we could—"

He holds up a hand. "For every memory they destroy, they lose one of their own. Is that right? Is it fair? There's a reason things are done the way they're done." He slides the glass I didn't take toward me anyway. "Drink up."

The brown liquid burns my chest. But my disgrace burns hotter.

"Jordan, there is no easy answer for what you're asking. Sometimes we just have to dig deep into our hearts, rely on what we know, and trust that." He leans back in his chair.

My grip tremors on the glass. *That's what I did. At that house. I swear, that's what I did. And everything feels different now.*

"Take the rest of the morning," he says. "Try to get some rest. You look like you need it. Then back at it."

"Thank you, sir." I gulp down the well of emotions and gaze at the folded paper again, noticing the date. "It's the final day of Trials at House Perl."

"Ah, your aunt—"

"My cousin, Adola. I have to be there. I'm sorry, sir, I'll be back first thing tomorrow."

He doesn't push back. Not much good it would do him. *I'm going.*

Regardless of how I'm feeling, I'm not missing the chance to be there for Adola. When I return to my workspace, I have a dozen missed messages from my aunt. Yani skips by then, plops herself on my desk, polishing her purple-studded silver diadem. She hands me a stack of scribbled-on papers.

"First six places on my list. Not one of them has heard of that girl."

"Have you heard from Charlie? How's his list going?"

"No, actually. He's been hard to reach. Busy with Mother, probably."

"Of course."

"My team and I are going to check out this last location tonight." Her fingers play on my shoulder, then drop to the dip in my shirt. "What do I get if I'm the one who finds the girl?"

"Yani, please." I remove her hand and stand, putting distance between us. "Keep me posted on what you find tonight. I'll be at Hartsboro." I leave her there, moving to exit the room.

"You're not as fun as you used to be," she says to my back. "You've changed."

Tell me about it.

TWENTY-EIGHT

Quell

Hartsboro swarms with people. I tuck my purpled fingers in the pockets of my dress; pain pulses in my bones, up through my hands, radiating into my arms. I hurry through the crowd to find Beaulah's Healer. I intend to try my magic again. If that's what I could do the first time I pushed my magic, how much more could I do with practice? But I can't do anything with this much pain. On the door is a note: IN THE NORTH WING ALL DAY.

Adola's map of the grounds takes me past large windows; outside, oversized tents are being erected on the grass. A large tapestry woven with Adola's face hangs in the Sphere room. The whole estate buzzing with anticipation; I can't imagine how she must be feeling. There is no sign of her anywhere. Across the estate the entire wing of student and maezre dorms are roped off with caution tape.

"Hello?" I'm listening for a heartbeat or footsteps when a door flies open and Beaulah's Healer comes storming out.

"The whole wing has to be fumigated *again*." She huffs. "Miss Marionne?"

"I'm sorry to bother you." I hold up my hands.

She straightens her glasses. "Anywhere else?"

"I don't think so."

She sighs.

"If it's a bad time—"

"No, come along." She leads me into one of the rooms and has me sit down and hold out my hands. Still stewing, she examines them on both sides before pulling threads of magic between her fingers and massaging them along my skin. It takes several tries; she seems to grow only more frustrated, muttering under her breath. But when she finishes, the pain has subsided, and the bruises appear to be lessening.

"On the mend." She looks over my hands again. "Sorry for being so short with you. Headmistress's pets. One of them bit one of my staff and it took a whole week to heal their arm."

"Thanks, I'm sure you're busy," I flex my hands as she tidies up before opening the door for us to exit.

"It's *all* the people! We never get a break, on or off Season. Events, parties—the overflow's spilled into my own private quarters!" She closes and locks the door behind her. "And more are coming in today. I was hoping the wing was finally ready to be opened up for the influx. It's been closed for months with an infestation of fleas, as if their biting wasn't enough. Anyway, please find me again, if needed."

"Thank you." I curtsy and am about to head back toward the Instruction Wing when her words stop me dead in my tracks.

"Wait, you said the north wing has been closed?"

"Yes, for months."

But Charlie . . . He said he stays in the north wing. *He was sick in bed all day on the day my mother left a few weeks ago.* "Isn't Charlie's room in here somewhere?"

"Charlie Huston? He rooms in the guesthouse. Have a good afternoon." She hurries off.

I nod, unable to find words, and leave. I'm hurrying toward my room when I spot Della watching me. She scurries off before I can catch her. *Charlie is staying in the guesthouse?* He said he couldn't tell my mother goodbye. But he was really in the same house with her the whole time? Charlie lied to me.

And I want to know why.

By afternoon, the bruises on my hands have faded and I've managed to flag a few pages in my Darkbearer books that describe magic I'd like to try. A sharp knock pulls me from my studying. I'm grabbing for the knob when I hear Charlie's voice on the other side of the door.

I freeze.

"You said she was here," he grumbles.

"She must still be out on the grounds," Della says. "Sometimes she visits the gardens."

"Find her and bring her to me."

They leave and I can't breathe.

Exhausted from lessons and the anxiety of the afternoon, I retreat to the bathroom. I turn the spigot until my bathwater is as cold as it can be and I step inside. I hug my knees to my chest and slip my head underwater to quiet everything until I can't hold my breath anymore. I should sneak back to the guesthouse and take a more thorough look around. But there are people all over the grounds. Outside my window, I can hear the festivities ramping up.

This party will be on the cover of *Debs Daily* tomorrow. And not with the headline Beaulah thinks. Adola failing is going to make a mess of this tonight. I wish there was a way I could help her. If she'd even accept it.

Then it hits me.

Everyone will be hyper focused on Adola and celebrating afterward. If I want to get another look at that guesthouse, my best chance is *tonight.*

The door to my bedroom opens suddenly. *Charlie!* But before I can move, Jordan's voice floats into the bathroom.

"Thank you," he says. "I can handle it from here."

"I'll be outside the door should you need anything, sir."

I clamp my mouth shut and slip out of the tub, trying my hardest to not slosh the water. The door closes and something heavy hits the floor. Wrapped in a robe, I peek into the bedroom through the bathroom doors, which, thankfully, are only slightly ajar. And there he is, standing in my—*his*—room!

He pulls a tux out of his bag and lays it across my bed. My mind races. All my things are neatly put away, thanks to Della. The only sign someone has been here is a glass of water on the bedside, some notes in a drawer, and a wardrobe full of dresses. He takes off his coat. Then he pulls his shirt off over his head. I'm dripping wet on the marble floor. My heart is in my throat.

I glance back at the balcony doors, torn on which would be worse: to have Jordan catch me in this bathroom or to have random houseguests see me climbing down the side of the estate, basically naked. Panic takes flight in my chest.

Jordan stops, holding his own chest.

His expression sharpens with concentration.

The trace.

My grip on the door tightens, and I take a deliberate, long breath. My pulse slows. He doesn't move for several moments before unbuckling his belt, tossing it aside, and grabbing a fresh towel from the folded stack beside the bed. He rolls his neck, the hard lines of his body flexing. I look away. He is perfect in every way and it pricks me like a needle. A reminder that he fits in this world in a way that I never will.

My toushana purrs awake. The more I stare at him half dressed, the angrier I become. I could take him by surprise right now, drown him in shadows until I choke the life out of him. I could hurt him before he hurts me. *Trust your instincts.* Beaulah's words resound in my head. My toushana roils, and cold fills my bones when Jordan wanders to the bedside table and finds my half-empty glass. He grimaces, then checks the wardrobe, before marching toward the door.

"Sir?" He disappears down the hall, and I take the chance to dart into the bedroom and grab clothes. Their voices are muffled, but I perk up my ears as I slip on underclothes and throw a silk dress over my head.

"Is there someone staying in my room?"

His crisp tuxedo shirt and fine tailored jacket both lie across my bed. A red gem more brilliant than any I've ever seen hangs from a silver chain.

"I know the Headmistress is filled to the brim with guests," Jordan goes on. "Have they spilled into the House?"

I try to listen but their conversation quiets. The pendant is the shape of a heart, smooth and shiny. *How endearing.* A heart pendant for a man without one. He must be so proud. I could spit. And I consider doing so when I spot a colorful something peeking out from beneath his suit. I slide the items over and find a half-eaten bag of candy. Time seems to still. I take a green one, and a wave of emotion wells up in me as I remember. A heaviness settles in my chest. Somehow my cheeks are wet. I swipe beneath my eyes, wishing I could claw away the memories.

I dash back toward the bathroom, but then I think better of it and hide behind the trick bookcase instead. I pull it closed just as he returns. Through the peepholes I see him; the green candy is still crushed in my fist. His brow is furrowed and his hand grazes his chest. *How can he still do this to me?* I crush the candy and watch him.

He studies the opened bag with an etch between his brows.

I don't move.

Knock. Knock. "Mr. Wexton, I've found you a room."

He glances around once more before opening the door.

"The starting horn will blow in a matter of minutes," the attendant says.

"I'm going to need another favor." Jordan's jaw hardens as they depart.

I sag against the wall. *No distractions. Focus on what's important. What do I want?* I hustle down the hidden corridors for the hunting grounds. Next stop: the guesthouse.

TWENTY-NINE

———✳———

Jordan

The minute I reach the doors of the cigar lounge, I smell dirt.

Dirt in the air. Dirt all over my clothes. Dirt on the framed portraits and on the rows of diadems and masks in glass cases. I steady myself against a wall, fending off curious gazes of guests entering the lounge as I clip my last cuff link in place.

There is no dirt in here. There is no dirt anywhere.

The last time I listened to my instincts—as the Dragunhead advised—and relied and trusted on what I knew, I left here as Ward four years ago, and I never regretted it. But I never made a stand. Even now, Beaulah doesn't know what I think about her. Sometimes the truth feels safer as a secret. I blow out a long breath before checking my phone for messages, but there are none. The final warning horn for Trials blew ten minutes ago. My hands are slick when I grab the door handle. I exhale sharply once more before stepping inside.

Heads turn in my direction, a few at a time, until the entire room stands, applauding me. My gut twists. I am proud of all I've accomplished but embarrassed it had anything to do with this place. My thoughts drift to the raid two nights ago. Beaulah parts the crowd. She halts, taking all of me in, then opens her arms for me to come to her. My feet are leaden. *And there is that dirt smell again.* I approach her, one begrudging step at a time.

"You look well, dear nephew." She holds up my arm to the crowd, and the applause roars louder. "*My* nephew! The Dragunheart."

My skin burns from all the stares. Beaulah bares a cheek for me to kiss. I oblige even though it sickens me. I'm just one of her prize show dogs and it sets my teeth on edge. She touches the heart pendant against my chest, tracing its engraving.

"It's simply mesmerizing."

I move my shoulder, taking the lavaliere away from her touch.

She startles. I've never upset her on purpose. I've never done anything but avoid her. The one time I did disobey her, I was thirteen, and she made me sleep in the hunting ground for three nights without contact with anyone.

"I was just admiring. I'd love to hold it in my hands. That's only fitting, given I trained you, don't you agree?" She strokes the virtue pins shining on my coat and I'm reminded of my conversation with my brother.

I glare at her, the truth hanging on my lips. Beaulah resolutely meets my stare and reaches for the red pendant again. I move away. Her mouth bows, but no creases reach her eyes. This gesture is about power. A game she's used to winning.

"I just want to touch it, Jordan."

I can't risk angering her too much. I need to be here for Adola.

"It's never supposed to be in anyone's possession other than the Dragunheart. I hope you understand."

"You've always been one for the rules." She links her hands, radiating annoyance. "It is good to see you back home. Don't stay gone so long." She tidies my coat, and for Adola's sake I don't pull away. "You don't want to forget who you are. Oh, and your room is occupied. We've found ourselves overrun with guests for Trials. Brisby can find you another one."

"I can't stay the night, so it doesn't matter."

"Oh, but we have the band here until midnight. And then there's—" She sighs. "You're busy, I know." Her lips purse with pride. "You're all grown up now. Shall we?" She offers her arm; I take it. "There are many here I'd like you to say hello to. And while I have you, I was thinking we should talk about reinstating you to the House's family name. Jordan Richard *Perl*. There's no reason your father's punishment should still be yours."

I slip my arm from hers. "I am going to try to find Adola and wish her luck."

"Evening, Mother." Charlie approaches with wide-open arms, and I almost don't recognize him. His skin hangs from his bones, as if he's aged a decade in days. His eyes have all but disappeared into their sockets. *What the hell is wrong with him?* I want to ask. But Charlie's never wanted a brother in me: he wanted a son. He walks with a limp, falling into Beaulah's hug. She helps steady him before dusting him off. He kisses her cheek.

"Jordan," he says.

"Charlie."

"I have updates on that list of places you had me check out. I'll get it to you. Been busy. I'm sure you understand." He turns back to Beaulah.

"Did you sleep well after dinner last night?" she asks, roping herself onto his arm. "And that tea I told you about should help—"

I leave them, moving through the crowd toward the glass windows that look out on the grounds below.

"It's him," someone whispers to their companion, pointing as I pass. Both are dark-haired, with the same round, wide noses—sisters, judging by their resemblance. The back of my neck heats at how my very presence here is an endorsement I'm loath to give. *But Adola.* My precocious little cousin, who is gifted at everything but the things our aunt wants her to be proficient in. She wears her mask well, carrying the burden of heir, but she won't face Trials alone.

I check my watch, then my phone. A few more hours of this and I'm out of here.

I circle the room, minding my business as best I can, but the clinking of glasses, cheerful laughter, and overall revelry makes me want to claw at my skin. Dancing on graves and all that . . . I rush out onto the balcony, which is mostly empty of people. A few are immersed in conversation, tittering behind gloved hands, nibbling from plates of hors d'oeuvres. The fresh air hits me and my breath comes a bit easier. Below are three raised platforms where candidates are being prepared. My cousin's long hair is roped into a braid and twisted into a bun behind her head. She's wearing fitted pants and a long-sleeved top. I swallow a dry breath and grip the balcony railing.

"Adola!"

She gazes up at me, hand at her brow. I wave and reach out to her. She reaches up toward me. Music streams from the open doors at my back, the party fully in motion. A server offers me a glass of champagne, and it takes everything in me to push him away.

"I'll be right here," I shout down to her.

She nods.

A camera flashes.

"Have some class. You didn't even ask," I say as the cameraman sulks back inside.

"I require the balcony," I say to no one in particular. And the smattering of guests retreat inside. Adola presses her palm to her heart and waves once more, before being escorted toward the luminous forest. My nails dig into stone railing.

When she disappears into darkness, I slip a hand into my coat and find the spot beneath my arm, where the flesh is raised and scarred from my lowest right rib, around my side, to my spine. Through my shirt I feel it, and remember. The air grows colder. It's suddenly hard to breathe. I hold on to the railing more tightly, biting down on my lip, but my mouth tastes like dirt. I inhale deeply, trying to fend off the memory that's coming. But when a howl rips through the forest, my pulse thuds. I can see snapping jaws and sharp teeth as the memory, long buried, takes me.

I can see a moonlit clearing up ahead, with the oak tree, where my aunt wants me to retrieve the relic. Eyes gleam at me and low snarls rattle the forest. One wolfhound steps forward. With my heart in my throat I pull at my magic; a warm tingle tickles my belly. Then my jaw shifts. Sharp teeth tear through my gums, parting my lips, as my head morphs into a mirror of the monster before me.

To defeat the monster, you have to pretend to be the monster.

I step toward them; they bare their teeth. So I bare mine. I close my eyes and focus on the rustle of the leaves through the trees, picturing each crinkle as a note of sound I can grab. Magic burns deep down inside me and I tense all over, shoving together the two sensations: the noises I hear and the magic unfurling in me. I shudder as they collide. Suddenly the trees thunder with a chorus of menacing growls; my magic works to transform the sound.

One wolf retreats, then another, before each pair of glowing eyes disappears back into the forest. I collapse, shaking. I did it. *I release the warm sensation, and my features bleed back to normal before I race to the oak clearing.*

A chest of things is burrowed in a hole within the old oak. Inside are stacks of coins like the ones Draguns wear at their throats. But these are gold. There is also a velvet pouch of enhancer stones and a leather-bound book. I flip through its brittle pages carefully. Some of the handwritten words are confusing, but the name on the first page, I know. Dysiis.

The sun will rise soon. The book is the only thing that seems truly rare. I grab it and dart back toward home.

But the sound of wolves grows louder. I don't look back until I run right past them, circling their prey. I glance their way and put my eyes on their meal. My heart stops.

Ollie, my Labrador retriever, cowers tethered to a tree, trembling. Surrounded.

His blue leather collar hangs from his neck, and the world blackens at its edges.

There are no perfect choices. Choose properly, *my aunt said.*

I need to keep going.

But Ollie.

Tears fill my eyes. I set the tome down carefully and pull at the warm feeling in my body until I have a wolf's head again. I dart toward Ollie, pulling on the sound of the night, covering my footsteps in growls. I throw myself in

front of him, and a dozen wolves stare back at me. Stalking me. Angry that I
just interrupted their supper. I plant my feet firmly, choking on tears. They'll
have to kill me to have him. Ollie whimpers. A few wolves back away, but a
large one steps forward. Fear like I've never felt buzzes through me.

He lunges through the air.

A sharp, cold bite sinks into my skin.

Just as a curious black substance I've never seen before streams through the
air to my fingers.

"MR. WEXTON?"

I realize I'm on the ground, hugging my knees. The cameraman is
back, staring at me. He snaps the camera in my face before I can get up.
And I shoo him away. I lean against the balcony railing, eyeing the time,
ignoring my racing pulse.

An hour has passed.

The other two participants have returned, bloody and fatigued, and
are now limping up to the lounge for their pinning. My heart stutters in
my chest, then pounds, and I'm overcome with the weight of a fear that's
foreign to me. I clutch my chest. *The trace.* Quell, nudging me. I pound
my fist on the stone railing. There's still no sign of Adola. I slip off my
coat, then my tie. I'm not leaving her.

"Jordan, why are you concerned?" Beaulah asks, joining me on the
balcony.

"Aren't you?"

She turns the ring on her hand. "Your father stood in that cigar lounge,
worrying about the same things, when you were down there. Adola's a big
girl. I let her wait, as long as she wanted, to be sure she was ready. She
will be fine."

I untuck my shirt.

"If she doesn't come out soon, I'm going in there to get her."

My aunt's jaw tics, but she says nothing.

THIRTY

Quell

When the starting horn blows, I'm already in the forest.

But nothing looks the same as it did when Adola led me to the guesthouse the first time. I find the worn path and follow it. Fog wreathes the thick nest of trees. Cold simmers beneath my skin, my toushana awake and ready. *Trust my instincts. Focus on what I want.* Beaulah's words urge me forward. I pick up my pace to a light jog.

Voices echo in the distance. A thud, proceeded by grunts.

I still. Toushana coils in my chest, snaking its way through my arms, and when I open my hands, a cloud of darkness is there. I abandon the trail but follow it from a distance, keeping an eye on its winding bends, looking for Della or Charlie. By the time my throat burns from the cold winter air, I still haven't spotted the guesthouse. *Did I make a wrong turn?* A pair of glowing eyes appears in the distance and it stops me dead in my tracks. *Easy now. Calm.* I stand firm, but when I blink, it's gone.

I'm about to keep going when a husky voice not unlike Charlie's pricks my ears. A coppery scent hits my nose. Besides the burial, I wonder what other terrors Beaulah has them face in there. I never asked her. Heavy footsteps plod in my direction, and I watch as an unfamiliar pair dressed in House robes trudges through the forest. Thick ropes are slung over their shoulders and red-stained sacks drag behind them. Whatever is in there reeks of blood. I can hear Beaulah's voice in my head. *The path to a breakthrough is paved in fear.*

They walk past without noticing me, then veer off the path. When they're out of sight, I find the trail again. Howls and rustling leaves send a chill up my spine. But there is no sign I've been followed. I jog until the path abruptly ends. Every intersection of the woods looks like the one before it. My heart rattles with panic. Charlie knows his way around these woods better than anyone. I need to find that guesthouse, fast. I pick a direction and sprint.

The woods thin. Up ahead is a clearing with a sprawling, oversized oak, its tall, thick branches sweeping the ground. I slow, realizing I've gone the wrong way again, and a shrill scream rips the air.

"You have to pile it all in, you fool," someone says. "Can't make it too easy to get to the finish line." The hardness in his tone renders me straight as a board. I hold in a breath, listening. But I only hear the scrape of metal, followed by a dull thud. Then another scrape and thud in a steady motion.

Scrape.

Thud.

Scraaaape.

Thud.

The commotion pulls my attention in that direction, as I try to make sense of the eerie sounds. Beneath the oak is a man holding a giant shovel. He shoves it into a mountain of dirt, using his shoe to deepen its scoop. Then he heaves the dirt into a hole—*a grave*—in the ground. Another man beside him watches.

Someone is buried alive under there.

"That should be good." The one holding the spade unties the bloodied sack slung over his back. He spills chunks of raw meat around it. I swallow but remember that these guys aren't going anywhere. I turn to tear myself away, to keep looking for some sign of the guesthouse, when the men pick up their shovels and jog past me.

"The girl's next."

Adola.

Where are you going?!

They stop and squint in my direction, and I realize I said that out loud. I step into the moonlight. "What the hell are you doing in here?"

"You're leaving them here!" I look for other men hiding in the brush, but there are none.

"We've got other graves to dig." He checks his watch. "You should get out of here." They rush off in opposite directions with their shovels and half-filled sacks. How will Adola escape? She has got to be pushed out of the nest someday. Maybe the sheer terror of it will awaken something ferocious in her like it did in me. *And if it doesn't?*

A sudden scream.

An explosion of dirt and ash.

The grave is no longer filled. A hand rises from it, clawing its way up and out of the ground. A boy lifts himself, breathless and trembling. I'm trying to release a tight breath when a blur rushes past me.

Snapping growls collide with shrieks.

The boy hollers again; an animal's whimper follows. The scene at the foot of the oak has changed. The boy and the beast wrestle, tumbling one over another. I look around again, waiting for help to step in, but there is no one. Toushana streams through the air, connecting with his hands. A shrill shriek tears from his throat as he pins the wolf. He brings a rock down on its head so hard it doesn't move again. Back on his feet, he charges at the wolf pack, his own teeth bared, darkness thrashing in his grip. I look away just before they slam into one another.

A vicious bark.

Howls of pain.

Whimpers.

Then silence.

I dare look, and the boy's knees hit the dirt. He's covered in blood. Four wolves lie around him, unmoving. I feel sick. He pulls himself back up to his feet. His clothes are ripped to shreds and he limps away. Still, no one slips from the shadows to help. Either they're awful at their jobs or Beaulah lied. *The guesthouse. Charlie lying.* But my legs are like lead.

Adola will never survive this.

I groan and race off through the forest in the direction the men went. I want many things, and her surviving this is one of them.

I'M OUT OF breath and everything hurts by the time I find them. Adola stands between an empty grave and a mountain of dirt. Just beyond her, I can faintly make out the pointed eaves of the guesthouse. My heart skips a beat.

"No!" Adola holds the shovel overhead. Then she swings it at the one who is supposed to be burying her. I chew my lip, moving through the forest around the unfolding scene. The guesthouse, the answers I want, are *right there*.

He yelps, narrowly skirting the blow. "You're supposed to cooperate."

"*Get away from me!*" Adola swings again, and this time the spade slams into his leg. He stumbles, dropping his sack of bloodied meat. It spills on the ground.

"You're nuts!" He scurries up and dashes off.

I check the surroundings. I know what's coming. She has *seconds* to get away. And I have a choice to make. I don't know if Beaulah realizes how unprepared her niece is. How close help needs to be. But I'm not going to sit and watch while someone who is trying to find the courage to be okay with being different is killed. I turn my back on the guesthouse and run to her.

"Adola!"

"Quell?"

She drops the shovel and bursts into sobs. Wisps of toushana are on her hands. She holds them out to me.

"I'm trying," she sobs. "I swear, I'm trying—"

"Listen, you have to—"

Low growls snap our mouths shut.

Adola's eyes widen.

"*Run!*"

She hesitates. "No, I can't. You—"

A wolf bounds toward us and leaps. It slams into Adola, knocking her to the ground. I draw the deathly magic to my hands, and my palms fill with darkness. I grab the wolf by the scruff of his neck and lock my arm around his head. His fur burns away, my toushana turning it to wisps of nothingness. Then I bear down on his throat. When a burning smell hits my nose, he tries to jerk away. I release him and he runs off, tail between his legs.

"Go! Get to the finish line. I will draw them out."

"Quell!" Adola balls her fists.

"You've much worse odds than I do."

"Hurry, please."

"I will."

She darts away.

The circle of wolves around me tightens. There are four here, but more are in the forest. I swallow, holding my toushana fiercely in my grip. The world blackens at the edges, my magic begging for release. I back away slowly and my foot nudges a chunk of meat on the ground. My toushana zips through me and I unleash it, turning the meat to rot. The wolves watch, licking their chops between their bared teeth.

A distant whimper.

A horn blows.

I gather all the meat and destroy each piece.

"Go!" I say. "There's no food here anymore. It's gone."

They close in around me with snarls in their throats.

My fingers are icy and their tips are bruising. With everything I have, I pull at the braid of ice wrapped around my ribs. Fog forms at my lips as toushana seeps from every part of me, engulfing us in shadows, singeing everything it touches. One mutt backs away. Another follows him. But the largest one, with a grizzly brown mane and a head bigger than mine, crouches, preparing to lunge. I stagger my feet, ready to catch him, though my bones are still aching.

Suddenly, the world becomes a haze of sharp teeth, of scratching, ripping. I pummel my fists into anything that touches me. The world tips sideways. My back slams the ground. A mouth chomps at my face.

"Help! Someone, please!"

Another wolf grabs hold of my leg. I brace for the bite. But it just grabs me by the pants and pulls. I kick, screaming and clawing at the ground, leaving dark trenches in the wake of my toushana-filled hands. But it's no use. They are too big and too strong. Two have me now, dragging me deeper into the forest. I aim a kick at one wolf's head, but he shakes with all his might and the world rocks as my body shakes in the power of his jaws. I'm pulled faster across the rough ground, and the guesthouse looms into view.

Teeth grab me by the hair and slam my head to the ground.

The world goes black.

THIRTY-ONE

Jordan

Adola bursts through the trees and I rush down to greet her. She slams into me, her body shaking. Cuts and scrapes litter her skin. She sobs and I hold her as the crowd joins us on the lawn, shouting in celebration. Fireworks pop in the distance. Drinks pass around on trays, and string lights illuminate a festive tent across the lawn. Tears streak down Adola's face. She could have been killed in there. *This is madness.*

I hold her tighter. "It's over. It's all over."

Something nudges my elbow. Beaulah beams as she hands me two small boxes.

"Adola, dear, I am so proud of you." She pats her on the back.

"Pin, pin, pin!" the crowd chants, and Adola's sobs turn to stutters as she tries to slow her breath. Her attendant throws her riband over her head.

"You don't have to do this," I tell her. "Say the word and I'll make an excuse."

She shakes her head and wipes away the evidence of her humanity from her cheeks. Her gaze hollows and it sends a shiver up my spine. The girl she's become in the last few years at Hartsboro is a phantom of who she was when we were small. Her emptiness radiates in my own chest, as if it were yesterday that I stood in her place. As if it were me out there, again, starved for breath under pounds of earth, wrestling mongrels to the death. Adrenaline buzzes in my veins, then and now.

I close my hands over the box. Nothing in me wants to put this pin on her chest, a silent salute to the practices that earned it. I look at my lapel, and the shame I've already been carrying intensifies.

How have I not realized this before? As long as these pins mean something to me, Beaulah means something to me. Her opinion means something to me. That's why I've never fessed up to her about how I feel about her and this place. Running from Hartsboro was easier than looking her in the eyes and telling her the truth.

Trust my gut. Which is screaming, "This is madness!"

"I can't do this to you, cousin."

"Please—" With a weak grip, she lifts my hand holding the box. I take out the pin; its carved gold shape is a twin to the one on my own lapel.

"Come on, Jordan."

"The scars will heal, but the nightmares never will."

"I don't care," she says through gritted teeth. She presses her shoulders back, straightening her posture.

"Whenever you're ready, nephew," Beaulah says. And I may as well be twelve, standing over Ollie's lifeless body.

My own pins catch my eye, and a reckless anger burns through me. My brother's words come to mind again. *There is more to the pins than accomplishment.* They've linked me to this place, and its practices, for far too long. Maybe that's what he meant. My phone buzzes in my pocket.

Yani: You need to see this. Location incoming.

"You don't need this," I tell her, holding up the box. "I understand you want it. I wanted it, too."

"Pin me, Jordan, *right now*," she says. The watching crowd begins to whisper. There's nothing I can say to make her change her mind. The entire House is on the line. Hartsboro would be better in her hands. It's the consolation I hold on to as I grab her sash.

"Adola Perl, Marked daughter and heiress of House of Perl, you've earned two distinct honors for valor and loyalty. Pin or not, you are the bravest person I know. And one day you will be the most heralded leader this House has seen in a century."

I feel the burn of Beaulah's stare on my skin.

"If you receive this honor, say *I accept*."

"I accept!"

I press the pin through the fabric and the crowd explodes in excitement. *Blind, all of them.* Beaulah shoves a cup in Adola's hand and urges it to her mouth.

None of this is okay. And turning my back on it doesn't make it go away. This was my home, a House of great history. But it's run like a cult. My phone buzzes again.

Yani: Pls hurry

"Jordan, are you sure you can't stay?" Beaulah presses.

The sight of her face only boils my rage. Heeding my gut instinct, I snatch the six virtue pins off my chest, one by one. In at least this *one* thing, she will know I don't approve.

Adola gasps.

"What are you—" Beaulah starts.

I hug my cousin one more time and whisper, "You're better than her. *Be* better than her."

"Jordan?" Beaulah still gapes at me, flabbergasted. The crowd watches. She shifts uncomfortably. "Everything's fine, friends. Please make your way to the celebration. Adola, run along and get cleaned up."

No one moves.

I toss the gold pins at Beaulah.

And something over me breaks.

THIRTY-TWO

Quell

I awaken and the world is quiet. My body pinches with pain all over. A rocky ceiling towers above me, and the floor beneath me is hard. The time in the forest comes back to me in a rush and I sit up. That's when I spot it: a wolf licking an oversized bone. He notices me and bares his teeth. I try to pull on my toushana, but only a whiff of cold answers from my purpling fingers.

I lug myself to my feet and the beast stalks toward me. A few others shift from the shadows. I summon every ounce of anything I have left and tighten from my center, pulling at the thread of cold. It roils in me a little stronger. I put more distance between us, skirting piles of bones littered all over the ground.

"Come on," I summon my toushana again, but my magic is spent. I grab and brandish the largest bones I can find, waving them in the air.

"Go on! Get out of here!"

The beast lunges at me and I run.

The cave brightens and I pound my feet harder toward what I hope is an opening. I skirt another pile of bones, this one with a scent that makes my eyes water. Barking wolves urge my feet faster. I spot a trapdoor in the rocky ceiling above. I wedge my foot in a cleft to climb the wall. But the rock is slick and I fall, smacking the ground. Teeth nip at the hems of my clothes. *Up. I have to get up.* But what I tripped over makes my heart knock into my ribs.

The spilled contents of a familiar pink bag, ripped to shreds.

A pen with a checkered pattern and purple eraser that I've seen before.

A chewed pocketbook with worn blue leather and broken zipper.

These are my mother's.

She—

Bile burns its way up my throat and my knees hit the ground hard.

The wolves watch, heads cocked.

My mother, she . . .

"No."

Charlie said she left. Beaulah said the same. A ringing screeches in my ears, flooding my ability to think straight. My mother wouldn't leave her bag: in all my life she never went anywhere without it. Bile rises in my throat. *They lied to me.* They lied, and that means . . . I slap a hand to my mouth. I can't finish the thought. I can't see the horror of the ground between my tears.

The dogs snap their teeth, and suddenly I'm gathering the shred of her belongings, scrambling backward, away from the dogs, away from the darkness—as if climbing to the light can wipe away the image seared on the back of my eyelids, as if it can stop this inescapable nightmare from forming as a full thought in my mind. I scale the rocky wall, cleft by cleft, to the latched door in the ceiling.

I push upward on the door but it doesn't budge. Desperate, I pull on my magic, and faint shadows bleed through my skin. *Please be enough.* My toushana connects with the wooden door and sears a small hole through it before blowing away. Tears prick my eyes as I realize what my mother's shredded things mean. I pummel my fist into the hole in the door, slowly breaking its already fractured panel. I pound it again and again until the hole is wide enough that I can force my arm through, reach inside, and undo the lock. The door buckles open into a room, and I lift myself out.

I slam it shut, latch it, and collapse on the floor.

Everything hurts, but I check that I have each of my mom's effects, then pull myself up onto my feet. I recognize the room around me. The quaint bed, the trunk of blankets.

My mother's room in the guesthouse.

The furniture and big rug have been pushed aside. The hatch in the floor that I just came out of was beneath the bed.

"No!" I stare at her things, these pieces of her, and realize it's all there is left. The wall holds me up. I should have written more, I should have asked her more questions, I should have left Chateau Soleil sooner. Faced my fears sooner. My world frays at its seams. I run my hands along the bed where she slept and press the linens to my nose. But any scent of her is long gone. Anger roils through my body, and my toushana flutters faintly in my chest.

Someone is going to answer for this. I'm about to grab the knob when my gaze snaps to the hatch in the floor. The door lies in pieces, but wedged in its boards is a tiny white scrap of paper. It's stuck in the grooves of the wood between the floorboards. I pull it out and unfold it.

Follow the lair to its darkest corner.
Climb, it'll take you to the far end of the forest.

"She thought . . ." I choke on the words. *This was a way out.*

My knees go out from under me. I hold them, rocking back and forth. A burning like I've never felt blooms in my chest. Blinding rage. Someone wrote that note. Someone sent her to the wolves, and I don't think it was to help her. I see red and force myself up to grab the knob to leave. The door won't move. I turn and tug, but it won't open. I reach for my magic despite its exhaustion but it answers in wisps. I ram the door with my shoulder. It doesn't budge. Then, with the dregs of energy I have left, I heave a small table overhead at it. But even that doesn't damage the door enough to get it open. I shove every piece of furniture, shatter every lampstand against it. And when I'm out of furniture, I pound the wall until my fists are sore and red. When suddenly the door opens.

And on the other side of it is Adola.

THIRTY-THREE

Jordan

The wind cuts deeper than a fall evening in Virginia should.

Yani: Enter around back.

She hasn't offered much more information since I left Hartsboro. Just that this was a safe house and there was something here I needed to see as soon as possible.

"Took you long enough," she says when I open the back door.

There isn't a sound in the house and no one's in sight. The mudroom smells like paint. We pass through a bare kitchen and a scantly furnished dining room. *We've finally found one.*

"How many?"

"Five adults."

"Where are they?"

"I separated them. Caught them trying to get their story straight. Upstairs in the main bedroom." A door beneath the stairs is slightly ajar. She opens it for me to go through. I enter the basement and the light of thousands of candles nearly blinds me. The walls are covered in pinned papers. A narrow path snakes between the candles, around the room's perimeter.

"It looks like some kind of shrine," she says. "Weird, right?"

"Did you examine those?"

"No. If a single one of those tips over, everything on these walls would be up in flames in minutes."

"I think that's the point."

Carefully, I navigate the path for a closer look, snuffing out the flames I pass. At first the wall hangings appear to have no connection to one another, just a smattering of collected clippings. Most have torn edges, as if they were ripped right out of old books. Others are sketches, maps, diagrams of the Sphere, profiles about its casing engineers, myths about sun tracking. Each is hand annotated with intricate details. I grab my phone but think better of it. This isn't something just anyone should see.

"This isn't a shrine. It's research." Carefully plotted and thorough. I remove a stapled stack from the wall for a closer look. *Sphere Health: Four Key Critical Signs of Distress. Gem Mining. Enhancer Composition. Binding and Unbinding. Perilous Truths About Toushana.*

I study a diagram that is hand drawn. The page itself looks so old, its inked markings are hard to read. But someone's gone over it in pencil, retracing what's been lost to age.

A place like this would have to be watched constantly. "When you found this room, was someone in here?" I ask.

"Yes." She points to a cot I overlooked in the corner.

I point out another paper that's familiar. "This one is from Dysiis's original findings."

"But those are locked away in the hidden library at Yaäuper Rea."

Yani says the words before I can get them out. The fellow in the red ball cap was stealing things with information similar to this. The next wall is full of notes on the chemical composition of the matter inside the Sphere, how it intersects with tracing magic and tethers it to the magic inside all of us. The whole place is more of the same.

Everything points back to the Sphere.

"They're trying to find out if magic will indeed be lost if the Sphere bleeds out."

"Why do people in a safe house care about the Sphere?" she asks.

"They don't."

UPSTAIRS, THE FIVE people are huddled in a single bedroom with wall-to-wall beds. The windows are covered with thick sheets of fabric nailed to their frames.

"There were four doors off the hall; what's in the other rooms?"

"Nothing," Yani says.

"You searched them thoroughly?"

"I did."

One of the women fidgets, her eyes darting to a curtain nailed to a wall barricaded by a bed. The thud of her heart rages as I approach the blocked window and drag the bed out of the way. I rip off the curtain and behind it is not a glass but a narrow door.

No one moves.

I pull on the knob but the door doesn't open. I tug dark magic to my hands and press it to the wood until it rots in my fingers. The door dislodges and opens. Inside is a small bedroom. A petite desk sits beside a little bed the right size for a very young kid. The walls appear singed, as if the room's survived some kind of fire.

"Where is the child who slept in this bed?"

The woman whose fidgeting gave away the hiding spot sobs quietly until a gentleman pulls her into a tight hug.

No one speaks.

"Are they hiding somewhere else?" I ask.

The woman wails.

"Did they die?"

"We've been raided before," the gentleman says.

"No one is raided and lives to talk about it." Black tickles my palm. "Last chance—the truth."

"It's *true*, we have been raided," another says.

"Then *why* aren't you dead?" Yani asks, black spooling in her hands.

"We were told we'd survive if we gave up the boy!" The woman buries her face, shaking with grief.

"What's so special about the boy?"

"He's a . . ."

"*Hush, now*, Rosie," an older fellow who hasn't spoken chastises her.

"We can't hide it anymore. He'll kill us!" Her voice cracks. "We knew the risk taking him." She meets my eyes. "He's a descendant of a family line that was cursed with . . . with toushana."

"A Darkbearer's child."

"She swore she wouldn't hurt him," Rosie goes on.

She.

"Who is *she*?"

"She didn't give a name," the older fellow speaks up. "We never saw her face. But she said she'd keep quiet about our little operation here if we gave her the boy and occasionally did favors for her. *Errands*, she called them. And then she had us keep track of her research, which I think you've seen in the basement."

Yani's eyes meet mine.

"She said she would raise the boy to have a better life," Rosie says. "So, as a house, we agreed. She even sends pictures from time to time."

"Show me," I say.

Rosie grabs a photo book from beneath a mattress and hands it to me. I flip past a bunch of unknown faces and stop at a man wearing a red ball cap: the man from Yaäuper Rea. Rosie turns a few more pages and points. "We got that one about nine months ago."

I gasp at the picture of a young boy in a fine tuxedo, with dark messy hair, shimmering hazel eyes, and reddened cheeks. He is unmistakable.

"Stryker." My heart rends.

"You know him?" Rosie smooths away her tears. "Is he alright?"

"Beaulah." *The headmistress of House of Perl is raiding safe houses to collect Darkbearer descendants.* I try to ask why but the question dies in my throat. I know the answer. A shiver runs down my spine as the pieces of the puzzle begin to fit together.

"The Sphere is cracked, Yani. If it bleeds out, the Headmistresses—"

"Are dead," she finishes.

"Would Beaulah, in particular, leave anything that big to chance?"

Yani gazes around the room, her hands moving to her mouth. Beaulah prefers control in *her* hands. That's why she's tried to fill the brotherhood ranks with so many from her own inner circle. She intends to use these descendants to do something to the Sphere to save herself. Somehow that is her plan.

I order everyone to stay put until I've come up with what should happen next. Then I pull Yani into the hall.

"Did you know about this?" I ask her.

"No, I swear."

"You had no inclination that Beaulah was *raiding* on her own, exploiting these people to steal secure information, using Draguns from the brotherhood to *barter* for children, and storing her evidence here to incriminate *them,* if found?"

"Jordan, you and your high horse. She is just like anyone else, taking what she can to get what she wants."

I flinch. "You . . . *admire* her."

"You should try it."

"You disgust me."

"Not entirely." Her teeth pull at her lip and I regret ever looking at her any other way than I do now. I leave her there. Stryker, the little boy we took on the museum raid. That eager gleam in his eyes. He earnestly listened to my counsel. He seemed so innocent. Beaulah stole him and is blackmailing these people to plot treason. While carefully keeping her hands clean.

If Quell is a monster in the making for binding with toushana, for hunting the Sphere, what does that make Beaulah?

Quell.

The weight of her name ricochets through me like a bullet in search of a target.

"Oh my god."

If Beaulah is collecting Darkbearer descendants, she would want Quell most of all.

"I know where Quell is."

I thought I was hunting the greatest living threat to the Sphere.

I was wrong.

THIRTY-FOUR

———※———

Quell

"Quell!" Her brows kiss as she takes in the ruined room. "I've been looking for you!" Adola is covered in scrapes and bruises, but two shiny pins gleam on her collar. She scans me up and down. "I've been so worried. Are you alright?"

I search for the words but everything that comes to mind feels impossible to say out loud. All I can manage is to hold out the nearly shredded pink handbag.

She eyes it in confusion.

"My mother's things," I choke. "The wolves."

She gasps, then grabs my hand. "We have to get out of here before Charlie gets back."

The trip through the forest is a blur. In the distance, the commotion of loud revelry rattles beneath a tent strung with lights. But, given what I know, they may as well be floodlights on a graveyard. Once we're inside Hartsboro, Adola leads me upstairs to her room. She checks that we haven't been followed before closing us inside and turning the door's dead bolt. I pull out the note from the guesthouse and study the handwriting again. I'm going to find out who wrote this.

"What happened?" She examines what's left of the pink bag, which I've dropped on the ground. Her mouth moves, but I don't hear what she says. Then somehow I'm sitting down.

"Quell, please talk." She hugs around herself, eyeing the bruises on my hands. "I want to help."

"She's dead. Ripped apart by—" The words lodge in my throat. "I think someone sent her to be killed." I show her the note.

Adola reads it and her brows draw together. There's a glint of real sadness in her eyes. She stares off.

A tightness tries to well up in my chest, but I stand and pace, stoking my rage instead. Someone did this. When I find them, they're dead. My toushana, still weakened, stirs. There aren't many potential culprits. It was someone here, with guesthouse access. Someone who talked to my mom enough for her to believe they were trying to help her. I read the words again.

"It makes it sound like she was a prisoner here." Which is a very different story from the one Charlie and Beaulah painted.

"I'm so sorry, Quell. I don't know what to say." She offers to hug me but I don't move, so she wraps around me. "Deep breaths. You're so strong. You're going to get through this." She pulls over a blanket. "You're so cold. Can I put on a fire?"

I walk past her and run a cold bath, opening the window to let the autumn wind inside. She watches, her calmness uncanny. The longer I soak, the stronger I feel. And the bruises on my fingers begin to fade. After some time, I climb out of the tub and find Adola writing at her desk. She stands.

"Are you hungry?"

"For blood."

She swallows. "There are no right things to say after something like this, I'm realizing." She hooks her hands. "Maybe try to think of things that give you hope. Like the beach."

A chill skitters up my spine.

"You like the beach, right? The sand and the sounds of the water."

"When did I tell you I liked the beach?"

She goes pale. "Y-you must have told me. Something about how you and your mom loved it."

"I never told you that."

Adola trembles.

"Talk."

She sighs. "I shouldn't have lied. Charlie saw me with her, and I was worried that only made things worse. And then when I saw you and my aunt getting closer, I worried you would tell my aunt anything I told you."

I don't believe my ears. *"Sit."* I push her into a seat. "The whole truth. Out with it."

She pulls at the threads on her dress as she talks. "I met your mom one evening at a private dinner my aunt hosted for her closer friends and family. Afterward, Rhea approached me—"

Hearing about her memories with my mother feels like a dagger in my chest.

"She told me that I reminded her of you. That was our only interaction for a while. Then I noticed she hadn't been around. Charlie was keeping her at the guesthouse, not letting her wander the grounds. So I visited her and that's when we talked about your love of water and sand. And how she had this whole trip planned once you left your grandmother's."

My whole body quakes.

"Charlie caught us chatting and he shooed me away. I never saw her again. And next thing I know, my aunt told me she left."

"You've held this back, all this time. I trusted you. I tried to help you, relentlessly!"

"I've learned in *this House* to *not* ask questions, alright!" She storms away, raking a rough hand through her hair. She starts to cry but it only kindles my anger more. *How is* she *the one who gets to be sad?* Her chin slides over her shoulder, and she starts to speak but stops.

Toushana hums beneath my skin. My fury rises with each step. I've been played, lied to, by all of them.

"Did you write this note?" I hold it in front of her face, seething.

"No! I would never. I didn't even know she was interested in leaving."

"Who else was my mother communicating with?"

She shakes her head.

"*Who?* Charlie, Yagrin, *Jordan?* Whoever it was earned her trust enough that she believed that note."

"You don't know what you're asking." Tears stream her cheeks. "What they would do if they found out I betrayed them? We are 'family first' in this House. Our bonds run deeper than loyalty to any Order. I am a Perl."

"You don't want to be a Perl on their terms. You curtsy to their music, but you curse them under your breath. Loyalty doesn't bind your tongue. Fear does."

She glares at me.

"Which one of them gave her this note, Adola? Who did she trust?"

She rocks back and forth. "Stop, *please.*"

"*Tell me.*" Cold claws at my bones, writhing and unsettled. A sickening feeling lurches inside as I realize I know the answer. "Say it."

She marches up to me, eyes rimmed with tears. "You don't know what you're asking me to do!"

"I'm asking you to stand for something."

"You think the truth is worth dying for? You think that's so easy? Let me see you do it."

"I didn't say it was easy. Say the name, Adola." I need to hear it. To be sure. I poke the pins on her chest. "You owe me that much."

She balls her fists.

"*Who—*"

"Mother! Mother gave the order, alright!" She holds up the note. "This is Charlie's handwriting, but my aunt had him write it. She tried to convince Rhea to bring you here. And she refused. So she ordered Charlie to." She gestures at the note. "I overheard them fighting about it a night ago." Adola's eyes are bloodshot. "She caught me eavesdropping. She told me she'd feed me to her dogs, too, if I told you."

There it is. The truth I suspected. The world bleeds red. Boiling, bubbling, the shade of death. Toushana burns inside, begging to seep through my skin. Adola tries to rush past me, but I grab her by the arm.

"Get out of this House. Fast. Before I burn it to the ground."

HARTSBORO IS SILENT. The Trial celebration festivities officially ended, but the after-party thumps in the distance. I enter the smoking room, then slip behind one of the bookcases, determined to find Beaulah's bedroom. When she's asleep, when she feels safe, is the best opportunity to press my toushana into her skin and do to her what she did to my mother: tear her apart.

The bookcase closes and I imagine my mother's screams ringing in my head. My hands are slick and the walls of the hidden corridor close in. I pull at my toushana, playing with it, urging it to freeze me down to the bone. So I can't feel my racing heart or the sting in my eyes. But my mother's smile forces its way into my thoughts.

Dead.

She's dead.

I urge myself up and run the length of the estate. Picturing Beaulah's shock drives my feet faster. When she thinks she's safe, I'm going to take her by surprise. Maybe I'll tie her up to ensure she can't get away. I want to savor the terror of the unknown in her eyes. I want to make her feel every burst of fear and pain my mother must have felt in her last minutes of life. *Trust my magical instincts*, she'd said. They're loud and clear right now.

Her bedroom is in its own wing of the House. I climb rungs welded into the inside of the walls.

I pull myself up onto the second floor and race behind the walls, burning tiny holes, room by room, until I find a bedroom that is lavishly outfitted in cracked-column decor and House colors. Framed portraits cover the walls above a large bed. In the middle of the room is Beaulah, asleep in a freestanding tub filled with ice water.

Her head rests backward. I knock along the wall, listening for a break in the hollow sound indicating there's a bookcase on the other side. My fingers find a seam and I nudge the secret door forward. It opens silently. My bones burn with an icy, violent appetite I've never felt before. And

I lean into it. Inside the room, my chest tightens, my toushana ready to strike. Beaulah's eyes are closed, her breath slow and even. I stretch open my hands. Blood pools in my ears as my magic awakens, hungry to release this pressure chamber in my chest.

Know what I want.

Trust my instincts.

Break through the fear.

I thirst, imagining the shock in her eyes. The wounded way she will look at me when she realizes she *made* me this way. She pushed me to this edge. And it killed her.

I take another step. Someone grabs me firmly by the arm.

I know the touch before I see him. Murder darkens his green eyes.

"Hello, Jordan."

THIRTY-FIVE

Jordan

Quell's wrist rotates in my grasp as she turns to face me. Her eyes are bloodshot and she seethes with anger. Beaulah shifts in the tub, still fast asleep. Quell tries to tug away, toushana thrashing in her free hand. *We're not doing this here.* I jerk her into an iron hold, with my hand over her mouth, and drag her back to the hidden corridors. The shadows in her fist dissolve. The door closes, engulfing us in near darkness. She claws at me to let her go, but I hold on tighter when teeth sink into my fingers.

"You!" I pull out my fire dagger and bring the blade near her throat. "Who else have you hurt?"

"If you want to know my crimes, you'll have to find their bodies first."

I stiffen. A bluff. I think? The timid girl eager to make a good impression on her grandmother is gone.

"Don't seem so surprised. I'm exactly what you expected." She tenses, and as I hold her back pressed against me, a black diadem emerges from her head. "A monster, right?"

"You mock our rules, but they keep this Order together." I try very hard to not think about the rules I've broken as Dragunheart. The lies I've told. The protocol I didn't follow. The kid on the raid I couldn't kill. Admitting to myself for the first time makes me sick to my stomach. Shame has wrapped its way around my throat. Not because I regret my decision. But because I don't.

If I were a good Dragun, I would.

I'm hesitating. I'm a disgrace. That's what my brothers would say. I tighten my grip on the blade. Her traitorous stare burns into me as if she sees into my soul. I could redeem myself to my vows right now with a sharp flick of my wrist. My pulse picks up. My hands are slick. I've hunted and waited for this moment for so long. And here it is. I pull her head aside, exposing more of her neck.

"Do it!" she says. "I dare you!"

But my grip on the handle slacks.

Spilling her blood here accomplishes nothing and sacrifices everything. Beaulah has to be dealt with. It irks me to no end. But to stop the greatest threat, I need Quell's help.

"I'm going to let you go," I say. "Do not fight me."

"I'm not going to fight you. I'm going to kill you."

I turn my grip to look her right in her eyes. "Threaten me again and I will send your grandmother your ashes as a farewell present." I shove her away. Her hair is wild, her clothes ripped; cuts and scrapes cover her skin. A bloody nick leaks down her leg. She looks at me a moment, then bolts back toward Beaulah's room. I catch her around the waist and put myself between her and it.

"What's she done to you?"

She fumes, pacing in a circle, shadows pooling at her feet. Then she turns to me, stare alight with rage, and opens her arms. "Come on, Jordan. *Fight me!*" She growls but all I sense in her is pain, and it dents my anger. The seconds stretch and every thought I had moments ago abandons me. Her freckles taunt me like a sparkling night sky. Beautiful to behold but far out of reach. I hate her for making me feel these things. I hate her so much, I don't want to look at anything else. I just want to stew in this swelling rage until it burns away every nerve of feeling in my body. Until I can *do* and no longer *feel.* I clench my fists and she raises her hands, magic thrashing in them again.

"I've waited for this," I tell her. "And yet I can't—"

"You've always been a coward."

"Because I need your help, Quell."

"That's what I liked about Yagrin. He was never scared."

"Don't ever say that name to me again."

"Get out of my way!" She charges at me, shadows growing in her fists. I dodge her, dashing aside, and twist my dagger. It erupts in flames. She pushes her magic together and the void of darkness grows. I bring my blade down hard, stabbing the magic between her hands, to cut through her toushana with fire. The shadows vanish.

Her nostrils flare as she comes at me again, but the toushana in her hands is a faint whiff of what it was. That's when I notice bruises all over her hands. She groans in frustration and puts more distance between us. But this is my chance. I lunge at her, blade swiping at the remnants of her magic. She backs away. I press on, winding the dagger down, up, and around, its blade slashing the air in every direction. She backs up again, still trying for her magic, until her back hits a wall.

I close in on her, slipping my blade into my sleeve before grabbing her wrists, crushing them together. She's strong. But I am stronger. And with her magic not cooperating, she's lost her advantage. I press against her, holding her body against mine, and pin her arms overhead. She's so close her scent surrounds me. A bouquet of jasmine with singed petals.

Her breath is ragged, but at least she's not fighting me anymore. I clear my throat, trying to remember what I was going to say and exactly how I was going to say it. But every time I look at her, into those eyes, I'm assaulted by memories.

"I hate you," she says.

"I hate you, too."

"I'm going burn the bones out of your body and dance on your grave for taking this away from me." She glares at the wall we came through.

"What did she do to you?"

She blinks slowly. Then looks off, ignoring the question.

"You're coming with me."

"To be burned? No, thank you. You'll have to kill me here, before I kill you." In a burst of strength, she tries to spin away, but my fingers snag on her hair and I grab a fistful, pulling her back to me. Her chin hits my chest. She glares up at me. I press the flaming dagger at her throat again.

"I am not having you burned. *Yet.*" Her heart races and I feel it rending my chest.

"So what *is* your plan?" She eyes the knife.

"Beaulah is after the Sphere. And she intends to do something worse than break it."

Quell's body stills beneath mine and a part of me is relieved.

"I suspect she intends to take its power for herself, which risks the Sphere bleeding out and ending all magic. Or worse, if she succeeds, someone like *her* would be in control of it." It's the only plausible possibility, given how desperate she's been to study the Sphere. "She has to be stopped. The future of the Order, the future of *all magic* is at risk."

She meets my eyes, listening intently.

"I was hoping you might know more about her plans from your time here."

"I don't. If you want her dead, let me go. I'll take care of that now." She pulls away from me, and because she's calmed, I let go of her.

"I can't let you do that," I go on. "I want evidence of her crimes. I want to catch her in the act so she can be taken in and made to answer for all the heinous things she's done. To her, being removed from power is a fate worse than death."

"You have a whole brotherhood. Why do you need to partner with a fugitive?"

"We're going to beat her to the Sphere and catch her in the act of trying to steal its power. You can track the Sphere faster than anyone. Yagrin says you're the best." The anger inside her has been replaced by something much heavier.

"Something bad happened to you here," I say. An olive branch of sorts.

"I don't need your sympathy."

Her dismissiveness incenses me. "Whatever costs you had to pay for that poor decision are your own doing."

She's silent.

"We're going." I grab her wrist. She doesn't budge.

"You can take my corpse. If I go alive, it will be because I choose to."

"You're a walking dead girl. Choice isn't a luxury you have."

"A dead girl doesn't fear ultimatums."

"Demonstrating loyalty to the Order can only help your case."

"I thought you wanted me dead."

I release a sharp breath, my patience waning. "I want what the Order requires. And for a bit longer, that's you, *alive*."

"I don't know, ripping your heart out of your chest, in the bowels of your childhood home, sounds a bit more entertaining."

"Fine!" I'm done trying to do this the nice way. I press the blade so hard against her it forces her chin up. "You thought you had it figured out, didn't you? You flitted from Darragh Marionne's cage to Hartsboro's, like a little sparrow, with your sorrowful songs about how oppressed you were there."

Pink rushes to her cheeks.

"Beaulah made you feel safe, cared for. Then she turned on you. Is that what happened? You think because you have dark magic you're safe." I chuckle dryly. "You're still weak. Because you don't even begin to understand what you're capable of. And by the time you do, I'll make sure you're dead."

THIRTY-SIX

Quell

Jordan's eyes swarm with shadows, and it's like staring at a ghost of the person he once was. Still, I can't help but search for that boy I used to know. The one I loved. The one who showed me where to find my magic and how to believe the best about myself. Who held my hand and taught me to dance. But there's an emptiness to his glare, as if a whole part of him that used to exist has been ripped out. Not going to lie—after the last few hours, part of me envies being able to exist that way.

"*What* did Beaulah do to you?" he asks again.

And again, I ignore him. He doesn't know about my mom, and I can't bear to hear those words come out of my mouth once more. He wouldn't care anyway. "You mean, what was I going to do to her? How much detail would you like?"

His gaze traces me. First my clothes, then my head, where my diadem is, then the bruises on my hands. Finally, he meets my eyes and I can hear the patter of his heart speed up. He glares, but those viridescent moons swim with desperation. I lean into his blade at my neck, calling his bluff.

"Afraid of actually having to use that knife?"

He white knuckles its handle. "Go on, lie to yourself. You're good at that." A stranger hovers over me, clinging to duty to the Order as if it's all he has left.

"I see nothing has changed," I say.

"Everything has changed."

"And yet you're errand boy for another model citizen in the Order. Hope this one doesn't disappoint."

His jaw clenches.

"You hate me because I see through your mask."

"I hate you because you exist."

Partly true. I did break his heart.

He brings the fire dagger closer to my face. Magic, still weak, flutters in my hands. The blade's heat is warm, and part of me wonders what it would feel like to touch the fire and let it consume me. To shake this deep nothingness that aches in my chest. But my toushana writhes in me, and the only thing that I can think about is severing Beaulah's head from her body. I draw in a breath, balling my fists, and my magic seeps back into me.

Something he said a few moments ago piqued my interest. He's right: losing power is a reality Beaulah fears more than death. But he wants to bring her in and allow the Order to lock her up or something. Handing over her fate to the Order is far too generous.

"What makes you think she can even get the Sphere's power?"

"She's been collecting Darkbearer descendants. I suspect she is trying to learn about their connection to toushana, steal it, and somehow put it in another person. So she can use those loyal to her even more lethally."

His words lasso like a noose around my neck. *Me.* That's what she was doing in our experiments? All this time, I've just been part of Beaulah's collection.

"She is vile, like my grandmother."

He lowers the blade, sheathing it. "We agree on one thing, I see."

"How is the magic in the Sphere connected to the magic in all of us?" I circle him, pondering. Beaulah needs more than just justice. I want her to feel seething fury when she becomes powerless. She needs to know the pain of loving something more than life itself, and losing. I try to think past my revenge for some idea of what's next, after she's dealt with. But there is only bleakness beyond it.

"It works similarly to the trace," he says. "We're bound."

"If the Sphere drains, we lose our magic, I know. But if she takes the power for herself, what happens to us?"

"Depends on what she does with it. As long as magic is contained, it concentrates its power, keeping it stable for us." Something dark shades his expression. "The Sphere's casing was supposed to maintain the perfect equilibrium to keep magic in balance. But it's blackening on the inside. I'm not sure if that'll make it easier or harder for Beaulah."

"What's causing the blackness?"

"Too many of your kind out there using toushana."

I think of Knox, Willam, and the others in safe houses. Knox wouldn't let me stay in the safe house unless I agreed to abandon magic completely.

"You're wrong."

"About?"

"Many things."

His mouth purses, those disgustingly perfect cheekbones pushing up under his eyes. He shrugs me off with that air of arrogance I found revolting when we first met. It reminds me why loathing him—my instinctual reaction—was the right choice.

"You're going to help me get Beaulah arrested. Do we have an understanding?"

An idea strikes me so fast, I almost laugh. If Beaulah can take the power into her possession, that means I could, too. I could drain the Sphere into something in my possession to steal the one thing she loves most. I bite away the twisted smile curling my lips.

"I am interested in witnessing Beaulah's downfall," I say.

He lowers the blade. It's not a lie, more of a half-truth. One of the more useful things I learned at Hartsboro. We will track down the Sphere before Beaulah. But when we find it, I'm going to take its innards for *myself*. And enjoy watching Beaulah's horror when all the magic she once had, the power she holds, is in *my* hands.

I offer a hand to shake on it. "I'll help you track the Sphere."

PART THREE

THIRTY-SEVEN

Nore

Nore ignored the feeling of the ancestors watching her as she strode toward the glittering lights and soft music emanating from the main house. Her stomach sloshed. She was close. If her plans proceeded as she hoped, she would have that Scroll tonight. She watched the time.

While back in her cottage, Nore had researched what the Immortality Scroll supposedly looked like. She pored over volumes of legend and lore, some by Caera Ambrose, the inaugural Headmistress of House of Ambrose, who discovered the Scroll. Caera had published the most information on the topic. But Nore also read writings from several other Ambrosers, some who doubted the Scroll existed at all. Many thought it was a myth, believing that, if such a thing did exist, it would be extraordinarily difficult to achieve. Jealousy often bred doubt. That didn't worry her.

But there was one question in all her research that made her heart tremor.

Caera Ambrose discovered the secret to immortality and inked its instructions on the legendary Scroll. Their House held this secret for centuries, and yet there was not record of a single Headmistress ever trying to use it. It probably required the rarest elixirs, and strongest strains of magic. But literally no one had tried. When Mildred Ambrose died during childbirth, leaving no one to take over in her absence, her husband let the House pass on, out of their immediate family, instead. And during the early years of their House, when Caera's great-grandchildren fought to the blood over an assumed illegitimate daughter, they allowed the leadership to pass to the next generation instead of resurrecting the woman. Or at least trying to.

The cost of using such magic must be *high*.

Nore swallowed. Darragh hadn't expressed any reservations about what the Scroll's magic would cost her. She just wanted the Scroll, and Nore was going to give it to her.

Tonight.

She checked the time again as she entered the large ballroom. The tables were adorned with royal-blue linens and copper-colored plates. Surprisingly, there was a single white flower at the center of each table. Onstage an Audior quartet played. Classical notes streamed from the magic at their fingertips like a symphony. Nore moved through the crowd and squeezed the crushed nixelweed petals in her pocket. Nixelweed was used by Retentors to expel digested magic by inducing a rapid succession of sneezes. It basically upset people's seasonal allergies. But, for her purposes tonight, a little sneezing was all she needed.

Ellery was talking with Mr. Hargrove surrounded by an audience, all with cigars in hand, each wearing their own rendition of the drab gray suit. Nore spotted her mother, deep in conversation as well, with a familiar woman in a gray laced corset and a single pearl resting on the metal diadem arced above her head. Mrs. Hargrove caught her staring and waved her over. Nore's throat went dry. Showtime. *Please let this work.*

"Mrs. Hargrove, a pleasure to see you again. Mother." Nore curtsied, careful to hold her head painfully still so that her curled hair didn't show her earrings. But her mother's gaze was fixed on her ears.

"Nore," Mrs. Hargrove greeted her warmly. "You look quite nice." Her mother had sent over a simple gown made of rough linen fabric. A burlap ribbon lined its capped sleeves and another tied around her waist. She was fluffing her locks when her mother reached for her hair and pulled it behind her shoulder. Mrs. Hargrove's eyes widened.

"You really have no respect," her mother spit. "Here of all places."

Isla snatched Nore's hook earrings out of her ears before she could move. She clenched her fists. Yagrin gave her those! Mrs. Hargrove watched them while fiddling with the hem of her sleeve. Keeping up appearances was the opposite of what their House stood for. Public shame was welcomed.

Nore held her composure despite the biting pain in her earlobes. She was getting in that vault tonight. Nothing would ruin her plan. She pulled her fist out of her pocket, careful to keep her fingers tightly together. Nore waited until they began to chat again, as if she weren't there. She brought her hand to her mouth and opened it ever so slightly. She blew a sharp burst of air through her fist. The petal dust trickled through the air, so fine it was hardly noticeable in the dim room. She held her breath. Her mother's and Mrs. Hargrove's noses wriggled.

"Oh, goodness. I— *Achoo!*" Her mother's sneeze flew out of her nose and into her gloved hands before she could open her purse for a handkerchief. Mrs. Hargrove sneezed as well, but Nore watched as her mother's eyes squinted and watered. Her mother sneezed violently into her hands twice more before frantically apologizing.

Nore opened her hand. "Your gloves," she said, offering to take both of theirs. She couldn't be too considerate or Mother would suspect her. "I'll get a fresh pair for both of you."

"Such a mannerable young lady, Isla," Mrs. Hargrove said, handing Nore her gloves. "You must be so proud."

Her mother eyed Nore strangely.

"Any excuse to get out of here," Nore said, low enough that only her mother would hear. Her mother snatched off her gloves and handed them to her. "Be quick. I've worked in the labs this afternoon for hours; my hands should not be exposed."

Nore excused herself and carefully folded her mother's gloves to preserve the palm, where her mother had made the most mess. She scanned for Ellery. He was occupied. But she darted over and pinched his arm gently.

"Talkative tonight, aren't you?"

"No time to breathe."

"You don't have to go through with this."

"I'm doing this. You're the heir. I have to get power where I can." He looked away.

She sighed, unsure how to take that, but remembered she had a timeline to keep. "Well, I pray to the Sovereign she is at least tolerable." She pulled him aside. "I have what I need," she whispered, dangling the folded gloves.

His nose scrunched in confusion.

"I've made a minor adjustment to the schedule for the evening," their mother said. The audience began to whistle and applaud, their eyes moving to Ellery. Rumors spread fast. "My dear son has an announcement."

The color drained from Ellery's face. He tugged at his coat, pressed his shoulders back, and plastered on a smile before striding up to their mother. Nore fumed and found the door. She wasn't watching this.

"Elena, where are you, darling?" Her brother's voice boomed over the microphone. "Would you join me up here?" The crowd swooned as Nore exited the ballroom.

THE HALL OF Discovery was empty. The long corridor that bridged the specialty labs and session wings was usually teeming with débutants, even despite the off Season. At Dlaminaugh, students were welcome to stay and study year-round. But tonight everyone was at the ball. The glass boxes in the corridor showcased relics with detailed inscriptions, each tied to some lesson or moral quandary that was discovered or studied by a débutante of their House. Nore waited, watching her wristwatch. And after what felt like forever, Darragh Marionne finally came around the corner.

"I'd worried you didn't get my message."

"Well, do you have it?" Darragh folded her arms, and Nore noticed the gray hair on her head had gone almost all white. She wore a dark traveling shawl over a long dress. "Your letter made it sound like you have it."

Nore's heart ticked faster. As if Darragh could read the panic on her face, she dangled a copy of *Debs Daily.* "I assume you saw this? If I die without that Scroll in my possession, the world will know your secret. The brotherhood will kill you for that poison in your veins even if it hasn't matured." Her chin rose. "You save both of us, or neither."

"I will keep up my end of the bargain." Nore pointed to the wall between two glass display cases. "That's the family vault. I'm getting it now. *We're* getting it now."

She gestured for her to go on.

"Stay close."

Nore ran her gloved hands along the seams of the walls, applying pressure to the spot where the wall seemed to dip, bowing in ever so slightly. She laid her gloved palm on that spot, and the surface heated, feeling hot even through the satin. She pushed against the wall. And its hardness softened.

She leaned with all her strength, and a seam in the wall split, opening to a hidden metal box of a room. She grabbed Darragh by the wrist and they hurried inside. The poorly lit vault, with its piles of chests and bins, was covered in dust. Urns, ornate vases, sculptures, and paintings were stacked, in no precise order, on shelves and on the floor. Nore scanned the vault. There was so much to take in: trinkets, jars, elixir vials. She didn't see anything that looked like parchment.

When her eyes landed on a raised marble pedestal with a glass box on top, she gasped.

Inside was a thumping red organ. *A heart.*

She stumbled backward and bumped into Darragh, who was searching the room even more feverishly than she was.

"I don't see it anywhere," Nore said. But Darragh's stare, too, landed on the beating heart. A storm of questions raged in Nore's head. Beside the glass case was some kind of journal. She grabbed it and flipped open its cover, when her mother's voice sent an icy chill into her bones.

"Don't touch that!"

It was the first time Nore had felt her toushana flicker in a long time. As panic tried to take over, her mind sharpened like a laser. She slipped the journal into her pocket as her mother rushed past her, putting herself between them and the glass box. "Get out of here, *right now*." Her mother was talking but Nore hardly heard her. The organ beating behind her . . .

"Mother—is that yours?"

Isla's throat bobbed and Nore had her answer.

"*What* did you do?"

"*Shh.*" She gazed around. "The ancestors."

"What does this mean? Are you . . . dead?" She couldn't believe her ears.

"I'm very much alive. But as long as I'm Headmistress, the ancestors require it." She picked up the glass box and held it tightly to her body.

"*The Immortality Scroll*," Darragh said.

Her mother looked at Darragh, bewildered, then at her.

"I'm looking for the Scroll, Mother."

"There are records of people trying, for generations, to find where Caera Ambrose hid it." Her mother's voice cracked and it unsettled Nore. She'd never seen her this way. "You'll never find it. "

"She's lying," Darragh said.

"I am *not*. Do you think if I had that Scroll, my heart would be in this *box*?"

Nore wasn't sure what that meant, but it didn't sound good at all. Darragh stared daggers at Nore and she thought her heart would beat out of her chest.

"Nore, we had a deal," Darragh said.

"What are *you* even doing here?" Isla asked. "The Dragunhead intends to have your head."

"He can intend all he likes," Darragh retorted. "When I found Nore hiding in the middle of nowhere, she was bruised and bloody. Draguns had ravaged wherever she was staying and were trying to find her. She saw me and all she could manage was a feeble '*Please help.*'" Darragh straightened her collar. "Had you seen the value of protecting your family *first*, at any cost, as I advised, your daughter wouldn't have run to me for help."

Her mother snarled. "*Help?* What help could you possibly give her? You're a dead woman."

"And yet the glory of this House is going to preserve *my* legacy."

"Enough of this!" Isla raised her arm in the air, and only then did Nore realize she was wearing a purple Cultivator ring. Her mother twisted her wrist and balled her fist, then opened her palm. The air in her hand rippled, magic streaming from it. Her mother reached to touch the nearest wall. The room rumbled, the wall fracturing beneath her Shifter magic. Debris rained from overhead. Nore shoved Darragh aside before dashing out of the vault. When they spilled into the Hall of Discovery, the walls of the vault closed up with her mother still inside, holding the glass box and sobbing. She still had so many questions. But they had to wait until she found that Scroll.

Celebratory cheers rang in the distance; her brother's party was still underway. Nore almost headed in that direction but a sour smell stilled her in her tracks. She peered down the hall and glimpsed dark shadows rising. The ancestors were inside the house. Her heart knocked into her ribs. She and Darragh ran, away from the ballroom. The shadows followed closely behind them. But when they reached the grass, then the expanse of lawn, and finally Nore's porch, the ancestors fell back.

"Those spirits want you, child," Darragh said. But Nore wasn't listening. She was flipping furiously through the journal she had pocketed. Its pages were filled with crossed-out latitude and longitude coordinates, inked in various colors and various handwritings, all on paper that—if its yellowing was any indication—was very old. Beside each scratched-out coordinate were notes.

43.6971° N, 114.3517° W *Ear ringing. Lots of blood. Didn't make it far. (aud)*
43.6807° N, 114.3637° W *Got close. Skin started peeling away from bones. (anat)*

Air changed quick. Got harder to breathe. Couldn't shift it back. (shif)

From what Nore recalled of her House history and estate geography sessions, these coordinates all appeared to be within Ambrose territory. One coordinate was circled many times, in every color of ink. She pointed it out to Darragh, whose jaw clenched. Nore couldn't read the woman's expression, as she was too steeped in her own shock. But she could feel Darragh's anger. The circled location had dozens of notes about the magical injuries people had suffered.

Nore flipped through the pages again, paying close attention to the annotations on the side. *Aud* for Audior. *Anat* for Anatomer. Each was a different type of magic, followed by symptoms or reactions. *There are records of people trying to find where Caera Ambrose hid it for generations,* her mother had said.

"Every single person who tried this had some kind of magic," she told Darragh. Magic which seemed to backfire. Audiors transfigured sound, but their ears started ringing. A few Anatomers, who could transfigure bodily anatomy, had their skin start to peel away. Nore's mind raced. She could do this. Because she *didn't* have magic.

"I can figure this out. I can find the Scroll. The Dragunhead comes for you in five days. Give me three."

"You're the presumed heir. Getting away from here is that important to you?" Darragh asked.

"More than anything." A thought struck Nore. "Are the rumors about your granddaughter true?" she asked.

"You wouldn't ask if you didn't already know."

"Why not offer her the freedom you're offering me?"

Darragh's jaw ticked. "I offered her freedom of another kind. Our agreement comes with a steep price."

"That you didn't want her to pay . . ." The wind picked up outside. "You should get out of here, quickly. The ancestors are wary of outsiders." She was growing certain they were wary of *her*, too. "So, we have a deal still?" she pressed.

Darragh *tsk*ed, refusing to take her hand. "I do hope your mother will be alright."

Nore didn't know what to say. She'd never seen her mother so shaken. "I am not thinking about her right now. I don't fit her mold. I was never good enough for her." The admission left Nore's lips before she could stop it. She didn't care what her mother thought. She didn't want her mother's approval. She didn't care why her heart was in that box.

"The more I've seen in my life, the more I've realized that it's *the world* that isn't good enough for people like us. People who don't fit the mold, as you say." Darragh moved a rogue hair out of Nore's face. "Some lose sight of that and destroy the things that matter most."

Nore considered her earnest expression. In one evening, the woman had gone from the object of her blackmail to a partner in crime.

"Are you the villain everyone says you are?"

"You are always someone's villain, Nore." Darragh buttoned her traveling shawl. "I'll give you until tomorrow. If you have nothing to show by then, I *will* go to my contact at *Debs Daily* with everything that's happened here tonight. I have to protect my interests, and heat on Ambrose takes the heat off Marionne. I'm sure you understand."

"You'll have the Scroll by then."

THIRTY-EIGHT

——✳——

Quell

All the confidence I felt at Hartsboro abandons me as Jordan marches toward the elevators of the swanky hotel housing Dragun Headquarters. Yagrin visited here, wearing my mother's persona. *Was that before or after she was . . .* I stop. The world swims.

"Ma'am?" The attendant behind the desk stands.

"She's fine, Joel." Jordan's foot taps. "Quell, this way."

I don't move. I can't. Then my knees go out from under me. Jordan's jaw clenches.

"What are you playing at?" He tugs me up and I snatch my hand away from him.

The concierge watches, his smile waning.

"What is wrong with you?" Jordan asks.

"I need a minute." I blow out a long, slow breath and bury any thoughts of my mother. I need to focus on finding out how to get the Sphere's magic into something else. Something in *my* possession.

Jordan stares, brows cinched, and his hand hovers near his chest.

I ram the call button for the elevator and it takes an eternity to show up. If he knew what I really wanted to do with the Sphere's magic, he'd put that dagger through my throat. "So what do you know about Beaulah's plans so far?"

"Let me worry about Beaulah."

I scowl. The elevator doors open and we step inside, along with a few others. We ride in silence. More join us, and Jordan and I end up wedged together in a corner, far too close for my comfort. His scent assaults me and it kindles memories of when I used to love being close to him like this. Memories that should be long dead. Our eyes meet. The knot at his throat bobs. I look away until, finally, the elevator doors open and the car empties again. We put as much distance between us as possible. Jordan slides a key out of his pocket and a hidden button appears. The elevator plummets.

"Do you know where you want to start tracking?"

"I'm still thinking. You could also show me everything you have on Beaulah and the Sphere. You look like you could use all the help you can get."

The elevator car reaches the ground. Jordan presses a button to keep the doors closed.

"My brother will be coming with us."

"I'm sure the brotherhood has no shortage of Draguns to supply, but—"

His brows dent, then his gaze widens.

"What?"

"Nothing. Get me a list of the resources you need and I'll take care of it. Figure out where you want to start. Once we have the Dragunhead's approval, we cloak at dusk. Now turn around."

"Excuse me?"

"I'm going to secure you with restraints so that you appear within control. I brought you in through the front doors on your own, out of respect for our partnership."

"If this is a trap—"

"It's not a trap. It's a formality." He pulls a metal circle from his pocket and shifts it into some kind of handcuffing contraption with three ovals: two smaller and one larger. I offer my wrists begrudgingly. He fits the cuffs on one wrist first, then the other. When he grabs my hips to fit the third brace, his fingers graze my belly, and my body betrays me, tingling at his touch. When he finishes, my arms are rigidly straight, held in place at my sides. I can hardly move my hands. I couldn't spool toushana in them if I wanted to.

The elevator doors open to a busy office full of Draguns, coins glimmering at their throats. A mousy secretary in orange heels shuffles toward us. Heads swivel in my direction as Draguns greet Jordan. His grip on me tightens.

"Maei, I need to see the Head immediately. And prep prisoner 23821 for release."

Her blue eyes dart from me to Jordan. She clicks a pen on her clipboard. "I—I don't think that's going to be possible, sir."

"Maei, we're not doing this today." He walks me into a glass room where there is a maze of desks. Maei follows and hands him a file. Jordan casually flips through it and I catch a glimpse of something about the Sphere.

"Get me in with him, Maei. Now."

Their words are drowned out by the growing chatter as more Draguns come and go. But my gaze is still glued to the folder in Jordan's hands.

"Wait here," he tells me, setting the file on his desk before marching across the lobby toward a closed office door, with Maei on his heels. They disappear inside. Everyone's attention moves back to their own work and I graze my fingertips over the folder. Moving is impossible in these cuffs. But after a couple of tries I manage to flip it open.

Inside is a compilation of ripped papers, scribbled notes, sketches of the orb, calculations, and folded pamphlets about the Sphere. Curious eyes flick in my direction. I lean on the edge of Jordan's desk, loitering as nonchalantly as one can in handcuffs tethered to a harness. Once their curiosity moves on, I shove some of the papers around and read. Travel logs show that someone named Francis Clemon Hughes traveled to Aronya dozens of times in 1781. Stamped in red on each document is the word RESEARCH.

Aronya . . . The name is so familiar, but I can't place it.

I pull the folder closer to the edge of his desk so I can better sift through its contents. Beneath it all is a photo of human remains in a garden beside a cement house. A shiver slides down my spine when I realize Jordan is standing nearby.

"That file is confidential." He is collecting the papers I've mussed up, when I spot another note about Aronya on a paper that fell to the floor. It appears to be a list of items, which— As I squint to read, Jordan snatches the list.

"No!" I stomp on his hand, craning for a last look.

He growls in pain. *Lumen. Decibel. Strength.* A list of enhancers, like the ones I folded into my blade for Second Rite. Along with all manner of resources: herbs, various types of petals, peckle leaves. *That's where I know the name.* The caves of Aronya, where enhancers are mined, are an internship option for débutants. I remember my grandmother talking about it.

Jordan snatches me away from his desk.

"Those notes could've included things that help me sun track. I shouldn't have to sneak behind your back."

"And yet you did."

"If we're going to do this, you have to trust me. At least a little bit."

His jaw works.

Maei eyes us warily, clicking her pen faster. "The Dragunhead wants to see her, sir. Should I have her taken to the Shadow Cells? He can visit her there."

Jordan rubs his injured fingers, then pulls me by one of my cuffed wrists and smooths his magic along the metal. The contraption shifts into a thin silver ribbon and falls to the floor. Now that I'm no longer restrained, he hands me the file folder. But when I grab it, he doesn't let go.

"You will not defy my authority again."

A million ways to cut him with words flit through my mind. But I swallow them all. *Beaulah. My focus has to be on Beaulah. That's how I avenge Mom.* Before I can think of what to say back, I realize we have an audience.

The Dragunhead has joined us.

THIRTY-NINE

Jordan

I lead Quell into the Dragunhead's office. This may have been a mistake. If I can't convince him to allow us to track the Sphere together, Beaulah will get to it first. *How will I ever look at myself in the mirror again?* He has to see reason.

"Let me do the talking," I whisper to Quell as she shuffles past me, then sits.

The Dragunhead's gaze doesn't leave her. But, interestingly, there is more curiosity in it than anger. I slide to the edge of my seat. "Sir—"

He raises a hand to silence me. "I want to hear from Miss Marionne directly."

I smooth my clammy hands on my pants.

"You're a highly sought-after target." The Dragunhead leans back. "I've sent multiple Draguns to hunt you down on the word of my Dragunheart here, and it appears you outsmarted them all."

"I have no interest in being captured," Quell says.

"And yet you're here."

She tenses beside me.

"Tell me," the Dragunhead goes on. "Why did you leave Chateau Soleil?"

Quell stops twisting a fraying hem on her shirt and stares at me with a question in her eyes. Why haven't I told the Dragunhead about her binding with toushana? Because I'm a fool, that's why. Quell fidgets. *Don't tell him.* I stare intently at Quell, wishing she could read my thoughts. Her pulse picks up.

"At Cotillion I bound to the toushana inside me," she says, white knuckling her chair. My grip tightens on mine. The Dragunhead doesn't move. But the creases in his expression have smoothed. He's not surprised.

"So the rumors are true."

"What rumors, sir?" I ask.

He hasn't ever mentioned hearing anything about Quell.

"If this made it to my ears, I know it made it to yours." My neck flushes with heat. *He's never going to trust me again.* "And yet you didn't bring her in for sentencing. She's not even cuffed. You're requesting to allow her *more* freedom, *more* opportunity to evade us. This surprises me, Mr. Wexton."

"I brought her in here uncuffed because—"

Quell's gaze burns my skin.

"I trust her with this task."

The Dragunhead grazes his knuckles under his chin. "First you want to delay Yagrin's sentencing and now you want me to allow you to gallivant around the globe with two fugitives. She should be in the Shadow Cells."

"Sir, Beaulah Perl has been planning to steal the Sphere's magic for some time. I believe she was at Quell's Cotillion to recruit her and offer her safe haven."

Quell's jaw clenches, but the tightness burning in my chest—*her* chest—shifts to sadness.

"If she gets to that Sphere before us, she could drain the innards and *lose them.*" My heart rams in my chest. "For all we know, she could have concocted some twisted way to alter the Sphere's magic to affect all of us. You *cannot put anything* past Beaulah Perl. You have to—"

"Let me be clear," Quell cuts in. "I'm going to find this Sphere with or without your approval. You won't detain me alive. So make your decision quickly." She flexes her fingers.

I watch the Dragunhead for some indication of how upset he is that a person bound to toushana is sitting in his office instead of a cell. But he drums his fingers on his desk, watching her more with curiosity than irritation. His body language is unreadable.

"He is asking me to believe that you have no ulterior motives and will honor your word to help us bring Beaulah Perl in to answer for this very serious allegation. Someone who just gave you safe haven. You can see how I'm struggling with that, can't you?"

"I don't care what you believe. You're wasting my time." She stands.

The Dragunhead shoots up from his seat, too.

"Quell, we had an agreement," I say, refusing to stand and let this situation escalate any further than it already has.

The Dragunhead's hand curls around his hip to his sheathed fire dagger. "*Quell.*"

She leans across his desk. "Beaulah Perl offered my mother safe haven, too. Then she fed her to her dogs. Either get on board or get out of my way."

The air in the room drops to a chill.

Beaulah killed her mother.

A hurricane of my own feelings blows through me. My gaze hits the floor.

The Dragunhead's glassy stare moves beyond our conversation. "That is grave news, Miss Marionne." The warring emotions burning through her finally make sense.

The Dragunhead's attention is still somewhere else.

"Sir, Beaulah is the greatest living threat to this Order," I say. He lets out a giant sigh. "The fact of it is, I *cannot* track the Sphere quickly without the help of a Darkbearer." I can't believe my ears. "She is the only one of them I trust."

"And what sort of guarantees are you expecting for Quell after she's done what you asked?"

Quell's heart rams in her chest and I feel it like a dagger in mine. Despite her tragedy, she is still wrong for binding to toushana and defying the rules of this Order.

"What you do with her afterward is not my concern. You're a fair judge."

Her heart hammers harder. I avoid her gaze.

After a long silence, he says, "I can see how this could be an opportunity, Quell, to use all that dark power to accomplish something helpful. But I can't give you that chance. I'm sorry."

"Sir!"

"Enough!" The vein at his jaw pulses. "There are cells *full* of safe house inhabitants waiting for burning. *Any* number of them could have the poison in their veins! Why do you insist on working with *her*?"

His question unsteadies me. "Beaulah killed her mother. And that's good fuel."

"Judging by your reaction, you just learned that."

I swallow.

"Maei," he says in a raised voice, and the door to his office opens. "Lock down Headquarters, all exits and entrances sealed, until Mr. Wexton and I finish this meeting."

My heart skips a beat.

"Take Miss Marionne to the waiting area, please. If she gives you a hard time, do whatever you need to have her restrained."

Quell rises, seething. I take advantage of the moment to hold the door open for them. "I'm going to fix this," I whisper to her. "Don't do anything stupid."

"I trusted you."

"Trust me *now*. We are walking out of here together."

Worry knots through her, and it feels like a thick chain linking together in my chest. I close the door behind Maei and Quell. The Dragunhead lights a cigar and paces, his skin still flushed. "I lost my temper with you. I apologize."

"I brought you an impossible request. But it's our only hope of saving this Order. If she dies now, we are at a loss." The words are bitter. "We need her. Just for a time."

His back is still to me when he says, "I can't go along with something like this in front of her or anyone."

I cease breathing.

"I'm having a guards' meeting tonight, on the hour of the shift change. The cells will be unguarded and your brother's might malfunction. And, son, you have a weakness for her." He takes a long pull of his cigar. He cups my shoulder. "Destroy it or she will destroy you."

I open my mouth to respond, but think better of it. I thank him again and exit the office. I have it in hand. Quell is a means to an end. Someone I will use. The way she used me. The crowd in Headquarters has thinned. The red light glaring above the doors flickers out, signaling the lockdown is over. I find Quell flipping through the file folder on Francis's grandfather along with Maei's notes on the Sphere.

Her mother is dead.

I reach my desk and she gawks at me as I stare back, speechless.

Her mother is dead because Beaulah killed her.

Words claw their way up my dry throat. "We're all set to go."

She gathers the papers nonchalantly, as if there isn't a chasm of pain gaping in her chest.

"Jordan, did you hear what I said?" She is resolute. Still, the urge to say something, anything about her mother, bites at my lips.

"Quell, about—"

"Don't." She's like glass: hard, but fragile. And now that I know what Beaulah's done, I can see through her clearly. "I said we're going to start in Aronya. It has a tall mountain peak and clear skies, and it's fairly remote, so we should be undisturbed."

I let the urge to say something about her mother go.

Why Aronya? I almost ask. But we've thrown enough daggers today. If we're going to work together, she is right: we have to trust each other. A little bit. Quell's gaze moves past me to someone entering Headquarters.

She tenses beside me as Charlie rounds on us, and I can feel her heart pounding. His skin is blotchy and pale and his stare is glassy. He looks like death. Yani is with him. Charlie struts toward us, as bullish as ever. Angry bruises are all over his hands. He catches me staring and stuffs them in his pockets.

"I see you've chosen your side, *Dragunheart*," Charlie says.

"Charlie," Quell mutters, and shadows shift between her fingers. I step between them.

"Charlie, do you really want to do this here?"

"No, not here. Not yet."

Maei clears her throat.

"You surprise me." He addresses Quell, and I can feel her shake with fury behind me. "And after all the bonding we did."

I shove him in the chest. "Leave."

Charlie throws his hands up, smirking as Maei gathers a stack of files and hands them to him before retreating back into the Head's office.

"Let's go, Yani," Charlie says. "Duty calls."

"Yani," I say.

She turns at the sound of her name, and a fire I haven't seen in her in a long time has returned.

"You're choosing the wrong side."

She grabs me by the jaw. Then she gazes between Quell and me. "I'll take my chances."

Once the door closes, I try to slow my raging pulse. *This isn't good. This isn't good at all.*

"I despise him almost as much as that witch he serves."

"She knows."

"That girl?"

"*Beaulah*. I don't know how, but she knows that we're onto her. Which means she's onto us."

FORTY

·· ———✳——— ··

Quell

Jordan moves closer to me, and my hand tightens on my copy of *The Anatomical Difference: Darkbearers' and Multistrand Magic.* The dimness washes the alleyway behind Headquarters in an orange glow.

"You're blocking the streetlight." He doesn't move, so I stand back, putting more space between us. I turn the page, skimming a section on the chemical anatomy of toushana. I turn another page, thinking of Knox and the others, wondering what happened to them. A part of me aches. I share a connection with them in a way. And yet, I abandoned them.

Jordan eyes me.

"Not a fan of my reading preferences?"

A vein at his jaw pulses. He checks his watch again, then he pulls out an inscribed vial. "Don't lose this."

I unscrew it. Inside are fine glowing granules. *Sun Dust.*

"How'd you get this?"

Jordan only raises a brow. *He stole it. Jordan Wexton broke a rule.* I won't give him the satisfaction of my being impressed.

"What time is Yagrin supposed to be able to slip out?"

"Any moment."

I return to my book and he groans. "This is going to be a long trip if you're going to grumble every time I read a page."

The streetlamps reflected in his eyes shimmer golden. He reaches in his pocket. "You're welcome to do something other than fill your head with that propaganda nonsense."

He pops a green candy into his mouth. His mouth puckers and his cheeks rise, defining their sleek craters, and it makes me dizzy. I glare at my book. *Two can play this game.* I turn to a section in the text that I'm sure will irritate him and clear my throat.

"'The prevalence of toushana has been denied by the Order since its inception. The official response has been that it poses too great a risk to consider giving it any credibility. Though that only seems to underscore its importance.'"

Jordan walks away and I follow, projecting my voice.

"'The Order fears that binding with toushana is an awakening of *boundless* power.'" I snap the book closed and rest against the building, utterly satisfied with myself.

"Are you finished being incorrigible?"

Cold yawns in my chest, and I urge it through my bones and into my hand. Black drips from my fingers and I coil it playfully in the air.

"You should reserve your energy for what's ahead."

"I can spare a bit to get under your skin."

His head cocks. "This isn't some game we're playing at. This is the life and livelihood of members all over. You should take that seriously and *prepare.*"

"You prepare your way, I'll prepare mine."

He marches up to me, snatches my book, and presses his palm across my stomach.

"Is this where your toushana lives in you?" His hand moves across my body to my lower hip, leaving a trail of heat in its wake. "Or is it here?"

"What are you—"

"It's one of those two places. Toushana attaches to the stronger organ in either place, burrowing a home for itself inside you. *En domum* it grows, until it's strong enough to attach to each and every part of you." His hand traces up my body, grazing my ribs. "First, it explores your neighboring organs." His knuckles stroke the bone between my breasts, careful to avoid touching either one.

My neck breaks out in cold sweat.

"There, it can latch on to the ventricles of your heart, changing your body chemistry drop by drop until your blood bleeds black." His fingers walk up my chest and pause at the hollow of my neck. "Before it finally moves on to exercise its power over your brain."

I swallow a dry breath.

"*Binding Mechanics,* volume two, around chapter five or so." He hands me back my book. "If you're going to read that poison, read both sides."

When air moves between us again, I'm not breathing. What he said can't be the full truth. He's just trying to sway me to his twisted way of thinking—to hate myself, like I used to.

"I have it under control," I say.

He lifts his shirt to show me the handle of his fire dagger.

"Underneath your veneer is fear," I say. "You wouldn't carry a weapon otherwise."

He drums up another snappy reply, and I realize we'll never get anywhere if we're at each other's throats like this. "The Dragunhead mentioned Yagrin. Of all people, why him?"

He picks his nails. "He knows the most about sun tracking. I'm not taking any chances out there."

I frown in confusion before realizing both Yagrin and Jordan finished at House of Perl. So they must have been at Hartsboro around the same time.

"He *lied* to me, pretended to be one of his personas to gain my trust. He knew my mother was at Hartsboro and never said anything. I'm not working with him." A strangled laugh escapes my throat. I did all I could to get away from Yagrin and yet here I am.

"You don't have a choice."

"You can't trust him. He wants to bleed the Sphere out of spite."

"He can't bleed the Sphere. He's tried. He wasn't strong enough. He needs you to do it. Lie to him, I don't care."

"So we're using him?"

He chuckles, a real laugh that creases around his eyes. "You act like you're above such a thing."

"All this time you've been thinking I *used you*?"

"I don't spend any time thinking about you at all."

His words cut, even though they shouldn't. He is tossing his bag of candies in the trash when the alleyway door to Headquarters opens and Yagrin appears. His pallor is worse and his hair is longer. A thin scruff of a beard shadows his face.

"This is a surprise," Yagrin says. "What's happened?"

"We were just talking about how I never wanted to see your face again. But Jordan insists that, of all the brotherhood, we have to drag *you* along with us because you're good at sun tracking."

"The best," Jordan says.

"Ah. Who better than his spiteful, sorry-excuse, waste-of-space brother?"

"Enough, Yagrin." Jordan glances at me. "Quell, are you ready?"

Yagrin's brows bounce, his features curling into a smug expression I know well. Beside him, Jordan huffs with impatience, his expression twisting in the same pompous way.

Almost the *exact* arrogant way . . .

Jordan's taller, with lighter eyes, fuller lips, and more melanin, but if that were taken away, he'd look a lot like Yagrin.

"No. There is no way."

Yagrin and Jordan look at each other, and the slopes of their profiles match.

"You're—"

The sharp cheekbones, the deeply set eyes, the aquiline noses. Genetics are a funny thing. I hardly look anything like Mom.

"*Brothers?*"

"How could you not tell her?" Yagrin mumbles.

"I thought *you* had," Jordan mutters back. Before I realize it, I'm stomping in his brother's direction. The slap shocks both of us and leaves my hand stinging. Yagrin's cheek is bright red.

"You rat. Are you just made of lies?! And *you!*" I turn to Jordan.

"I thought—" he starts.

My hand flies at his face. He catches my wrist before my palm slams into his cheek.

"I thought you knew."

"Let's get this over with so I never have to look at either of you again."

FORTY-ONE

*

Jordan

The trip to the caves of Aronya is a nightmare. It takes three days to get there because of the resting time required to hold cloaking magic for that long. I don't know what I was thinking, choosing to be stuck with these two. A patch of rocky earth wreathed by mountainous boulders is where we've made camp for the night. It only has room for a single tent, which I've set aside for Quell. The moment we left Headquarters, Yagrin transformed back into Liam. But he decided to lay his sleeping pack right beside mine. I can't stretch my arms without hitting his.

"Again," he says, nudging me with his elbow. Despite Liam's persona, Yagrin's brown eyes stare back at me, and seeing a part of the real him is some small consolation. I want him to realize I'm honestly trying to save him. "Oh, come on. What about the time Father whipped you at the governor's party in front of everyone?"

"I said, no more. We're done."

The mirth playing on his lips dies as if the curtain just closed on his favorite show. I leave him there. I'm about to douse the fire with a bucket of dirt when I catch a pair of curious eyes peering at me between the flaps of her tent. Once I'm upon Quell, she retreats back inside. I open the tent, letting firelight stream in.

"Is it too cold in here?"

"I'm reading. Go away."

I clench my fists. *Her stubbornness knows no bounds, I swear.* "You need to keep your body fairly cool so that *magic* of yours doesn't start to act up."

"I said I'm fine. Go away."

"You'll slow us down if you start having issues."

"The only issue I'm having is your insistence that you know my magic better than I do. Go back to reminiscing with your brother. You two deserve each other."

Her pupils dilate normally, the moonlight catching on the lighter brown of her eyes. Her lips are full of color. And her skin is smooth, as if freshly oiled. She doesn't appear sickly. Toushana's affinity for the cold can make it flare up without warning in warmer climates. She must have struggled at Chateau Soleil. And yet I was so mesmerized by her facade that I missed all the signs.

"I'll check on you again in a few hours. Answer when I call or I'll drag you out of that tent."

"Touch me without my permission and I'll burn your eyes out of their sockets while you sleep." She snarls as she zips the tent closed. Her anger stirs like a furnace. Choices have consequences. But as I walk back to my pack, all I can think about is how devastated Quell felt when she told the Dragunhead what happened to her mother. Her rage is a mask.

It's not hard to imagine how Beaulah weaseled her way into Quell's trust. She is good at manipulating what people want. I look back at the tent and think of returning to Quell, of telling her that I'm sorry she had to endure Beaulah for a single day, let alone several. But sympathy is useless. When I return to my pack, my brother's waiting for me. *This is going to be a long trip.*

The second day takes us to a jungle buzzing with thick air and colorful foliage. We make camp in a nest of grass. I tug the triple knot secured to the large rings of a hammock roped between a pair of trees.

"Yags." I walk over and take his bedroll from him, rolling it back up. "Sleep off the ground. We're not in the desert anymore."

"Why do you have us in the jungle on this island anyway? Sleeping out in the open would be better. Like a beach."

Beyond my brother, Quell stands with her back to us.

"No beaches."

"It's better than whatever's going to slither down these branches while we sleep."

"If I say no beach, it's no beach. You had your chance to get Quell to the Sphere and you failed."

The brown in my brother's eyes shifts to Liam's blue, and a whole stranger stares back at me. I sigh. I can practically see our father visiting Hartsboro the day he realized Liam was one of Yagrin's personas. A part of childhood I'd buried. But the more we rehash the past, the harder it's becoming to ignore.

My father had chewed Yags out for his low marks, right in front of me. My brother cowered and the walls seemed to clatter with our father's thundering voice. When he finally stormed out, I tried to hug my brother, like I always did. But that time he shoved me off, his eyes dry, his lip quivering. My brother's magic wasn't very strong then, but in that moment he rolled his shoulders and strained, wrinkling his nose in determination. Suddenly he looked like a different person, like a young Liam with a shadow of Yagrin underneath. Then he gazed at himself in the mirror and sobbed. Father raged back in, calling him a coward. The scar Father's ring left etched on his face is still faintly visible on his cheek now, so many years later.

"Come on." I squeeze him by the shoulder. "Enough with this. Let me see your face."

Liam shrugs me off and the knot in my chest deepens. But whenever I reach to undo it, it slips out of my grasp. I leave my brother to his musing and look for Quell. She busies herself, preparing to hang a hammock.

"I can do that."

She doesn't respond but sighs in frustration when she rips a tear in the fabric. I smooth my Shifter magic over the frayed threads, and they bind themselves back together.

"Those trees over there are a bit stronger." I walk in that direction. To my surprise, she sticks to my heels. Once we find a shaded spot, I stop.

"Well? Are you going to set it up?"

"Oh, now you want my help."

"Just do it already." Her stomach churns loudly. When I finish the tent, I offer her a hard sausage from my bag and a drink from my canteen. She needs her strength to sun track.

"I'm not hungry."

"Eat."

She snatches the meat out of my hand and shoos me away.

One more day of this.

FORTY-TWO

Quell

I've slept terribly the last two nights and my toushana isn't happy about it. It slips over my bones, chilling them to the core. Then it pricks me in the ribs over and over, for a long while, before fading away. An hour or so later it's at it again.

The promise of sunrise lurks beyond the trees that my hammock's swung between. The color has drained from the world, but it's like the biggest, grayest, heaviest cloud sits squarely on my chest. I force in a big breath and feel my lungs swell. Breathing takes effort. *Everything* takes so much effort. I'm summoning Beaulah's face to my mind, to urge some motivation to my limbs, when Jordan pops up like a ghost.

"Get up."

He offers me a piece of bread that looks as hard as a rock. I roll onto my other side to look at something other than his face. The hammock shifts near my feet. I catch a glimpse of Jordan fiddling with the rings and suddenly the support goes out from under me. My stomach drops as the hammock and I plummet. My butt slams onto the ground.

"I said *get up*."

He steps back to give me room to stand, but I anticipate his movement and stick my leg behind his feet. He stumbles, and despite his gracefully flailing arms, gravity wins and he falls. And just like that I'm having a stellar morning.

"It's time to go." Jordan dusts himself off. Yagrin saunters over, looking like someone else. I bundle up my hammock and stuff it in my bag, keeping my back to him. I'm not dealing with another one of his personas. No way.

"Quell."

"Leave me alone, Yagrin, or Liam, or whoever you are."

"We cloak to Aronya today," Jordan says, taking my hammock and slinging it over his arm with the other two. Yagrin holds on to Jordan, then he reaches to hold on to me. I bristle at his touch, but I stuff down my annoyance and call on the cold to take us where we need to go.

THE MINING TOWN off the coast of Aronya smells like potpourri with a crude, sour scent underneath. Cargo ships line the modest harbor, where a flood of tourists loiter beneath signs for cave tours; they meander in and out of trinket shops and eateries. I hadn't pictured the remote island as a bustling center of commerce. Its skies are clear almost year-round, I read, and it has a high-altitude peak, *perfect* conditions for sun tracking undisturbed. But most importantly, Aronya is also where enhancer stones are mined . . . And enhancer stones hold magic! At first the throng of tourists are just a blur. Then I notice many of them tout House colors and subtle House symbols in some form or fashion.

"Is everyone on this island Marked?" I say to Jordan's back as we snake through the crowd and up the harbor.

"No."

A mountain looms in the distance. Its highest peak draws up to a wide crater and disappears into the clouds. "They used volcanic resources to build the Sphere?"

"Sort of."

The closer I look, the more the Order's world reveals itself. People in long dark coats too warm for this weather navigate the throng. A circular imprint or hole in the fabric at their neck gives them away. *Draguns.* Greedy Traders posing as finely dressed world travelers are scattered throughout the crowd, making eyes at anyone willing to meet theirs.

Jordan reaches for my hand.

I don't take it, but I walk faster, keeping in step with him. Workers covered in grease stains haul carts loaded down with goods to and from waiting ships. Each cart is branded with some kind of symbol. Three thorny branches woven together. A smudged dollop of paint. Several symbols I recognize, but some I do not.

"Where are those going?" I ask Jordan, pointing at a cart full of shipping crates marked on its side with thorny branches and a dark sun.

"Brotherhood business. That's not your concern."

Farther along the harbor, the cave's entrance is more visible. A line of gondolas drifts across shallow teal water toward a gaping entrance in the solid rock. Long crystalline formations with sharpened points line the rim of the cave's mouth, leaving an open space only large enough for a small boat to pass. I crane for a better view.

"I didn't anticipate so many people," I say.

"Something has to fund our research."

Snooping here is not going to be easy. Jordan pulls me aside, out of the way of the crowds.

"Where do you want to set up?"

"Up there somewhere," I say, scanning the wilderness around the mountain beyond the town.

"Tourists aren't allowed to stay on the island overnight," Yagrin adds. "After sunset, Aronya's a whole different place. There's a nice bed-and-breakfast for Marked patrons in the mountains."

"You've been here before?"

He nods but doesn't offer any more details. "We could track on the be—"

Jordan cuts Yagrin off. I take their bickering as a chance to slip into the stream of people rushing by us. I want a close look inside that cave. That has to be where the magical stones are mined. Down the harbor is a gaggle of people waving LINE STARTS HERE signs.

"Excuse me," I ask a fellow in a bright turquoise-and-gray tunic as he fans patrons in his direction. *Oralia.* "Do you offer private tours?" I fiddle with my fleur-de-lis earring.

"*Fratris fortunam*," he says under his breath. "You'll need to access our evening schedule, madam." His lips pucker in a smile. "Is this your first time to Aronya?"

"It is."

"From Second Rite enhancers to commemorative Cotillion gifts, retail shops to the mines, we have it all."

Jordan shoulders his way through the crowd toward us.

"I'm dying to see all Aronya has to offer, especially the Sphere."

"You and so many. Tourism has been up with all the nasty rumors about the Sphere cracking." He glances at a pocket watch.

"Do you expect magic to all be gone imminently?"

"What is magic for, if not to be used until the very last drop," he says out of the side of his mouth.

I wait for him to guffaw, but he doesn't.

"Magic serves the user, after all." He swipes two fingers in the air, left, then right, and it reminds me of House of Oralia's sigil—two smeared dollops of paint.

Unsure what to say to that, I move things along. "Are you able to lead my tour?"

"Meet me at Betty's bauble shop at sundown."

"It's a plan."

"What's the plan?" Jordan is behind me. I wave at the tour guide and lead Jordan away before saying, "I was asking some questions about the Sphere. The rumors of it breaking have increased tourism. People know what's happening."

"Which breeds fear. Fear breeds desperation." Jordan's jaw clenches. "Did he say anything else?"

"Just that he believes the Council and the Dragunhead have it in hand."

"This is useful intel. But don't run off from me like that again."

"I think I've proven I should have a longer leash."

"I'm keeping it short for your own sake." He steps closer and heat rushes through me. "Nothing is going to get in the way of you sun tracking that Sphere."

"My *entire* focus is on sun tracking."

He walks away and I swear I hear him mutter, "She's lying."

JORDAN REFUSES TO let us stay near the harbor. Instead we hike up the mountain and watch as the little city bloats with patrons milling around like worker bees. Once we're settled, Jordan leaves me alone to stew. I recline against a rock and let it hold me up. From this vantage point the shoreline is a dot in the distance. The horizon is ocean in every direction.

I stand. "I'm going back into town." It's a little early, but hiking back down beats sitting up here. Staring at a stupid beach. Jordan tears himself from whatever he's spent the last few hours doing and joins me.

"I'm going alone."

He eyes the shore. I walk off, and though I expect to hear his steps behind me, I don't.

"You have an hour," he shouts. "Don't make me come find you."

I flash him a choice finger in response.

When I reach the village at the bottom of the mountain, shops eclipse the view out to the water. The central artery of the retail district, appropriately named Main Street, is sparsely littered with people. I head toward a quaint pink building with a swinging sign that reads BETTY'S. The clock on a tower chimes six times in succession. Then suddenly the colors of Main Street shift and sharpen. Shades draw up in windows, and the letters on shop signs transfigure. A shopkeeper dusts her Shifter magic across the windows of Harbor Reads bookstore; each of its grand windows transfigures into a doorway with stairs heading in hidden directions. Myrtle's window front shop is now Misa Memorabilia, every inch of its walls covered in stickers, magnets, and tees. Graffitied on the side of a building is a burning fleur-de-lis, my grandmother's House sigil. I walk faster. The farther I go, the more the air fills with cinnamon and spice:

pastry shops appear where there had been boarded-up doors moments before.

Every several paces is a flickering lamppost with huge flames. I give them a wide berth, gawking at every kind of store imaginable. A dagger polisher. A swath of Vestiser boutiques. Flower crafters. Cartographers. Street artists and their muses, crafting portraits with nothing but their bare hands. A conglomerate of stationery needs. Jewelers. A smelly forge. And that's just what I can see.

The next person I pass boasts a magnificent ruby-red-and-silver diadem. For a moment, I imagine letting go of the tightness at the meeting of my ribs and showing my own diadem. My heart twists. The real Misa, where Knox's family was from, was a place for everyone. I skim for any sign or hint that this could be the same. But when I stop to read the signs hanging on the lampposts, I have my answer.

KEEP THE TOUSHANA AWAY

I almost trip over an elderly couple, arm in arm at a bistro table. The one thing I'll miss about Hartsboro is that I didn't have to hide there. My insides urge to release my toushana, nestled beneath my ribs. That entire part of my body is as cold as death, and it's reassuring.

"Quell!" The whisper comes from an alleyway between two shops. Out pokes Liam's head.

"What are you doing?"

He hops in stride with me. "I've known him longer than you have. He's not as clever as he thinks."

I smirk, then remember I'm annoyed with him and frown instead. "I don't forgive you for lying to me."

"You don't have to forgive me. You just have to help me bleed the Sphere. I know that's what you're up to. You see I was right all along, don't you?"

"I don't know what you're talking about."

"Quell, it's me."

"Precisely."

We walk a full block in silence.

"You know, I was thinking, we could tell my brother our real plan. Try to get him over to our side, now that you're on board, too. He'll do anything you say."

I guffaw. "Hardly. And *we* are not planning anything. I am locating the Sphere. That is all."

"He's been different these last several days." He goes on about a fight they had, but I have my eye on the bauble shop. It's up ahead and I need to lose this leech before then.

"Jordan's a coward." How Yagrin can see anything else in his brother, I'll never understand. "He's as rotten as the Order he serves."

"Then why are we here and not dead?"

My stomach twists at his suggestion. "Jordan is the enemy."

"There I must disagree with you. The Order is the only true enemy." To my relief, he meanders in another direction, just in time for me to slide into Betty's. But the tour guide is not there. I wait for a moment, then another, before hurrying off toward the cave myself.

After leaving town, I traipse around the base of the volcano. There has to be another way into that cave. I follow the strong wall of rock until I find an area where its foliage is loose. I peel back a curtain of overgrown vines and summon my toushana. Cold vibrates in my chest and I press it out through my hands, carving a decaying hole inside the mountain. When the dusty haze settles, I crawl through. Inside, only a shard of moonlight from the cave's mouth cuts across the teal water. But even in the dimness, everything sparkles. An earthy pungency pricks my nose. Thick, salty air gusts inside. And all I see is earth covered in gems.

"I knew it!" But no sooner than I think I've found enhancer stones, I realize nothing here looks as if it's ever been touched, and certainly not mined. I take a step, careful to set my foot firmly on flat ground. The whole place glitters. Brilliant stones in a rainbow of hues cover each inch of the rocky dome above. Blues deeper than the clearest ocean, greens brighter than any forest I've ever seen, yellows so shiny they look like gold, and regal purples. I can't resist running my hands along the jagged walls as I walk. The majesty of it all drags me along, one foot in front of the other. This place *feels* like magic. My toushana stirs inside, sidling against my organs with something that feels like comfort. Gardens of gems cover the ground, clustered in pointed, rocky formations.

A narrow river cuts through the rocks before winding around itself and emptying into the cave's mouth. *The gondola route for tourists.* But the cave goes deeper, meandering out of sight. I hurry that way, following a path lit by thin tapers on the walls. The path narrows and smooths. When I reach a gate that's been welded shut, I use my toushana to get through it. Past a narrow cleft in the rock, over a barricaded passageway, the cave opens up again, this time to an underbelly of shiny rocks, barrels overflowing with gems, and drums of kor elixir. My heart rams my ribs. The stones here are arranged methodically in neat rows as if they were planted here. And much appears to be picked over. The precise colors of the stones are consistent from gem to gem, reminiscent of rings maezres wear. There's enough here to make thousands of rings.

Cultivator rings hold magic, too.

Maezres use them to help bolster students' magic. *Many* students. Over *several* years, which means they can hold *much* more magic than simple enhancer stones. My heart skips a beat and my dark magic stirs. I've found something I can use.

I touch a stretch of bright green stones so vividly colored it looks like grass made of glass. Carefully, I pull on the thread of cold humming through my body and stream toushana toward it. Black touches the stone's glossed surface and it withers into blackened rot.

"No!" I stumble up and away and into a plot of red stones covered in soot with my thudding heart in my throat. I need this to work. I need something to hold the Sphere's magic so *I* can take it myself. Studying the bed of blood-hue stones, I notice the ground around the whole plot is blackened as if it's been burned. *As if it's been touched by toushana.* I closely inspect the rocks caked in ash. My toushana stirs. I smooth my thumb across one stone and its red color gleams beneath. My toushana shudders again. I shiver with a warning chill like I haven't felt in a long time.

Despite this mess, some of the stones are intact. Audior green. Shifter purple. Anatomer blue. Retentor colorless. I've never seen a red-stoned Cultivator ring in any of the Houses before. *Which could mean . . .*

Ice ripples inside me, my toushana two steps ahead of my mind. I have to know if I'm right. I rest a single fingertip on a red stone and watch, hardly breathing, as black seeps from my skin to form a thread of smoke. Instead of decaying the rock, it siphons inside, beneath the glassy surface. The cold in my chest teases with a sharp ache and I watch as the magic streams out of me and into the stone. It feels like an insistent tugging at the very marrow of my bones. My heart skips a beat and I close my fist. I should stop.

But my toushana still bleeds.

Rivers of black run between my fingers and into the rock. It tugs again, lassoing my heart. I tighten all over to restrain my magic. But it won't halt. Deadly cold sludges through me, like a massive weight being pulled along by a shoestring, up through my chest and toward my hand that's still connected to the gem.

I yank my arm back with all my strength, but the magic outside my body is stronger than a manacle. Panic rocks in my chest. I claw at the ground with my free hand and pull away with all my might. My bones scream. The world sways and I'm hot. So very hot.

My breath shortens.

Black glimmers beneath the gem's red surface.

My magic. It's taking my—

The world is heavy.

"Help," I manage, when Jordan's narrowed eyes find me.

FORTY-THREE

---*---

Jordan

Quell shrieks again and I'm at her side, trying to pry her hand from the stones on the ground. They appear to be sucking the toushana *and life* out of her. I then grab her by the wrist, tugging her arm backward. But the harder I pull, the louder she wails.

"Please, it hurts. I—" Tears bead in the corners of her bright eyes. I position myself behind her to hold her upright. She burns with fever.

"Quell?"

But she doesn't respond. Her head bobs and her lashes dip.

"Think of arresting Beaulah and how good that's going to feel."

Her heart races and I feel it inside. The pulsing stone is swelling in size, as is the darkness within it. My mind races. *Raw materials are more potent than refined enhancers. Once an enhancer is attached to something, it cannot be separated. Enhancers bind to surfaces because of their need to exist in balance. Like the Sphere.* The stone is feeding on her toushana, trying to equalize the magic disparity between it and her. And she's resisting, which only makes the enhancer work harder. She writhes against my chest.

"You have to overwhelm it. Get it to work to *de*tach from you."

"What?" She pants, growing heavier in my arms. Holding on to her is like cuddling a furnace. She claws at me. And that's when I notice the unnatural color of her tethered hand. It's the color of dried blood.

"Jordan, *ple—*"

"Push toushana into the stone, faster than it can take it."

"I don't under—" She blinks slowly and I feel her heart's cadence slow.

"*Use* your toushana. As hard as you can, *now.*" I tighten my hold on her frail body. She oscillates between cold and hot. Moaning in pain, she grits her teeth. Black gushes out of her tethered hand into the stone. It swells at first, the rock growing faster.

"*More.*"

"I can't—"

"You *can.*"

Her curled body lunges forward.

The flow of black gushes out, swallowing the red stone.

Toushana bleeds all over her fingers.

The stone shatters.

Rivers of darkness crawl across the ground, pooling together before rushing back inside her.

Quell collapses in my arms.

I dab her scorching forehead with my sleeve and pour a bit of my water in her mouth. She doesn't move, and the heart in my chest feels like stone. Then she nestles against me, her head cradled in my arm, and my heart races. She blinks, dazed, and everything else in the cave ceases to exist for me.

"Are you alright?"

She tries to get up. I help her, steadying her with an arm around her waist. She holds on to me, her fingers wrapped around mine, until she's back up on her feet. When she sees our hands intertwined, she snatches hers away. I clear my throat.

"What just happened?" she asks.

"I think that stone was sucking the life out of you. First, your magic; then the rest of you."

She hugs herself, staring at the charred bed of red stones still gleaming on the ground.

"How do you feel?"

"Hot. And tired." She inspects her hands. Their color has mostly returned, but they're dry, cracked, and blotchy with bruises.

"What were you doing in here?"

"I thought I might take one of those red gems."

"For?"

She shifts on her feet, jaw ticked with irritation.

"Forget it. Let's just get out of here." Trusting her was always a risk. Once Quell can stand without much swaying, I offer her a hand to help guide her over the uneven ground. She reluctantly slips her hand into mine. The rest of her body boils, but her fingers are still ice. I rub them between my hands to warm them. She watches me curiously.

"The mission. We need you fully recovered."

"I told you, I'm alright," she retorts, but doesn't pull away. As we traverse the cave's narrower passages back toward the entrance, I keep a close eye on her. My heart races; I'm still a bit worked up.

"There you are!" A tour guide approaches. His gaze snaps to the pendant on my necklace. "Good evening, Dragunheart, sir. Aronya sends its warmest greetings to the brotherhood."

"Pleasure. I should be getting her back." I try to move past him, bringing Quell along. He steps in our way, eyeing her hands.

"What happened?"

She laces them behind her back. "I don't know what you mean."

"The mines are inspected for any abnormalities, chemical or otherwise, and—"

"There's no need for an interrogation. I found her trying to steal. But I've apprehended her, and I assure you she will receive consequence for her infraction. It's been handled."

Quell grumbles an exhausted groan.

"I'm sorry, sir, but I'm required to search her person in a case like this. I must insist." He grabs her and I see red.

I heave him away from her and flatten him against the wall. "You don't have the authority to insist." I straighten his disheveled clothes. "On the honor of my position, you'll find everything in there in good order. Are we understood?"

"Yes, sir." Sweat beads on his forehead. "Forgive me if I—"

"It's forgotten. Like our visit here tonight." I gesture for him to lead the way to the exit. I usher Quell with a hand on her waist to steady her, and her skin is still fire.

"It's good for morale to have you here on the island, sir, with everything going on."

I clench my teeth.

"What do you make of the latest gossip?"

I ignore him, helping Quell over the uneven ground.

"I hear a House is marching from the east in search of the Sphere."

Beaulah.

"And another House has joined the search."

I stop.

Quell and I meet eyes.

"Tell me everything you know."

BEAULAH ISN'T WORKING *alone.* Logs crackle in the fire. Quell stares into it, in a daze. We've been here for an entire day and she hasn't counted a single sun spot. Nor is she in any shape to. Beaulah has help. I know she's done research on how to manipulate the innards of the Sphere. What we discovered in that safehouse is clearly only a piece of a larger plan. And if I know anything about Beaulah, it's that she is loyal to one person— herself. *This is not good.* My brother turns a stick with some kind of bug on the end over the flames.

"Which House do you think is marching to help her?" I ask.

"How do you know they're an ally?" Liam asks. "Couldn't they be marching against her?"

I sit back. I hadn't considered that.

"When you say *marching*, what do you mean?" It's the first time Quell has spoken since we left the cave. She refused food and has only been sipping water.

"Their residence is formally closed," I say. "Security protocols are in place for an extended time away. By the books it means that sixty percent or more of a House's staff is on the move with the lady of the House."

"Is that unusual?" she asks. "Has it been done before?"

"Twice." Liam gently strums his guitar.

"When Misa fell," I say. "The early days of the Houses were violent. House of Marionne, actually, feared that families of those who were cast out would want revenge. The Headmistress left when rumor of a serious attack reached her."

"And the other time?" she asks.

My brother and I share a glance. "The Order wasn't always run by Council of Mothers. A cabinet of twelve used to run it: the Upper Cabinet. The Council was supposed to attend an annual meeting with them. Before attending, Beaulah marched—closing her House down and taking mostly everyone with her."

"She was scared of something," Quell says. "What happened at the meeting?"

"Tragic accident," Liam jumps in. "The Uppers went into the hotel where the meeting was held but never came out. No bodies were ever discovered. The Headmistresses and the Dragunhead were the only leadership the Order had left."

I nudge the logs in the fire, and the flames swell. I don't have proof that Beaulah conspired to kill the Uppers, so I've never said anything. But it's one more reason she needs to finally be brought to justice, *with* evidence.

"Do you have eyes on Beaulah, reporting back to you?" Quell asks. "We can't rely on random tidbits we pick up while out here."

"You're asking if I'm spying on her?"

"You said she's onto us somehow. She is most certainly spying on you. Are there any Draguns from her House that you could turn your way?"

Yani comes to mind. When we were . . . close she used to listen to me.

But the dark gleam in her eye at Headquarters suggests she will do the opposite of what I say just to spite me.

"You don't understand the reach of Mother's indoctrination if you think they can be turned," my brother says.

"You two broke away," she says.

"You sure he's broken away?" A smirk very unlike Liam's plays on his lips.

"Funny, brother."

"How are you two even related?" Quell asks, fanning herself.

"Can you feel your magic?" I ask, ignoring the dig. She's right: we couldn't be more different. And I'm not sure who to blame for that anymore.

She holds her side. "It's there. I'll be fine."

"If you can't reach it, you're not fine." *I can't believe this has devolved to me counseling her on how to take care of her illegal magic!*

"This makes me think of a story," Liam starts, but I douse the fire before he can get started.

"Off to bed, both of you," I say.

Quell stands, still unsteady on her feet. I get up to help her and press the back of my hand against her neck. "You're still scorching."

"I'm going to sleep it off," she says, shrugging away from my touch before sauntering toward the tent. I follow her, leaving Liam behind. She disappears through the flaps and shouts, "I intend to be well enough to start sun tracking at sunrise."

A million thoughts run through my mind. But I return to the fire to ensure it's out. Once that's cleaned up, Liam prepares for bed.

"We're behind," I tell my brother, swallowing my annoyance that he still won't face me as himself. "I need you to help her with tracking tomorrow, with whatever energy she has."

He rolls in his covers and our makeshift camp is silent. But the events of the evening keep me sitting up and keep my mind going. If I hadn't shown up when I did, she would be dead. I drag my pack right in front of the entrance to her tent.

"Are you going to get some sleep?" Liam props himself up on his elbows.

"Eventually. I'm just thinking about tomorrow."

"You're thinking about Quell. The way you feel about her."

I can still feel the heat of her skin against my hand. "Shut up and sleep." I clench my fists. "You don't know what you're talking about."

"People who don't have the privilege of lying to themselves get real good at seeing the truth." He buries himself in his bed and I settle in mine. But sleep doesn't come. I can still hear the fear in her voice when I found her, and feel her relief when I held her. Maybe I imagined it. Maybe I wanted her to turn to me. I glare at the dark sky. Then I glare at my brother, sleeping so peacefully.

He's right.

The Dragunhead was right. I have a weakness for her. She is all I think about. And not just because of the mission. The flaps to Quell's tent ripple in the wind. Tucked into my bed, I pull the covers tighter around myself. I have to stay away from her. My brother shuffles in his blankets. I suppose there are worse things in the world than having a brother who's determined to be a pain and tell me the truth.

"Yags, do you remember the time we found all those dead rats in the country house?"

My brother answers with snores. *Tomorrow. We'll talk about that story tomorrow.*

FORTY-FOUR

*— * —*

Quell

I hang on Jordan's breaths until they slow and his body is still. Then I unzip my tent and step over him onto my shaky limbs. I thought he'd never fall asleep. But my throat is parched. And my dry skin itches all over. The burning sensation that tugged at my bones in that cave still rages inside me. I need to get to the ocean and cool down. I force my knees to lock, engaging every muscle to keep me from collapsing.

My toushana flutters as I stumble down the rocky mountainside. The streets of the town at the base of the hill are barren of people. I hurry past the harbor and don't stop until my feet hit sand.

Cold water crashes against my toes and a comforting chill shivers up my legs. But my body is still slick with sweat. I rip off my outer layers until I'm down to just underclothes and wade deep into the water, letting the coolness wash over me. With my eyes closed, I let myself sink into that weightlessness the ocean gives me, the feeling I love so much. The motion of the water rocks me back and forth. The gentle cadence soothes me, and I can feel the chilly water chipping away at my body temperature.

Finally, I open my eyes. And the island stares back at me. There's no one there waiting on the shore. There's no pink-striped towel with a cooler of snacks.

No little house with little windows. No safe haven.

Momma.

Suddenly the water is too cold and the salt in my eyes stings. The world is heavier. I swim back to the shore and try to exhale.

But the memories shatter me.

I can see a tiny jar that used to hold our money, covered with the swirls of blue fingerpaint. I can see the look on Mom's face when she handed me her dagger—one that I had to barter to save my life. One she could have used to save herself from the wolves. My knees go out from under me. The roar of the waves crashing around me is too loud. The moon is too bright. And the water is far too cold.

Moisture wells in my eyes but I hold in the tears. I have to be strong or I'll never peel myself up off this sand. I crawl the rest of the way to the shore, my hands digging in the sand. I can see the castles she and I were supposed to build. The ones made of sand and the real ones we daydreamed of having. *How do I do this without you?* Droplets fall on the back of my hand. And the longer I cry, the more it hurts. I lie there, hugging my knees, imagining that if I curl up into a ball tightly enough, I could disappear. Maybe this is all some kind of terrible dream. But I squeeze and squeeze and the only thing I feel is more hollow.

The pain hurts, deep inside. In a place I never reached. One I didn't know existed. A hole so vast and so deeply unreachable, it can never be filled.

I cry out to the waves but they only lap gently in response. I pound the sand until my fist is red. Every part of me hurts—the parts I show the world, and the parts I've never seen. I try to remember the last thing she said to me or the last thing I said to her. But it's all a haze of shadows.

"A house. With tiny windows. On the beach." I shake with a guttural pain so deep I expect to see the bloodstains on the sand. "You were supposed to be *here.*"

I dig for anger but only find more tears.

Enough to drown the ocean behind me.

And it's still not enough.

FORTY-FIVE

·· ──✳── ··

Jordan

A jolt slides against my ribs like a sharpened knife. I sit up, blinking. I check the time. I was out for an hour or two—it couldn't have been more. Yagrin's sack hasn't moved. The tent, however, is unzipped, and I don't have to peer inside to know Quell's gone.

Then my heart pangs with a deep ache of sadness, with a heaviness like I've never felt. The trace knocks in my chest, wedging deeper, then twisting so hard that it urges me to my feet. I inhale, pushing breath to all my heightened senses. But there isn't a whiff of lilac or jasmine. Quell is nowhere near here. The trace jabs my heart again, and the grief is so strong I can feel the weight pressing on my shoulders.

Only one place would make her feel like this.

I find Quell staring out at the water, hugging around herself. Her skin bathes in the moonlight, and breath sticks in my chest. *I shouldn't be here. Not when my head is this cloudy. Not when I feel her pain so strongly.* My hands find their way into my pockets, and every urge to back away from the sand, from the crash of the waves, from her, abandons me.

"Quell." The word falls out of my mouth.

Her chin slides over her shoulder.

"Do you prefer to be alone?" My pulse picks up and whatever else I was going to say blows away with the wind.

"Stay if you want, I don't care." Her gaze moves back out to the water.

A knot in my chest tugs down sharply like an anchor. The same knot that brought me here: the enormity of her grief. It sits on me and I cannot breathe. I close the distance between us despite my best judgment—hoping, wanting, wishing I could ease this writhing discomfort that's hers and somehow also mine.

I reach for her, and to my relief and surprise she doesn't move.

My next breath is a stutter. I'd almost forgotten how it feels when we're not fighting. I freeze, waiting for her to tense or give me the slightest indication that she doesn't want me touching her this way. But she doesn't move. So I don't either. We stay like that, with my hand gently cupped around her arm, until my feet are buried in the sand from the tide rolling in.

Something violent rears up inside me. *This is wrong.*

I begin to pull my hand away. But her fingers find mine.

And the whole world seems to still.

She turns, lifting her chin, and meets my stare. Her fingers work their way between mine and we stand there. Tears stream down her freckled cheeks, and the next one that falls does something confusing to my insides. It rolls down her face, streaming across her parted lips before dangling from her chin. I tighten my free hand into a fist, resisting the urge to catch it.

But then I can't resist anymore, and I smooth my thumb across the tear before it falls. *I should have said something before about her mother.* She leans into the palm of my hand. First her head, then her entire body folds into my chest. I wrap around her, holding on to her tightly, and the pain billowing inside us both eases like the calming of a raging storm. I bury my face in her hair and inhale, and it's like taking my first breath in a long time.

She is darkness.

But somehow she warms me like the sun.

My senses abandon me, and I pull her chin up so that we can see each other fully. I start to speak but her hand rises to my face, pressing my mouth closed gently. She leans back on my chest. She doesn't have to speak. The minute we shatter this silence, this moment will sift through our fingers quicker than sand. Stealing it is the only way it can exist.

I hold on to her tighter.

She cries a bit more, off and on, but after a long while, the tangle of her sadness unravels and she lets out a long exhale. She wriggles in my grip, and for a second I consider refusing to let her go. Holding her is the only thing that feels right in all this chaos. But I release her and she puts more distance between us.

"Thank you."

Her words carve a chasm the size of the Sphere inside me.

What have I done?

FORTY-SIX

Quell

Jordan left me after I told him I needed a bit more time at the beach, alone. When I make it back to camp, the chill on my skin from the ocean has nearly worn off. It was not nearly cold enough. The sun is on the horizon. Jordan is sitting by a fire. I don't have to ask to know he hasn't been able to go back to sleep. I give the flames a wide berth, wanting to hold on to the damp chill on my skin as long as possible. I'm not as hot, but I am weak.

"I'll be ready," I tell him when his head swivels in my direction. "The sun should crest the volcano soon."

"Quell, if you need to rest—"

"I'm fine."

"Stop saying that. We both know that isn't true." A war wages in his eyes.

"I'm tracking when the sun comes up."

There's much he doesn't say; I can tell by the look on his face. Resigned, he looks for his brother. "Yagrin."

It's only then I realize Yagrin, who still looks like Liam, is also fully awake. "There's a split in the trees to the south that has a really nice angle. I scoped it out earlier. Tried and counted to about twenty before my magic wouldn't let me see anymore."

"Great. But I'm going to try here first." I sit down and my head swims, but I hold still. Jordan calls him over for a word. They chat at a volume too low to hear. Jordan throws up his hands in frustration.

Suspend, count, flare, cloak. When the sun rises over the trees, I pull on the wedge of cold that slumbers at my side. When the brothers notice me, their fighting stops and *I* have all their attention again. I pour a hill of Sun Dust in my hand and toss it in the air. Iciness simmers in my veins but my toushana doesn't move. I hold my side and try again. But the cold resting inside is like a block of ice. I shift in my seat.

Jordan watches. Liam stands over me. I resituate myself and try again, willing my toushana to move, react, do *something*. It stirs weakly. I pull at the faint threads of its motion and try to force it into my hands, just to see what happens. But not even a wisp of magic appears.

"Concentrate on the cold," Liam says. "Picture it growing."

"Could you be quiet?"

I try twice more but it goes nowhere. I could scream. Jordan paces. Tears sting my eyes but I'm done crying. "I need space." I stand but wobble a moment to catch my balance. Both boys freeze as if I'm a piece of glass that might shatter. "Find something else to gawk at!"

To my relief, Jordan gives me some space, instead watching from a distance. But Liam doesn't move.

"I'm going farther up the mountain for a clearer view." I shoulder my bag and it only makes the world more topsy-turvy. I stumble into Jordan.

"That's it." His tone brokers no argument. "We're taking you to the bed-and-breakfast near here. You need an ice bath and proper rest."

My grip tightens on my bag strap. "No, I need to sun track. Beaulah's already ahead of us."

"I'm not asking you, Quell."

Yagrin opens his mouth to speak but snaps it shut, looking between us.

I drop my bag; the world is still a bit fuzzy at the edges. "Who exactly do you think you are?"

Jordan blows out a slow breath, then grabs my tent and starts packing it. "I'm not changing my mind on this. It's what's best for you."

"Oh, because you suddenly want what's best for me."

"Don't pretend like I didn't care."

"*Deal!* I won't pretend. Because you *didn't*."

"It was real for me. Every single moment of it was real for me. *You* were the liar. The master manipulator, twisting my feelings to help you shine as a débutante." He snarls. "We were something that should have never been."

"You couldn't be more right."

Yagrin stuffs his hands in his pockets. "The inn has a nice porch that you could—"

"Shut up!" we shout at Yagrin. He backs away just as Jordan pulls the tie tight on the last of my things. He takes my bag from me roughly.

"*I* say when I need to rest. *I* say when and where I'm going to sun track. I have to do this myself!" My voice cracks and it burns me with rage. "Don't you understand? It's just me now. Just me, *all alone!*"

I try to wrangle my bag from him but his grip is iron.

"*You are coming* to the inn." He wraps his arms around my legs, lifts me up off the ground, and throws me over his shoulder. The world tips upside down.

I kick and beat on his back, but he turns to his brother and says, "Keep watch here. Hopefully by midday, Quell is better. I was reading up in one of her Darkbearer books, and the ice bath should help."

"You went through my things!" I beat his back harder.

He grabs the rest of our stuff and starts up the hill.

I pound his back as hard as I can, but it's no use. He hikes up the hill with one arm clamped around my thighs. Eventually I run out of steam and hang there, limp, the rest of my energy zapped. After a long while, Jordan stops, and the world turns right side up as he sets me on my feet.

"If you're done fighting me, you can walk."

But the sudden weight on my feet is too much, and I almost fall.

He sighs and picks me up again; this time, one arm is cradled around my back and the other is beneath my knees. I try to muster the energy to argue, but my head lolls to his chest. I exhale, watching the sway of his necklace, losing myself in his cadence, when the stone of the Dragunheart pendant catches a glimmer of light. Beneath its surface are wisps of shadowed darkness. My heart skips a beat. I peer harder. His pendant is trimmed in metal with silver filigree. But the faceted stone itself is a radiant, unforgettable shade of red.

Like the gem from the cave.

My fingers twitch. I smile. One step closer to my plans for the Sphere.

FORTY-SEVEN

· ——✳—— ·

Jordan

Quell's body cooks in my hands. The longer I carry her, the warmer she becomes. Her head rests on my chest and I lengthen my stride to get down the hillside faster. She lifts her head every once in a while and takes a look around. After the first mile or so, she grows heavier in my hands, and I have to adjust my hold on her.

"I can walk, really."

"Save whatever strength you have for sun tracking."

"Right." There's no fight in her voice this time, as if she spent every ounce of it sobbing her eyes out at the ocean all night and used whatever dregs she had left trying to break my back with her fists. I'm not going to fight her anymore. The time it takes, the energy it requires—it's draining her and wasting time.

"We need you well."

"For the mission."

A half-truth. I want her well. I want many things, I'm realizing. Things I shouldn't. I give her a curt nod and she lies against me again. Her hair grazes my neck; the scent of it is a gritty mix of jasmine and sweat.

"I should have said something sooner, but I was very sad to hear about your mother." I hold my breath, waiting for a shift in her comfort at being in my arms. But she doesn't say anything.

"Quell?"

"I heard you."

"We're going to take Beaulah down." And yet my mouth keeps moving. "You're going to get well. Track that Sphere and she is ours."

She nestles against me.

"Are we almost there?" She turns the chain of my Dragunheart pendant necklace. I stop, setting her lightly on her feet, and shake out my arms. Before picking her up again, I tuck my pendant inside my shirt. She eyes the spot on my chest where it just was.

"It shouldn't be too much farther." The hike to the bed-and-breakfast is several miles. It's a petite two-story inn with intimate charm but grand, sweeping ocean views. I set her on her feet gently, but stay nearby.

"People might get the wrong idea," she says, steadying herself on the steps of the inn. "The Dragunheart grabbing a room with a girl."

"The mission is what matters. Not people's opinions."

She relents, allowing me to escort her up the porch and inside. We're greeted by a concierge with a festive pair of suspenders and a radiant mask of rose petals. Once I check her in under my name, I request every cube of ice in the entire inn be sent to her room. He agrees, befuddled, before directing us there.

Quell pushes the door open and I follow her inside. The room isn't anything like Chateau Soleil or Hartsboro, but its plush furnishings and spacious layout are much better than the campsite's. Quell sits on the edge of the bed and the tiniest exhale escapes her lips. An entire wall is covered in windows that extend into the bathroom. Quell reclines on the bed and her eyes close.

"I'm going to draw your bath."

As the tub fills, I unlatch the window, pushing against the bottom pane until it juts out. A breeze whips in, filling the room with salty air. The combination of an ice bath and the cool air should get her temperature down fast.

A knock at the door pulls me away. In minutes, the quickly filling bath is loaded down with buckets of ice. When I return to the bedroom, Quell is curled in a ball, fast asleep. I can feel her body heat before my hand even touches her back. She hardly moves in response.

"Up you go." I sit her up and her lashes bat lazily.

"I don't think I can." She's languid in my grip.

"You have to. The—"

"Mission. I know." She sighs, exasperated, and pushes one shoe off. But the second one isn't coming off easily. She holds it out to me. I pull the laces, loosening them one by one, then slide my hand inside the boot to guide her foot out of it gently. She pulls at her blouse, gesturing for my help. My throat bobs. Steeling myself, I undo the small buttons, then help her get it over her head. I avert my eyes and wrap her in a towel quickly and usher her to the bathroom. She tests the water and I wait outside the door. Another few items of clothing hit the ground before water sloshes and skin skids against porcelain. Finally, I hear another long exhale.

"How long should I stay in?"

"Until you can feel your magic strongly again."

"But the water, what if I—"

"I'll be right here. I'm not going to leave until you're feeling better."

Silence.

Some time passes. I peer through the cracked door, and Quell's head rests back on the tub, her arms braced along the top.

She pulls a hand out of the water, and droplets run down her arms. She opens her hand and a wisp of black spools there before vanishing. "I think it is helping."

"Good."

"Jordan?"

"Yes."

"When the time comes for me to avenge my mother, don't get in my way."

She settles deeper into the bath. I watch until her breaths are steady and I'm sure she's fallen asleep. Then I rest my head against the doorframe and exhale.

FORTY-EIGHT

Quell

I wake the next morning with a stiffness in my limbs. The ice in the tub has melted, but the water is still cold. I tighten at my center, feeling the spot where my toushana slumbers.

Answer me.

A cold sensation in my bones shudders like a boulder that's never been moved. Then it rolls through me and pressure gathers in my chest. I sit up in the water as the quake shoves through me. When I reach for my magic, it answers, and shadows thrash in my palms. I let out a sharp exhale, but an ache buried inside me twists. What use is all this magic if it couldn't save my mother?

I drag myself out of the tub. I scrub myself dry, wishing I could rub hard enough to get rid of the stain of grief. I sit on the vanity's stool and wade through the sadness, because I have to let myself feel it. After some time I pull myself together, trying to focus on why I'm here. *I need a closer look at that pendant on Jordan's necklace.* Thoughts of my mother recede to the hollow, hidden place inside me where I bury them.

When I open the door to the bathroom, my clothes from the trip are laid out near a window left ajar. They smell like fresh lemons. The bed looks untouched.

"Jordan?"

The deck outside stretches from the bedroom to the bathroom, but the only sign of him is a muddied pair of shoes. *This is my chance.* If he changed, maybe he took his pendant necklace off? I slip into my clothes before flipping through his things, looking in the room's every nook and cranny. The wardrobe is full of cobwebs; a small bag he carries is tucked inside. I tear through it, looking for some trace of his pendant, when I spot a note on the bedside table.

Stay put.

Lying down on the bed, I watch the fan spin. Jordan's obstinance got me to this room, to that bath. He is technically the reason I feel so much better. He even washed my clothes by hand. Who does that for someone they don't care about? How does the mission mean that much to him? My gut says it doesn't. That he is lying to himself. But even that is a choice.

I bury my face in a pillow, trying to think of something besides the look in his eye when he coached me through pulling away from that stone. But no matter how hard I try to *not* picture his green eyes, they are all I can see. He held me on that beach as if I were the only thing in the world. It felt real. It felt *good* to believe for a second I wasn't alone. I vent my frustration into the pillow.

None of this should matter. He is a means to an end. Brooding over a boy who *might* still care for me, but wishes I were dead. *I'm an idiot.* ~~Hate is safer. Because hate I know what to do with.~~ I fill my thoughts with the Dragunheart pendant instead. It's small, but if it can expand like the stones in the cave . . . I look for the file on Francis to see if any of the notes mention the red stone, but the only note I find says it was a prominent part of the process used to create the Sphere's casing. My tongue pokes my cheek. *It might work.*

Sun crests the horizon outside my balcony window by the time I am done rummaging through the notes I made from the file. And it hits me: we won't even find the Sphere if I don't keep an eye on the number of sunspots so we don't miss the next flare. Holding the balcony doors ajar, I toss a bit of Dust in the air. The glowing speckles suspend in a hazy cloud between my line of sight and the sun. Cold needles prick behind my eyes, keeping them open. The haze of nothingness suddenly pops with dots of color; a few at first, then a surge of spots almost all at once. I count up to forty-three before I lose track. I finally allow myself a blink and when I open my eyes the dots have gone. The last time I checked there were a little more than a dozen spots. *It's doubled.*

I look for my shoes. I have to find Jordan and Yagrin. A flare is imminent. We have a couple of days, maybe—no more.

The inn's lobby is full of people waiting to dine, and the explosion of chatter stops me in my tracks. It's morning again, which means the island is open to visitors. Magic is hidden. I check myself in a mirror. My diadem is tucked away.

From the hall, I scan for Jordan and garner a few stares. My grip on my skirt tightens when I spot someone who, from far away, looks a bit familiar. I crane for a better view and my heart stumbles. The gentleman's unkempt hair, piercing blue eyes, and devilish smirk are unforgettable. *Felix.* Shelby kissed him in the forest outside Chateau Soleil one moment and he turned her into ash the next. He converses with a lady who twists pearls around her finger, listening intently.

Felix hasn't looked up. But another scan of the room sends my heart racing. Across the parlor, Mynick and two other men are being escorted to a table. There are silver coins being turned mindlessly in several people's hands all across the dining room, coins sitting on a table here and there, and a few bold Draguns with coins at their collar. The walls close in as I reconsider every person's wardrobe. Black, there's so much black with hints of red and the occasional embroidered column on a sock, the hem of a sleeve. Beaulah's Draguns. *Everywhere.*

I'm backing away when a firm hand finds my lower back and urges me along. I smell him before I see him and the flutter of my heart calms. He leads us into a stairwell and jams the door.

"Were you seen?" Jordan asks.

"No."

"Are you sure?"

"Positive. I came to tell you the number of sunspots is increasing quickly. A flare is imminent. Then I saw Felix!"

"And *many* others."

"How many?"

"Two dozen. Maybe more. A war is brewing."

"Are they following us?"

"Perhaps." His jaw ticks. "Or Yagrin's not really on our side."

"That's not it."

"You don't know how much of a screwup my brother can be, even on accident."

I fold my arms. "You shouldn't talk about him that way. If you want to be frank, the most logical leak in our trio is *you*. Because I certainly have no love for Beaulah, and I *know* Yagrin hates that woman."

"The audacity, that you think you know my brother better than me."

"You know him, but you don't see him. Funny, the way he talks, it sounds like he thought that was changing."

His mouth hardens, and I can feel him tense beside me. Then his shoulders sink. "Look, drop this. None of us are working with Beaulah." Something like regret glints in his eyes. "I don't know how Beaulah figured out we're here. The concierge may have recognized you even though we didn't give your name. She has eyes everywhere. If they're here, they're either planning to follow us when we catch a flare to the Sphere or stop us. We need to adjust our plans."

My toushana nudges me. "We can damage their numbers . . ."

His brows crease.

"If they try to follow us when we catch a flare to sun track, neither of us will be able to stop them. There are too many of them. If we want to make out of here with an advantage over Beaulah, we have to do something drastic."

His expression darkens. "What exactly are you suggesting?"

"We attack them before they attack us or get in our way. We can wait until they're asleep and do it."

"You want to raid my own brotherhood? *Me,* the Dragunheart."

"Jordan, you said yourself, like Charlie, they've chosen their side."

"We take an oath, sealed in bone and blood, unto death."

"And yet they are here. Marching for Beaulah to steal the Sphere's magic." I hate when he does that. When he gets too scared to actually *do* something. Our back is up against a wall, can't he see that? I'm getting to that Sphere before Beaulah. *Without* dozens of her Draguns following me.

He sighs.

"Have them arrested, send them to the Dragunhead. We have to do *something* to get rid of some of them. There are three of us!"

His knuckles scrape his jaw. "They'll deny it. We can't prove they are here with treasonous intent. Our hands are tied."

I unleash a cloud of shadows before siphoning it back into myself. "*No,* they're not!"

FORTY-NINE

—✳—

Jordan

I storm out of the stairwell. Almost all of the lobby crowd has moved into the dining area. I spot Felix dining with an Unmarked. Eyes follow me through the restaurant, but no one dares say a word.

"Felix. What are you doing here?"

"Brother." He looks up from his copy of the *Daily* and greets me with a well-rehearsed smile. The woman at the table looks over at me and blushes.

"Rosalind," he says in an awful Italian accent, "questo e mio fratello. Brother, meet Rosalind. She's visiting for the day from Sardinia."

"Piacere di conoscerti." She holds out her hand, and I oblige it with a kiss.

"I require a word."

He turns a page in the paper. "Begonia Terrace has gone on the market. Sixty-eight million. House of Oralia is selling. What do you think of *that*?"

"Per favore scusaci un attimo," I say to the woman, with perfect pitch and flawless intonation. She thanks Felix, rises from the table, and leaves.

"You just ruined what was looking to be a very promising morning."

More eyes are on us. Draguns I haven't seen in years. I snatch the paper away from him.

"Is Charlie here?"

"Do you see him?"

"Yaniselle?"

He quirks a brow. "Aye."

I lean across the table. "I'll ask once more. Why are you here?"

Felix shifts. He clears his throat and tosses his napkin on his plate. "Broom closet near the fire exit on the south side of the inn."

I exit the restaurant first and find the broom closet. He joins me moments later, the playfulness on his face gone.

"Why are you here? What is Beaulah playing at?"

"Sunspots are aggressively growing in number."

"You wouldn't have passed Maezre Tramaine's session if it wasn't for my brother doing your work. Don't talk to me about things you don't know anything about. How much longer do you think Beaulah's going to be able to hide where her loyalties really lie?"

Felix dusts off my shoulder. "Making your father proud, I see."

I tighten a fist. "I urge you to see reason and uphold your vows."

"Funny. I was going to give you the same advice." Felix straightens his coat and reaches for the broom closet door. "Many understand Mother's position and are passionate about her cause."

The other House that's marching.

I pin him in place. "You will give me something or you won't leave here at all."

Felix swallows. "I've heard Chateau Soleil is a ghost town."

"Darragh Marionne would never march in support of Beaulah." It can't be House Ambrose. They'd see allying with Beaulah as beneath them. Headmistress Oralia never troubles herself with anything. "There aren't any other Houses. Duncan? Their House has been dissolved."

"Grudges outlive people, Jordan. I'm surprised you of all people don't realize that."

"They could not care less about House of Marionne."

They have nothing to lose.

"You dated the Duncan girl," I say. "The one who died."

"Aye."

"Did you kill her?"

"You wound me. I'm still sick with grief."

This reeks of Beaulah's plotting. Shelby Duncan was the first Duncan to be admitted to a House for magic training since the House fell decades ago. If she died on Marionne territory, that would cement Duncan as an enemy and put a target on Darragh Marionne's back. This was calculated, cold-blooded murder. For power.

I snatch the coin from his throat. "Beaulah gave the order, didn't she? To get rid of Shelby at Chateau Soleil."

Felix sucks his teeth.

I open the door. "Leave."

"My coin."

"Be grateful you're leaving with your life."

His nostrils flare, his cheeks flush. "I heard about your visit to the Trial ceremony. How Jordan Wexton threw his virtue pins. You're out, brother. Exposed. Go bark up another tree. Try Marionne—I hear you like getting underneath their skirts." He storms off. I drop his coin in my pocket, my pulse thundering.

A war is brewing.

And we're the only ones without allies.

THE CHAIR WHERE I spent the night outside Quell's room is still there. I sit, pondering some kind of solution to this impending chaos. We can't stoop to Beaulah's level of violence. I understand Quell wants to make sure Beaulah doesn't get to the Sphere before we do, but there has to be another way. We can outsmart them somehow. *What if there is no other way,* I can almost hear Quell say. I rake a hand through my hair, still able to see the Dragunhead's face when I asked him to go on this mission. He won't be happy to hear about this development. My gut sloshes as I slip my phone out of my pocket. I see no other option than to update him and get his wisdom. I fire off a message requesting Maei have him call me.

The door to the room opens.

"You're not leaving this room until it's time to cloak to the Sphere," I say, and I feel anger rising inside her. "What's the latest count of sun-spots?"

"Approaching the hundreds. So I'm your prisoner now?"

"You become my prisoner each time you don't do what I say."

She slams the door just as the phone buzzes. I stand, too frazzled to sit.

"Sir?"

"I hear there's trouble in Aronya."

"Three on the march."

"Three! By god."

"Sir, we need to talk about the brothers matriculating from Hartsboro."

"I'm listening."

"I have concerns about their loyalties. They're all over this inn. I believe they're helping *her.*"

The line is silent for so long, I clear my throat to ensure he's still there.

"I . . . I don't know what to do."

"Keep your brothers in line, whatever it takes. *That's* what you do!"

"Yes, sir."

The line goes dead.

The day whirls by and I can hardly focus. By the time the inn empties of visitors, I've eased back into my seat outside Quell's room. The island is ours again. Ours, and Beaulah's team of Draguns'. My eyes are heavy and yet my mind won't stop. I need to think. But I can't think without rest. I rattle a fist on the door. I hope she's calmed. I'll tie her down to keep her in this room, if I must, in order to steal a nap. I knock again, but there's no response. She could be asleep. With a cursory glance around, I pull on the chill of dark magic in the air and cloak, slipping through the door. Once I'm inside, it's completely dark.

I pull back the covers but there's no sign of Quell. The trace on her is also silent. My heart knocks into my ribs. If I've lost her or if someone's hurt—

Creak.

The noise is coming from outside, on the balcony. Over the ledge, a floor below, Quell lowers herself using a makeshift rope. I'm halfway over the rail as she disappears inside the room. By the time I make it there and peer through the window, the room swells with a cloud of shadows. When the haze clears, a dark figure darts out the door. I force my way inside and a biting cold is in the air. I look around, expecting to see bodies. There are two beds, a Dragun in each, and neither moves.

I touch one and he is still warm. To my relief, he's blinking at the ceiling, frozen in shock. His hands are purple, as if they've been badly bruised.

"I can't . . . My magic . . . It won't . . ." He gapes in horror. The other Dragun is in bad shape, too.

"Stay here," I tell them both, and rush out the door. She is using toushana to bruise their hands so badly it stops their ability to access magic. *If we use magic selfishly, to hurt people, then we're no better than Darkbearers.*

The hall is empty. I try the next door, listening before slipping between its seams. There are two Draguns in this room as well, scantily clad and in the same bed. She wails at the sight of her hands. *I'm too late.*

"Did you see who did this?" I ask. *How big of a hole has Quell dug for herself?*

"It was dark."

"The room went cold as ice."

I still may be able to fix this if I can find her before she harms anyone else. I have them stay put before returning to the hall. A head of wavy hair darts around a corner and I'm on her tail. She dashes inside a room. By the time I enter, there's a Dragun wide awake in bed, holding the covers to himself. Water runs in the bathroom.

"Dragunheart, sir." He swallows. "What—um—what brings you here so late?" His gaze darts to the wardrobe, then to his clothes, and to the dagger all the way across the room. I move slowly in that direction, shadows spooling in my fist. I reach for the handle and the door flies open. Quell bursts out of the cabinet, but she's startled by the magic in my hands. And it gives me the moment I need. I tackle her, and her toushana fizzles out as I wrestle her arms behind her back, one after the other.

"I am not the enemy! Look around."

"How many rooms have you visited?" I ask, pinning her wrists together.

"Not enough."

"Quell, you have to stop this." It isn't right!

"I've shown mercy." She wriggles an arm free, then lassoes it around my neck with monstrous strength. And suddenly she's behind me, tightening her grip on my neck. "They've done terrible things for that woman. We both know it." She seethes, tightening her hold on me. This is not about their magic. This is not about the Sphere. This is about hurting anyone even remotely connected to Beaulah.

"You're not thinking clearly. Your magic, it's too riled up. And this isn't our plan. Quell, please." I tug at her arms around my neck, which are making it hard for me to breathe.

"I've never been clearer in my entire life."

I slam myself backward into the cabinet, and her grip loosens enough for me to twist in her hold and grab her firmly by the wrists. "You're ruining everything."

A hungry look rages in those honey-brown eyes.

"Please, you have to trust me."

Her jaw hardens. But her body relaxes against me, and I let her arms down.

"Get back to the room," I whisper. "I'll clean this all up. Somehow I'll fix it."

"I don't need you to cover for me, Jordan." She pushes me off her and paces the full length of the room, stopping at the bed beside the Dragun, who watches her with wide eyes.

"I need you to *help* me," she says.

The Dragun fumbles in his covers behind her.

"That *is* helping you!"

She shakes her head.

Then she gasps as metal protrudes through her shirt, sprouting a flower of blood.

FIFTY

Jordan

I see red.

The Dragun's gleaming eyes glint with ambition as dark magic whirs in his hand. Quell's knees hit the ground, and I'm on top of him in a blur of motion. My fist connects with his face, and I keep smashing until my knuckles are wet with his blood. I crush his windpipe, summoning the cold. He sputters as the choke takes him.

"Traitor," he mutters. Shadows urge the toushana into him. My heart thuds; shoving it at such a fast rate makes my fingers numb. He tries to writhe, but the choke stiffens him beneath me. He gazes up, frozen, with a wide-eyed stare. His skin begins to bruise beneath mine, and I snatch my hand away. I stumble up and off him, swallowing hard.

The urge to climb back on top of him bites at me, but I reach for the cuffs. He's not moving. I nudge him with my foot and his hand twitches. I rush to Quell. Her shirt is soaked. But she motions for me to help her up and I do. Once on her feet, she lifts her shirt to show her wound. The tip of a long metal knife protrudes from her abdomen. The gash above her navel is weeping red, when something strange happens.

Quell's hand swells with toushana. She grips the dagger's tip and winces. But when she pulls it out, the blade dissolves, inch by bloodied, silver inch. The dagger handle falls from her back, clattering to the ground, but I can't tear my gaze away from her wound. She works shadows across her trunk again, and the gash narrows until it's closed completely and her stomach is smooth and soft.

"I don't understand."

She stares in disbelief. "I wasn't sure it would work."

"Toushana destroys everything it touches," I say.

"Except itself. I realized it when I was studying how Darkbearers used to bind with dark magic. They used toushana on itself and it *healed* the impurities in Darkbearers' blood. My magic decomposed the blade. But when it touched my skin, it sensed itself and rebuilt what was dying."

This is some kind of trick. A lie. But the only thing that's changed is the pace of my heartbeat. She lays my hand on her skin where the wound just was. "I'm okay."

"Are you sure?"

"I think so. Are *you* okay?" She eyes the unmoving Dragun on the ground.

"Healers should still be able to help him."

A wild look still gleams in Quell's eyes.

"You can't do this," I say, remembering how we got in this mess in the first place.

"They're not dead. Every Dragun I stopped is one of Beaulah's that won't be in our way tomorrow. At least I think they'll wake up tomorrow." She shows me a paper with ripped edges. "There are several more rooms full of Draguns. I intend to clear them all."

"Do you hear yourself?" I take the paper. It's a guest log she's apparently stolen from the front desk. "Quell, this is wrong."

"It's not. Somewhere, deep down, you know that." She moves to the door. "You won't stop me. So help me or look the other way." She leaves, and all I can think of is some kind of harm coming to her. It boils me with rage but cuts like fear. *I will not lose her. Not like this.* I rush out the door behind her. Quell is about to slip inside the seams of the next door when I grab her by the wrist. "Only maim them *as little* as you have to. Restrain them. I'll cuff them."

"Fine." She tugs her wrist out of my hold. With my heart in my throat, I follow her into the next dark room.

An hour races past, and by the time we finish, we've made sure a whole floor of Draguns can't use their magic. When we stumble out of the last room, Quell's own hands are covered in deeper bruises; they travel all the way up her arms. We stop at the door to her room. Her clothes are disheveled, her hair is a mess, and the look in her eyes is untamed. But she is smiling. I've only seen her move with that much passionate determination one other time. And it had been ridiculous.

Then we ran through the kitchens of my father's hotel, and she shoved cake in my mouth. So utterly ridiculous. Embarrassing, frankly. And yet I don't think I ever laughed so hard. My father was furious when he found out what we did, which only made it more delicious. There was something unbridled in her expression then, and that same person stares at me now. She is untethered and free. I move closer to her. Her lashes dip. *How is it that she's never been more beautiful to me than in a moment like this?*

The thought sinks my heart with such regret.

She grabs the knob behind her and opens the door, but I linger in the doorway, adrenaline coursing through me like a hungry lion. After a moment I realize I don't have anywhere else to go and follow her inside. She disappears into the bathroom. I sit on the edge of her bed, and the heaviness of the night sits on my chest. On the one hand we minimized the threat; we upheld justice. But on the other, I've just abused my power by aiding and abetting a fugitive.

The bathroom door opens, and she stands in the doorway, wrapped in a towel, hair dripping wet. "Oh." She cinches her towel tighter. "You're still here."

"You're right, I should go." I stand, my muscles complaining at the teasing rest I just gave them.

"Jordan, you need to sleep. It's been two days." She has a point. She grabs her pile of clean clothes that I hang-dried for her. On her way back into the bathroom, she stops close to me and fixates on my pendant dangling on my chest.

"It's so radiant."

The smell of her incenses me. She is a hillside of honeysuckle, a garden full of roses, and the acridness of my hopes and dreams I had so many months ago, burning. There's a bookshelf in the room. I put some distance between us and trail a finger along the spines. "Like any of these?"

"That one was my plan for tonight, actually." She pulls a book by Dickens with a tattered spine.

"*Oliver Twist*. How fitting."

We share a laugh. I rock back and forth on my heels, unsure what to do with the silence.

"You can stay here if you want." That is somehow the worst and most intoxicating idea she's ever had. I have to keep my head on straight with Quell. But every moment I'm with her, I only want to be with her more.

"I'll get my own room." I leave before she can protest.

The lobby of the inn is silent, but before I can even get my question out the concierge says, "I'm sorry, sir. If you need a room, we're all booked for the night." He smiles timidly, and I can sense his stress. "I must be getting back to an urgent matter, if there's not anything else."

I drag myself back to Quell's room. *This isn't a good idea.* She opens the door dressed for bed in an oversized tee. *My* oversized tee. She allows me inside, and I stand there with my hands in my pockets. She clears the decorative pillows off the bed.

"I don't want to sleep in the same bed any more than you," she says. "But we have to rest."

"I know. I know."

"Well, it doesn't have to be weird."

"It won't be weird. Why would it be weird?"

"Well, you're acting as if—"

Fire crackles in the fireplace, and a silence settles between us.

"Never mind." She pulls the outer and under covers off the bed and hands me one. "Tomorrow there could be a flare. We have to be ready."

"You're right. Beaulah always seems two steps ahead."

She smiles darkly. "Not after tonight."

Shame burns my cheeks, but I can't help but smile back. I join her at the bed, on the opposite side. "Ladies first."

She rolls her eyes and slides into her covers. I take off my shirt and catch her staring. She promptly looks away. I get in beside her, keeping a wall of blankets between us. I stare straight up at the ceiling and keep my hands clasped across my chest so there's no chance I can touch her by accident. I'm about to close my eyes when she clears her throat.

My heart twinges, fluttering with nervousness. But it's not mine. It's hers.

"Relax," I say.

"I'm fine."

"Liar."

"Shut up!"

A smile tugs at my lips, and I can hear the mirth between her words.

"Are you asleep?"

"Quell, it's been ten seconds."

"Okay, good." She rolls on her side and faces me, propping her head on her elbow. "I was thinking. I never said thank you earlier. So, thank you." She pushes her diadem through her head, and I've never seen it so close. It's a rich ebony metal. Intricate details coil around sharp spires ornamented with radiant dark-pink stones. Clusters of them sparkle like a thousand stars.

I shift uncomfortably.

"I'm just glad you didn't get hurt," I say.

"That's the nicest thing you've said to me in months."

"The mission."

"Don't pretend you didn't enjoy it. It's *okay*, Jordan. You didn't do anything disloyal. If anything, you upheld the Order."

"Respectfully, you're wrong."

The pressure inside me tremors. How do I lie here and pretend that I am not weak for her? I went with her tonight because I couldn't fathom someone raising a hand to harm her. If any of those Draguns had overcome Quell, even if she were at fault, I can't be sure I wouldn't have wrapped my hands around their throats until the light went out of their eyes.

"Quell—"

"Yes?" She bites her bottom lip and pulls at the ends of her hair. When she catches me watching, she shoves her hand away, trying to hide her nervousness. But I can feel it shaking in my chest. I can feel mine, too.

I stare at her and take all of her in. The girl who destroyed me. Made a fool of me. Made me love her after I vowed to never love anyone again. And yet all I want to do is hold her once more, like I did on that beach.

And believe that I deserve to be as free as she is.

The admission unravels something tightly woven in me, unspooling everything I am. My stupidity gets the better of me, and I reach for her face, tracing the slope of her cheeks, the rise of her jaw, the delicateness of her neck. She turns into my touch, and it ruins me.

"Tonight, I went against everything I stand for. And yet, I would betray my vows a thousand times to never leave this moment."

The brown of her eyes glimmers with determination, like it did the first time we met. I try to look away but can't. Are we just forever destined to exist this way? On the opposite ends of possibility? At either end of a deadly blade?

"What are you thinking?"

I roll onto my back and glare at the ceiling. "That I wish I could be free. Free of worrying about the Order. The pressures of my position. Free of carrying the weight of magic on my shoulders. Free to be reckless. Free to make mistakes. To breathe the world in, Quell."

"That makes two of us."

I laugh. "You're so free already."

"Not nearly enough. I hate hiding."

I don't know what to say. I can't change who she is. And no matter what I want, I can't change who I am either. She scoots closer to me and I stop breathing.

The word *don't* hangs on my lips. "I am the most wretched person I know."

"No." Her fingers play on my chest. "I am." She twists the chain at my throat and tugs *hard*, bringing me closer. I drown in the bronzed sands of her eyes and grab a fistful of blanket.

"I want to kiss you. But it would ruin everything."

She touches my lips with delicate fingers, and tears well in my eyes. It's more than a kiss: it's a choice. A choice to forsake who I am for who I wish I could be. She leans forward, trembling. She stops before my mouth and I don't breathe. The hollow of her throat begs for a kiss. We've never been this close. And the way she shakes, I'm sure she hasn't ever been this close to anyone.

"Kiss me, Jordan." She closes her eyes. I touch the tips of her diadem before taking her face gently in my hand, considering the weight of this decision. Her breath is warm on my palm. It sends bumps up my arms. I graze her lips with mine, and it feels like the first time. There were no other kisses before this one. No one other than her. No moment or decision that mattered more.

Her mouth melts into mine, and a shudder rushes through me.

I pull her closer, and she deepens the kiss, exploring my mouth. Our tongues tangle. Our breaths hitch. There is a dance made of our music. Every ounce that she gives of herself makes me want to give her that much more of me. She bites my lip, and I nibble at hers before we bury our mouths together again. Her body curls around mine, and I break the kiss and lift her off me. Her teeth pull at her swollen lips.

"What are we doing?"

"Choosing freedom." She wrestles free of my hold, and our mouths crash together; the world reddens with passion. Her legs untangle from her covers and wrap around mine. My hand snakes up her back, to the base of her neck. She breathes my name, and I yearn with an ache to give her a reason to say my name again and again. Teach her secrets she's never learned, far more rare and special than magic. She grinds her body on top of mine and passion jolts through me. So sharp, I have to come up for air. I swallow. She pants. But I reestablish a sliver of space between us, a force field repelling us from going any further. I have to remind myself to breathe.

"What's wrong?"

"Nothing, I just . . . this is moving fast."

She plays with the necklace on my chest and the sight fully knocks me back to my senses.

I am the Dragunheart.

I sit up. "I'm a leader in this Order. I have to get hold of myself, which starts with being honest."

The sparkle in her eyes dies, and I burn with shame.

"Quell. I don't hate you. I never have, not even when I found out your secret. I don't think I could ever hate you. But in the morning, I still have a duty that I cannot escape. I thought I could do this, but I lied to myself. I can't."

"What are you saying?"

"I'm saying Yagrin is going to accompany you the rest of the way. I'll travel alone and meet you there."

"No."

"Quell."

"Jordan!" She sits up.

"What do you expect to come of this? Look at what we did to my brothers tonight."

"So you regret it?"

"Part of me does, yes! I don't know if that will ever go away. But it's no matter now. I have to live with it. And look at what we were about to do *here,* now. I don't want to hurt you any more than I already have."

"You just want to kill me." Her nose crinkles, and I can feel her hurt radiating in my chest.

"I've never wanted to do that!" I stand and pace, unable to look at her anymore when she's staring at me like that. "We don't work."

"Oh, get over yourself," she says. The soft parts of her are gone. And the fire I've known since we started this journey is back in full force. "All I'm asking is for you to stay through the next leg of this trip. *Please.*" She fluffs her pillow, settling down to go to bed. "You know, I hated you for what you did to me at Chateau Soleil. But it did set me free. A multitude of truths can exist. The justice that you, the Dragunheart, and I, a Dark-bearer, served tonight made the Order safer. And made Beaulah weaker. You want to stop lying to yourself? Start with that."

She tugs the lamp cord and I can't see the hurt in her eyes anymore. It should make me feel better, but instead it keeps me up all night.

FIFTY-ONE

Quell

I lie there waiting for Jordan to fall asleep. The plan was to rest and prepare for tomorrow. But then he looked at me with those green eyes, and it set me on fire, taking me back to feelings I was sure I had buried. Then we kissed and it reminded me what it felt like to truly be alive. It felt good to not care who I was, for once, and take what I want. I hate him for running. But I love him for all he sees in me.

Frustration tangles in my chest. *How, after everything, can he still choose to be a coward?* I toss and turn, trying to think of something, *anything* other than Jordan Wexton, but the last few hours won't let me go. I slip out of bed and pad to the window as quietly as I can. But the minute I open the balcony door, he props up on his elbows in bed.

"Quell, I didn't mean to upset you. Are you okay?"

If he asks me that one more time, I'm going to scream. I ignore him, stepping outside, letting the breeze from the ocean whip through my hair, imagining I could take flight on the wind. And disappear from here. Go to wherever my mother is. My heart pangs and I immediately regret allowing myself the space to think of her. But grief doesn't seem to follow any of my rules; it refuses to stay in the box I put it in. I sit on the balcony's railing.

"Quell, please come back to bed. You really do need rest." He stands in the doorway; his body glistens in the moonlight. A scar across his ribs disappearing behind him is his only glaring imperfection. But it helps to make him human.

"Well, thanks to you, I can't sleep." I storm past him, back inside, and sit up in the bed. "Did you ever tell me how you got that scar?"

He looks down. His fingers trace it.

"When they buried me during one of my Trials, the fool shoved the spade too deep in the ground and it caught me in the ribs."

I wince. The things he's survived . . . it's miraculous he's not a complete monster.

"My aunt called the scar a badge of honor."

For the first time in a long time, when I look at Jordan, I don't see the veil he holds so firmly in place. He sits in the chair by the fire. "I can sleep here if that makes it easier for you to rest."

"That's not helpful. I'm fine." My irritation thrums, remembering his decision. I don't want him to leave. I want him right here. Beside me. *How else will I* . . . I glare at the red pendant. Then look away. He meets my eyes, and staring into them renders me immobile because of the way he gazes at me. As if he's probing my soul. As if he wants to know me in the deepest way. As if he wants to see me inside and out and love every part of me.

And as if he finally has the courage to.

It takes my breath away.

He looks at me like no one else ever has. My heart patters as I drink in his stare. It feels like all I've ever truly wanted was to be known fully and to hear that I'm okay. Tears well in my eyes and he rises from his seat, joining me at the bedside in a breath, tracing away each tear before it falls. I wish I could tell him that he thinks I'm the powerful, unapologetic, and carefree one. But the truth is I live in terror every day of being alone forever.

"You're not fine. I always know how you're really feeling." His fingers leave my face and draw circles on my hands.

"I don't like the idea of you leaving Yagrin and me to finish this trip together."

"Why not?" Something hides between his words.

"He isn't helpful in the ways you are." Fear keeps me from admitting the full truth.

"Yagrin is good company. The times I couldn't sleep when we were kids, he'd tell me stories. When my aunt found us, she dragged me from his room and gave me three nights with the wolves. She told me to cuddle them." He shrugs nonchalantly. Hurt is etched in a notch between his brows. He doesn't try to hide it.

Beaulah really broke him. Somehow I hate her more.

"The Healer had me for almost a month."

"She is an awful person. She deserves what's coming to her."

"I've realized there's something broken in my aunt. Instead of trying to fix it in herself, she tries to break it in other people."

"I will break *her* more." The truth of my plan sticks to my lips. I search him, wondering if maybe he could be convinced to help me take the Sphere's magic and put justice in *our* hands.

He peels back the covers and climbs back in bed with me. I turn my back to him, hugging my pillow. This is always how it is with us. He connects to something inside me, and it holds on to me like a tether.

"Are you really going to leave?"

His hand rests on my back gently. I raise my elbow, allowing his arm to slip around me. He pulls me tight against him. My head nestles in the space beneath his jaw. "For now, let's just both rest."

He strokes the hairs beside my face. And in a breath I'm fast asleep.

I AWAKEN WITH Jordan's body wrapped around mine. He sleeps so peacefully. We've shifted in the night, and I'm sprawled across his chest. Outside our door is faint commotion. But I bury my head back in the covers, not wanting this to end. His hand strokes my back. Outside, the sky is a dim blue with the promise of morning. Last night feels like a dream.

"How sure are you there will be a flare today?" he asks.

"I would bet my toushana on it." I have to tell him the truth about my plans for the Sphere's magic. Otherwise, last night meant nothing.

"I need to get Yagrin so he can cloak with us." He stirs beneath me, and I eye the pendant on his chest.

"I think I know where Beaulah is going to store the magic from the Sphere."

"What do you mean?"

"The stone in the cave—I touched it because I suspected it was like Cultivator ring stones and could contain toushana." I hold up his pendant. "I think this is made of the same stone."

"I know for a fact it is. Why do you think I don't let you ever touch it?"

"Jordan, I want to beat Beaulah at her own game. I want us to take the innards of the Sphere and hold them in your pendant."

He goes rigid and my heart stumbles. Then he unfurls himself from me, and we sit up side by side in bed.

"*See me*, Jordan. *Please.* I don't have any desire for power over the Order or anything ridiculous like that. I am not Beaulah."

He breathes harder, watching me. Silent.

"You know me better than anyone."

His chin slides over his shoulder, looking away from me. After several moments, he says, "I do see you, Quell. But have you considered what possessing something so powerful could do to you, especially with your affliction? And for someone still facing a death sentence, it feels a bit reckless to be—"

"Forget I said anything." I get out of bed. I can't listen to what sounds like rejection from him. Not now, not after last night. "If you'll excuse me, I have revenge to accomplish."

He gestures for me to go.

Outside I pace. He is entirely frustrating. He won't stop my plans. I'm going to get that pendant from his neck. Beaulah *will be* tormented to know the power she loves so much is in my hands. The sun glares at me, and I use the last of the Dust in the vial around my neck. I suspend it in the air and once the haze settles, magic surges through me, up from the place where it sleeps, freezing my chest before pushing its way behind my eyes. I shift my line of sight to look through the Dust at the sun and blink. Colorful spots bleed through the dusty haze. I count. There are so many, I lose count at one hundred.

"Jordan!"

"What is it?"

"Get Yagrin now."

FIFTY-TWO

━━━━✳━━━━

Nore

Nore's heart thundered as she snuck through Dlaminaugh. The crowds from the ball had cleared the estate, but it wasn't until the moon hung high in the sky that she dared venture out to find the journal's circled coordinates in one of their graveyards. She walked along the balustrade of the staircase down to the first floor, watching for the occasional shift of a shadow that didn't quite make sense with the light. She knew her ancestors were there. And after seeing her mother's fear when she asked about the heart, Nore wanted more than ever to avoid them.

She dashed down the hall, past the labs, and through the Hall of Discovery, bridged between the buildings. The corridor looked untouched. But shrouded around its base, against the wall they had gone through just hours earlier, was a pile of black rose petals. Nore pressed one to her nose, but all she smelled was the lotion on her hands. The only person she knew with a garden of the strange flower was Darragh Marionne. She furrowed her brow and backed away, the journal tight in her grip. Was her mother still in there? If she wasn't, where had she gone? *I don't care.*

Nore hurried off but didn't get far before she heard a pair of hushed voices coming toward her. She smoothed her clothes and tidied her hair as Maezre Tutom and her mother's maid came around the corner, arm in arm. Her mother's maid was pink from crying. The maezre's expression was riddled with lines as well, but she looked more agitated than worried. She threw a glance over her shoulder before meeting Nore's eyes.

"Maezre. Mrs. Shoom." She curtsied, then noticed what had her maezre's attention. A pair of Draguns with talons at their throat and sapphire rings on their knuckles were coming up the hallway behind them.

"Have you seen your mother, Nore?" one Dragun asked. He appeared to be the leader of the two. She'd seen him patrolling the grounds. *Head of security*, she guessed.

"I haven't seen her since the ball," she lied, avoiding Maezre Tutom's insistent stare.

"No one can find her. She was last seen exiting this hall. She did not notify Mrs. Shoom her bedtime would be delayed. Also, the lock on her personal safe in her bedroom was found broken. The Dragunhead's been notified."

Her heart skipped a beat. Who would do *that*?

Mrs. Shoom tightened her grip on Maezre Tutom's arm, who petted her hands.

"That is concerning," Nore managed.

The Dragun's glare narrowed as he stepped closer to her. "It is not a secret that you have no love for your mother. But by morning, if there is trouble lurking, you should at least behave as if you do."

Nore's jaw worked. "You are overreacting. She's probably in her lab." ~~No, that didn't make sense. She spent afternoons in lab. She bit her lip. Her~~ improv garnered her a few quizzical glances. She took a deep breath.

"It's our job to prepare in case she doesn't reappear."

"What do you mean, exactly?"

"Sovereign forbid, upon Isla Ambrose's final breath, the heirship passes automatically to her next of kin in the line of succession. You."

This prison was determined to keep her in.

"The House becomes yours; as Headmistress it would be your seat on the Council and your life tethered to the Sphere." The lead Dragun eyed her warily but signaled for the others to depart.

Maezre Tutom pulled Nore closer and whispered, "The ancestors are angry. Everything hangs on your mother being found. *Everything.*" Nore glanced at the trick wall, where she knew the vault was. She didn't know if her mother was still in there or had run off somewhere else. She had been so distraught over Nore learning about the glass box. She bit her lip. How bad would it be to mention that her heart was being held in a glass box? Could that help their searching? The last secret her mother had kept—about Nore being Unmarked—hadn't seemed very serious, but Nore was dead wrong about that. "I'm sorry, I wish I was more help."

Nore hurried off to Maezre Tutom, who whispered comfort to Mother's wailing maid. The lead Dragun followed. She cut a left, then a right. But he stayed on her heels. Her brother intersected with them in the next hall.

"Mr. Ambrose, we need constant eyes on Nore." It was the lead Dragun who spoke.

"I need a word with my sister. *Alone.*"

Her brother pulled her aside. "What are you doing?"

"Do you trust me?"

"I want to. But you are worrying me."

Nore tried to hold her face still as stone, but her brother knew her too well.

He sighed. "What have you done?"

"If you want to know, come with me. *Help* me."

"Nore, no." He pulled her to a halt with a rough grip that was unlike him. "This has to stop. You're the *heir.* You can't—" He raked a hand through his long hair. "Tell me the truth, *everything.*"

"Only if you'll have my back regardless, like you said."

"That's an impossible ask."

"It didn't used to be."

His mouth hardened and he looked past her. She couldn't be sure he wouldn't stop her. Or worse, enlist the Draguns to help him stop her.

"Sorry, Ell. I have to do this. For me."

She ran away from her brother's shouts, but he didn't follow her. That was something, at least.

DARING SHOOK HIS mane when Nore approached. She ran a hand down the crest of his neck and gave his nose a scratch. His hoof pawed at the hard ground. She dug out a treat and held it out on her palm.

"Today we go on our biggest adventure yet," she whispered to him as she gathered his tack and grabbed a shovel. Daring's ears twitched. "I'll figure out a way to take you with me. You have my word." She checked her map once more. The coordinates were on the westernmost graveyard on the sunset side of the mountains, miles away. If the Scroll was at those coordinates, she'd be free. Once the girth was tight under his belly, she slipped the reins over his head, put the bit in his mouth, and climbed on. She guided him out the gate and then rocked her hips forward. He took off. The wind whipped through her hair and her heart squeezed. She wasn't a little girl or Red anymore, but in this moment, she felt as if she could be just as free.

Nore rode Daring hard across the estate, through the trails along the lake's edge of the property, then down into the valley that rimmed their vast estate. By the time the graveyard came into view, Nore was sore. She sat back in the saddle and Daring slowed. Her nose and fingers were ice.

"Easy," she said, gripping the reins with one hand and moving tree branches out of the way with the other. A tall fir was planted each time an ancestor was buried; there were firs all over the place. As they rode farther, the snow was cleared off an expanse of headstones, placed closely together. The pungent scent in the air grew sharper. Nore dismounted and led Daring the rest of the way. The forest shook, and then shadows shifted in the light. The ancestors had followed her here. As if they could sense her panic, their presence tightened around her.

"Come on!" She pulled Daring. He refused to move. But when she spun around, she saw what he was looking at.

Ellery appeared from the trees on horseback, light gleaming on the slick hide of his black stallion. He was always much faster than Daring. His gray gloves were dark with blood. Daring reared. Nore let him go.

"You followed me. Why?"

"I'm here to help." Her brother's stare deadened. He lifted two sealed pails from his horse's pack and spilled the steaming liquid onto the icy ground before handing Nore a shovel with jagged teeth. "You're here to dig up the coordinates. Get started."

Nore took the spade, her mind full of questions, but when she jabbed the ground with it, and felt the anticipation of freedom thumping in her chest, any concerns faded away. Ellery watched, his arms folded, and Nore almost asked why. But if her suspicions about the magical malfunctions she had read about in the journal were true, he *couldn't* help—because he had Anatomer magic.

"How did you know about the coordinates?"

"You've always hidden books in your stove. Once I found what you'd been reading, it wasn't hard to deduce what you've been researching. Darragh Marionne was also seen exiting the estate. It wasn't hard to put the two together. You're helping her."

"But that doesn't explain how you knew where to find this spot." She stopped digging and met her brother's eyes. There wasn't a hint of malice, but there was something she had never seen before in him. She didn't have words for it, but her clammy hands slipped on the shovel.

"The legend of the Immortality Scroll is known, Nore. You'd know that if you were around this place. People have written about trying to dig up this spot. Keep going."

She worked furiously until her muscles ached. *He knew about the Scroll, but said nothing before. Why?* The sun was fully awake when she shoved the spade in the dirt and hit something hard. Her brother watched and didn't blink. She fell to her knees, her hands and legs numb, digging at the earth, clearing it so she could see what was underneath. Then she did, and her stomach curdled. *Bones. Human ones.* Beside them, an empty glass box like the one that held her mother's heart. "The ancestors required Caera's heart, too . . ." She stumbled up, an eerie feeling all over her skin. The dead around her hovered over the open grave, then explored inside. Chills raced up her arms as she paced, trying to force down a sick feeling.

Finally her brother smiled, and said, "Thank you."

She blinked, not understanding.

"Have you ever wondered why Ambrose can push our strands of magic farther than any other House?"

He pulled a dog-eared book from his satchel and handed it to Nore. "Because the House has a pact with our dead—we give up the Headmistress's heart in exchange for help with magic. With Mother missing, you, dear sister, are next."

FIFTY-THREE

· · ———— ✳ ———— · ·

Quell

By the time Jordan returns with Yagrin, I'm on the balcony rehashing my plan. When we find the Sphere, I won't have much time. Jordan isn't going to give me his necklace and he'll be even more on guard.

Yagrin enters as himself and that's some small relief. He and Jordan must have not argued the whole journey up the peak. Maybe they've made some kind of peace.

"How many sunspots were there this morning?" he asks.

"Hundreds."

"All of Beaulah's Draguns are gone," Jordan cuts in, his expression harried. I guess their sun tracking wasn't as bad as he'd thought.

"What about the ones we detained?"

But before he can respond, the morning sky ripples with plum and orange streaks. A light flashes, shooting across the sky.

The flare.

It's time.

"Now!"

Jordan and Yagrin latch onto me. I pull at my toushana and picture my magic grabbing hold of the bright light, wrapping us in it, taking us with it. We disappear.

⚜

WE APPEAR ON a snowy field between mountains, where a thicket of sturdy conifers are frosted with snow. A barren field of headstones stretches out before us against an ominous gray sky. And far in the distance, the tip-top of a glass-and-stone building disappears into the clouds.

"House of Ambrose," Jordan says.

"*There* she is." Yagrin nudges me. I turn all the way around and the sight knocks the wind out of me. A sea of sloping hillside graveyards stretches ahead of us as far as I can see. There are thousands of headstones, maybe more. The way the snow is lumped, I wouldn't be surprised if there are more flat headstones than tall ones. But the expanse of dead isn't what rattles my pulse.

The Sphere hovers over them like a dark moon.

Its insides undulate violently, cracking like whips of electricity. Jordan and Yagrin stare, unmoving. I step out from the shade of the trees, my eyes adjusting to the colorless landscape.

That's when I see them.

Cloaks appear—pops of shadows, all across the graveyards. Then they dissolve, leaving a person behind. On the Sphere's left flank are Draguns in dark colors, forming themselves in neat rows. With every blink of my eyes, it seems another joins them.

"House of Perl," I say. They are dots in the distance, but Beaulah is hard to miss, her deep red coat billowing. Beside her, opposite the Sphere, is a ragtag band of people wearing pale green robes marked with a sigil I've never seen before. On the Sphere's right flank is another hefty formation. I can spot my grandmother even from several fields' distance away. She's wrapped in a bright gold coat marked with a fleur-de-lis. Near her is someone who could, from far away, be Abby. She has her dark hair and dainty frame.

There *is* a war brewing.

Jordan was right.

And it's right here.

FIFTY-FOUR

·· ———✳——— ··

Nore

Nore stood over the hole in the earth beside the ancient fir tree, her heart ramming in her chest. This graveyard was where the eldest Headmistresses were buried. There was much commotion in the distance, but she couldn't tear her eyes away from the matter at hand.

"I don't understand," she said, looking at the page Ellery saved. It was a diagram of a heart, surrounded by shaded figures with streams of magic, connected to it. She dropped the book and stared at the empty glass box beside Caera Ambrose's remains in the grave.

"In exchange for the Headmistress's heart," he went on, "the ancestors gave parts of their own dead magic to us. When a member of this House uses magic, we channel not only our own, but the magic of our House's dead. This Pact we have with them is unbreakable, sister."

Nore braced herself and stepped inside the hole to retrieve the glass box. Beneath it was a piece of dry parchment. She pulled, and out of the ground came a rolled scroll.

Her brother's eyes glittered.

"Give it to me."

But before she could refuse, she unrolled it and realized the paper was ripped at its edge. Her heart rended. IMMORTALITY was in gold letters across the top.

The price of a life that never ends
is one that should have never begun.
When the half-moon's passed and the full moon awaits,
you'll find a hunchbacked orb that wanes.
Beneath it bring blood, bone, and

The rest of the scroll had been ripped off. She looked back in the grave and dug around, but there were no other scraps of paper.

"It's not all here."

Ellery snatched for the Scroll.

"No!" She skirted his reach.

"Who is the most magically superior Ambrose?"

"The Headmistress. Otherwise they wouldn't be fit to lead the most cutting-edge House in the Order." The recitation was out of Nore's mouth like an instinct, before she realized what she was saying.

"And that's the heart the Pact promises the ancestors. Don't you get it? If you become Headmistress, your heart won't have the magic they require." The blue in his eyes became a storm-tossed sea. "They'll devour you. *Give me* that Scroll!" He pulled out a blade, and Nore's bones shook in her skin. "It'll be quick and painless, like falling asleep. I'll bring you back immediately, I swear."

It all made sense now, but it shook her bones in horror. "You're asking me to let you kill me."

"I will follow the instructions on the Scroll. Mother will die."

The words bounced around in her skull. *Mother will die.* Had she been found? Was she hurt? Did he have her somewhere? Was she going to— The blood on his gloves. Her heart raced.

"The heirship will pass to me because there are no other girls in the near line. And I'll bring you right back. You know I honor my word. This gets the House out of your hair."

She put more distance between them, struggling to form words.

"This is everything you could possibly want."

"*Stop. Stop* talking!" She couldn't breathe: the last several hours blew through her memory like a snowstorm. She couldn't quite put into words how she knew this wasn't the answer. But she was sure. If she died and came back with toushana, then what? And being the sister of the heir to House of Ambrose did *not* sound much better than being heir. She trusted her brother.

But she trusted herself more.

She whistled for Daring and he emerged from the brush. She'd fooled herself into thinking there was a way she could detach herself from this world and her family, but there was no escape. Every option only buried her deeper in her fate. She was tied to this world, whether she had magic or not. The only choice she had was what she would do with that existence. She was smarter than all of them. If she played their game, she'd win. She would find a way to outsmart this Pact.

"No, Ellery. My answer is no!"

Shadows rose from the grave and surrounded her.

"I love you, dear sister. But I'm not asking." Her brother swung into his saddle. She held tight to the Scroll in one hand and grabbed Daring's reins with the other.

"You think you're so clever, Nore." Her brother rode up to her; his hands moved like lightning, unlatching his dagger. She yanked hard on Daring's reins, pulling his nose down sharply, the way he hated. He reared up on his back legs, knocking Ellery's stallion in the face, and it gave her the seconds she needed. She swung into her saddle and squeezed her knees tight. But her brother's steed dashed in the way. Daring spurred into motion. She tightened her grip on the Scroll. Ellery rode up beside her. He leaned sideways in the saddle, raised his blade, and drove it downward right into her fist.

"*Ah!*" The scream tore from her throat. Blinding pain ripped through her limbs. But she tightened her hold on the Scroll. He'd have to cut off her hand to force her to let go. He grabbed the Scroll, pulling it away from her. She held on. He tugged.

It ripped.

She kicked in her heels. Daring rode like the wind as Nore stuffed her bloody piece of the scroll into her dress. She rode hard through the graveyard, meandering. Daring tired, but she didn't let up. Ell's horse was faster, but she knew trails her brother didn't. Rivers of blood ran down her arms, but she dared not look too closely. She had to get far, far away.

A sharp light cut through the sky.

Daring reared up. He whinnied, backing away as the world warmed pink, then purple, the colors fluttering like a midmorning sunset.

Then a black moon appeared.

And the whole world darkened beneath its shadow. Violent matter sloshed under its glossy surface. The face of it was riddled with spider-webbed cracks.

The Sphere.

Before she could move, bursts of shadows appeared in snappy succession. Armies of people. She saw sigils and House colors, and her heart froze in her chest.

Everyone had their eye on the Sphere.

PART FOUR

FIFTY-FIVE

Jordan

The Sphere hangs in the air, bobbing above the ground like an angry storm, splintered with endless cracks. It's a wonder it has held up this long. My grip on Quell tightens. The world is silent; these buried mountains are suffocated by a blanket of snow. But everyone here can probably hear my thudding heart. We may have held back a dozen of Beaulah's Draguns, but two dozen more are sprawled out across the graveyard. Behind us, the angular, architectural wonder that is Dlaminaugh is eerily silent, as if the entire House of Ambrose is sitting behind their stone-and-glass walls, watching. The last time I visited here, I was a boy, traveling with my father. But seeing this place, *feeling* its mysterious aura, even from a great distance, is impossible to forget.

"Relocate," I mutter.

"It won't yet. Not until it's been attacked," my brother says. "And if strong enough magic is lassoed to it, it won't be able to move, even then. That's how I cracked it."

My heart thuds when I see Quell listening. I look for some indication that she's let this idea go. That after last night she's learned that I do trust her. I could never see her as a monster. But her plan is reckless. She knows nothing of the innards, magical composition, the fickle way it reacts with oxygen. A million things could go wrong. I only want her to see reason. I consider reaching for her, but her expression is ironclad.

"Wait here under the trees, please," I say to her. "It's far enough away, with plenty of cover. It should be fairly safe." But she pulls away from me, her expression darkening, before I can finish.

"I'm sorry." She grabs my necklace and tugs. Time and motion seem out of balance as the chain snaps. Our late-night talks, the way we slept tangled up together, the way it felt to tell her the things I haven't told anyone rush through my mind like some kind of fever dream. Before I can form words, she dashes off down the hillside toward the Sphere. And it feels like a part of me goes with her.

"Jordan," the Dragunhead says, and his voice spins me around. He's running toward me. "You're here. I'm so glad you're here." He jabs a thumb backward. "Ambrose won't come out. I've asked and Isla will not come to the gate to speak with me. Whatever happens here, we are on our own." His gaze falls to my chest. "Where is your pendant?"

"Quell." A rush of heat surges through me, and I clench my fists. "But Beaulah . . ."

He grabs me by the shoulders. "Where did the girl go?" He looks past me to the impending doom, and something shades his expression. Beaulah's forces move, surrounding the Sphere. *It's happening.* I look for Quell but don't see her.

"We have to let Beaulah get far enough in her plan to implicate herself. She is going to shatter the Sphere." My heart thuds. I swallow.

"And so is Quell, it seems," the Dragunhead says.

My chin hits my chest. How do I hide her intentions? How do I protect her now? But she's out in the open, defying everything we'd planned. He responds, but I don't hear a word he's saying once I realize I don't see my brother.

The Dragunhead shakes me. "You take care of Beaulah; I'll apprehend the girl."

Just past him, in the distance, Quell skirts past Duncan's forces, going around their perimeter, which is clever since everyone's attention is on the Sphere. *I should have seen this coming.* Word spread our world is fracturing, and every rat from the corners of the Order has come to make their claim on it. I look for House of Oralia, but there is no sign of them. I watch the other Houses. No one moves—like they're at some kind of standoff. Marionne has dozens in plain clothes. It appears Darragh just grabbed as many members from her House as she could.

And then there's Duncan, with much smaller numbers. But even from here, I can see daggers swirling with flames in their fists. Their attention is not on the Sphere, not on Beaulah, but on House of Marionne. Darragh is a dead woman.

One of House Duncan steps forward and the silence on the hillside somehow grows quieter. My heart thuds. All at once House Duncan lower to their knees. And raise their hands.

Things happen very quickly.

Shadows ribbon through the air to them, connecting with their hands. They all slam both hands of dark magic together and bury them in the snow.

The ground rumbles.

From their hands, a crack rips across the ground, right in Darragh's direction.

The air rings with shrieks. People shove one another out of the way. Darragh steps aside, glaring not at Duncan but at Beaulah Perl, whose House has linked hands and formed a circle around the Sphere. Duncan huddles again, doing something else. Pressure builds in my chest, but I can't tear my eyes away from the impending chaos. The Dragunhead doesn't move beside me.

"How do I protect the Sphere?"

The seconds are ticking by like hours when something dark is flung through the air at Darragh and her House. It hits the snow and explodes. Ash and snow, broken bits of earth, shoot through the air. And in a radius around everything the toushana bomb touched, the ground blackens. My heart stumbles. *Toushana*. Duncan's using dark magic. They've allied themselves with Beaulah. As if they've learned nothing from their past.

I look for Quell but don't see her. More explosions rain from the skies.

"Go to Beaulah!" The Dragunhead shoves me forward.

My body responds before my words can. Darting across the snowy graveyard is like navigating a minefield. Darragh Marionne marches toward Beaulah, dodging explosions. Black thrashes in her hands and my throat goes dry. *She has toushana. Quell was telling the truth.*

Bombs stream through the air, and I run faster.

Eruptions of darkness and wails leave my ears ringing.

My nose stings with the scent of burned earth.

I pull at the cold, trying to summon enough toushana to cloak closer to Beaulah. But the mist that floats toward me scatters, pulled in every direction by the battle. I urge my feet faster, dashing past bleeding, decaying bodies ornamented in blush and gold. The hillside reeks of death. *Yagrin, where are you?*

Those who don't have weapons shift them out of whatever they find on the ground. The violence only seems to roil the black matter inside the glassy orb, making its waves crash harder. Below it, Beaulah stoically watches the mayhem she caused. Yani, Felix, and the rest of them are rigid by her side. I look once more for my brother, but I run smack into Charlie. Or some hollowed-out version of him, no more than skin and bones. His hand thrashes with toushana and I reach for mine again.

"I'm not your enemy, Charlie."

"It's looking that way."

I try to charge past him but he shoves me back, hard. My arm burns as his magic tears the fabric of my shirt. He's so fragile, he loses his step. I grab him by the shirt and throw him to the ground.

"Stand down!"

His ripped shirt reveals a purpled body with a sutured cut at the meeting of his ribs, black at its seams.

"What have you done?"

He scrambles backward, trying to get up, and winces.

"Jealous? That she could make me into what you will never be." He spools shadows in his fist, and they do not come from the world around us. They come from inside him. I swallow. Somehow she's bound him to toushana.

He tries to stand, but whatever experiment Beaulah has done to him has overwhelmed his body.

"Magic is eating you from the inside," I breathe, unable to stomach the words. Unable to accept what I'm seeing. This is *Charlie,* my mentor, the stand-in uncle who taught me the way of things when I arrived at Hartsboro. He took me on my first raid and made sure I didn't get hurt.

When he manages to get to his feet, I don't have the heart to stop him. He's done more damage to himself than I could ever do. He will be dead in days.

"Out of my way," I say.

He widens his stance.

I step forward; he reaches for me. And I bury my dagger in his belly, in mercy. He slumps over my shoulder, and I hold him, tears pricking my eyes. I lower him to the snow, close his hollow stare, and force myself to keep moving.

That's when I spot Quell. She's almost made it past the other Houses to the Sphere. Her clothes are a mess; she must have had an altercation with someone on the way. *I don't know what to do.* Do I go after her? Or do I go after Beaulah, who's watching the chaos from beneath the Sphere, her Draguns formed up beside her? Waiting. Watching. As Quell darts around their perimeter, Beaulah's head follows her. And an eerie feeling slithers around my throat.

They're waiting.

Waiting for Quell to break the Sphere. Beaulah was never going to do it herself. Having Quell do it was her plan all along.

"Quell, don't!" But she's too far away to hear. The sights and sounds of clashing bodies dull, and all I can hear is the thud of Quell's heart. I clutch my chest, wishing the trace worked in reverse. Wishing I could get her attention faster.

"Quell!"

I dash across the graveyard, between Duncan and Marionne's blood-bath, and shout for her until she turns in my direction. Her body bleeds dark magic as she prepares to direct it to the Sphere. I dodge bodies slamming into one another. When she gets within shouting distance of Beaulah, she comes to a sharp halt. I catch up to her. But her magic whirls violently around her, shadows swallowing her like a swarm of locusts. I can't get very close.

"Quell, stop!" I plead. "Don't do this. Beaulah's played you. This is a suicide mission. This is *not* what you are!"

Beaulah watches greedily. Her Draguns could be statues, standing around the Sphere.

Staring at Quell on the edge of demise makes my soul feel like it's being ripped in two. "Maybe, for you, everything between us wasn't real. But it is for me. Somehow you are both heart and darkness, which should be impossible! But defying the impossible is what you're best at. *Please.*" *Don't leave me to fight for freedom in this world alone.*

Quell shakes her head, her cheeks stained with tears. "If I don't do this, Mom died for nothing." She rotates her arms together and casts her magic onto the cracked Sphere like a net. Shadows hook onto its glass surface, and the orb shudders. Beyond her, Beaulah's mouth bows in a smirk. In the distance the Dragunhead races toward us. She has *minutes.*

Quell tugs downward, pulling on the tether of her magic.

The orb hits the ground, and the earth quakes. The black matter inside the Sphere is shaken up. When the matter settles, it churns in a counter-clockwise motion, growing slower and thicker with each rotation. My brother appears out of nowhere and joins Quell's side, unleashing his magic. *Beaulah wants this.* She's played them both, using their hatred of her to manipulate them into doing exactly what serves her purposes.

"*No!*" The Sphere's innards harden into a sludge.

"Get out of the way," the Dragunhead shouts.

"Sir, give me a minute—" I spin just as the Dragunhead's dagger slams into my chest.

FIFTY-SIX

———✳———

Quell

Jordan's knees hit the ground and a scream rips from my throat. I glare at the Dragunhead, who is now beside Beaulah, watching my magic attach to the orb. Beaulah's Draguns are staying put like obedient little minions.

"*Jordan!*" Magic streams from my trembling fingers. I want to let go. But Beaulah. *My mother.* "Yagrin!"

But he is already lugging Jordan's bleeding body away. When I turn back to the Sphere, even several hundred paces away, the sight of it stills my pulse. A piece of its glassy casing has broken free. Matter in the Sphere rolls to the gash in its exterior. A trickle of magic seeps from the crevice where the Sphere meets the earth.

It hits the air.

Then vanishes.

Evaporating.

And just like that, a whiff of magic is gone . . . forever.

"She's done it!" someone screams.

The Sphere's insides writhe. *I can do this.* I can get my revenge.

"Get rid of the girl." Beaulah gives the order, shoving Felix, Yani, and a few others in my direction. The linked hands around the Sphere break as Beaulah's Draguns come for me. I feel my pockets for Jordan's pendant as Draguns encircle me. I pull it out when the Dragunhead shouts, "Hurry!"

Draguns assault me, their toushana streaming through the air. When their magic hits me, it pummels the wind from my chest and the pendant from my grasp. Somewhere Yagrin howls. Another person shrieks. I scramble across the snowy ground, clawing through the snow, scratching at cement headstones in the pavement, for some sign of the red stone. I stagger up, still looking. But there is no sign of Jordan's necklace.

It's gone.

And so is my shot at forcing Beaulah to know my misery.

Tears try to pry their way from my eyes but I have none left to cry. The Draguns don't relent. Clouds of magic close around me so thickly, even the snow appears blackened. Toushana moves through me, comforting me as it twists around my bones like a hug. I pull at it harder, wishing it could numb the hollow ache where my heart used to live. I don't move. I'm waiting to be destroyed when something hits me right in the stomach. I narrowly catch it.

A ball of dark swirling mist.

I drop the bomb but it explodes, and it feels like a fire erupting in my hands. The force of it punches me in the chest. I stumble back, lose my footing, and trip. I blink, and somehow the world is still there. I wait for the sting of wounds or debilitating pain. But nothing happens. I pull myself up on my feet, my body colder all over. Beaulah's Draguns watch me, gaping, before hurling more magic.

Everywhere is death.

Everywhere is darkness.

And somehow I am existing despite it all.

The silver blade.

An ice storm stirs beneath my skin as I remember the small amount of toushana saving my life. A smile curls my lips.

The darkness can't hurt me.

Because I am the darkness.

I defy every lie about toushana they've built.

I am their villain, their scapegoat, the mask to their own monstrosity. Because without people like me, there would be no one to blame for the Order's horror but themselves.

The Draguns tire. And I am wholly intact. They cease their assault, backing away, as if they've had the same revelation.

"What are you doing?!" Beaulah snatches Yani by the arm. "I did not say retreat!" She looks around. *"Charlie?"*

The Dragunhead turns in to himself, cloaking and disappearing.

I glare at Beaulah. Then the Sphere. There is still one way I can avenge my mother. Toushana recoils in me with a vengeance. I hold my magic in, like I did at Hartsboro, letting it build up. When I release, I'm going to shatter the Sphere.

FIFTY-SEVEN

Jordan

I writhe on the frozen ground, trying to make sense of the world. Graves are still all around me, and I hear faint commotion in the distance. I'm still on Ambrose grounds. A fir tree that looks older than the Order blurs into the sky above me.

"Quell?" The word comes out cracked. I struggle to turn, but moving makes my body feel like it has split in two. *Is she alright?* I try to lift myself but collapse, and the last moments I remember come back in a rush. The Dragunhead set me up. He sent me to Beaulah without backup, knowing she'd try to kill me when I tried to stop her. He wanted me out of the way. Even if that meant *dead*.

The throbbing ache in my chest is still wet and warm around the base of the dagger. The blade isn't pushed in too deeply because, when I felt what was happening, I shoved away. Still, it feels like there's a log in the center of my chest, and every time I shift, it turns into a razor.

I hold breath in my chest and try once more to hoist myself up, to get a better idea of where I've been taken. Upright, with my back against a headstone, I can see more clearly. The stone walls of Dlaminaugh tower over me, no more than a few hundred paces away. I peer around for my brother. I could have sworn he grabbed me. But there's no one. I feel my pockets for any elixirs I might have on hand. Something for pain, or healing cuts, anything that could help. But I find nothing. I am going to die here. Alone.

I picture Quell's face. I want her to be the last thing I see. Tears come. I don't fight them.

Every person in the Order I gave my loyalty to has let me down. Beaulah. Darragh. Now the Dragunhead. My chin hits my chest.

I did everything right.

And the Order stabbed me in the back.

I rest my head back, letting myself feel whatever this chaos is. As I replay the past several weeks in my mind, a prick of something unfamiliar blooms inside. Parts of me that have been riddled with holes my entire life feel like they're finally filling in.

And then I close my eyes and let myself relive the final moments of the raid on the Unmarked house. The child we found had seen magic. I swallow, remembering, still able to feel the chill that rose on my arms when I told my men to clear the perimeter.

As I approached the small bed, my foot nudged the child's stuffed bear—like the one Yags used to drag everywhere. I stood in that little bedroom and drew the cold to myself. Shadows thrashed in one hand, and I held the bear in the other. Recitations ran through my head of protocols and drills, expectations. I could hardly breathe. But as I watched their little chest rise and fall, the rules didn't matter.

I laid the bear beside the child.

And snuffed out my magic in a tight fist.

Then I left the house.

And said nothing of it to anyone.

I couldn't sleep or eat, my training was a constant voice in my head, bashing me, that I couldn't escape. It was the Dragunhead's words, ironically, that helped. *Dig deep in the heart, rely on what I know, and trust it.*

Memories come in a flood. Diminishing Beaulah's ranks at the inn last night. Attacking my own men. Cheating, lying, stealing for my brother when we were little because that's what it took to protect him.

Disloyalty.

And yet, it feels . . . good.

More tears come as I glare at the spot on my chest where my Dragunheart pendant used to rest. It was all meaningless. The Dragunhead's position, his expertise, his experience—none of it made him worthy of magic. His betrayal today proved that. And the brotherhood. Most of them are just more pawns on a chessboard.

The Order is a game of power. One I never wanted to play.

None of the titles I've earned make me worthy of magic. My choices prove who I am. It is a seed of a thought I had so long ago, an inkling I dared not fully feel. But it's as true as the bleeding Sphere.

Magic could do so much good in the world if it weren't so feared. I think of Quell and Knox. I'm not sure what the answer is anymore. But forcing people to erase parts of themselves isn't it.

Magic deserves to be preserved. It's part of who we are as Marked people.

But the Order can burn.

I try again to stand, putting the brunt of my weight on the headstone. But it's no use. I lie on my side that doesn't ache, trying to stomach the pain. I need to get to Quell. I have to know if she's okay. A horse whinnies. Pounding hooves come to a screeching halt right before me. I blink, trying to make sense of the rider's face. And a person with windblown red hair who I've never seen before stares back at me.

FIFTY-EIGHT

Nore

The gentleman's robes suggested he had quite a high station in the Order. But the fine handle of the dagger protruding from his chest bore a coat of arms with each House sigil and a Dragun talon. Commotion roared in the distance; she gazed over her shoulder in the direction of the graveyard where she had just fled the confrontation with her brother. After gaping at the Sphere and the fight ensuing beneath it, Nore fled. Staying as far from the chaos as she could, she followed trails around to the opposite end of the estate, where there were courtyards instead of graveyards.

How did he get here?

She eyed the man again, took another wary glance over her shoulder, and dismounted. His skin was slick with sweat and blood.

"Excuse me. Are you—" She turned him from his side to his back, laying him flat on the ground. He groaned but opened his eyes. The wound in his chest was fresh. She knew where he'd come from.

"What exactly is the status of the Sphere?" She needed whatever information she could get on whether it would break. The moment it did, her mother would be dead and *she* would be Headmistress, which complicated everything. But the gentleman only moaned in pain, his eyes rolling in their sockets. She tapped her foot. Ellery could be on her tail. She pushed away Daring's reins, then whistled, and he ran off. The misdirection should buy her some time.

She sat the man up as best she could, trying to keep him from slouching and deepening the wound. "I need answers, and you're going to give them to me." Her mind raced with all she knew from her reading about healing magic. Back when she hoped Shifter magic would favor her. His eyes opened fully. They were green but dark. Like a hurricane ripping apart a meadow.

"Who are you?" he asked, his voice weak. She eyed the blade in his chest again. The knife must have hit bone because its tip was stiffly wedged in place.

"We can't take that out of you without massive blood loss." Her tongue poked her cheek. He grabbed her hand with a shocking amount of strength, given his state.

"*Who* are you?"

She straightened, considering how she should answer. She didn't need Red's face to be bold. She was talking to a dead man. "I'm Nore Emilie—"

"Ambrose." His grip tightened. "The red hair and inquisitive determination. I should have known."

"How do you know my name?"

"I'm Jordan Wexton."

"The *Dragunheart*." She eyed the blade again.

"You thought you'd captured a vigilante."

"You have no heart pendant." Red ran from the tear in his chest, and his grip on her slacked. "This blade is exquisitely crafted." It wasn't a fire dagger, which had a wider hilt to protect the hand from flames. If it were, Jordan Wexton would be dead. The blade was a honing-style dagger, but a fine one, with intricate detailing and the brotherhood's sigil burned into its handle. There was no doubt in her mind who it belonged to. "The Dragunhead stabbed you, his Dragunheart. Why?" It sounded preposterous. But nothing the Order did surprised her.

"My best guess is that he and Beaulah Perl are working together to bring down the Sphere."

Her eyes grew.

He shifted, grimacing, his hand moving to his wound.

"Careful!"

"Do you know any Shifter magic? Healer specialty would be great."

She swallowed. The truth came devilishly close to leaving her lips. "I don't. Sorry." She wasn't sure why she apologized. This wasn't her fault. But she'd stumbled upon someone very high up in the Order, with much power, who was fresh out of help. She gnawed her lip and whistled for Daring. "If we can get you to my cottage, I may have something that could help."

"I can't move, and you'd never be able to lift me up from here."

"Let me try."

"Out of my way," someone yelled. A girl with a cropped dark haircut and an irritated scowl shoved her aside. With magic streaming from her hand, she smoothed over Jordan Wexton's wounds. At the same time she gripped the dagger's handle and tugged carefully. The dagger came out in a rush of blood. She worked both hands over him now. His exposed skin tugged together, but the area soaked with blood failed to move. The girl tried again. Nore stood to get out of her way and backed into someone else.

"Oh, excuse me." She turned, and Yagrin stared back at her.

Nore couldn't move. Her heart squeezed. The sounds of the forest blared in her ears and the entire world faded. His dark hair hung loosely over his shoulders; it was longer than she remembered. The angles in his face had thinned with fatigue or something. But his dark eyes glittered as they always had, the right one more golden than brown. His strong, lean frame filled her with memories of them lying together, basking in the sunshine. She released a tight breath, relieved to see him alive and unhurt, and a lump of joy rose in her throat. Her heart pattered in a way she hadn't thought it ever would again. She stepped forward in disbelief. He was a dream. This wasn't real. But when he set his bag down, he stared at her with brows slashed downward. Like she was a stranger.

And then she remembered: she was.

"Who the hell are you?" he said, and it felt like her heart would rip in two. She choked down her feelings and put more distance between them.

"Show some manners, brother. That's the heir to House Ambrose. Nore."

She took another step backward. The last year by his side, as Red, flew through her mind, and it unsteadied her. She looked for Daring. She couldn't do this. She couldn't look at him and accept that, though she stood right there, he had no idea she even existed.

"Sorry," he said. "I'm Yagrin Richard Wexton, House of Perl, Dragun. Well, *ex*, I suppose. The brotherhood doesn't want anything to do with me now."

"What brotherhood?" Jordan said.

Nore still could not move.

"Are you alright?" Yagrin asked.

No, no, I'm not. She wanted to scream. But if she told him the truth, he would either not believe her or see that she was a fraud, a liar, a pretender—another dishonest cog in their toxic, broken world. If he knew her lie, he would write her off as being just like the rest of them. And that would shatter whatever fragments of her that were left.

First her brother, now this. Her knees felt weak beneath her. She needed to get out of there. *Where is*— She turned and her shire was galloping toward her through the trees.

Daring nudged her and she gripped his reins.

"He looked like he needed help, but you all have it handled." She turned quickly to hide the tears burning her eyes. She stepped into one stirrup, hoisted herself up, and then swung into the saddle.

"Nore, please stay," Jordan rasped. "The Order. Fracturing."

"We can use all the help we can get is what he's trying to say," Yagrin cut in.

The girl worked over Jordan's wounds still, but there was too much blood.

"I don't think I can," she said, with more honesty than they even realized. She could not be near Yagrin another second without crying.

"Where could you possibly have to go?" The girl stopped working, exasperated.

"Abby, please," Jordan said. "This is the heir of the House you insult."

"No, I'm sick of 'Rosers acting like they're superior. Is there an encyclopedia that's going to cry if you don't get back to it immediately?" She cut a glare at Nore, and for the first time, it occurred to her that Abby and Yagrin could be an item. She felt sicker. Too sick to even respond to the girl's retort.

"I didn't mean to upset your lady friend. I apologize," she said.

Yagrin cocked his brow.

"What? No. Abby just, um—doesn't deal with Ambrosers, not anymore."

"*Trash*, all of them," Abby grumbled to herself, still working furiously over Jordan's wound while ranting how awful 'Rosers were. It was almost endearing. Nore's heart squeezed. It shouldn't, but the tiniest beacon of hope shone in the darkest crevices of her soul. It didn't mean anything. But knowing that Yagrin and Abby weren't an item calmed the raging storm inside her. She watched Abby frustrate herself again.

"You're doing it wrong," Nore said. "That's why the bleeding won't stop."

"Excuse me?" Abby stared.

"Move." Nore joined Abby on the ground. Jordan was pale and he took longer to blink. "Give me your sweater."

Abby did. Nore balled it up and pressed it against Jordan's chest. She leaned, laying the full weight of her body against his. "It needs pressure. The wound was gushing faster than the magic could keep up. You have to slow the bleeding." She held him there, counting, checking the wound intermittently. And sure enough, though Jordan's head lolled backward, the wound wasn't swimming in blood as it had earlier.

"Now try to heal it."

Abby spread her hands across the tear in his chest, and the air between them wrinkled. His skin responded beautifully to her command, pulling itself back together. The bone beneath his chest shifted. He sucked in a huge breath and his eyes shot open.

"Shallow breaths," Nore told him. He listened. And in a few moments, his chest was moving normally; the wound was smooth skin, with only a faint scar. He was going to be okay. Jordan's fingers felt his chest. He pulled himself up on timid elbows.

"I'm . . . sorry for what I said about Ambrose," Abby said.

"I don't like them much either, if I can be honest."

Mirth creased around Abby's eyes. "What kind of Healer are you?"

"I'm not a Healer."

"Well, whatever you are, we could use your help," Jordan said. "Will you stay?"

They watched her, waiting for her answer.

FIFTY-NINE

Nore

Nore didn't know what to say. They awaited her response. But Jordan didn't know what he was asking her. To stay and help them was to live in perpetual torture.

"Well?" Yagrin oozed impatience, as he often did.

"I'll take your silence as a yes," Jordan went on. "First, I need your horse. My brother and I need to get back to the Sphere."

Yagrin's dark eyes glowed with ambition. Her insides warmed with excitement for him. She wanted him to know that she was proud of him for sticking it to the Order. She wasn't sure what it had taken to get to this moment, but freedom was what he'd wanted for so long, deep down. He'd just never had the courage to say it. Her lips parted as she warred with what to do.

"I can't give you my horse, I'm sorry."

Jordan stared at her dubiously, as if she hadn't just rescued him an inch from death. Yagrin, on the other hand, appeared disgruntled, irritated that she couldn't see their needs were obviously far greater than her own. But that was the farthest thing from true. If the Sphere bled out, Nore's mother would die, and the ancestors would expect her heart to be in that glass box. She needed that Immortality Scroll if she was going to outsmart the Pact.

"The world is literally on fire," Yagrin said. "But please, take your time."

"I'll ride out of this graveyard and never look back. I don't care about the Order." It was a bluff, but they didn't know that. The more she thought about it, the more she wanted them to protect the Sphere. But she needed help, too. Jordan stood now, fully healed. He turned the Dragunhead's dagger in his hand.

"An heir to a great House who doesn't care for the Order," Jordan said. "Our interests may be more aligned than you think, Miss Ambrose. Share your request."

"I want you to promise to help me in a matter, on your honor as Dragunheart." They watched her. She wet her lips. This was the boldest she'd ever been in her own skin. She was wearing her own face and she'd just admitted she had no love for the Order. There was no turning back now.

"My needs are twofold. Kidnap the Headmistress of House Ambrose and bring her to me. My brother may have plans to kill her, so it's a mercy, in a way. And help me find the rest of the pieces to this." She held up the Scroll.

Yagrin didn't speak. She bit down on her lip, wondering what he thought of her request. Too savage? Too hopeful?

"That's not a fair trade," Yagrin said.

But Jordan took the scrap from her hands. "*Intellectus secat acutissimum.*" His expression darkened. "Your House doesn't have the knowledge it's known for." He breathes a laugh.

~~Yagrin snatched the paper from his hands, greedily reading every mark~~ on it. When he looked up, he gazed off.

"This can bring back anyone from the dead?" he asked.

Her heart ticked faster. *He still loved her.* Or the lie that he knew.

"Within a certain amount of time after death, yes," she said.

"How much time?"

"That's unclear. Months. Maybe a year. I—I'd have to do more research."

~~"She doesn't have the full Scroll, Yags," Jordan said.~~

"We do have it," she said. "Or we did." She explained how Caera Ambrose uncovered the secret, then parts of it were lost somehow, leaving only this scrap and the one her brother had.

"If we find it, you have to give it to us," Jordan said.

Yagrin's mouth hardened. Even if she could give Yagrin the Scroll, the girl he loved was dead. Red was the one thing Nore couldn't give him. *She* needed the Scroll. But to get it she needed their help. She stuck out her hand.

"Deal," she said to Jordan.

He shook her hand. "Yagrin, after we push Beaulah back, you'll go with Nore. Abby—"

Abby cleared her throat. "You don't speak for me. What do I get out of this?"

"What do you want?" Nore responded.

"I want my magic." She folded her arms.

Jordan squeezed Abby's shoulder before he and Yagrin climbed up on Daring. Nore stroked his nose and scratched his neck before slapping him on the hind. They rode off toward the darkening calamity on the horizon.

SIXTY

Quell

The graveyard is engulfed in a cloud of darkness. Shouts scratch my ears, but it's the moans of people writhing in pain that stirs the bile in my stomach. The brooding sky has only grown darker, and the chaos has filled the air with ash. When mixed with the fog of toushana, the murk is so thick I can hardly make out the Sphere, now a bit away. But I can see wisps of magic evaporating into the chilled air. I keep my eyes fixed on it and the magic whirring in my chest. I hold my focus there, churning it faster, letting it build in me until my lungs feel as if they might explode.

In the haze I spot Beaulah's Draguns still arranged neatly around the Sphere. But as she breaks ranks with them and moves closer to me, several follow. My heart rams in my chest. I pull at the icy chill in my bones, urging it to stir harder.

When I release on the Sphere, she'll be dead.

"Get back!"

She steeples her hands.

That's when I see it.

A familiar ring on her knuckle. Once stoneless, now with a bright red heart-shaped stone at the center of its nest of gold. The stone from Jordan's pendant. *No! How?* I step backward, trying to think of something to say. Or something to do. That stone will draw my magic to it! I can't use toushana anywhere near it.

"I am so proud of you," the wretch says, moving right beside me.

I tighten at my core, trying to hold on to the weighty cold begging for release. Beaulah moves past me, motioning for her Draguns to get back to the Sphere. Near the opening. The window of chance is narrowing.

"Tell me, darling, why do you need to attack the Sphere to kill me? I'm right here."

Bile rises in my throat.

"If you're truly a Darkbearer, face me fearlessly. Release *on me*."

She doesn't want me to hurt the Sphere. She still has hope that she will make it out of here with the Sphere's power. Her ring flickers like the glow of a hungry flame. She waves her hand in front of me, near my chest. The magic growing in me shifts, compelled by the ring's nearness. Toushana moves through me in her direction. I am out of choices.

I put some distance between us before forcing out the cold clawing beneath my skin in one sharp gust, thrusting it in her direction. Hoping I can attack her with enough magic that it will also overwhelm the ring. Shadows rush at her. She meets them with her fist in midair, and the stone gleams.

Then several things happen at once.

Magic hooks in my chest.

Darkness bleeds out of me, reaching across the graveyard like an outstretched arm.

It touches Beaulah's fist.

And a tether of toushana pulls taut between us.

"Back to the Sphere," she orders Felix. "Leave her to me." The rest follow and she marches toward me. Shadows swirl beneath the surface of her ring. But the magic siphoning out of me snatches the breath out of my chest. The red rock on her finger swims with my toushana, growing larger. So large, she detaches it from the metal ring.

Fight. My mom deserves better. Beaulah watches the stone transform, filling with darkness. I try to pull away.

Somewhere, someone yells.

Beaulah grunts as something knocks her forward. And the tether of toushana between us breaks. She turns and is pulled into fighting. My heart twinges with hope. I look for Jordan or Yagrin. When my vision clears, my grandmother is holding a flaming dagger to Beaulah's throat.

SIXTY-ONE

* * *

Quell

Darragh has Beaulah frozen in her grasp, her arm tight across her chest and her blade's edge firmly at her throat. My *grandmother*— who tethers people to her House and who has murdered débutants who she accidentally gave toushana to. I can't move. She is the only living family I have left.

"Leave my granddaughter *alone*," she says.

Beaulah holds the red stone tight in one fist. None of Beaulah's Draguns are here to save her. She sent them back to the Sphere, and we're at least a hundred paces away. As hope twinges in my chest, Beaulah's free hand slips into her robes. Silver glints in her hand and she slams the metal into Grandmom's wrist in a flash. Grandmom howls in pain and Beaulah spins away. They circle one another. I search for the cold inside me, desperate to do something. But my skin is clammy and warm, my magic exhausted from Beaulah's pull on it.

"You traitorous witch," Beaulah spits.

"Says the woman trying to steal magic. I also know about *all* the bodies you've buried. Francis Clemmon Hughes, the reporter, the Cabinet!"

"You can't prove a thing." She dashes toward me. I scamper backward. My grandmother jumps in the way, jabbing her dagger at Beaulah's face while blood runs down her arm.

"I *said*, get away from Quell."

Beaulah narrowly misses the attack from my grandmother's blade. I stumble up and back away. They deserve each other. I consider running to the Sphere, trying to salvage something for myself out of this mess. But the cold only answers in wisps. If I want to survive at all, I have to get out of here.

"I could see the betrayal in your eyes the day we made the pact, Darragh."

"Murdering the Upper Cabinet and blackmailing the rest of us to go along with you is not my idea of good leadership," Darragh says.

I freeze.

"And robbing your members of their memories to cover for your worthless granddaughter *is*?"

Covering for me? She altered Abby's and the others' memories to protect her secret tether she has on her House. Abby had no idea I was even there at Cotillion. *Which gave me a ballroom full of guests who would swear I had nothing to do with the chaotic fallout of House Marionne.*

"Don't act like you're above such things. I know about those pins you use. The way it softens the memories of your débutants so they can't fully recall the horrors of those Trials."

"Sending Jordan to you was a mistake."

"It saved his life."

"Too bad it'll cost your granddaughter hers. You're not half the woman I am. I do what is *necessary*."

"Beaulah, darling, how long have we known each other? *So do I*." My grandmother turns to me. "I am so sorry, Quell. Secrets destroy everything."

I shake my head, my words not coming fast enough.

"Find Nore. She will see you through this."

"Nore Ambrose is dead." She told me that herself.

"So many are," she says. "Find them."

She puts herself between me and Beaulah.

"*Wait.*" I reach for her but she shoves me out of the way, *hard*, before dropping her blade. She opens her hands, where blackness writhes angrily.

"*Devour her*," Beaulah yells to her Draguns, forgetting she sent them back to the Sphere. My grandmother slams her hands together, and the toushana between them combusts. Darkness explodes like a cloud of dust. The snow blackens, the ground burns. Beaulah growls, then lunges at my grandmother, her dagger poised to stab. Darragh dashes aside and grabs Beaulah with her dark, magic-filled hands. A shrill scream rips through the air. The air rots with the stench of burning flesh. Beaulah cries out in pain, fumbling the stone. It rolls. I'm dashing for it when Beaulah throws off my grandmother, making her stumble. Then Beaulah kicks the gemstone farther out of my reach. She snatches up my grandmother's blade. Now doubly armed, she stands over Grandmom, her eyes bloodshot.

Grandmom shouldn't die like this. Not when I still have so many questions for her. Not when she was the one to come to my aid. As I rush to help her, Beaulah grabs her by the throat and shoves the dagger in her belly. She lets her go and my grandmother falls like a tree. I'm trembling as I pull at her unmoving body while Beaulah dashes for the stone.

When suddenly the Sphere crackles like a clap of thunder.

The whole world stills.

Its dark undulating matter shimmers.

I lose all feeling in my limbs. The numbness moves to my chest. The scar from binding with my toushana throbs. Then a trickle of warmth runs down the crown of my head, slipping over my whole body.

Suddenly, my skin shimmers the same way the Sphere does.

Beaulah gasps. And so do I, as I realize what's happening.

The Headmistress to House of Marionne is dead.

And so is her only daughter.

It's passed to me.

I am now Headmistress of House of Marionne.

SIXTY-TWO

·· ——— ✳ ——— ··

Jordan

With Dlaminaugh at our backs, we ride fast until we reach the patch of conifers where we first cloaked. I tug hard on the reins, and the horse comes to an abrupt halt. My brother's heart races as he stares over my shoulder. Despite the haze and the distance, it's clear the Sphere is still bleeding. It shimmers and my grip tightens on the reins. *What's happening?* We slip out of the shade and get closer. I spot a body on the ground that looks a lot like Darragh Marionne. I look away. What an awful way to die.

Quell.

Darragh is dead. Quell is Headmistress.

My heart rends. *I've failed to protect her before. I won't fail again.*

"This changes everything," I say. We're no longer just protecting magic for the sake of magic.

My brother stiffens at my back.

"You understand that, don't you?"

He hesitates, and I turn as best I can in the saddle so he can look me in the eye. "Quell's life is tethered to the Sphere now. If it empties, she—" But I cannot say it. I will not say it. Ever again.

"I know!" To be so close to the revenge he's long hungered for, just to have it snatched away.

"I'm sorry, Yagrin." I hope he knows how much I mean it. I hate how long it took me to see the Order for what it is. "I wanted to see the look on Beaulah's face when she realized her plan would not work. And this was truly the end."

"But she's won again," Yagrin spits, and his words stoke a flame that's already burning in me.

"Not yet."

We risk riding closer. Duncan's and Marionne's forces are everywhere. As the haze around the Sphere begins to clear, I pull back on the reins, careful to stay unseen. Beaulah leads Quell from Darragh's body toward the looming Sphere, where Draguns appear to be waiting.

"She is going to make Quell drain the Sphere," I say.

"Won't that kill her?" my brother asks.

"She must have a plan to put the magic in something."

"But what?"

I don't know. I need to get closer.

"Let me at her," he says.

"No." The last thing I need is my brother dying.

"I'll distract her. You get Quell out of here. We can meet up some-where safe."

"The Tavern? The one near Chateau Soleil."

I let Yagrin down and he disappears into the haze. I hear the commo-tion near the Sphere before I'm close to it. I kick in my heels and the horse trots. Darkness is a thick fog at the heart of the fighting. But the closer I get, the clearer I can see that the top of the glassy orb is empty. Black matter seeps from the hole at its base. The magical innards blow away in a fine mist, evaporating.

"Easy," I say to my mount. I swallow as I approach. It feels like eyes are following me through the shadows. When I find Quell, my heart stops. Beaulah has her in her grip. She holds Quell with one hand and cradles a pulsing red stone in the other.

"Go on," she urges. "Make it bleed faster."

Quell doesn't respond. Something about the way she staggers forward doesn't seem like her. I feel for her emotions inside my chest, but there's nothing there. She is calm, or half-dead already. I have to act fast.

"Beaulah Mavis Perl," I say. "By order of the Dragunhead and the Prestigious Order of Highest Mysteries, you are under arrest for dereliction of duty, Uniform Code of Dragun Justice, article four, and conspiracy to commit treason, article seven."

"I don't see a pendant around your neck." She smiles darkly and strokes my pendant gem. "It's grown nicely, thanks to this one here." Quell meets my eyes, and I finally can feel her again. *Panic. Fear.*

"I think I'll put it on my mantel when I'm finished."

"Do you agree to come peacefully?"

Beaulah's smug expression melts into a glare.

"Get off that horse and face me like the man you pretend to be."

I tighten my grip on Daring's reins.

"As I thought. Still the coward."

I dismount. I cannot be rash. That's what she wants. I grab the cuffs in my pocket and hold them out to her. "You can come along with dignity, or I will drag you from this graveyard by your throat if I must."

She marches toward me. Daring trots off to a faraway whistle. Beaulah's Draguns break formation around the Sphere and instead tighten around me. I walk backward away from them. They move with me. Away from the Sphere. Away from Quell, who stands there staring at me in confusion.

"Mother, watch him," Felix says. Yani is beside him. She avoids my gaze. Amid the distraction, Quell slinks backward, farther away from the Sphere. I spot Yagrin with Daring's reins in hand, beckoning for her attention.

"Even they are afraid for you," I say to Beaulah, desperate to keep their attention straight ahead, on me.

"He killed Charlie," Yani spits.

Beaulah's jaw works. "It's your arrogance, not your competence, that inspires you to behave so recklessly, Jordan. I know you better than you know yourself." Her words are poison. Still, my gut sloshes.

"You're wrong." I stop walking.

They come closer. Beaulah still holds her stone. Felix and Yani stick to Beaulah's flanks. Daring whinnies in the distance, but I keep my eyes fixed on Beaulah. In my periphery, my brother and Quell swing into the saddle. My heart squeezes.

"I'm not the boy you raised anymore. Nor am I the Dragunhead's. I'm arresting you because I want to and I can."

Felix puts himself between us.

"Mother, let me cut him," Yani says. Beaulah shushes her. Yani watches with more envy than anger.

"Give us some space," Beaulah says, her head swiveling. Then her brows slash downward. She tightens her grip on the stone cradled in her arm. "Where is she? Where is Quell?" She shoves Felix. "Standing around trying to protect me from this imbecile instead of keeping an eye on the girl. Get the dogs and *find* her now."

Draguns shift to shadows, and it's just the two of us.

"You'll die a Wexton. Never a Perl." She assumes *I* care because she does. It's the only thing left she has to hold over me.

"And you'll die alone. With no witnesses. No legacy. And no power." I roll up my sleeves and summon the cold.

SIXTY-THREE

※

Quell

Yagrin's horse comes to a stop beneath thick green trees covered in snow, where my ex–best friend and a redheaded girl are waiting. Dlaminaugh Estate looms in the background, touching the clouds. My body still writhes with a dull heat. I dismount, still haunted by my grandmother's final words to me.

The girl's hands are not gloved and her posture isn't timid. Her sharp shoulders are pressed back and her lips are in a thin line. I only saw the girl once. But she looks like Nore.

"Quell." Abby hooks her hands. I stare, unsure what to say.

"I've got to help my brother," Yagrin says.

"Meet at my cottage on the south end of Dlaminaugh Estate."

She sounds like Nore.

She steps forward, fidgeting with the pockets of her dress.

Nore Ambrose is alive.

"Right," Yagrin says. "Quell, Jordan will meet you at the Tavern down south, the one by your gran— You know the one."

Abby's gaze falls to her feet as Yagrin rides off.

"Good to see you again, Quell." Nore offers a hand.

"You are supposed to be dead."

She tosses her chin over her shoulder at the Sphere, tiny in the distance. "Draguns are all over these woods. We should get going. You both have a long journey. Abby doesn't know how to cloak, and you're probably too weak to. We can stop at my cottage. Traveling by night is safer."

"*Quell.*" It's Abby. "You have to say something to me."

"Do I? The last I saw you, your boyfriend plotted to have me killed. And you ran off." I fold my arms, a bit stunned by my upwelling frustration at Abby. I'd shut out those feelings; I didn't think I'd ever see her again.

"I didn't know, alright? Mynick didn't tell me."

"We need to get out of here," Nore says, looking around warily.

"And when it happened, I was scared," Abby goes on. "So I ran. I'm a coward. I was trying to get away from the chaos at the Sphere when Yagrin found me and took me to Jordan. I heal people; I don't battle Draguns. And what about you! I hear you have toushana? When were you going to tell me that?"

Nore grabs me by the wrist. "We need to leave *now*."

Abby's and my eyes meet, and we stick to Nore's heels. She leads us across a snowy stretch of graveyard, gazing over her shoulder every few moments.

"What is it?" I ask, but she only urges me to come along. Her estate grows larger the faster we run. When the gate comes into view, she cuts a sharp right.

"This way." We stop at the stables, where she offers Abby reins. "Do you ride?"

She nods. I shake my head before she can even ask and swing into the saddle behind Nore.

"No questions. Let's go."

We ride quickly, the Sphere's commotion at our backs, around the wooded perimeter of Dlaminaugh Estate. We squeeze through a break in the stone wall, which Nore has concealed with shrubbery. Once inside the grounds we stop at a small house. The minute my feet hit the ground, everything feels different. An eerie feeling of being watched covers me in shivers as I tie up my horse.

"Get inside," Nore says.

"I don't under—"

A whoosh of wind sweeps past, so strong it knocks me forward. The howling wind blows again, and I realize it doesn't feel like wind at all—it's more like *something* is pushing me around. The hair on my neck rises. Nore grabs me and Abby and dashes up the porch steps. The bones of the rickety wood creak and the sky seems to darken. She whips the door open and shoves us inside just as her porch chair comes flying and smashes into the door. She barricades her back against it, breathless.

Abby is frozen in shock.

"What is it?" I ask.

"I think the ancestors of my House are after me." She peeks out the shuttered windows; the wind hasn't stopped its assault. "Stay away from the windows. Just in case."

I huddle on a spot on the floor with my back to the wall.

"What does that mean?" Abby asks. "Are we safe in here?"

"Are we safe anywhere?"

Bang!

I jump. Abby shrieks. Nore peeks out the window, where a thick branch just cracked the glass. As she stares outside, Nore sucks in a breath but doesn't let it out.

"What is it?" I ask.

"Can you see them?" she says.

I look but only see a violent windstorm destroying the outside of her house. "See what?"

"The shadows. They're here. They're everywhere." She chews her nail.

"Oh my goodness, it's gone!" Abby rubs the spot where the scar pierced her at Cotillion. "Quell! There was a cloudiness in my head, a kind of fog, whenever I'd think back on certain things. But it's gone."

"My grandmother's dead. So her curse would be, too."

"Dead?" Nore clutches her chest. "Darragh?" She looks as if she might actually cry.

"We didn't know the same person, clearly." I feel sick thinking of my grandmother's atrocities. "She accidentally gave toushana to girls. And then killed them."

"Darragh Marionne killed girls with toushana?" Nore says. "I'll never believe that."

The window shutters rattle.

"It doesn't matter now, I suppose." I pull a blanket from her couch and hold it to my chin, realizing I need to stop dwelling on the past and start preparing for what's next—starting with how to get out of this cottage. The Order is in shambles. I'm not even sure if, come morning, I'll have magic.

After a long silence, Abby asks, "What do you think is going to happen with the Wexton brothers and the Sphere?"

"Beaulah is a demon they've been battling most of their lives," I say. "Today was a long time coming. They better win."

"The Sphere can't break," Abby says, and I can hear the fear between her words.

"The innards of the Sphere can be preserved in something else," Nore says. "It just needs the right magical composition. Stones, a blade, even, depending on how it was forged. There are options. What does Jordan have on him?"

"Nothing," I say. "He has nothing."

SIXTY-FOUR

«——✳——»

Jordan

The Sphere's innards are waning. Its glassy surface is half-empty. Halfway to destruction. Halfway to the end of magic as we know it. I have to get what's left of the Sphere's matter inside *something*. Beaulah holds on tight to the gleaming red stone full of shadows. She eyes the Sphere. I glance at it; still emptying. I don't know how much magic that stone can hold. But every bit that doesn't evaporate is magic we can hold on to—and figure out how to build on. If I just had something strong enough to put it in.

"I've already thought of five different ways this ends. You're still trying to figure out one."

She's bluffing. Like Draguns . . . "People remember the burning." I circle her. I need that stone or some other vessel for a new Sphere. Something that will keep magic intact and the Headmistresses alive. *Quell* alive. "Your magic isn't particularly strong. You're not bound to toushana. The only real power you have is fear. But that's broken."

She stiffens.

"I see you clearly." Words I've buried my entire life force their way out. "You take children and preach to them about all the magnificent things they can do, while coaxing them into desperation for your approval, warping their sense of who they are. You're all the same—you, the Dragunhead, and my father."

"You father would be dead if it wasn't for me. This whole House would be gone. It was *my* blood, sweat, and cunning that rebuilt this House. So *puff your chest out* at all the skills you have. But remember, you owe *everything you are* to me. I *own you*, little boy."

I used to tell myself that I worked so hard because I wanted to make the House proud, to do my duty, to shine as a Dragun, to be selected as Ward. But I was working for what those things would save me from: their judgment. Now that it doesn't have a hold over me anymore, I can see Beaulah more clearly.

"You use your position to make others cling to you. Because, without your power over others, you are no one. And if you are no one, what were all the starving years for? The poisoning of your father and sister so you could scare your mother away and become heir? It means nothing if you become nothing."

She reddens.

"Yes, I know. I've always known." My father told me once, when he was drunk, in that short window of time when he didn't hate me and I thought that was the same as loving me. He went on about how she kept him fed when he was an obedient little brother, helping her slip the poison into their food little by little for days. I buried the memory with everything else, remembering it only when my brother forced me to stop running from the past.

Her glare flicks to the Sphere, its darkness evaporating into mist. I eye her stone.

"My cousin couldn't be more unlike you. The House she runs will be *great*. And it's about time you got out of her way."

"You talk of Adola like you know her. *I* raised that girl as *mine*."

"I've learned that knowing someone and seeing them are not the same thing." I am close to Beaulah now. So close I could reach out and touch the stone in her hands. A familiar face lurks distantly behind her.

"I see *you*," she goes on. "A has-been who's just lost everything he's spent his entire life working for. All because of a girl who sunk her claws into you."

"Better her than you."

She steps closer to the Sphere; I block her path.

"When this is all over, before I let the light leave your eyes, nephew, you will beg me. *Dear Mother*, you'll say, *please have mercy.*"

"You're delusional."

"Ha!"

"Because the person you discount most is about to wrap his hands around your throat."

Yagrin grabs our aunt from behind in the choke. Her eyes are moons. He squeezes, rushing toushana into her. She drops the stone and claws at his wrists, trying to speak, but her speech comes out as a sputter. Her body begins to stiffen as the choke works. Beaulah Perl's eyes darken with fear for the first time I've ever seen. I dash for the stone. It's so large, I need both hands to lug it to the base of the Sphere's opening and use it to stopper the hole. But the moment the black matter inside the Sphere crashes against it, the stone cracks and breaks into pieces.

No . . . no, please.

Felix, Yani, and several others appear. I glance at the Sphere; its thrashing matter looks exactly how I feel inside. *Half-empty. Half of magic, gone.* I call to my magic, and it answers in a quiet thrum. I try again, but it's even weaker than it was before, the Sphere emptying—magic disappearing—taking its toll. Yagrin fights off another Dragun, holding Beaulah as a shield. The world frays at its edges.

I must do something. The totality of magic, both forbidden and proper, rides on this decision. *Oh my goodness, that's it.*

A stone is too easily possessed.

Beaulah's freed herself from Yagrin. She and the Draguns barrel toward me. I have seconds. I snatch up a broken shard of the red gemstone and unsheathe my dagger. I'm done trusting others with magic.

I press the tip of the blade into the chest wound that Abby just healed. It reopens. I hold the broken gem near the Sphere's opening. The dark innards rise like a charmed snake, as if magnetically drawn toward the stone.

When its innards nearly touch the stone, I shove it into my chest.

And the Sphere's magic follows.

A siphon of darkness streams through the air, from the Sphere into the gash in my skin. I burn all over as magic fills me. Slowly, at first— then my body convulses and my blood pumps harder. My body oscillates from warm to cold and then cold to hot. Blackness dents the edges of my vision as my body drinks in the Sphere's magic with a rabid thirst. The Sphere's level plummets. My body writhes. My bones shift. I hold still as the world bleeds of color.

When the final drop of matter falls from the glass, I shudder and collapse.

The last thing I feel is cold.

A bloodthirsty cold.

All over.

APPENDIX

THE HOUSES AND THEIR HISTORIES

MEMENTO SUMPTUS

HOUSE OF PERL

Est. 1822

At Hartsboro Estate

Territory: East and Northeast

Hartsboro Estate, located in Connecticut, was originally the operating Headquarters of the Order's governing body: the Upper Cabinet. In 1822, on the heel of the Sorting Years, to support the development of the Order's growing member numbers, Upper established a formalized magic-studying system using a boarding school model. Members would continue in the débutante tradition, which had been in practice since the onset of the Industrial Revolution, but be organized into Houses and territories. Houses would be overseen by a Headmistress.

The Upper Cabinet relocated their Headquarters and commissioned its first House: House of Perl, naming Beatrice Perl inaugural Headmistress. At the time, Beatrice had been serving in the Cabinet. Before agreeing to sign on, she insisted that the seat of the House pass down in family lineage by the matriarch. Upper agreed, and so it remains. The House of Perl sigil is a cracked column.

HOUSE OF MARIONNE

Est. 1874
At Chateau Soleil
Territory: Southern

House of Marionne was the second established House of the Order as their numbers swelled, with more and more showing a propensity for magic. The origins of the philosophies that shaped House of Marionne are rooted in the Era of Indulgence.

After the fall of Yaäuper Rea Universitas, the Silent Years followed. Formal magical education had come to a screeching halt as it was forced to shift to underground. It is said generations of magical people lost their magic because of sparse access to training, study, and development until a lowly but studious Order member, Loken Delosu, was sought out by King George I of England. He was courting Loken's affections, as he'd heard rumors his family dabbled in sun magic. George was in a long-standing war with the French and wanted any edge he could get. Around that same time, King Louis XIV, the "Sun King," heard of George's interest in Loken and sent his own parties to sway Loken. Louis, being a man of abundance, showered gifts and hospitality at the feet of Loken and his family, his friends, anyone he knew, in exchange for one thing—his company.

King Louis XIV was incredibly ambitious and eventually pressed Loken directly to know more about magic, but Loken refused. He held to the age-old tenet that magic should be kept far away from government. Louis beheaded him. The Order was divided on how to feel about the French and English years of courtship. But the years dabbling in French culture had left its mark evident in House of Marionne's architecture, culture, traditions, and art. The Upper Cabinet commissioned Claudette Marionne as inaugural Headmistress. The House of Marionne sigil is a fleur-de-lis.

COGITARE DE PRETIO

HOUSE OF DUNCAN

Est. 1875

At Wigonshire Estate

Territory: West and Midwest*

House of Duncan was established on the heels of House of Marionne at the urging of Upper Cabinet members who were rumored to favor House of Perl's Dysiian influences. The House was intended to be a replica in culture and architecture of House of Perl but located in Colorado. The estate's inaugural Headmistress was Maisie Duncan. In 1938, an explosion in the Midwest killed thousands of Unmarked. The news reported that the accident was the result of an industrial explosion. However, House of Duncan, whose new Headmistress was experimenting with using toushana to mine gold, was behind the tragedy. The dark magic she'd been illegally using spiraled out of control, and twenty-three hundred barrels of kor elixir leaked into an oil shipment being transported west. The result was catastrophic. The Upper Cabinet shut down the House immediately and required each member within its territories to reapply. Most were denied on grounds of distrust. The then Headmistress, Beil Duncan, was publicly beheaded, a rare but symbolically vicious act at the time. The House of Duncan sigil was a scale and darkened sun.

---

*The Midwest territory, formerly under House of Duncan, was initially moved to House of Ambrose. In later years the Midwest was split, its northern side under Ambrose territory and its southern side under Oralia.

HOUSE OF AMBROSE

Est. 1877

At Dlaminaugh Estate

Territory: Northwest and parts of the Midwest

House of Ambrose, nestled in the tallest peaks of central Idaho, was the fourth established House of the Order. Its inaugural Headmistress was Caera Ambrose, a well-known member of the Order who had built her reputation on leading efforts to push the bounds of understood magic. Her views were seen as outlandish, but she received the votes needed from the Upper Cabinet. Caera's ancestors were immigrants to America with a strained and hostile history with Europeans. Thus, Dlaminaugh Estate was erected as a neo-Gothic replica of Yaäuper Rea Universitas and commissioned to be the first House in the Order that defined itself as distinctly separate from European influence. Caera desired to usher forward a generation of débutants who would be known for their supreme intellect, not ostentatious shows of wealth. The House of Ambrose sigil is three yew leaves intertwined.

HOUSE OF ORALIA

Est. 1942
At Begonia Terrace
Territory: West and parts of the Midwest

House of Oralia was the fifth and final established House, located in northern California. Donya Oralia was its inaugural Headmistress. Her grandmother had been a candidate for Uppership but was ultimately passed over because of her progressive views on women's rights at the time. In 1942, House of Oralia was commissioned by a slim majority vote, as the world was engrossed in World War II. They are known for using magic as a means of artistic expression and enjoyment, believing magic serves the wielder and not the other way around. The House of Oralia sigil is two smudged dollops of paint.

THE DRAGUN BROTHERHOOD

Est. Late nineteenth century
Headquarters: Wexton MidCenter Hotel

Dysiis was a student of Yaäuper Rea Universitas who believed that to understand the full breadth of magic's capacity to be a positive influence, one had to understand the full intricacies of its darker parts. He studied toushana until he died. His studies were stored in the university library, despite much concern at the time that they could inflame if they fell into the wrong hands. Several decades later, a faction grew among magic pupils who were fascinated by Dysiis's teachings. Dysiisians took his teachings further, believing there was a place for the destructive magic in their world. Since so little was understood about the dark, powerful magic, the faculty at Yaäuper Rea Universitas forbid the study. Groups continued to meet about toushana in secret, and for a century, Darkbearers, a rebel group of toushana-users, used the destructive magic to terrorize villages, amass their own power, and infiltrate the highest levels of Church and State. This era is known as the Second Coming, referring to the Age of Vultures returned. It persisted until a group of Yaäuper Rea alumni banded together (referring to themselves as "Sunbringers") to bring Darkbearers to justice. Sunbringers used toushana, but only as needed to apprehend Darkbearers. They found burning the rebellious dark-magic users was the only way to ensure they and their toxic magic were dead, earning them the nickname Draguns.

When the city of Misa fell, the Order began building the House system. The next century was called the Sorting Years, when safe houses were illicitly erected to harbor toushana-users who'd fled Misa. The Upper Cabinet recruited descendants of Sunbringers, or "Draguns," to serve in an official capacity as a security, protection, and intelligence force: the brotherhood. In the early years, Houses were allowed to nominate débutants for the brotherhood before it shifted to by invite only. Some Draguns can trace their lineage to original Sunbringers.

LEXICON

·«———✳———»·

BINDING—the process of joining the enhanced magic, now held within the dagger's blade, with the magic user by plunging the magical dagger into the user's heart.

COTILLION—a formal ball at which débutants are presented for membership into the Order, a ceremony which includes completing Third Rite in front of an audience of members and publicly agreeing to the membership oath.

DARKBEARER—a group of magical persons in the thirteenth century who bound to toushana.

DRAGUN—a nickname for a Sunbringer, a uniquely skilled member of the Order trained to hunt and eradicate threats from the Order, primarily those with forbidden magic.

DRAGUN BROTHERHOOD—the community of Draguns across Houses, which collectively makes up the law enforcement and security force of the Order.

DRAGUNHEAD—the senior member of the Dragun brotherhood, a rank equal to the Headmistresses in authority, but with a separate and autonomous jurisdiction over all Draguns.

DRAGUNHEART—the senior understudy to the Dragunhead, a rank with second-in-command authority over all Draguns.

ELECTUS—a neophyte débutant who has not yet completed First Rite.

EMERGING—the manifestation of one's magic as either a jeweled mask across the top half of the face or a diadem arced above the head, proving one's magic is strong enough to be molded and used. Each person's magic is unique, and how it manifests will vary according to the magical heritage, skills, and talents of the magic user.

ESSENCE—the translucent aroma temporarily left behind where a magical person dies.

FIRST RITE—emerging a diadem from one's head or a mask on one's face.

HEADMISTRESS—the lady in charge of a magical training school.

HONING—the process of refining a dagger by forging it with gems to enhance its magical effectiveness.

MARKED—a person with a demonstrated capacity for proper magic use.

PRIMUS—a débutant who has passed First Rite and is actively working on Second Rite.

SECOND RITE—honing a dagger by folding specified enhancers into a blade to infuse one's own magic with added power.

SECUNDUS—a seasoned débutant who has passed Second Rite and is actively working on Third Rite.

SIGIL—an inscribed or painted symbol that represents a particular House and its set of values.

THE SPHERE—a magically encased orb that houses a connection between ancient magic and all magical people.

THE UPPER CABINET—established in the early eighteenth century, the Upper Cabinet was the original governing body of the Prestigious Order of Highest Mysteries, consisting of twelve all-male members.

THIRD RITE—binding with one's magic by plunging a fully honed dagger into one's heart in front of an audience of members at a Cotillion ceremony.

TOUSHANA—a forbidden, destructive magic.

UNMARKED—a person without magic.

ACKNOWLEDGMENTS

··——✳——··

The unexamined life is not worth living.

—Socrates

This book took *so* much out of me, but it gave me even more. When I think of the mark I want this series to leave on readers, I hope that falling in love with murderous assassins and rooting for the girl with a heart of darkness sparks a determined resistance to villainizing those who are different from us. Also, I hope we are able to see one another's created humanity before anything else. But most of all, I hope this story ignites the courage to look inside ourselves, deeply and critically; to know what we believe and why we believe it—and to hold the powers that be to the same standard.

I hope this book was as wild a ride for you as it was for me. I tried really hard to make this story even more satisfying than the first. Unveiling Red as Nore is one of my *favorite*-ever twists. Before I went on tour for book one, I'd planned for Yagrin to die in the final battle. But after hearing how much readers loved him, I rewrote his ending. The story is better for it. Writing can be such an isolated process. Thank you for being a part of my storytelling!

Bringing this book into the world wouldn't have been possible without an army of support. My biggest thank-you is always to God for this gift of words. And to my husband, who has let publishing upend his entire life (ha ha!) and only complains minimally. Thank you, my love. And to my three children, who are so sweet to share me so generously with the world. Being your momma is my favorite job.

To Jodi, who I'm convinced is my literary fairy godmother, thank you for always going to bat for me. Your advocacy and support are unparalleled.

And to my publishing team: Ruta, your fierce support brought this series to where it is; you are a dream to work with. Thank you for all you do: the long nights, the *detailed* emails, indulging my wildest ideas, spur-of-the-moment Zooms, and believing in me, draft after draft. <3 Simone, thank you for always being willing to jump in to help! To Jen L. and Jen K., thank you both for being Team Jess. I hope to make you both very proud! To Alex, Felicity, Shannon, and James, whose brilliance knows no bounds, you rocked the socks off this one, too. Endless love to each of you. To design extraordinaires Tracy and Theresa, whose patience must be limitless, these books wouldn't be where they are without the exceptional work you put in. Thank you, Virginia, for the gorgeous map, and Eleana, for the beautiful cover. Thank you, Kaitlin, Jaleesa, Shanta, and the rest of publicity. Thank you, Sales and Marketing, for all the time you put in despite your very full plates. I am beyond thankful to each and every person who worked double time, into the wee hours of the night, on their off days, to get this book out. There will never be enough thank-yous, Team Penguin. I am floored by the attention you give. Thank you for the full team embrace.

And to my dearest friends. Thank you, Emily, for literally holding me up through every draft, and through life! None of this author stuff would be happening without you in my ear daily. To Bailey B., your morning grins made every revising day brighter. And to the incomparable Sabaa Tahir, for being the literary sister I never knew I needed. For the constant calls, way too many cookies, flowers, tears—so many tears. And the way you love me so graciously. To my author buddies: Jessica O., Jessica F., Ayana G., Ally G., Sarah M., Ronni D., Nic, Dhonielle, Victoria A., Stephanie G., Ali H., Adalyn G., Rachel G., Shelby M., Jordan G., and others, who are always just a message away to encourage me or listen to me rant. To Del, Lisa, and Andonnia for letting me harass you with questions. To Sandra and Sara Kate, who love this series with a passion—you keep me going! To my sisters from other misses, Denean B. and Diarra F., thank you both for picking up my bags and carrying them alongside me. Dawna, your constant support of my work means the world to me. To my grandpa, Mom, Paigey, my cousins, Aunt Jackie, Tom, Beth, Andrea G., and the entire Bennett clan, who keep me fed without notice; my sweet Destiny, Erin H., and Courtney B. (not L., ha!); Laura Sue for her Photoshop genius at the drop of a hat; and the many others who pour into me so that I can pour out—I couldn't do any of this without you.

The biggest and warmest thank-you goes to you, reader. I could not tell stories without your support. Thank you for every purchase, library checkout, social media post, like, comment, or share. It might seem small, but it is not. I am thrilled that you've come back to this world, eager for more! I hope I get to meet many of you in person. Hearing what these characters have meant to you is the real gift in all of this. Writing for you has been an unbelievable joy!

Stay tuned, there's more.

Until then, keep your hair coiffed and your dagger *sharp*.